MOMENT OF TRUTH

The crucial moment had arrived. Dandy had come in and stood before the stove, his back to the mantelpiece. He was deathly pale and it was observed that his hands were trembling. The strain suddenly became almost unbearable. Why had Mrs. Dandy put such a roaring fire in the stove, even on a chilly October day? But she was always a little mad, anyway.

Dandy had once looked forward to this moment, when, clothed with authority, he should stand up before them all and announce Aunt Becky's decision. And how he wished himself dead.

"Come, come, Dandy," said William Y. impatiently. "Step on the juice. We've had enough of suspense. Tell us who's to get it and have it over."

"I—I can't," said Dandy, moistening his lips.

"Can't *what?*"

"Can't tell you who's to get the jug. I—I—don't know. Nobody ever will know—now."

"Look here, Dandy—" William Y. rose threateningly. "What does this mean?"

"It means"—the worst was out and Dandy had a little more courage—"I've lost the letter Aunt Becky gave me—the letter with the name in it."

For a few minutes everybody said nothing very rapidly. Then—

A
TANGLED
WEB

▼

L. M. MONTGOMERY

BANTAM BOOKS
NEW YORK · TORONTO · LONDON · SYDNEY · AUCKLAND

RL 6, IL age 12 and up

A TANGLED WEB
*A Bantam Book / published by arrangement with
the author's estate*

PRINTING HISTORY
*Copyright 1931 by McClelland and Stewart Limited
Canadian Favourites edition 1972
Bantam edition / September 1989*

ISBN 0-553-28050-3

*Bantam Books are published by Bantam Books, a division of Bantam
Doubleday Dell Publishing Group, Inc. Its trademark, consisting of the
words "Bantam Books" and the portrayal of a rooster, is Registered in U.S.
Patent and Trademark Office and in other countries. Marca Registrada.
Bantam Books, 666 Fifth Avenue, New York, New York 10103.*

PRINTED IN THE UNITED STATES OF AMERICA

RAD   12 11 10 9 8 7 6 5 4 3

TO
MY GOOD FRIENDS
MR. AND MRS. FRED W. WRIGHT
IN MEMORY OF
A CERTAIN WEEK OF LAUGHTER

CONTENTS

▼

A
TANGLED
WEB

1
AUNT BECKY'S LEVEE

▼

I

A dozen stories have been told about the old Dark jug. This is the true one.

Several things happened in the Dark and Penhallow clan because of it. Several other things did *not* happen. As Uncle Pippin said, this may have been Providence or it may have been the devil that certainly possessed the jug. At any rate, had it not been for the jug, Peter Penhallow might today have been photographing lions alone in African jungles, and Big Sam Dark would, in all probability, never have learned to appreciate the beauty of the unclothed female form. As for Dandy Dark and Penny Dark, they have never ceased to congratulate themselves that they got out of the affair with whole hides.

Legally, the jug was the property of Aunt Becky Dark, *née* Rebecca Penhallow. For that matter, most of the Darks had been *née* Penhallow and most of the Penhallows had been *née* Dark, save a goodly minority who had been Darks *née* Dark or Penhallows *née* Penhallow. In three generations sixty Darks had been married to sixty Penhallows. The resultant genealogical tangle baffled everybody except Uncle Pippin. There was really nobody for a Dark to marry except a Penhallow and nobody for a Penhallow to marry except a Dark. Once, it had been said, they wouldn't take anybody else. Now, nobody else would take them. At least, so Uncle Pippin said. But it was necessary to take Uncle Pippin's speeches with a large pinch of salt. Neither the Darks nor the Penhallows were gone to seed as far as that. They were still a proud, vigorous, and virile clan who hacked and hewed among themselves but presented an unbroken front to any alien or hostile force.

In a sense Aunt Becky was the head of the clan. In point of seniority Crosby Penhallow, who was eighty-seven when she was eighty-five, might have contested her supremacy had he cared to do so. But at eighty-seven Crosby Penhallow cared only about one thing. As long as he could foregather every evening with his old crony, Erasmus Dark, to play duets on their flutes and violins, Aunt Becky might hold the sceptre of the clan if she wanted to.

It must be admitted frankly that Aunt Becky was not particularly beloved by her clan. She was too fond of telling them what she called the plain truth. And, as Uncle Pippin said, while the truth was all right, *in its place*, there was no sense in pouring out great gobs of it around where it wasn't wanted. To Aunt Becky, however, tact and diplomacy and discretion, never to mention any consideration for anyone's feelings, were things unknown. When she wanted to say a thing she said it. Consequently Aunt Becky's company was never dull whatever else it might be. One endured the digs and slams one got oneself for the fun of seeing other people writhing under *their* digs and slams. As Aunt Becky knew from A to Z all the sad or fantastic or terrible little histories of the clan, no one had armour which her shafts could not penetrate. Little Uncle Pippin said that he wouldn't miss one of Aunt Becky's "levees" for a dog-fight.

"She's a personality," Dr. Harry Penhallow had once remarked condescendingly, on one of his visits home to attend some clan funeral.

"She's a crank," growled Drowned John Penhallow, who, being a notorious crank himself, tolerated no rivals.

"It's the same thing," chuckled Uncle Pippin. "You're all afraid of her because she knows too much about you. I tell you, boys, it's only Aunt Becky and the likes of her that keeps us all from dry-rotting."

Aunt Becky had been "Aunt Becky" to everybody for twenty years. Once when a letter came to the Indian Spring post-office addressed to "Mrs. Theodore Dark" the new postmaster returned it marked, "Person unknown." Legally, it was Aunt Becky's name. Once she had had a husband and two children. They were all dead long ago— so long ago that even Aunt Becky herself had practically forgotten them. For years she had lived in her two rented rooms in The Pinery—otherwise the house of her old friend, Camilla Jackson, at Indian Spring. Many Dark and Penhallow homes would have been open to her, for the clan were never unmindful of their obligations, but Aunt Becky would have none of them. She had a tiny income of her own and Camilla, being neither a Dark nor a Penhallow, was easily bossed.

"I'm going to have a levee," Aunt Becky told Uncle Pippin one afternoon when he had dropped in to see her. He had heard she was not very well. But he found her sitting up in bed, supported by pillows, her broad, grid-dled old face looking as keen and venomous as usual. He reflected that it was not likely there was much the matter with her. Aunt Becky had taken to her bed before now when she fancied herself neglected by her clan.

Aunt Becky had held occasional gatherings that she called "levees" ever since she had gone to live at The Pinery. It was her habit to announce in the local papers that Mrs. Rebecca Dark would entertain her friends on such and such an afternoon. Everybody went who couldn't trump up a water-tight excuse for not going. They spent two hours of clan gossip, punctuated by Aunt Becky's gibes and the malice of her smile, and had a cup of tea, sandwiches, and several slices of cake. Then they went home and licked their wounds.

"That's good," said Uncle Pippin. "Things are pretty dull in the clan. Nothing exciting has happened for a long time."

"This will be exciting enough," said Aunt Becky. "I'm going to tell them something—not everything—about who's to get the old Dark jug when I'm gone."

"Whew!" Uncle Pippin was intrigued at once. Still he did not forget his manners. "But why bother about that for a while? You're going to see the century out."

"No, I'm not," said Aunt Becky. "Roger told Camilla this morning that I wouldn't live this year out. He didn't tell *me*, the person most interested, but I wormed it out of Camilla."

It was a shock to Uncle Pippin and he was silent for a few moments. He had had a death-bell ringing in his ear for three days, but he had not connected it with Aunt Becky. Really, no one had ever thought of Aunt Becky dying. Death, like life, seemed to have forgotten her. He didn't know what to say.

"Doctors often make mistakes," he stammered feebly.

"Roger doesn't," said Aunt Becky grimly. "I've got to die, I suppose. Anyhow, I might as well die. Nobody cares anything about me now."

"Why do you say that, Becky?" said Camilla, betraying symptoms of tears. "I'm sure *I* do."

"No, you don't really. You're too old. We're both too old to care really for anybody or anything. You know perfectly well that in the back of your mind you're thinking, 'After she dies I'll be able to have my tea strong.' There's no use blinking the truth or trying to cover it up with sentiment. I've survived all my real friends."

"Come, come, what about me?" protested Uncle Pippin.

Aunt Becky turned her cronelike old grey head toward him.

"You!" She was almost contemptuous. "Why, you're only sixty-four. I was married before you were born. You're nothing but an acquaintance if it comes to that. Hardly even a relative. You were only an adopted Penhallow, remember. Your mother always vowed you were Ned Penhallow's son, but I can tell you some of us had our doubts. Funny things come in with the tide, Pippin."

This, reflected Uncle Pippin, was barely civil. He decided that it was not necessary to protest any more friendship for Aunt Becky.

"Camilla," snapped Aunt Becky, "I beg of you to stop trying to cry. It's painful to watch you. I had to send Ambrosine out because I couldn't put up with her mewing.

Ambrosine cries over everything alike—a death or a spoiled pudding. But one excuses her. It's about the only fun she's ever got out of life. *I* am ready to die. I've felt almost everything in life there is to feel—ay, I've drained my cup. But I mean to die decently and in order. I'm going to have one last grand rally. The date will be announced in the paper. But if you want anything to eat you'll have to bring it with you. I'm not going to bother with that sort of thing on my death-bed."

Uncle Pippin was genuinely disappointed. Living alone as he did, subsisting on widower's fare, the occasional meals and lunches he got in friends' houses meant much to him. And now Aunt Becky was going to ask people to come and see her and wasn't going to give them a bite. It was inhospitable, that's what it was. Everybody would be resentful but everybody would be there. Uncle Pippin knew his Darks and his Penhallows. Every last one of them would be keen to know who was to get the old Dark jug. Everybody would think he or she ought to have it. The Darks had always resented the fact of Aunt Becky owning it, anyhow. She was only a Penhallow. The jug should be the property of a born Dark. But old Theodore Dark had expressly left it to his dearly beloved wife in his will and there you were. The jug was hers to do as she liked with. And nobody in eighty-five years had ever been able to predict what Aunt Becky would do about anything.

Uncle Pippin climbed into what he called his "gig" and drove away behind his meek white horse down the narrow, leisurely red side-road that ran from Indian Spring to Bay Silver. There was a grin of enjoyment on his little, wrinkled face with its curious resemblance to a shrivelled apple, and his astonishingly young, vivid blue eyes twinkled. It would be fun to watch the antics of the clan over the jug. The thorough-going, impartial fun of one who was not vitally concerned. Uncle Pippin knew he had no chance of getting the jug. He was only a fourth cousin at best, even granting the dubious paternity about which Aunt Becky had twitted him.

"I've a hunch that the old lady is going to start something," said Uncle Pippin to his white nag.

II

In spite of the fact that no refreshments were to be served, every Dark and every Penhallow, by birth, marriage or adoption, who could possibly get to Aunt Becky's "levee" was there. Even old rheumatic Christian Dark, who hadn't been anywhere for years, made her son-in-law draw her through the woods behind The Pinery on a milk-cart. The folding doors between Aunt Becky's two rooms were thrown open, the parlour was filled with chairs, and Aunt Becky, her eyes as bright as a cat's, was ready to receive her guests, sitting up in her big old walnut bed under its tent canopy hung with yellowed net. Aunt Becky had slept in that bed ever since she was married and intended to die in it. Several women of the tribe had their eye on it and each had hoped she would get it, but just now nobody thought of anything but the jug.

Aunt Becky had refused to dress up for her guests. She wasn't going to be bothered, she told Camilla—they weren't really worth it. So she received them regally with a faded old red sweater pinned tightly around her shrunken throat and her grey hair twisted into a hard knot on the crown of her head. But she wore her diamond ring and she had made the scandalised Ambrosine put a little rouge on her cheeks.

"It's no more than decent at your age," protested Ambrosine.

"Decency's a dull dog," retorted Aunt Becky. "I parted company with it long ago. You do as you're bid, Ambrosine Winkworth, and you'll get your reward. I'm not going to have Uncle Pippin saying, 'The old girl *used to have* good colour.' Dab it on good and thick, Ambrosine. None of them will imagine they can bully me as they probably would if they found me looking lean and washed-out. My golly, Ambrosine, but, I'm looking forward to this afternoon. It's the last bit of fun I'll have this side of eternity and I'm going to lap it up, Ambrosine. Harpies all of 'em, coming here just to see what pickings they're going to get. Ay, I'm going to make them squirm."

The Darks and Penhallows knew this perfectly well, and every new arrival approached the walnut bed with a secret harrowing conviction that Aunt Becky would certainly ask any especially atrocious question that occurred to her. Uncle Pippin had come early, provided with several wads of his favourite chewing-gum, and selected a seat near the folding doors—a point of vantage from which he could see everybody and hear everything Aunt Becky said. He had his reward.

"Ay, so you're the man who burned his wife," remarked Aunt Becky to Stanton Grundy, a long, lean man with a satiric smile who was an outsider, long ago married to Robina Dark, whom he had cremated. Her clan had never forgiven him for it, but Stanton Grundy was insensitive and only smiled hollowly at what he regarded as an attempted witticism.

"All this fuss over a jug worth no more than a few dollars at most," he said scornfully, sitting down beside Uncle Pippin.

Uncle Pippin shifted his wad of gum to the other side of his mouth and manufactured a cheerful lie instantly for the credit of the clan.

"A collector offered Aunt Becky a hundred dollars for it four years ago," he said impressively. Stanton Grundy *was* impressed and to hide it remarked that *he* wouldn't give ten dollars for it.

"Then why are you here?" demanded Uncle Pippin.

"To see the fun," returned Mr. Grundy coolly. "This jug business is going to set everybody by the ears."

Uncle Pippin nearly swallowed his gum in his indignation. What right had this outsider, who was strongly suspected of being a Swedenborgian, whatever that was, to amuse himself over Dark whimsies and Penhallow peculiarities? It was quite in order for him, Pippin Penhallow, baptised Alexander, to do it. He was one of the tribe, however crookedly. But that a Grundy from God knew where should come for such a purpose made Uncle Pippin furious. Before he could administer castigation, however, another arrival temporarily diverted his attention from the outrageous Grundy.

"Been having any more babies on the King's Highway?"

Aunt Becky was saying to poor Mrs. Paul Dark, who had brought her son into a censorious world in a Ford coupé on the way to the hospital. Uncle Pippin had voiced the general clan feeling on that occasion when he said gloomily,

"Sad mismanagement somewhere."

A little snicker drifted over the room, and Mrs. Paul made her way to a chair with a burning face. But interest had already shifted from her to Murray Dark, a handsome middle-aged man who was shaking Aunt Becky's hand.

"Well, well, come to get a peep at Thora, hey? She's here—over there beyond Pippin and that Grundy man."

Murray Dark stalked to a chair, reflecting that when you belonged to a clan like this you really lived a dog's life. Of course he had come to see Thora. Everybody knew that, including Thora herself. Murray cared not a hoot about the Dark jug but he did care tremendously about a chance to look at Thora. He did not have too many of them. He had been in love with Thora ever since the Sunday he had first seen her sitting in the church, the bride of Christopher Dark—drunken ne'er-do-well Chris Dark, with his insidious charm that no girl had ever been able to resist. All the clan knew it, too, but there had never been any scandal. Murray was simply waiting for Chris to pass out. Then he would marry Thora. He was a clever, well-to-do farmer and he had any amount of patience. In time he would attain his heart's desire—though sometimes he wondered a little uneasily how long that devil of a Chris *would* hang on. That family of Darks had such damn' good constitutions. They could live after a fashion that would kill any ordinary man in five years, and flourish for twenty. Chris had been dying by inches for ten years, and there was no knowing how many inches were left of him yet.

"Do get some hair tonic," Aunt Becky was advising William Y. Penhallow, who even as a baby had looked deadly serious and who had never been called Bill in his life. He had hated Aunt Becky ever since she had been the first person to tell him he was beginning to get bald.

"My dear"—to Mrs. Percy Dark—"it's such a pity you haven't taken more care of your complexion. You had a fairly nice skin when you came to Indian Spring. Why, *you* here?"—this to Mrs. Jim Trent, who had been Helen Dark.

"Of course I'm here," retorted Mrs. Jim. "Am I so transparent that there's any doubt?"

"It's a long time since you remembered my existence," snapped Aunt Becky. "But the jug is bringing more things in than the cat."

"Oh, *I* don't want your jug, I'm sure," lied Mrs. Jim. Everybody knew she was lying. Only a very foolish person would lie to Aunt Becky, to whom nobody had ever as yet told a lie successfully. But then Mrs. Jim Trent lived at Three Hills, and nobody who lived at Three Hills was supposed to have much sense.

"Got your history finished yet, Miller?" asked Aunt Becky.

Old Miller Dark looked foolish. He had been talking for years of writing a history of the clan but had never got started. It didn't do to hurry these things. The longer he waited the more history there would be. These women were always in such a confounded hurry. He thankfully made way for Palmer Dark, who was known as the man who was proud of his wife.

"Looks as young as ever, doesn't she?" he demanded beamingly of Aunt Becky.

"Yes—if it's any good to look young when you're not—" conceded Aunt Becky, adding by way of a grace note, "Got the beginnings of a dowager's cushion, I see. It's a long time since I saw you, Palmer. But you're just the same, only more so. Well well, and here's Mrs. Denzil Penhallow. Looking fine and dandy, too. I've always heard a fruit diet was healthy. I'm told you ate all the fruit folks sent in for Denzil when he was sick last winter."

"Well, what of it? *He* couldn't eat it. Was it to be wasted?" retorted Mrs. Denzil. Jug or no jug, *she* wasn't going to be insulted by Aunt Becky.

Two widows came in together—Mrs. Toynbee Dark, who had had her mourning all ready when her third and last husband had died, and Virginia Powell, whose husband had been dead eight years and who was young and tolerably beautiful but who still wore her black and had vowed, it was well known, never to marry again. Not, as

Uncle Pippin remarked, that any one was known to have asked her.

Aunt Becky let Mrs. Toynbee off with a coldly civil greeting. Mrs. Toynbee had been known to go into hysterics when snubbed or crossed, and Aunt Becky did not intend to let any one else usurp the limelight at her last levee. But she gave poor Virginia a jab.

"Is your heart dug up yet?"

Virginia had once said sentimentally, "My heart is buried in Rose River churchyard," and Aunt Becky never let her forget it.

"Any of that jam left yet?" asked Aunt Becky slyly of Mrs. Titus Dark, who had once gathered blueberries that grew in the graveyard and preserved them. Lawyer Tom Penhallow, who had been found guilty of appropriating his clients' money, was counted less of a clan disgrace. Mrs. Titus always considered herself an ill-used woman. Fruit had been scarce that year—she had five men to cater for who didn't like butter—and all those big luscious blueberries going to waste in the lower corner of the Bay Silver graveyard. There were *very* few graves there; it was not the fashionable part of the graveyard.

"And how's your namesake?" Aunt Becky was asking Mrs. Emily Frost. Kennedy Penhallow, who had been jilted by his cousin, Emily, sixty-five years before, had called his old spavined mare after her to insult her. Kennedy, happily married for many years to Julia Dark, had forgotten all about it, but Emily Frost, *née* Penhallow, had never forgotten or forgiven.

"Hello, Margaret; going to write a poem about this? 'Weary and worn and sad the train rattled on,'" Aunt Becky went off into a cackle of laughter and Margaret Penhallow, her thin, sensitive face flushing pitifully and her peculiarly large, soft, grey-blue eyes filling with tears, went blindly to the first vacant chair. Once she had written rather awful little poems for a Summerside paper, but never after a conscienceless printer had deleted her punctuation marks, producing that terrible line which haunted the clan forever afterwards like an unquiet ghost which refused to be laid. Margaret could never feel safe from hearing it quoted somewhere with a snicker or a bellow. Even here at Aunt Becky's death-bed levee it must be dragged up. Perhaps Margaret still wrote poems. A little shell-covered box in her trunk might know something about that. But the public press knew them no more, much to the clan's thankfulness.

"What's the matter with you, Penny? You're not as good-looking as you generally believe you are."

"Stung on the eye by a bee," said Pennycuik Dark sulkily. He was a fat, tubby little fellow with a curly grey beard and none too plentiful curly hair. As usual, he was as well-groomed as a cat. He still considered himself a gay young wag, and felt that nothing but the jug could have lured him into a public appearance under the circumstances. Just like this devilish old woman to call the attention of the world to his eye. But he was her oldest nephew and he had a right to the jug which he would maintain, eye or no eye. He always felt that his branch of the family had been unjustly done out of it two generations back. In his annoyance and excitement he sat down on the first vacant chair he spied, and then to his dismay discovered that he was sitting beside Mrs. William Y., of whom he had the liveliest terror ever since she had asked him what to do for a child who had worms. As if he, Pennycuik Dark, confirmed bachelor, knew anything about either children or worms.

"Go and sit in that far corner by the door so that I can't smell that damn' perfume. Even a poor old nonentity like myself has a right to pure air," Aunt Becky was telling poor Mrs. Artemas Dark, whose taste in perfumes had always annoyed Aunt Becky. Mrs. Artemas *did* use them somewhat too lavishly, but even so, the clan reflected as a unit, Aunt Becky was employing rather strong language for a woman—especially on her death-bed. The Darks and the Penhallows prided themselves on keeping up with the times, but they were not so far advanced as to condone profanity in a woman. *That* was still taboo. The joke of it was that Aunt Becky herself had always been down on swearing and was supposed to hold in special disfavor the two clansmen who habitually swore—Titus Dark because he couldn't help it and Drowned John Penhallow, who could help it but didn't want to.

The arrival of Mrs. Alpheus Penhallow and her daughter created a sensation. Mrs. Alpheus lived in St. John and happened to be visiting her old home in Rose River when Aunt Becky's levee was announced. She was an enormously fat woman with a rather deplorable penchant for wearing bright colours and over-rich materials, who had been very slim and beautiful in a youth during which she had been no great favorite with Aunt Becky. Mrs. Alpheus expected some unpleasant greeting from Aunt Becky and meant to take it with a smile, for she wanted badly to get the jug, and the walnut bed into the bargain, if the fates were propitious. But Aunt Becky, though she said to herself that Annabel Penhallow's dress was worth more than her carcass, let her off very leniently with,

"Humph! Smooth as a cat's ear, just as always," and looked past her at Nan Penhallow, about whom clan gossip had been very busy ever since her arrival in Rose River. It was whispered breathlessly that she wore pajamas and smoked cigarettes. It was well known that she had plucked eyebrows and wore breeches when she rode or "hiked," but even Rose River was resigned to that. Aunt Becky saw a snakey hipless thing with a shingle bob and long barbaric earrings. A silky, sophisticated creature in a smart black satin dress who instantly made every other girl in the room seem outmoded and Victorian. But Aunt Becky took her measure on the spot.

"So this is Hannah," she remarked, hitting instinctively on Nan's sore spot. Nan would rather have been slapped than called Hannah. "Well—well—well!" Aunt Becky's "wells" were a crescendo of contempt mingled with pity. "I understand you consider yourself a modern. Well, there were girls that chased the boys in my time, too. It's only names that change. Your mouth looks as if you'd been making a meal of blood, my dear. But see what time does to us. When you're forty you'll be exactly like this"—with a gesture toward Mrs. Alpheus' avoirdupois.

Nan was determined she wouldn't let this frumpy old harridan put her out. Besides, she had her own hankerings after the jug.

"Oh, no, Aunt Becky darling. I take after father's people. They stay thin, you know."

Aunt Becky did not like being "darlinged."

"Go upstairs and wash that stuff off your lips and cheeks," she said. "I won't have any painted snips around here."

"You—why, you've got rouge on yourself," cried Nan, despite her mother's piteous nudge.

"And who are you to say I should not?" demanded Aunt Becky. "Now, never mind standing there switching your tail at me. Go and do as you're told or else go home."

Nan was minded to do the latter. But Mrs. Alpheus was whispering agitatedly at her neck,

"Go, darling, go—do exactly as she tells you—or—or—"

"Or you'll stand no chance of getting the jug," chuckled Aunt Becky, who at eighty-five had ears that could hear the grass grow.

Nan went, sulky and contemptuous, determined that she would get even with somebody for her manhandling by this cantankerous old despot. Perhaps it was at this moment, when Gay Penhallow was entering the room in a yellow dress that seemed woven out of sunshine, that Nan made up her mind to capture Noel Gibson. It was intolerable that Gay of all people should be a witness of her discomfiture.

"Green-eyed girls for trouble," said Uncle Pippin.

"She's a man-eater, I reckon," agreed Stanton Grundy.

Gay Penhallow, a slight, blossom-like girl whom only the Family Bible knew as Gabrielle Alexandrina, was shaking Aunt Becky's hand but would not bend down to kiss her as Aunt Becky expected.

"Hey, hey, what's the matter?" demanded Aunt Becky. "Some boy been kissing you? And you don't want to spoil the flavour, hey?"

Gay fled to a corner and sat down. It was true. But *how* did Aunt Becky know it? Noel *had* kissed her the evening before—Gay's first kiss in all her eighteen years—Nan would have hooted over *that*! An exquisite fleeting kiss under a golden June moon. Gay felt that she could *not* kiss any one, especially dreadful old Aunt Becky, after *that*. Never mind if Aunt Becky wouldn't give her the jug. What difference did it make about her old jug, anyway? What difference did anything make in the whole wide beautiful world except that Noel loved her and she loved him?

But something seemed to have come into the now crowded room with the arrival of Gay—something like a sudden quick-passing breeze on a sultry day—something as indescribably sweet and elusive as the fragrance of a forest flower—something of youth and love and hope. Everybody felt inexplicably happier—more charitable—more courageous. Stanton Grundy's lantern-jaws looked less grim and Uncle Pippin momentarily felt that, after all, Grundy had undoubtedly married a Dark and so had a right to be where he was. Miller Dark thought he really would get started on his history next week—Margaret had an inspiration for a new poem—Penny Dark reflected that he was only fifty-two, after all—William Y. forgot that he had a bald spot—Curtis Dark, who had the reputation of being an incurably disagreeable husband, thought his wife's new hat became her and that he would tell her so on the way home. Even Aunt Becky grew less inhuman and, although she had several more shots in her locker and hated to miss the fun of firing them, allowed the remainder of her guests to pass to their seats without insult or innuendo, except that she asked old Cousin Skilly Penhallow how his brother Angus was. All the assembly laughed and Cousin Skilly smiled amiably. Aunt Becky couldn't put *him* out. He knew the whole clan quoted his Spoonerisms and that the one about his brother Angus, now dead for thirty years, never failed to evoke hilarity. The minister had come along that windy morning long ago, after Angus Penhallow's mill-dam had been swept away in the March flood, and had been greeted excitedly by Skilly.

"We're all upset here today, Mr. MacPherson—ye'll kindly excuse us—my dam brother Angus burst in the night."

"Well, I think everybody is here at last," said Aunt Becky—"everybody I expected, at least, and some I didn't. I don't see Peter Penhallow or the Moon Man, but I suppose one couldn't expect either of them to behave like rational beings."

"Peter *is* here," said his sister Nancy Dark eagerly.

"He's out on the verandah. You know Peter hates to be cooped up in a room. He's so accustomed to—to—"

"The great open spaces of God's outdoors," murmured Aunt Becky ironically.

"Yes, that's it—that's what I mean—that's what I meant to say. Peter is just as interested in you as any of us, dear Aunt."

"I daresay—if *that* means much. Or in the jug."

"No, Peter doesn't care a particle about the jug," said Nancy Dark, thankful to find solid ground under her feet in this at least.

"The Moon Man's here, too," said William Y. "I can see him sitting on the steps of the verandah. He's been away for weeks—just turned up today. Queer how he always seems to get wind of things."

"He was back yesterday evening. I heard him yelping to the moon all last night down at his shanty," boomed Drowned John. "He ought to be locked up. It's a family disgrace the way he carries on, wandering over the whole Island bareheaded and in rags, as if he hadn't a friend in the world to care for him. I don't care if he isn't mad enough for the asylum. He should be under *some* restraint."

Pounce went Aunt Becky.

"So should most of you. Leave Oswald Dark alone. He's perfectly happy on nights when there's a moon, anyhow, and who among us can say that. If we're perfectly happy for an hour or two at a time, it's as much as the gods will do for us. Oswald's in luck. Ambrosine, here's the key of my brass-bound trunk. Go up to the attic and bring down Harriet Dark's jug."

III

While Ambrosine Winkworth has gone for the jug and a hush of excitement and suspense has fallen over the assembled clan, let us look at them a little more closely, partly through Aunt Becky's eyes and partly through our own, and get better acquainted with them, especially with those whose lives were to be more or less affected and altered by the jug. There were all kinds of people there with their family secrets and their personal secrets, their outer lives of which everything—nearly—was known, and their inner lives of which nothing was known—not even to lean, lank Mercy Penhallow, whose lankness and leanness were attributed to the chronic curiosity about everyone which gave her no rest day or night. Most of them looked like the dull, sedate folks they were but some of them had had shocking adventures. Some of them were very beautiful; some were very funny; some were clever; some were mean; some were happy; some were not; some were liked by everybody and some were liked by nobody; some had reached the stodgy plane where nothing more was to be expected from life; and some were still adventurous and expectant, cherishing secret, unsatisfied dreams.

Margaret Penhallow, for instance—dreamy, poetical Margaret Penhallow, who was the clan dressmaker and lived with her brother, Denzil Penhallow, in Bay Silver. Always overworked and snubbed and patronised. She spent her life making pretty clothes for other people and never had any for herself. Yet she took an artist's pride in her work and something in her starved soul sprang into sudden transforming bloom when a pretty girl floated into church in a gown of her making. *She* had a part in creating that beauty. That slim vision of loveliness owed something of its loveliness to *her*, "old Margaret Penhallow."

Margaret loved beauty; and there was so little of it in her life. She had no beauty herself, save in her overlarge, strangely lustrous eyes, and her slender hands—the beautiful hands of an old portrait. Yet there was a certain attractiveness about her that had not been dependent on youth and had not left her with the years. Stanton Grundy, looking at her, was thinking that she was more ladylike than any other woman of her age in the room and that, if he were looking for a second wife—which, thank god, he wasn't—Margaret would be the one he'd pick.

Margaret would have been a little fluttered had she known he was thinking even this much. The truth was, though Margaret would have died any horrible death you could devise before she admitted it, she longed to be married. If you were married you were somebody. If not, you were nobody. In the Dark and Penhallow clan, anyhow. She wanted a dear little homey place to call her own;

and she wanted to adopt a baby. She knew the very kind of baby she wanted—a baby with golden hair and great blue eyes, dimples and creases and adorable chubby knees. And sweet sleepy little kisses. Margaret's bones seemed to melt in her body as water when she thought of it. Margaret had never cared for the pack of young demons Denzil called his family. They were saucy and unattractive youngsters who made fun of her. All her love was centered in her imaginary baby and her imaginary little house—which was not quite as imaginary as the baby, if truth were known. Yet she had no real hope of ever owning the house, while, if she could get married, she might be able to adopt a baby.

Margaret also wanted very much to get the Dark jug. She wanted it for the sake of that far-off unknown Harriet Dark concerning whom she had always had a strange feeling, half pity, half envy. Harriet Dark had been loved; the jug was the visible and tangible proof of that, outlasting the love by a hundred years. And what if her lover had been drowned! At least, she had *had* a lover.

Besides, the jug would give her a certain importance. She had never been of any importance to anyone. She was only "old Margaret Penhallow," with fifty drab, snubbed years behind her and nothing ahead of her but drab snubbed old age. And why should she not have the jug? She was a real niece. A Penhallow, to be sure, but her mother had been a Dark. Of course Aunt Becky didn't like her, but then whom did Aunt Becky like? Margaret felt that she ought to have the jug—must have the jug. Momentarily, she hated every other claimant in the room. She knew if she had the jug she could make Mrs. Denzil give her a room to herself in return for the concession of allowing the jug to be put on the parlour mantelpiece. A room to herself! It sounded heavenly. She knew she could never have her little dream-house or her blue-eyed, golden baby, but surely she might have a room to herself—a room where Gladys Penhallow and her shrieking chums could never come—girls who thought there was no fun in having a beau unless you could tell the world all about him and what he did and what he said—girls who always made her feel old and silly and dowdy. Margaret sighed and looked at the great sheaf of mauve and yellow iris Mrs. William Y. had brought up for Aunt Becky, who had never cared for flowers. If their delicate, exotic beauty was wasted on Aunt Becky, it was not lost on Margaret. While she gazed at them she was happy. There was a neglected clump of mauve iris in the garden of "her" house.

IV

Gay Penhallow was sitting next to Margaret and was not thinking of the jug at all. She did not want the jug, though her mother was wild about it. Spring was singing in her blood and she was lost in glamourous recollections of Noel's kiss—and equally glamourous anticipations of Noel's letter, which she had got at the post-office on her way up. As she heard it crackle in its hiding place she felt the little thrill of joy which had tingled over her when old Mrs. Conroy had passed it out to her—his wonderful letter held profanely between a mail-order catalogue and a millinery advertisement. She had not dreamed of getting a letter, for she had seen him—and been kissed—only the night before. Now she had it, tucked away under her dress, next to her white satin skin, and all she wished was that this silly old levee was over and she was away somewhere by herself, reading Noel's letter. What time was it? Gay looked at Aunt Becky's solemn old grandfather clock that had ticked off the days and hours of four forgotten generations and was still ticking them relentlessly off for the fifth. Three! At half-past three she must think of Noel. They had made a compact to think of each other every afternoon at exactly half-past three. Such a dear, delightful, foolish compact—because was she not thinking of Noel all the time? And now she had his kiss to think about—that kiss which it seemed everyone must see on her lips. She had thought about it all night—the first night of her life she had never slept for joy. Oh, she was so happy! So happy that she felt friendly to everybody—even to the people she had never liked before. Pompous old William Y. with his enormous opinion of himself—lean, curious, gossipy Mercy Penhallow—overtragic Virginia Powell with her tiresome poses—Drowned John, who had shouted two wives to death—Stanton Grundy, who had cremated poor Cousin Robina and who always looked at everybody as if he were secretly amused. One didn't like a person who was amused at everybody. Dapper Penny Dark, who thought he was witty when he called eggs cackleberries— Uncle Pippin with his old jaws always chewing something— most of all poor piteous Aunt Becky herself. Aunt Becky was going to die soon and no one was sorry. Gay was so sorry because she wasn't sorry that the tears came to her eyes. Yet Aunt Becky had been loved once—courted once— kissed once—ridiculous and unbelievable as it seemed now. Gay looked curiously at this solitary old crone who had once been young and beautiful and the mother of little children. *Could* that old wrinkled face ever have been flower-like? Would she, Gay, ever look like that? No, of course not. Nobody whom Noel loved would ever grow old and unlovely.

She could see herself in the oval mirror that hung on the wall over Stanton Grundy's head, and she was not dissatisfied with the reflection. She had the colouring of a tea-rose, with golden-brown hair, and eyes to match it— eyes that looked like brown marigolds flecked with glints of gold. Long black lashes and eyebrows that might have been drawn in soot, so finely dark were they against her face. And there was a delicious spot here and there on her skin, like a little drop of gold—sole survivor of the freckles that had plagued her in childhood. She knew quite well that she was counted the beauty of the whole clan—"the prettiest girl that walked the aisles of Rose River Church," Uncle Pippin averred gallantly. And she always looked the least little bit timid and frightened, so men always wanted to assure her there was nothing to be frightened of and she had more beaus than you could shake a stick at. But there had never been anyone who really mattered but Noel. Every lane in Gay's thoughts to-day turned back to Noel. Fifteen minutes past three. Just fifteen more minutes and she would be *sure* that Noel was thinking of her.

There was a tiny dark fleck or two on Gay's happiness. For one, she knew all the Penhallows rather disapproved of Noel Gibson. The Darks were more tolerant—after all,

Noel's mother had been a Dark, although a rather off-colour one. The Gibsons were considered a cut or two beneath the Penhallows. Gay knew very well that her clan wanted her to marry Dr. Roger Penhallow. She looked across the room at him in kindly amusement. Dear old Roger, with his untidy mop of red hair, his softly luminous eyes under straight heavy brows and his long, twisted mouth with a funny quirk in the left corner—who was thirty if he were a day. She was awfully fond of Roger. Somehow, there was a good tang to him. She could never forget what he had done for her at her first dance. She had been so shy and awkward and plain—or was sure she was. Nobody asked her to dance till Roger came and swept her out triumphantly and paid her such darling compliments that she bloomed out into beauty and confidence—and the boys woke up—and handsome Noel Gibson from town singled her out for attention. Oh, she was very very fond of Roger—and very proud of him. A fourth cousin who had been a noted ace in the war Gay so dimly remembered and had brought down fifty enemy planes. But as a husband—Gay really had to laugh. Besides, why should any one suppose he wanted to marry her? *He* had never said so. It was just one of those queer ideas that floated about the clan at times—and had a trick of turning out abominably correct. Gay hoped this one wouldn't. She would hate to hurt Roger. She was so happy she couldn't bear to think of hurting any one.

The second little fleck was Nan Penhallow. Gay had never been too fond of Nan Penhallow, though they had been chums of a sort, ever since childhood, when Nan would come to the Island with her father and mother for summer vacations. Gay never forgot the first day she and Nan had met. They were both ten years old; and Nan, who was even then counted a beauty, had dragged Gay to a mirror and mercilessly pointed out all the contrasts. Gay had never thought of her looks before, but now she saw fatally that she was ugly. Thin and sunburned and pale—freckles galore—hair bleached too light a shade by Rose River sunshine—funny, black unfaded eyebrows that looked as if they had just lighted on her face—how Nan made fun of those eyebrows! Gay was unhappy for years because she believed in her plainness. It had taken many a compliment to convince her that she had grown into beauty. As years went by she did not like Nan much better. Nan, with her subtle, mysterious face, her ashgold hair, her strange liquid emerald eyes, her thin red lips, who was not now really half as pretty as Gay but had odd exotic charms unknown to Rose River. How she patronised Gay— "You quaint child,"—"So Victorian." Gay did not want to be quaint and Victorian. She wanted to be smart and up-to-date and sophisticated like Nan. Though not exactly like Nan. She didn't want to smoke. It always made her think of that dreadful old Mrs. Fidele Blacquiere down at the harbour and old moustached Highland Janet at Three Hills, who were always smoking big black pipes like the men. And then—Noel didn't like girls who smoked. He didn't approve of them at all. Nevertheless, Gay, deep down in her heart, was glad the visit of the Alpheus Penhallows to Rose River was to be a brief one this summer. Mrs. Alpheus was going to a more fashionable place.

V

Hugh Dark and Joscelyn Dark (*née* Penhallow) were sitting on opposite sides of the room, never looking at each other, and seeing and thinking of nothing but each other. And everybody looked at Joscelyn and wondered as they had wondered for ten years, what terrible secret lay behind her locked lips.

The affair of Hugh and Joscelyn was the mystery and tragedy of the clan—a mystery that no one had ever been able to solve, though not for lack of trying. Ten years before, Hugh Dark and Joscelyn Penhallow had been married after an eminently respectable and somewhat prolonged courtship. Joscelyn had not been too easily won. It was a match which pleased everybody, except Pauline Dark, who was mad about Hugh, and Mrs. Conrad Dark, his mother, who had never liked Joscelyn's branch of the Penhallows.

It had been a gay, old-fashioned evening wedding,

according to the best Penhallow tradition. Everybody was
there to the fourth degree of relationship, and every one
agreed that they had never seen a prettier bride or a more
indisputable happy and enraptured bridegroom. After the
supper and the festivities were over, Hugh had taken his
bride home to "Treewoofe," the farm he had bought at
Three Hills. As to what had happened between the time
when Joscelyn, still wearing her veil and satin in the soft
coolness and brilliance of the September moonlight—a
whim of Hugh's, that, who had some romantic idea of
leading a veiled and shimmering bride over the threshold
of his new home—had driven away from her widowed
mother's house at Bay Silver and the time when, three
hours later, she returned to it on foot, still in her dishev-
elled bridal attire, no one ever knew or could obtain the
least inkling in spite of all their prying and surmising. All
Joscelyn would ever say, even to her distracted relatives,
was that she could never live with Hugh Dark. As for
Hugh, he said absolutely nothing and very few people
ever dared say anything to him.

Failing to discover the truth, surmise and gossip ran
riot. All sorts of explanations were hinted or manufactured—
most of them ridiculous enough. One was that Hugh, as
soon as he got his bride home, told her that he would be
master. He told her certain rules she must keep. He
would have no woman bossing *him*. The story grew till it
ran that Hugh, by way of starting in properly, had made or
tried to make Joscelyn walk around the room on all fours
just to teach her he was head of the house. No girl of any
spirit, especially Clifford Penhallow's daughter, would endure such a thing. Joscelyn had thrown her wedding-ring
at him and flown out of the house.

Others had it that Joscelyn had left Hugh because he
wouldn't promise to give up a cat she had hated. "And
now," as Uncle Pippin said mournfully, "the cat is dead."
Some averred they had quarreled because Joscelyn had
criticised his grammar. Some that she had found out he
was an infidel. "You know, his grandfather reads those
horrid Ingersoll books. And Hugh had them all on a shelf
in his bedroom." Some that she had contradicted him.
"His father was like that, you know. Couldn't tolerate the

least contradiction. If he only said, 'It's going to rain
to-morrow,' it put him in a fury if you said you thought it
would be fair."

Then Hugh had told Joscelyn she was too proud—he
wasn't going to put up with it any longer. He had danced
to her piping for three years but, by heck, the tune was
going to be changed. Well, of course Joscelyn *was* proud.
The clan admitted that. No woman could have carried
such a wonderful crown of red-gold on her head without
some pride to hold it up. But was that any excuse for a
bridegroom setting wide open the door of his house and
politely telling his bride to take her damned superior airs
back where they belonged?

The Darks would have none of these crazy yarns. It was
not Hugh's fault at all. Joscelyn had confessed she was a
kleptomaniac. It ran in her family. A fourth cousin of
her mother's was terrible that way. Hugh had the
welfare of generations unborn to think of. What else
could he do?

Darker hints obtained.

After all, though these little yarns were circulated and
giggled over, few really believed there was a grain of truth
in them. Most of the clan felt sure that Joscelyn's soft
rose-red lips were fast shut on some far more terrible
secret than a silly quarrel over cats or grammar. She had
discovered something undoubtedly. But what was it?

She had found a love letter some other woman had
written him and gone mad with jealousy. After all, Joscelyn's
great-grandmother had been a Spanish girl from the West
Indies. Spanish blood, you know. All the vagaries of
Joscelyn's branch of the Penhallows were attributed to the
fact of that Spanish great-grandmother. Captain Alec
Penhallow had married her. She died leaving him only one
son—luckily. But that son had a family of eight. And they
were all kittle cattle to handle. So intense in everything.
Whatever they were, they were ten times more so than
any one else would be.

No, it was worse than a letter. Joscelyn had discovered
that Hugh had another wife. Those years out west. Hugh
had never talked much about them. But at the last he
broke down and confessed.

Nothing of the sort. That child down at the harbour, though. It was certain *some* Dark was its father. Perhaps Hugh—

Naturally, it made a dreadful scandal and sensation. The clan nearly died of it. It had been an old clan saying that nothing ever happened in Bay Silver. Rose River had a fire. Three Hills had an elopement. Even Indian Spring years ago had an actual murder. But nothing ever happened in Bay Silver. And now something had happened with a vengeance.

That Joscelyn should behave like this! If it had been her rattle-brained sister Milly! They were always expecting Milly to do crazy things, so they were prepared to forgive her. But they had never though of Joscelyn doing a crazy thing so they could not forgive her for amazing them. Not that it seemed to matter much to Joscelyn whether they forgave her or not. No entreaty availed to budge her an inch. "Her father was like that, you know," Mrs. Clifford Penhallow wept. "He was noted for never changing his mind."

"Joscelyn evidently changed hers after she went up to Treewoofe that night," somebody replied. "*What* happened, Mavis? Surely you, her mother, ought to know."

"How can I know when she won't tell me?" wailed Mrs. Clifford. "None of you have ever had any idea how stubborn Joscelyn really is. She simply says she will never go back to Hugh and not another word will she say. She won't even wear her wedding-ring." Mrs. Clifford thought this was really the worst thing in it all. "I *never* saw anyone so unnaturally obstinate."

"And what in the world are we to *call* her?" wailed the clan. "She *is* Mrs. Dark. Nothing can alter that."

Nothing *could* alter it in Prince Edward Island, where there had been only one divorce in sixty years. Nobody ever thought of Hugh and Joscelyn being divorced. One and all, Darks and Penhallows, would have expired of the disgrace of it.

In ten years the matter had naturally simmered down, though a few people kept wondering if the wife from the west would ever turn up. The state of affairs was accepted as something permanent and immutable. People even forgot to think about it, except when, as rarely happened, they saw Hugh and Joscelyn in the same room. Then they wondered fruitlessly again.

Hugh was a very fine-looking man—far handsomer now at thirty-five than he had been at twenty-five, when he was rather lank and weedy. He gave you a feeling that he was able to do anything—a feeling of great, calm power. He had gone on living at Treewoofe with an old aunt keeping house for him, and in agricultural circles he was regarded as a coming man. It was whispered that the Conservative party meant to bring him out as a candidate at the next election of the Provincial House. Yet his eyes with their savage bitterness were the eyes of a man who had failed, and nobody had ever heard him laugh since that mysterious wedding-night.

He had had one keen greedy look at Joscelyn when he had paused a moment in the doorway. He had not seen her for a long time. The tragic years had passed over her without dimming her beauty. Her hair, massed round her head in shining defiant protest against the day of bobs, was as wonderful as ever. She had left her roses behind her—her cheeks were pale. But the throat he had once kissed so tenderly and passionately was as exquisite and ivory-like as ever, and her great eyes, that were blue or green or grey as the mood took her, were as lustrous and appealing, as defiant and ecstatic as they had been when she had looked down at him in the hall up at Treewoofe, that night ten years before. Hugh clenched his hands and set his lips. That lean fox of a Stanton Grundy was watching him—everybody was always watching him. The bridegroom jilted on his wedding night. From whom his bride had run in supposed horror or rebellion over three miles of dark solitary road. Well, let them watch and let them guess. Only he and Joscelyn knew the truth—the tragic absurd truth that had separated them.

Joscelyn had seen Hugh when he came into the room. He looked older; that unmanageable lock of dark hair was sticking up on the crown of his head as usual. Joscelyn knew she wanted to go over and coax it down. Kate Muir was sitting beside him ogling him; she had always detested and despised Kate Muir, *née* Kate Dark, who had been an ugly swarthy little girl and was now an ugly swarthy little widow with more money than she knew what to do with. Having married for money, Joscelyn reflected contemptuously, she had a right to it. But was that any excuse for her sitting in Hugh's pocket and gazing up at him as if she thought him wonderful. She knew that Kate had once said, "I always told Hugh she wouldn't make him a suitable wife." Joscelyn shivered slightly and locked her slender hands, on which was no wedding-ring, a little more tightly on her knee. She was not—never had been—sorry for what she had done ten years ago. She *couldn't* have done anything else, not *she*, Joscelyn Penhallow, with that touch of Spanish blood in her. But she had always felt a little outside of things and the feeling had deepened with the years. She seemed to have no part or lot in the life that went on around her. She learned to smile like a queen, with lips not eyes.

She saw her face reflected in the glass beside Gay Penhallow and suddenly thought that she looked old. Gay, wearing her youth like a golden rose, was so happy, so radiant, as if lighted by some inner flame. Joscelyn felt a queer new pang of envy. She had never envied anyone in all these ten years, borne up by the rapture of a certain strange, spiritual, sacrificial passion and renunciation. All at once, she felt an odd flatness, as if her wings had let her down. A chill of consternation and fright swept over her. She wished she had not come to this silly levee. She cared nothing about the old Dark jug, though her mother and Aunt Rachel both wanted it. She would not have come if she had thought Hugh would be there. Who would have expected him? Surely *he* didn't want the jug. She would have despised him if she thought he did. No doubt he had had to bring his mother and his sister, Mrs. Jim Trent. They were both glowering at her. Her sisters-in-law, Mrs. Penny Dark and Mrs. Palmer Dark, were pretending not to see her. She knew they all hated her. Well, it didn't matter. After all, could you blame them, considering the insult she had offered to the House of Dark? No, it didn't matter—Joscelyn wondered a little dreamily if anything mattered. She looked at Lawson Dark, with the V.C. he had won at Amiens pinned on his breast, in his wheel-chair behind Stanton Grundy, for ten years a paralytic from shell-shock. At Naomi Dark beside him, with her patient, haggard face and her dark, hollow eyes in which still burned the fires of the hope that kept her alive. Joscelyn was amazed to find suddenly stirring in her heart a queer envy of Naomi Dark. Why should she envy Naomi Dark, whose husband didn't recognise her—never had recognised her since his return from the war? His mind was normal in every other respect, but he had forgotten all about the bride he had met and married only a few weeks before his departure for the front. She knew Naomi lived by the belief that Lawson would remember her some day. Meanwhile she took care of him and worshipped him. Lawson had grown quite fond of her as a nurse, but no recollection ever came to him of his sudden love and his brief honeymoon. Yet Joscelyn envied her. She *had* had something. Life had not been an empty cup for her, whatever bitter brew was mingled in it. Even Mrs. Foster Dark had something to live for. Happy Dark had run away from home years ago, leaving a note—"I'll come back some time, Mother." Mrs. Foster would never lock her door at night lest Happy come, and it was well known that she always left a supper on the table for him. Nobody else believed Happy would ever come back—the young devil was undoubtedly dead years ago and good riddance! But the hope kept Mrs. Foster going, and Joscelyn envied her.

She saw Murray Dark devouring Thora Dark with his eyes, satisfied if she gave him only one look in return. He would, Joscelyn knew, rather have one of those long, deep, remote looks of Thora's than a kiss from any other woman. Well, it was no wonder he loved Thora. She was one of those women men can't help loving—except Chris Dark, who had given up loving her six weeks after he had married her. Yet other women did not dislike Thora. Whenever she came into a room people felt happier. She lighted life like a friendly beaming candle. She had a face that was charming without being in the least beautiful. A fascinating square face with a wide space between her blue almond-shaped eyes and a sweet, crooked mouth.

She was very nicely dressed. Her peculiarly dark auburn hair was parted on her forehead and coronetted on her crown. There were milky pearl drops in her ears. What a wife she would make for Murray if that detestable Chris would only be so obliging as to die. The winter before, he had had double pneumonia and everybody was sure he would die. But he hadn't—owed his life, no doubt, to Thora's faithful nursing. And Matthew Penhallow at Three Hills, whom everybody loved and who had a family that needed him, died of *his* pneumonia. Another proof of the contrariness of life.

Pauline Dark wasn't here. Was she still in love with Hugh? She had never married. What a tangled, criss-crossed thing life was, anyhow. And here they were all sitting in rows, waiting for Ambrosine Winkworth to bring down the jug about which they were all ready to tear each other in pieces. Truly a mad world. Joscelyn was un-blessed with the sense of humor which was making the affair a treat to Tempest Dark, sitting behind her. Tempest had made up his mind on considered opinion to shoot himself that night. He had nearly done it the night before, but he had reflected that he might as well wait till after the levee. He wanted, as a mere matter of curiosity, to see who got the old Dark jug. Winnifred had liked that jug. He knew he had no chance of it himself. Aunt Becky had no use for a bankrupt. He was bankrupt and the wife he had adored had died a few weeks previously. He couldn't see any sense in living on. But just at this moment he was enjoying himself.

VI

Donna Dark and Virginia Powell sat together as usual. They were first cousins, who were born the same day and married the same day—Donna to her own second cousin, Barry Dark, and Virginia to Edmond Powell—two weeks before they had left for Valcartier. Edmond Powell had died of pneumonia in the training camp, but Barry Dark had his crowded hour of glorious life somewhere in France. Virginia and Donna were "war widows" and had made a solemn compact to remain widows forever. It was Virginia's idea, but Donna was very ready to fall in with it. She knew she could never care for any man again. She had never said her heart was buried in any especial place—though rumour sometimes attributed Virginia's famous utterance to her—but she felt that way about it. For ten years they had continued to wear weeds, though Virginia was always much weedier than Donna.

Most of the clan thought Virginia, with her spiritual beauty of pale gold hair and over-large forget-me-not eyes, was the prettier of the two devoted. Donna was as dark as her name—a slight, ivory-coloured thing with very black hair which she always wore brushed straight back from her forehead, as hair should be worn only by a really pretty woman or by a woman who doesn't care whether she looks pretty or not. Donna didn't care—or thought she didn't—but it was her good luck to have been born with a widow's peak and that saved her. Her best features were her eyes, like star-sapphires, and her mouth with its corners tucked up into dimples. She had bobbed her hair at last, though her father kicked up a fearful domestic hullabaloo over it and Virginia was horrified.

"Do you think Barry would have liked it, dear?"

"Why not?" said Donna rebelliously. "Barry wouldn't have liked a dowdy wife. He was always up-to-date."

Virginia sighed and shook her head. *She* would never cut off her hair—never. The hair Edmond had caressed and admired.

"He used to bury his face in it and say it was like perfumed sunshine," she moaned gently.

Donna had continued to live with her father, Drowned John Penhallow—so called to distinguish him from another John Penhallow who had not been drowned—and her older half-sister, Thekla, ever since Barry's death. She had wanted to go away and train for nursing, but Drowned John had put his not inconsiderable foot down on that. Donna had yielded—it saved trouble to yield to Drowned John at the outset. He simply yelled people down. His rages were notorious in the clan. When reproached with them he said,

"If I didn't go into a rage now and then, life here would be so dull my females would hang themselves."

Drowned John was twice a widower. With his first wife, Jennie Penhallow, he had quarreled from the time they were married. When they knew their first baby was coming, they quarreled over what college they would send him to. As the baby turned out to be Thekla, there was no question—in Drowned John's mind, at least—of college. But the rows went on and became such a scandal that the clan hinted at a separation—not divorce of course. That never entered their heads. But Drowned John did not see the sense of it. He would have to have a housekeeper.

"Might as well be quarreling with Jennie as with any other woman," he said.

When Jennie died—"from sheer exhaustion," the clan said—Drowned John married Emmy Dark, destined to be Donna's mother. The clan thought Emmy was more than a little mad to take him, and pointed out to her what an existence she would have. But Drowned John never quarreled with Emmy. Emmy simply would not quarrel—and Drowned John had secretly thought life with her was very flat. Yet, although he always had two sets of manners and used his second best at home, Thekla and Donna were rather fond of him. When he got his own way he was quite agreeable. Hate what Drowned John hated—love what Drowned John loved—give him a bit of blarney now and again—and you couldn't find a nicer man.

All sorts of weird yarns were told of Drowned John's young days, culminating in his quarrel with his father, during which Drowned John, who had a tremendous voice, shouted so loud that they heard him over at Three Hills, two miles away. After which he had run away to sea on a ship that was bound for New Zealand. He had fallen overboard on the voyage and was reported drowned. The clan held a funeral service and his father had his name chiselled on the big family monument in the graveyard. After two years young John came home, unchanged save for a huge snake tattooed around his right arm, having acquired a lavish vocabulary of profanity and an abiding distaste for sea-faring. Some thought the ship which had picked him up unnecessarily meddlesome. But John settled down on the farm, told Jennie Penhallow he was going to marry her, and refused to have his name erased from the monument. It was too good a joke. Every Sunday Drowned John went into the graveyard and guffawed over it.

He was sitting now behind William Y. and wondering if William Y. really was presumptuous enough to imagine *he* should have the jug. Why, there was no manner of doubt in the world that he, John Penhallow, should have it. It would be a damned outrage if Aunt Becky gave it to anyone else and he'd tell her so, by asterisk and by asterisk. His very long face crimsoned with fury at the mere thought—a crimson that covered his ugly bald forehead, running back to his crown. His bushy white moustache bristled. His pop-eyes glared. By—more asterisks and very lurid ones—if any one else got that jug they'd have to reckon with *him*.

"I wonder what Drowned John is swearing so viciously inside himself about," thought Uncle Pippin.

Donna wanted the jug, too. She was really quite crazy about it. She felt she ought to have it. Long, long ago, when Barry was just a little boy, Aunt Becky had told him she was going to leave it to him when she died. So she, Barry's widow, should have it now. It was such a lovely old thing, with its romantic history. Donna had always hankered after it. She did not swear internally as her father did, but she thought crossly she had never seen such a bunch of old harpies.

VII

Outside on the railing of the verandah Peter Penhallow was sitting, swinging one of his long legs idly in the air. A rather contemptuous scowl was on his lean, bronzed, weary face. Peter's face always looked bored and weary— at least in scenes of civilisation. He wasn't going in. You would not catch Peter mewed up in a room full of heirloom hunters. Indeed, to Peter any room, even a vacant one, was simply a place to get out of as soon as possible. He always averred he could not breathe with four walls around him. He had come to this confounded levee—a curse on Aunt Becky's whims!—sorely against his will, but at least he would stay outside where there was a distant view of the jewelled harbour and a glorious wind that had never known fetters, blowing right up from the gulf—Peter loved wind—and a big tree of apple blossom that was fairer to look upon than any woman's face had ever seemed to Peter. The clan wrote Peter down as a woman-hater, but he was nothing of the sort. The only woman he hated was Donna Dark; he was simply not interested in women and had never tried to be because he felt sure no woman would ever be willing to share the only life he could live. And as for giving up that life and adopting a settled existence, the idea simply could never have occurred to Peter. Women regretted this, for they found him very attractive. Not handsome but "so distinguished, you know." He had grey eagle eyes, that turned black in excitement or deep feeling. Women did not like his eyes—they made them uncomfortable—but they thought his mouth very beautiful and even liked it for its strength and tenderness and humour. As Uncle Pippin said, the clan would likely have been very fond of Peter Penhallow if they had ever had any chance to get acquainted with him. As it was, he remained only a tantalising hop-out-of-kin, out of whose goings-on they got several vicarious thrills and of whom they were proud because his explorations and discoveries had won him fame—"notoriety," Drowned John called it—but whom they never pretended to understand and of whose satiric winks they were all a little afraid. Peter hated sham of any kind; and a clan like the Penhallows and the Darks were full of it. Had to be, or they couldn't have carried on as a clan at all. But Peter never made any allowances for that.

"Look at Donna Dark," he was wont to sneer. "Pretending to be devoted to Barry's memory when all the time she'd jump at a second husband if there was any chance of one."

Not that Peter ever did look at Donna. He had never seen her since she was a child of eight, sitting across from him in church on the last Sunday he had been there before he ran away on the cattle-ship. But people reported what he said to Donna and Donna had it in for him. She never expected any such good luck as a chance to get square. But one of her day-dreams was that in some mysterious and unthinkable way Peter Penhallow should fall in love with her and sue for her hand, only to be spurned with contumely. Oh, how she would spurn him! How she would show him that she was "a widow indeed." Meanwhile she had to content herself with hating him as bitterly as Drowned John himself could hate.

Peter, who was by trade a civil engineer and by taste an explorer, had been born in a blizzard and had nearly been the death of three people in the process—his mother, to begin with, and his father and the doctor, who were blocked and all but frozen to death on that night of storm. When they were eventually dug out and thawed out Peter was there. And never, so old Aunty But averred, had such an infant been born. When she had carried him out to the kitchen to dress him, he had lifted his head of his own power and stared all around the room with bright eager eyes. Aunty But had never seen anything like it. It seemed uncanny and gave her such a turn that she let Peter drop. Luckily he landed unhurt on a cushion of the lounge, but it was the first of many narrow shaves. Aunty But always told with awe that Peter had not cried when he came into the world, as all properly behaved babies do.

"He seemed to like the change," said Aunty But. "He's a fine, healthy child but"—and Aunt But shook her head forebodingly. The Jeff Penhallows did not bother over her "buts." She had got her nickname from them. *But* they lived to think that her foreboding on this occasion was justified.

Peter continued to like change. He had been born with the soul of Balboa or Columbus. He felt to the full the lure of treading where no human foot had ever trod. He had a thirst for life that was never quenched— "Life," he used to say, "that grand glorious adventure we share with the gods." When he was fourteen he had earned his way around the world, starting out with ten cents and working his passage to Australia on a cattle-ship. Then he had come home—with the skin of a man-eating tiger he had killed himself for his mother's decorous parlour floor and a collection of magnificent blue African butterflies which became a clan boast—gone back to school, toiled slavishly, and eventually graduated in civil engineering. His profession took him all over the world. When he had made enough money out of a job to keep him for awhile, he stopped working and simply explored. He was always daring the unknown—the uncharted—the undiscovered. His family had resigned themselves to it. As Uncle Pippin said, Peter was "not domestic," and they knew now he would never become so. He had had many wild adventures of which his clan knew and a thousand more of which they never heard. They were always expecting him to be killed.

"He'll be clapped into a cooking-pot some day," said Drowned John, but he did not say it to Peter, for the simple reason that he never spoke to him. There was an old feud between those two Penhallow families, dating back to the day when Jeff Penhallow had killed Drowned John's dog and hung it up at his gate, because Drowned John's dog had worried his sheep and Drowned John had refused to believe it or to get rid of his dog. From that day none of Drowned John's family had had any dealings, verbal or otherwise, with any of Jeff Penhallow's. Drowned John knocked down and otherwise maltreated in the square at Charlottetown a man who said that Jeff Penhallow's word was as good as his bond because neither was any good. And Peter Penhallow, meeting a fellow Islander somewhere along the Congo, slapped his face because the said Islander laughed over Thekla Dark having once flavoured some gingerbread with mustard. But this was clan loyalty and had nothing whatever to do with personal feeling, which continued to harden and embitter through the years. When Barry Dark, Peter's cousin and well-beloved chum, told Peter he was going to marry Donna Dark, Peter was neither to hold nor bind. He refused to countenance the affair at all and kicked up such a rumpus that even the Jeff Penhallows thought he was going entirely too far. When the wedding came off, Peter was hunting wapiti in New Zealand, full of bitterness of soul, partly because Barry had married one of the accursed race and partly because he, Peter, being notoriously and incurably left-handed, had not been accepted for overseas service. Barry had been rather annoyed over Peter's behaviour and a slight coolness had arisen between them, which was never quite removed because Barry never came back from the front. This left a sore spot in Peter's soul which envenomed still further his hatred of Donna Dark.

Peter had had no intention of coming to Aunt Becky's levee. He had fully meant to leave that afternoon en route for an exploring expedition in the upper reaches of the Amazon. He had packed and strapped and locked his trunk, whistling with sheer boyish delight in being off once more. He had had a month at home—a month too much. Thank God, no more of it. In a few weeks he would be thousands of miles away from the petty gossips and petty loves and petty hates of the Darks and Penhallows—away from a world where women bobbed their hair and you couldn't tell who were grandmothers and who were flappers—from behind—and in a place where nobody would ever make moan, "Oh, what will people think of you, Peter, if you do—or don't do—that?"

"And I swear by the nine gods of Clusium that this place will not see me again for the next ten years," said Peter Penhallow, running downstairs to his brother's car, waiting to take him to the station.

Just then Destiny, with an impish chuckle, tapped him on the shoulder. His half-sister Nancy was coming into the yard almost in tears. She couldn't get to the levee if he wouldn't take her. Her husband's car had broken down. And she *must* get to the levee. She would have no chance at all of getting that darling old jug if she did not go.

"Young Jeff here can take you. I'll wait for the evening train," said Peter obligingly.

Young Jeff demurred. He had to hoe his turnips. He could spare half an hour to take Peter to the station, but spend a whole afternoon down at Indian Spring he would not.

"Take her yourself," he said. "If the evening train suits you as well, you've nothing else to do this afternoon."

Peter yielded unwillingly. It was almost the first time in his life he had done anything he really didn't want to do. But Nancy had always been a sweet little dear—his favourite in his own family. She "Oh—Petered" him far less than any of the others. If she had set her heart on that confounded jug, he wasn't going to spoil her chance.

If Peter could have foreseen the trick Fate had it in

mind to play him, would he really have gone to the levee, Nancy to the contrary withstanding. Well, would he now? Ask him yourself.

So Peter came to the levee, but he felt a bit grim and into the house he would not go. He did not give his real reason—for all his hatred of sham. Perhaps he did not acknowledge it even to himself. Peter, who was not afraid of any other living creature from snakes and tigers up, was at the very bottom of his heart afraid of Aunt Becky. The devil himself, Peter reflected, would be afraid of that blistering old tongue. It would not have been so bad if she had dealt him the direct thwacks she handed out to most people. But Aunt Becky had a different technique for Peter. She made little smiling speeches to him, as mean and subtle and nasty as a cut made with paper, and Peter had no defence against them. So he thankfully draped himself over the railing of the verandah. The Moon Man was standing at the other end, and Big Sam Dark and Little Sam Dark were in the two rocking-chairs. Peter didn't mind them but he had a bad moment when Mrs. Toynbee Dark dropped into the only remaining chair with her usual whines about her health, ending up with pseudo-thankfulness that she was as well as she was.

"The girls of today are *so* healthy," sighed Mrs. Toynbee. "Almost vulgarly so, don't you think, Peter? When I was a girl I was extremely delicate. Once I fainted six times in one day. I don't really think I *ought* to go into that close room."

Peter, who hadn't been so scared since the time he had mistaken an alligator for a log, decided that he had every excuse for being beastly.

"If you stay out here with four unwedded men, my dear Alicia, Aunt Becky will think you have new matrimonial designs and you'll stand no chance of the jug at all."

Mrs. Toynbee turned a horrible shade of pea-green with suppressed fury, gave him a look containing things not lawful to be uttered and went in with Virginia Powell. Peter took the precaution of dropping the surplus chair over the railing into the spirea bushes.

"Excuse me if I weep," said Little Sam, winking at

Peter while he wiped away large imaginary tears from his eyes.

"Vindictive. Very vindictive," said Big Sam, jerking his head at the retreating Mrs. Toynbee. "And sly as Satan. You shouldn't have put her back up, Peter. She'll do you a bad turn if she can."

Peter laughed. What did Mrs. Toynbee's vindictiveness matter to him, bound for the luring mysteries of untrod Amazon jungles? He drifted off into a reverie over them, while the two Sams smoked their pipes and reflected, each according to his bent.

VIII

"Little" Sam Dark—who was six-feet-two—and "Big" Sam Dark—who was five-feet-one—were first cousins. "Big" Sam was six years the elder, and the adjective that had been appropriate in childhood stuck to him, as things stick in Rose River and Little Friday Cove, all his life. The two Sams were old sailors and longshore fishermen, and they had lived together for thirty years in Little Sam's little house that clung like a limpet to the red "cape" at Little Friday Cove. Big Sam had been born a bachelor. Little Sam was a widower. His marriage was so far in the dim past that Big Sam had almost forgiven him for it, though he occasionally cast it up to him in the frequent quarrels by which they enlivened what might otherwise have been the rather monotonous life of retired seafolk.

They were not, and never had been, beautiful, though that fact worried them little. Big Sam had a face that was actually broader than it was long and a flaming red beard—a rare thing among the Darks, who generally lived up to their name. He had never been able to learn how to cook, but he was a good washer and mender. He could also knit socks and write poetry. Big Sam quite fancied himself as a poet. He had written an epic which he was fond of declaiming in a surprisingly great voice for his thin body. Drowned John himself could hardly bellow louder. When he was low in his mind he felt that he had missed his calling and that nobody understood him. Also that nearly everybody in the world was going to be damned.

"I should have been a poet," he would say mournfully to his orange-hued cat—whose name was Mustard. The cat always agreed with him, but Little Sam sometimes snorted contemptuously. If he had a vanity it was in the elaborate anchors tattooed on the back of his hands. He considered them far more tasty and much more in keeping with the sea than Drowned John's snake. He had always been a Liberal in politics and had Sir Wilfrid Laurier's picture hanging over his bed. Sir Wilfrid was dead and gone but in Big Sam's opinion no modern leader could fill his shoes. Premiers and would-be premiers, like everything else, were degenerating. He thought Little Friday Cove the most desirable spot on earth and resented any insinuation to the contrary.

"I like to have the sea, 'the blue lone sea,' at my very doorstep like this," he boomed to the "writing man" who was living in a rented summer cottage at the cove and had asked if they never found Little Friday lonesome.

"Jest part of his poetical nature," Little Sam had explained aside, so that the writing man should not think that Big Sam had rats in his garret. Little Sam lived in secret fear—and Big Sam in secret hope—that the writing man would "put them in a book."

By the side of the wizened Big Sam Little Sam looked enormous. His freckled face was literally half forehead and a network of large, purplish-red veins over nose and cheeks looked like some monstrous spider. He wore a great, drooping mustache like a horse-shoe that did not seem to belong to his face at all. But he was a genial soul and enjoyed his own good cooking, especially his famous pea soups and clam chowders. His political idol was Sir John Macdonald, whose picture hung over the clock shelf, and he had been heard to say—not in Big Sam's hearing—that he admired weemen in the abstract. He had a harmless hobby of collecting skulls from the old Indian graveyard down at Big Friday Cove and ornamenting the fence of his potato plot with them. He and Big Sam quarreled about it every time he brought a new skull home. Big Sam declared it was indecent and unnatural and unchristian. But the skulls remained on the poles.

Little Sam was not, however, always inconsiderate of

Big Sam's feelings. He had once worn large, round, gold earrings in his ears, but he had given up wearing them because Big Sam was a fundamentalist and didn't think they were Presbyterian ornaments.

Both Big and Little Sam had only an academic interest in the old Dark jug. Their cousinship was too far off to give them any claim on it. But they never missed attending any clan gathering. Big Sam might get material for a poem out of it and Little Sam might see a pretty girl or two. He was reflecting now that Gay Penhallow had got to be a regular little beauty and that Thora Dark was by way of being a fine armful. And there was *something* about Donna Dark— something confoundedly seductive. William Y.'s Sara was undeniably handsome, but she was a trained nurse and Little Sam always felt that she knew too much about her own and other people's insides to be really charming. As for Mrs. Alpheus Penhallow's Nan, about whom there had been so much talk, Little Sam gravely decided that she was "too jazzy."

But Joscelyn Dark, now. She had always been a looker. What the divvle could have come between her and Hugh? Little Sam thought "divvle" was far less profane than "devil"—softer like. For an old sea-dog Little Sam was fussy about his language.

Oswald Dark had been standing at the far end of the verandah, his large, agate-grey, expressionless eyes fixed on the sky and the golden edge of the world that was the valley of Bay Silver. He wore, as usual, a long black linen coat reaching to his feet and, as usual, he was bareheaded. His long brown hair, in which there was not a white thread, parted in the middle, was as wavy as a woman's. His cheeks were hollow but his face was strangely unlined. The Darks and Penhallows were as ashamed of him as they had once been proud. In his youth Oswald Dark had been a brilliant student, with the ministry in view. Nobody knew why he "went off." Some hinted at an unhappy love affair; some maintained it was simply overwork. A few shook their heads over the fact that Oswald's grandmother had been an outsider—a Moorland from down east. Who knew what sinister strain she might have brought into the pure Dark and Penhallow blood?

Whatever the reason, Oswald Dark was now considered a harmless lunatic. He wandered at will over the pleasant red roads of the Island, and on moonlight nights sang happily as he strode along, with an occasional genuflection to the moon. On moonless nights he was bitterly unhappy and wept to himself in woods and remote corners. When he grew hungry he would call in at the first house, knock thunderingly on the door as if it had no right to be shut, and demand food regally. As everybody knew him he always got it, and no house was shut to him in the cold of a winter night. Sometimes he would disappear from human ken for weeks at a time. But, as William Y. said, he had an uncanny instinct for clan pow-wows of any sort and invariably turned up at them, though he could seldom be persuaded to enter the house where they were being held. As a rule he took no notice of people he met in his wanderings—except to scowl darkly at them when they demanded jocularly, "How's the moon?"—but he never passed Joscelyn Dark without smiling at her—a strange eerie smile—and once he had spoken to her.

"You are seeking the moon, too. I know it. And you're unhappy because you can't get it. But it's better to want the moon, even if you can't get it—the beautiful silvery remote Lady Moon—as unattainable as things of perfect beauty ever are—than to want and get anything else. Nobody knows that but you and me. It's a wonderful secret, isn't it? Nothing else matters."

IX

The folks in the parlour were getting a bit restless. What—the devil or the mischief—according to sex—was keeping Ambrosine Winkworth so long getting the jug? Aunt Becky lay impassive, gazing immovably at a plaster decoration on the ceiling which, Stanton Grundy reflected, looked exactly like a sore. Drowned John nearly blew the roof off with one of his famous sneezes and half the women jumped nervously. Uncle Pippin absent-mindedly began to hum *Nearer My God to Thee*, but was squelched by a glare from William Y. Oswald Dark suddenly came to the open window and looked in at these foolish and distracted people.

"Satan has just passed the door," he said in his intense dramatic fashion.

"What a blessing he didn't come in," said Uncle Pippin imperturbably. But Rachel Penhallow was disturbed. It had seemed so *real* when the Moon Man said it. She wished Uncle Pippin would not be so flippant and jocose. Every one again wondered why Ambrosine didn't come in with the jug. Had she taken a weak spell? Couldn't she find it? Had she dropped and broken it on the garret floor?

Then Ambrosine entered, like a priestess bearing a chalice. She placed the jug on the little round table between the two rooms. A sigh of relieved tension went over the assemblage, succeeded by an almost painful stillness. Ambrosine went back and sat down at Aunt Becky's right hand. Miss Jackson was sitting on the left.

"Good gosh," whispered Stanton Grundy to Uncle Pippin, "did you ever see three such ugly women living together in your life?"

That night at three o'clock Uncle Pippin woke up and thought of a marvelous retort he might have made to Stanton Grundy. But at the time he could think of absolutely nothing to say. So he turned his back on Stanton and gazed at the jug, as everyone else was doing—some coveteously, a few indifferently, all with the interest natural to this exhibition of an old family heirloom they had been hearing about all their lives and had had few and far between opportunities for seeing.

Nobody thought the jug very beautiful in itself. Taste must have changed notably in a hundred years if anybody had ever thought it beautiful. Yet it was undoubtedly a delectable thing, with its history and its legend, and even Tempest Dark leaned forward to get a better view of it. A thing like that, he reflected, deserved a certain reverence because it was the symbol of a love it had outlasted on earth and so had a sacredness of its own.

It was an enormous, pot-bellied thing of a type that had been popular in pre-Victorian days. George the Fourth had been king when the old Dark jug came into being. Half its nose was gone and a violent crack extended around its middle. The decorations consisted of pink-gilt scrolls, green and brown leaves and red and blue roses. On one side was a picture of two convivial tars, backed with the British Ensign and the Union Jack, who had evidently been imbibing deeply of the cup which cheers *and* inebriates, and who were expressing the feelings of their inmost hearts in singing the verse printed above them:

> "*Thus smiling at peril at sea or on shore*
> *We'll box the old compass right cheerly,*
> *Pass the grog, boys, about, with a song or two*
>   *more,*
> *Then we'll drink to the girls we love dearly.*"

On the opposite side the designer of the jug, whose strong point had not been spelling, had filled in the vacant place with a pathetic verse from Byron:

> "*The man is doomed to sail*
> *With the blast of the gale*
> *Through billows attalantic to steer.*
> *As he bends o'er the wave*
> *Which may soon be his grave*
> *He remembers his home with a tear.*"

Rachel Penhallow felt a tear start to her eyes and roll down her long face as she read it. It had been, she thought mournfully, so sadly prophetic.

In the middle of the jug, below its broken nose, was a name and date. Harriet Dark, Aldboro, 1826, surrounded by a wreath of pink and green tied with a true-lover's knot. The jug was full of old potpourri and the room was instantly filled with its faint fragrance—a delicate spicy smell, old-maidishly sweet, virginally elusive, yet with such penetrating, fleeting suggestions of warm passion and torrid emotions. Everybody in the room suddenly felt its influence. For one infinitesimal moment Joscelyn and Hugh looked at each other—Margaret Penhallow was young again—Virginia put her hand over Donna's in a convulsive grasp—Thora Dark moved restlessly—and a strange expression flickered over Lawson Dark's face. Uncle Pippin caught it as it vanished and felt his scalp crinkle. For just a second he thought Lawson was remembering.

Even Drowned John found himself recalling how pretty and flower-like Jennie had been when he married her. What a hell of a pity one couldn't stay always young.

Everyone present knew the romantic story of the old Dark jug. Harriet Dark, who had been sleeping for one hundred years in a quaint English churchyard, had been a slim fair creature with faint rose cheeks and big grey eyes, in 1826, with a gallant sea-captain for a lover. And this lover, on what proved to be his last voyage, had sailed to Amsterdam and there had caused to be made the jug of scroll and verse and true-lover's knot for a birthday gift to his Harriet, it being the fashion of the time to give the lady of your heart such a robust and capacious jug. Alas for true loves and true lovers! On the voyage home the Captain was drowned. The jug was sent to the broken-hearted Harriet. Hearts *did* break a hundred years ago, it is said. A year later Harriet, her spring of love so suddenly turned to autumn was buried in the Aldboro churchyard and the jug passed into the keeping of her sister, Sarah Dark, who had married her cousin, Robert Penhallow. Sarah, being perhaps of a practical and unromantic turn of mind, used the jug to hold the black currant jam for the concoction of which she was noted. Six years later, when Robert Penhallow decided to emigrate to Canada, his wife carried the jug with her, full of black currant jam. The voyage was long and stormy; the currant jam was all eaten; and the jug was broken by some mischance into three large pieces. But Sarah Penhallow was a resourceful woman. When she was finally settled in her new home, she took the jug and mended it carefully with white lead. It was done thoroughly and lastingly but not exactly artistically. Sarah smeared the white lead rather lavishly over the cracks, pressing it down with her capable thumb. And in a good light to this very day the lines of Sarah Penhallow's thumb could be clearly seen in the hardened spats of white lead.

Thereafter for years Sarah Penhallow kept the jug in her

dairy, filled with cream skimmed from her broad, golden-brown, earthenware milk pans. On her deathbed she had given it to her daughter Rachel, who had married Thomas Dark. Rachel Dark left it to her son Theodore. By this time it had been advanced to the dignity of an heirloom and was no longer degraded to menial uses. Aunt Becky kept it in her china cabinet, and it was passed around and its story told at all clan gatherings. It was said a collector had offered Aunt Becky a fabulous sum for it. But no Dark or Penhallow would ever have dreamed of selling such a household god. Absolutely it must remain in the family. To whom would Aunt Becky give it? This was the question every one in the room was silently asking; Aunt Becky alone knew the answer and she did not mean to be in any hurry to give it. This was her last levee; she had much to do and still more to say before she came to the question of the jug at all. She was going to take her time about it and enjoy it. She knew perfectly well that what she was going to do would set everybody by the ears, but all she regretted was that she would not be alive to see the sport. Look at all those female animals with their eyes popping out at the jug! Aunt Becky began to laugh and laughed until her bed shook.

"I think," she said, finally, wiping the tears of mirth from her eyes, "that a solemn assembly like this should be opened with prayer."

This was by way of being a bombshell. Who but Aunt Becky would have thought of such a thing? Everybody looked at each other and then at David Dark, who was the only man in the clan who was known to have a gift of prayer. David Dark was usually very ready to lead in prayer, but he was not prepared for this.

"David," said Aunt Becky inexorably. "I'm sorry to say this clan haven't the reputation of wearing their knees out praying. I shall have to ask you to do the proper thing."

His wife looked at him appealingly. She was very proud because her husband could make such fine prayers. She forgave him all else for it, even the fact that he made all his family go to bed early to save kerosene and had a dreadful habit of licking his fingers after eating tarts.

David's prayers were her only claim to distinction, and she was afraid he was going to refuse now.

David, poor wretch, had no intention of refusing, much as he disliked the prospect. To do so would offend Aunt Becky and lose him all chance of the jug. He cleared his throat and rose to his feet. Everybody bowed. Outside the two Sams, realising what was going on as David's sonorous voice floated out to them, took their pipes out of their mouths. David's prayer was not up to his best, as his wife admitted to herself, but it was an eloquent and appropriate petition and David felt himself badly used when after his "Amen" Aunt Becky said:

"Giving God information isn't praying, David. It's just as well to leave something to His imagination, you know. But I suppose you did your best. Thank you. By the way, do you remember the time, forty years ago, when you put Aaron Dark's old ram in the church basement?"

David looked silly and Mrs. David was indignant. Aunt Becky certainly had a vile habit of referring in company to whatever incident in your life you were most anxious to forget. But she was like that. And you couldn't resent it if you wanted the jug. The David Darks managed a feeble smile.

"Noel," thought Gay, "is leaving the bank now."

"I wonder," said Aunt Becky reflectively, "who was the first man who ever prayed. And what he prayed for. And how many prayers have been uttered since then."

"And how many have been answered," said Naomi Dark, speaking bitterly and suddenly for the first time.

"Perhaps William Y. could throw some light on that," chuckled Uncle Pippin maliciously. "I understand he keeps a systematic record of all his prayers, which are answered and which ain't. How about it, William Y.?"

"It averages up about fifty-fifty," said William Y. solemnly, not understanding at all why some were giggling. "I am bound to say, though," he added, "that some of the answers were—peculiar."

As for Ambrosine Winkworth, David had made an enemy for life of her because he had referred to her as "Thine aged handmaiden." Ambrosine shot a venomous glance at David.

"Aged—aged," she muttered rebelliously. "Why, I'm only seventy-two—not so old as all that—not so old."

"Hush, Ambrosine," said Aunt Becky authoritatively. "It's a long time since you were young. Put another cushion under my head. Thanks. I'm going to have the fun of reading my own will. And I've had the fun of writing my own obituary. It's going to be printed just as I've written it, too. Camilla has sworn to see to that. Good Lord, the obituaries I've read! Listen to mine."

Aunt Becky produced a folded paper from under her pillow.

"*No gloom was cast over the communities of Indian Spring, Three Hills, Rose River or Bay Silver when it became known that Mrs. Theodore Dark—Aunt Becky as she was generally called, less from affection than habit—had died on*'—whatever the date will be—'*at the age of eighty-five.*'

"You notice," said Aunt Becky, interrupting herself, "that I say *died*. I shall not pass away or pass out or pay my debt to nature or depart this life or join the great majority or be summoned to my long home. I intend simply and solely to die.

"*Everybody concerned felt that it was high time the old lady did die. She had lived a long life, respectably if not brilliantly, had experienced almost everything a decent female could experience, had outlived husband and children and anybody who had ever really cared anything for her. There was therefore neither sense, reason nor profit in pretending gloom or grief. The funeral took place on*'—whatever date it does take place on—'*from the home of Miss Camilla Jackson at Indian Spring. It was a cheerful funeral, in accordance with Aunt Becky's strongly expressed wish, the arrangements being made by Mr. Henry Trent, undertaker, Rose River.*'

"Henry will never forgive me for not calling him a mortician," said Aunt Becky. "Mortician—Humph! But Henry has a genius for arranging funerals and I've picked on him to plan mine.

"*Flowers were omitted by request*'—no horrors of funeral wreaths for me, mind. No bought harps and pillows and crosses. But if anybody cares to bring a bouquet from their own garden, they may—'*and the services were conducted by the Rev. Mr. Trackley of Rose River. The pall-bearers were Hugh Dark, Robert Dark,*'—mind you don't stumble, Dandy, as you did at Selina Dark's funeral. What a jolt you must have given the poor girl!—'*Palmer Dark, Homer Penhallow*'—put them on opposite sides of the casket so they can't fight—'*Murray Dark, Roger Penhallow, David Dark, and John Penhallow*'—Drowned John, mind you, not that simpering nincompoop at Bay Silver—'*who contrived to get through the performance without swearing as he did at his father's funeral.*'"

"I didn't," shouted Drowned John furiously, springing to his feet. "And don't you dare publish such a thing about me in your damned obituary. You—you—"

"Sit down, John, sit down. That really isn't in the obituary. I just stuck it in this minute to get a rise out of you. Sit down."

"I didn't swear at my father's funeral," muttered Drowned John sullenly as he obeyed.

"Well, maybe it was your mother's. Don't interrupt me again, please. Courtesy costs nothing, as the Scotchman said. '*Aunt Becky was born a Presbyterian, lived a Presbyterian, and died a Presbyterian. She had a hard man to please in Theodore Dark, but she made him quite as good a wife as he deserved. She was a good neighbour as neighbours go and did not quarrel more than anybody else in the clan. She had a knack of taking the wind out of people's sails that did not make for popularity. She seldom suffered in silence. Her temper was about the average, neither worse nor better and did not sweeten as she grew older. She always behaved herself decently, although many a time it would have been a relief to be indecent. She told the truth almost always, thereby doing a great deal of good and some harm, but she could tell a lie without straining her conscience when people asked questions they had no business to ask. She occasionally used a naughty word under great stress and she could listen to a risky story without turning white around the gills, but obscenity never took the place of wit with her. She paid her debts, went to church regularly, thought gossip was very interesting, liked to be the first to hear a piece of news, and*

*was always especially interested in things that were none
of her business. She could see a baby without wanting to
eat it, but she was always a very good mother to her own.
She longed for freedom, as all women do, but had sense
enough to understand that real freedom is impossible in
this kind of a world, the lucky people being those who can
choose their masters, so she never made the mistake of
kicking uselessly over the traces. Sometimes she was mean,
treacherous and greedy. Sometimes she was generous,
faithful and unselfish. In short, she was an average person
who had lived as long as anybody should live."*

"There," said Aunt Becky, tucking her obituary under
the pillow, quite happy in the assurance that she had made
a sensation. "You will observe that I have not called myself
'the late Mrs. Dark' or 'the deceased lady' or 'relict.' And
that's that."

"God bless me, did you ever hear the equal of that?"
muttered Uncle Pippin blankly.

Every one else was silent in a chill of outraged horror.
Surely—surely—that appalling document would never be
published. It must *not* be published, if anything short of
the assassination of Camilla Jackson could prevent it. Why,
strangers would suppose it had been written by some
surviving member of the clan.

But Aunt Becky was bringing out another document,
and all the Darks and Penhallows bottled up their indignation for the time being and uncorked their ears. Who was
to get the jug? Until that was settled the matter of the
obituary would be left in abeyance.

Aunt Becky unfolded her will, and settled her owlish
shell-ringed glasses on her beaky nose.

"I've left my little bit of money to Camilla for her life,"
she said. "After her death it's to go to the hospital in
Charlottetown."

Aunt Becky looked sharply over the throng. But she did
not see any particular disappointment. To do the Darks
and Penhallows justice, they were not money-grabbers.
No one grudged Camilla Jackson her legacy. Money was a
thing one could and should earn for oneself; but old family
heirlooms, crusted with the sentiment of dead and gone
hopes and fears for generations, were different matters.

Suppose Aunt Becky left the jug to some rank outsider? Or a museum? She was quite capable of it. If she did, William Y. Penhallow mentally registered a vow that he would see his lawyer about it.

"Any debts are to be paid," continued Aunt Becky, "and my **grave** is to be heaped up—not left flat. I insist on that. Make a note of it, Artemas."

Aretmas Dark nodded uncomfortably. He was caretaker of the Rose River graveyard, and he knew he would have trouble with the cemetery committee about that. Besides, it made it so confoundedly difficult to mow. Aunt Becky probably read his thoughts, for she said:

"I won't have a lawn-mower running over me. You can clip my grave nicely with the shears. I've left directions for my tombstone, too. I want one as big as anybody else's. And I want my lace shawl draped around me in my coffin. It's the only thing I mean to take with me. Theodore gave it to me when Ronald was born. There were times when Theodore could do as graceful a thing as anybody. It's as good as new. I've always kept it wrapped in silver paper at the bottom of my third bureau drawer. Remember, Camilla."

Camilla nodded. The first sign of disappointment appeared on Mrs. Clifford Penhallow's face. She had set her heart on getting the lace shawl, for she feared she had very little chance of getting the jug. The shawl was said to have cost Theodore Dark two hundred dollars. To think of burying two hundred dollars!

Mrs. Toynbee Dark, who had been waiting all the afternoon for an opportunity to cry, thought she saw it at the mention of Aunt Becky's baby son who had been dead for sixty years, and got out her handkerchief. But Aunt Becky headed her off.

"Don't start crying yet, Alicia. By the way, while I think of it, will you tell me something? I've always wanted to know and I'll never have another chance. Which of your three husbands did you like best—Morton Dark, Edgar Penhallow, or Toynbee Dark? Come now, make a clean breast of it."

Mrs. Toynbee put her handkerchief back in her bag and shut the latter with a vicious snap.

"I had a deep affection for all my partners," she said.

Aunt Becky wagged her head.

"Why didn't you say 'deceased' partners? You were thinking it, you know. You have that type of mind. Alicia, tell me honestly, don't you think you ought to have been more economical with husbands? Three! And Poor Mercy and Margaret there haven't been able even to get one."

Mercy reflected bitterly that if *she* had employed the methods Alicia Dark had, she might have had husbands and to spare, too. Margaret coloured softly and looked piteous. Why, oh, why, must cruel old Aunt Becky hold her up to public ridicule like this?

"I've divided all my belongings among you," said Aunt Becky. "I hate the thought of dying and leaving all my nice things. But since it must be, I'm not going to have any quarreling over them before I'm cold in my grave. Everything's down here in black and white. I've just left the things according to my own whims. I'll read the list. And let me say that the fact that any one of you gets something doesn't mean that you've no chance for the jug as well. I'm coming to that later."

Aunt Becky took off her spectacles, polished them, put them back on again, and took a drink of water. Drowned John nearly groaned with impatience. Heaven only knew how long it would be before she would get to the jug. He had no interest in her other paltry knick-knacks.

"Mrs. Denzil Penhallow is to have my pink china candlesticks," announced Aunt Becky. "I know you'll be delighted at this, Martha dear. You've given me so many hints about candlesticks."

Mrs. Denzil had wanted Aunt Becky's beautiful silver Georgian candlesticks. And now she was saddled with a pair of unspeakable china horrors, in colour a deep magenta-pink with what looked like black worms wriggling all over them. But she tried to look pleased, because if she didn't, it might spoil her chances for the jug. Denzil scowled, jug or no jug, and Aunt Becky saw it. Pompous old Denzil! She would get even with him.

"I remember when Denzil was about five years old he came down to my place with his mother, one day, and our old turkey gobbler took after him. I suppose the poor bird thought no one else had a right to be strutting around there. 'Member, Denzil? Lord, how you ran and blubbered! You certainly thought Old Nick was after you. Do you know, Denzil, I've never seen you parading up the church aisle since but I've thought of that."

Well, it had to be endured. Denzil cleared his throat and endured it.

"I haven't much jewellery," Aunt Becky was saying. "Two rings. One is an opal. I'm giving that to Virginia Powell. They say it brings bad luck, but you're too modern to believe that old superstition, Virginia. Though I never had any luck after I got it."

Virginia tried to look happy, though she had wanted the Chinese screen. As for luck or no luck, how could that matter? Life was over for her. Nobody grudged her the opal, but when Aunt Becky mentioned rings many ears were pricked up. Who would get her diamond ring? It was a fine one and worth several hundreds of dollars.

"Ambrosine Winkworth is to have my diamond ring," said Aunt Becky.

Half those present could not repress a gasp of disapproval and the collective effect was quite pronounced. This, thought the gaspers, was absurd. Ambrosine Winkworth had no right whatever to that ring. And what good would it do her—an old broken-down servant? Really, Aunt Becky's brain must be softening.

"Here it is, Ambrosine," said Aunt Becky, taking it from her bony finger and handing it to the trembling Ambrosine. "I'll give it to you now, so there'll be no mistake. Put it on."

Ambrosine obeyed. Her old wrinkled face was aglow with the joy of a long-cherished dream suddenly and unexpectedly realised. Ambrosine Winkworth, through a drab life spent in other people's kitchens, had hankered all through that life for a diamond ring. She had never hoped to have it; and now here it was on her hand, a great starry wonderful thing, glittering in the June sunshine that fell through the window. Everything came true for Ambrosine in that moment. She asked no more of fate.

Perhaps Aunt Becky had divined that wistful dream of the old woman. Or perhaps she had just given Ambrosine the ring to annoy the clan. If the latter, she had certainly succeeded. Nan Penhallow was especially furious. *She* should have the diamond ring. Thekla Penhallow felt the same way. Joscelyn, who once had had a diamond ring, Donna, who still had one, and Gay, who expected she soon would have one, looked amused and indifferent. Chuckling to herself Aunt Becky picked up her will and gave Mrs. Clifford Penhallow her Chinese screen.

"As if I wanted her old Chinese screen," thought Mrs. Clifford, almost on the point of tears.

Margaret Penhallow was the only one whom nobody envied. She got Aunt Becky's *Pilgrim's Progress,* a very old, battered book. The covers had been sewed on, the leaves were yellow with age. One was afraid to touch it lest it might fall to pieces. It was a most disreputable old volume which Theodore Dark, for some unknown reason, had prized when alive. Since his death, Aunt Becky had kept it in an old box in the garret, where it had got musty and dusty. But Margaret was not disappointed. She had expected nothing.

"My green pickle leaf is to go to Rachel Penhallow," said Aunt Becky.

Rachel's long face grew longer. She had wanted the Apostle spoons. But Gay Penhallow got the Apostle spoons— to her surprise and delight. They were quaint and lovely and would accord charmingly with a certain little house of dreams that was faintly taking shape in her imagination. Aunt Becky looked at Gay's sparkling face with less grimness than she usually showed and proceeded to give her dinner set to Mrs. Howard Penhallow, who wanted the Chippendale sideboard.

"It was my wedding-set," said Aunt Becky. "There's only one piece broken. Theodore brought his fist down on the cover of one of the tureens one day when he got excited in an argument at dinner. I won out in the argument, though—at least I got my own way, tureen or no tureen. Emily, you're to have the bed."

Mrs. Emily Frost, *née* Dark, a gentle, faded little person, who also had yearned for the Apostle spoons, tried to look grateful for a bed which was too big for any of her tiny rooms. And Mrs. Alpheus Penhallow, who wanted the bed, had to put up with the Chippendale sideboard. Donna Dark got an old egg-dish in the guise of a gaily coloured china hen sitting on a yellow china nest, and was glad because she had liked the old thing when she was a child. Joscelyn Dark got the claw-footed mahogany table Mrs. Palmer Dark had hoped for, and Roger Dark got the Georgian candlesticks and Mrs. Denzil's eternal hatred. The beautiful old Queen Anne bookcase went to Murray Dark, who never read books, and Hugh Dark got the old hour-glass—early eighteenth century—and wondered bitterly what use it would be to a man for whom time had stopped ten years ago. He knew, none better, how long an hour can be and what devastating things can happen in it.

"Crosby, you're to have my old cut-glass whiskey decanter," Aunt Becky was saying. "There hasn't been any whiskey in it for many a year, more's the pity. It'll hold the water you're always drinking in the night. I heard you admire it once."

Old Crosby Penhallow, who had been nodding, wakened up and looked pleased. He really hadn't expected anything. It was kind of Becky to remember him. They had been young together.

Aunt Becky looked at him—at his smooth, shining bald head, his sunken blue eyes, his toothless mouth. Old Crosby would never have false teeth. Yet in spite of the bald head and faded eyes and shrunken mouth, Crosby Dark was not an ill-looking old man—quite the reverse.

"I have a mind to tell you something, Crosby," said Aunt Becky. "You never knew it—nobody ever knew it—but you were the only man I ever loved."

The announcement made a sensation. Everybody—so ridiculous is outworn passion—wanted to laugh but dared not. Crosby blushed painfully all over his wrinkled face. Hang it all, was old Becky making fun of him? And whether or no, how dared she make a show of him like this before everybody?

"I was quite mad about you," said Aunt Becky musingly. "Why? I don't know. You were handsomer sixty years ago than any man has a right to be, but you had no brains. Yet you were the man for me. And you never looked at me. You married Annette Dark—and I married Theodore.

Nobody knows how much I hated him when I married him. But I got quite fond of him after awhile. That's life, you know—though those three romantic young geese there, Gay and Donna and Virginia, think I'm talking rank heresy. I got over caring for you in time, even though for years after I did, my heart used to beat like mad every time I saw you walk up the church aisle with your meek little Annette trotting behind you. I got a lot of thrills out of loving you, Crosby—many more I don't doubt than if I'd married you. And Theodore was really a much better husband for me than you'd have been—he had a sense of humour. And it doesn't matter now whether he was or wasn't. I don't even wish now that you had loved me, though I wished it for so many years. Lord, the nights I couldn't sleep for thinking of you—and Theodore snoring beside me. But there it is. Somehow, I've always wanted you to know it and at last I've had the courage to tell you."

Old Crosby wiped his brow with his handkerchief. Erasmus would never let him hear the last of this—never. And suppose it got into the papers! If he had dreamed anything like this was going to happen, he would never have come to the levee. He glowered at the jug. It was to blame, durn it.

"I wonder how many of us will get out of this alive," whispered Stanton Grundy to Uncle Pippin.

But Aunt Becky had switched over to Penny Dark and was giving him her bottle of Jordan water.

"What the deuce do I care for Jordan water," thought Penny. Perhaps his face was too expressive, for Aunt Becky suddenly grinned dangerously.

"Mind the time, Penny, you moved a vote of thanks to Rob Dufferin on the death of his wife?"

There was a chorus of laughs of varying timbre, among which Drowned John's boomed like an earthquake. Penny's thoughts were as profane as the others' had been. That a little mistake between thanks and condolence, made in the nervousness of public speaking, should be everlastingly coming up against a man like this. From old Aunt Becky, too, who had just confessed that most of her life she had loved a man who wasn't her husband, the scandalous old body.

Mercy Penhallow sighed. *She* would have liked the Jordan water. Rachel Penhallow had one and Mercy had always envied her for it. There must be a blessing in any household that had a bottle of Jordan water. Aunt Becky heard the sigh and looked at Mercy.

"Mercy," she said apropos of nothing, "do you remember that forgotten pie you brought out after everybody had finished eating at the Stanley Penhallow's silver-wedding dinner?"

But Mercy was not afraid of Aunt Becky. She had a spirit of her own.

"Yes, I do. And do *you* remember, Aunt Becky, that the first time *you* killed and roasted a chicken after you were married, you brought it to the table with the insides still in it?"

Nobody dared to laugh but everybody was glad Mercy had the spunk. Aunt Becky nodded undisturbed.

"Yes, and I remember how it smelled! We had company, too. I don't think Theodore ever fully forgave me. I thought that had been forgotten years ago. *Is* anything ever forgotten? Can people *ever* live anything down? The honours are to you, Mercy, but I must get square with somebody. Junius Penhallow, do *you* remember—since Mercy has started digging up the past—how drunk you were at your wedding?"

Junius Penhallow turned a violent crimson but couldn't deny it. Of what use was it, with Mrs. Junius at his elbow, to plead that he had been in such a blue funk on his wedding-morning that he'd never had had the courage to go through with it if he hadn't got drunk? He had never been drunk since, and it was hard to have it raked up now, when he was an elder in the church and noted for his avowed temperance principles.

"I'm not the only one who ever got drunk in this clan," he dared to mutter, despite the jug.

"No, to be sure. There's Artemas over there. Do you remember, Artemas, the evening you walked up the church aisle in your nightshirt?"

Artemas, a tall, raw-boned, red-haired fellow, had been too drunk on that occasion to remember it, but he always roared when reminded of it. He thought it the best joke ever.

"You should have all been thankful I had that much on myself," he said with a chuckle.

Mrs. Artemas wished she were dead. What was a joke to Artemas was a tragedy to her. She had never forgotten—never could forget—the humiliation of that unspeakable evening. She had forgiven Artemas certain violations of his marriage vow of which every one was aware. But she had never forgiven—never would forgive—the episode of the nightshirt. If it had been pajamas, it would not have been quite so terrible. But in those days pajamas were unknown.

Aunt Becky was at Mrs. Conrad Dark.

"I'm giving you my silver saltcellars. Alec Dark's mother gave them to me for a wedding-present. Do you remember the time you and Mrs. Clifford there quarreled over Alec Dark and she slapped your face? And neither of you got Alec after all. There, there, don't crack the spectrum. It's all dead and vanished, just like my affair with Crosby."

("As if there was ever any affair," thought Crosby piteously.)

"Pippin's to have my grandfather clock. Mrs. Digby Dark thinks she should have that because her father gave it to me. But no. Do you remember, Fanny, that you once put a tract in a book you lent me? Do you know what I did with it? I used it for curl papers. I've never forgiven you for the insult. Tracts, indeed. Did I need tracts?"

"You—weren't a member of the church," said Mrs. Digby, on the point of tears.

"No—nor am yet. Theodore and I could never agree which church to join. I wanted Rose River and he wanted Bay Silver. And after he died it seemed sort of disrespectful to his memory to join Rose River. Besides, I was so old then it would have seemed funny. Marrying and church-joining should be done in youth. But I was as good a Christian as any one. Naomi Dark."

Naomi, who had been fanning Lawson, looked up with a start as Aunt Becky hurled her name at her.

"You're to get my Wedgwood teapot. It's a pretty thing. Cauliflower pattern, as it's called, picked out with gold lustre. It's the only thing it really hurts me to give up.

Letty gave it to me—she bought it at a sale in town with some of her first quarter's salary. Have you all forgotten Letty? It's forty years since she died. She would have been sixty if she were living now—as old as you, Fanny. Oh, I know you don't own to more than fifty, but you and Letty were born within three weeks of each other. It seems funny to think of Letty being sixty—she was always so young—she was the youngest thing I ever knew. I used to wonder how Theodore and I ever produced her. She *couldn't* have been sixty ever—that's why she had to die. After all, it was better. It hurt me to have her die—but I think it would have hurt me more to see her sixty— wrinkled—faded—grey-haired—my pretty Letty, like a rose tossing in a breeze. Have you all forgotten that gold hair of hers—such *living* hair. Be good to her teapot, Naomi. Well, that's the end of my valuable belongings—except the jug. I'm a bit tired—I want a rest before I tackle *that* business. I'm going to ask you all to sit in absolute silence for ten minutes and think about a question I'm going to ask you at the end of that time—all of you who are over forty. How many of you would like to live your lives over again if you could?"

X

Another whim of Aunt Becky's! They resigned themselves to it with what grace they could. A silence of ten minutes seems like a century—under certain conditions. Aunt Becky lay as if tranquilly asleep. Ambrosine was gazing raptly at her diamond ring. Hugh thought about the night of his wedding. Margaret tried to compose a verse of her new poem. Drowned John became conscious that his new boots were exceedingly tight and uncomfortable and uneasily remembered his new litter of pigs. He ought to be home attending to them. Uncle Pippin wondered irritably what that fellow Grundy was looking so amused about. Uncle Pippin would have been still more scandalised had he known that Grundy was imagining himself God, rearranging all these twisted lives properly, and enjoying himself hugely. Murray Dark devoured Thora with his eyes and Thora went on placidly shining with her own light. Gay began to pick out her flower-girls. Little Jill Penhallow and little Chrissie Dark. They were such darlings. They must wear pink and yellow crêpe and carry baskets of pink and yellow flowers—roses or 'mums, according to the time of year. Palmer Dark enjoyed in imagination the pleasure of kicking Homer Penhallow. Old Crosby was asleep and old Miller was nodding. Mercy Penhallow sat stiffly still and criticised the universe. Many of them were already sore and disappointed; nerves were strained and tenuous; when Julius Penhallow cleared his throat the sound was like a blasphemy.

"Two minutes more of this and I shall throw back my head and howl," thought Donna Dark. She suddenly felt sick and tired of the whole thing—of the whole clan—of her whole tame existence. What was she living for, anyhow? She felt as out of place as the blank, unfaded space left on the wall where a picture had hung. Life had no meaning—this silly little round of gossip and venom and malicious laughter. Here was a roomful of people ready to fly at each other's throats because of an old broken-nosed jug and a few paltry knick-knacks. She forgot that she had been as keen as anybody about the jug when she came. She wondered impatiently if anything pleasant or interesting or thrilling were ever going to happen to her again. Drowned John's early wanderlust suddenly emerged in her. She wanted to have wings—wide sweeping wings to fly into the sunset—skim over the waves—battle with the winds—soar to the stars—in short, do everything that was never done by her smug, prosperous, sensible home-keeping clan. She was in rebellion against all the facts of her life. Probably the whole secret of Donna's unrest at that moment was simply a lack of oxygen in the air. But it came pat to the psychological moment.

The sudden and lasting cessation of all the undertones and rustlings and stirrings in the room behind them at first arrested the attention and finally aroused the wonder of the outsiders on the verandah. Peter, who never knew why he should not gratify his curiosity about anything the moment he felt it, got off the railing, walked to the open

window and looked in. The first thing he saw was the
discontented face of Donna Dark, who was sitting by the
opposite window in the shadow of a great pine outside. Its
emerald gloom threw still darker shadows on her glossy
hair and deepened the lustre of her long blue eyes. She
turned toward Peter's window as he laid his arms on the
sill and bent inward. It was one of those moments all the
rest of life can't undo. Their eyes met, Donna's richly
quilled about with dark lashes, somewhat turbulent and
mutinous under eyebrows flying up like little wings, Peter's grey and amazed, under a puzzled frown.

Then it happened.

Neither Donna nor Peter knew at first just what *had*
happened. They only knew *something* had. Peter continued to stare at Donna as if mesmerised. Who was
this creature of strange dark loveliness? She must be one
of the clan or she wouldn't be here, but he couldn't place
her at all. Wait—wait—what old memory flickered tanta-
lisingly before him—now approaching—now receding? He
must grasp it—the old church at Rose River—himself, a
boy of twelve sitting in his father's pew—across the aisle a
little girl of eight—blue-eyed, black-haired, wing-browed—a
little girl, *sitting in Drowned John's pew!* He knew he
must hate her because she sat in Drowned John's pew. So
he made an impudent face at her. And the little girl had
laughed—*laughed*. She was amused at him. Peter, who
had hated her before impersonally, hated her now person-
ally. He had kept on hating her although he had never
seen her again—never again till now. Now he was looking
at her across Aunt Becky's parlour. At that moment Peter
understood what had happened to him. He was no longer
a free man—forevermore he must be in the power of this
pale girl. He had fallen in love fathoms deep with Drowned
John's daughter and Barry Dark's detested widow. Since
he never did anything by halves he did not fall in love by
halves either.

Peter felt a bit dizzy. It is a staggering thing to look in at
a casual window and see the woman you now realise you
have been subconsciously waiting for all your life. It is a
still more staggering thing to have your hate suddenly
dissolve into love, as though your very bones had melted

to water. It rather lets you down. Peter was actually afraid
to try to walk back to the verandah railing for fear his legs
would give way. He knew, without stopping to argue with
himself about it, that he would take no train from Three
Hills that night and the lure of Amazon jungles had
ceased—temporarily at least—to exist. Mystery and magic
enfolded Peter as a garment. What he wanted to do was to
vault over the window-sill, hurl aside those absurd men
and women sitting between them, snatch up Donna Dark,
strip off those ridiculous weeds she was wearing for another man, and carry her off bodily. It was quite on the
cards that he would have done it—Peter had such a habit
of doing everything he wanted to do—but at that moment
the ten-minute silence was over and Aunt Becky opened
her eyes. Everybody sighed with relief and Peter, finding
that all eyes were directed towards him, dragged himself
back to the railing and sat on it, trying to collect his
scattered wits and able only to see that subtle, deep-eyed
face with its skin as delicate as a white night moth, under
its cap of flat dark hair. Well, he had fallen in love with
Donna Dark. He realised that he had been sent there by
the powers that govern to fall in love with her. It was
predestined in the councils of eternity that he should look
through that particular window at that particular moment.
Good heavens, the years he had wasted insensately hating
her! Hopeless idiot! Blind bat! Now the only thing to do
was to marry her as quickly as possible. Everything else
could wait but that could not. Even finding out what
Donna thought about it could wait.

Donna could hardly be said to be thinking at all. She
was not quite so quick as Peter was at finding out what had
happened to her. She had recognised Peter the moment
she had seen him—partly from that same old memory of
an impudent boy across the aisle, partly from his photo-
graphs in the papers. Though they weren't good of him—
not half as fascinating. Peter hated being photographed
and always glared at the camera as if it were a foe. Still,
Donna knew him for her enemy—and for something else.

She was trembling with the extraordinary excitement
that tingled over her at the sight of him—she, who, a few

seconds before, had been so bored—so tired—so disgusted that she wished she had the courage to poison herself.

She was sure Virginia noticed it. Oh, if he would only go away and not stand there at the window staring at her. She knew he was leaving for South America that night—she had heard Nancy Penhallow telling it to Mrs. Homer. Donna put her hand up to her throat as if she were choking. What was the matter with her? Who cared if Peter Penhallow went to the Amazon or the Congo? It was not she, not Donna Dark, Barry's inconsolable widow, who cared. Certainly not. It was this queer, wild, primitive creature who had, without any warning, somehow usurped her body and only wanted to spring to the window and feel Peter's arms around her. There is no saying but that this perfectly crazy impulse might have mastered Donna if Aunt Becky had not opened her eyes and Peter had not vanished from the window.

Donna gave a gasp, which, coming after the universal sigh, escaped the notice of everybody but Virginia, who laid her hand over Donna's and squeezed it sympathetically.

"Darling, I saw it all. It must have been frightfully hard for you. You bore it splendidly."

"What—what did I bear?" stammered Donna idiotically.

"Why, seeing that dreadful Peter Penhallow staring at you like that—with his hate fairly sticking out of his eyes."

"Hate—hate—oh, do you think he hates me—really?" gasped Donna.

"Of course he does. He always has, ever since you married Barry. But you won't run the risk of meeting him again, darling. He's off tonight on some of his horrid explorations, so don't worry over it."

Donna was not worrying exactly. She only felt that she would die if Peter Penhallow did go away—like that—without a word or another glance. It was not to be borne. She would dare uncharted seas with him—she would face African cooking-pots—she would—oh, what mad things was she thinking? And *what* was Aunt Becky saying.

"Every one over forty who would be willing to live his or her life over again exactly as it has been lived, put up your hand."

Tempest Dark was the only one who put up his hand.

"Brave man! Or fortunate man—which?" inquired Aunt Becky satirically.

"Fortunate," said Tempest laconically. He *had* been fortunate. He had fifteen exquisite years with Winnifred Penhallow. He would face anything to have them again.

"Would *you* live your life over again, Donna?" whispered Virginia sentimentally.

"No—*no!!*" Donna felt that to live over again the years that Peter Penhallow had hated her would be unendurable. Virginia looked grieved and amazed. She had not expected such an answer. She felt that something had come between her and Donna—something that clouded the sweet, perfect understanding that had always existed between them. She had been wont to say that words were really unnecessary for them—they could read each other's thoughts. But Virginia could not read Donna's thoughts just now—which was perhaps quite as well. She wondered uneasily if the curse of Aunt Becky's opal was beginning to work already.

"Well, let's get down to business," Aunt Becky was saying.

"Thank the pigs," thought Drowned John fervently.

Aunt Becky looked over the room gloatingly. She had prolonged her sport as long as it was possible. She had got them just where she wanted them—all keyed up and furious—all except a few who were beyond the power of her venom and whom for that reason she did not despise. But look at the rest of them—squatting there on their ham-bones, pop-eyed, coveting the jug, ready to tear in pieces the one who got it. In a few minutes the lucky one would be known, they thought. Ah, would he? Aunt Becky chuckled. She still had a bomb to throw.

XI

"You're all dying to know who is to get the jug," she said, "but you're not going to know yet awhile. I did intend to tell you today who I meant to have it, but I've thought of a better plan. I've decided to leave the jug in keeping of a trustee until a year from the last day of next

October. *Then*, and not till then, you'll find out who's to get it."

There was a stunned silence—broken by a laugh from Stanton Grundy.

"Sold!" he said laconically.

"Who's the trustee?" said William Y. hoarsely. He knew who *should* be trustee.

"Dandy Dark. I've selected him because he is the only man I ever knew who could keep a secret."

Every one looked at Robert Dark, who squirmed uncomfortably, thus finding himself the centre of observation. Everybody disapproved. Dandy Dark was a nobody—his nickname told you that. It was a hangover from the days when he *had* been a dandy—something nobody would ever dream of calling the fat, shabby, old fellow now, with his double chin, his unkempt hair and his flabby, pendulous cheeks. Only his little, deep-set, beady black eyes seemed to justify Aunt Becky's opinion of his ability to keep a secret.

"Dandy is to be the sole executor of my will and the custodian of the jug until a year from the last day of next October," repeated Aunt Becky. "That's all the rest of you are to know about it. I'm not going to tell you how it will be decided then. It is possible that I may leave Dandy a sealed letter with the name of the legatee in it. In that case Dandy may know the name or he may not know it. Or it is equally possible that I may leave instructions in that same sealed letter that the ownership is to be settled by lot. And again, I may empower Dandy to choose for himself who is to have the jug, always bearing in his mind my opinions and prejudices regarding certain people and certain things. So in case I have chosen the last alternative, it behooves you all to watch your step from now on. The jug may not be given to anyone older than a certain age or to any unmarried person who, in my judgment, should be married, or to any person who has been married too much. It may not be given to anyone who has habits I don't like. It may not be given to anyone who quarrels or wastes his time fiddling. It may not be given to anyone addicted to swearing or drinking. It may not be given to any untruthful person or any dishonest person or any extravagant person. I've always hated to see anyone wasting money, even if it wasn't mine. It may not be given to anyone who has *no* bad habits and never did anything disgraceful"—with a glance in the direction of the impeccable William Y. "It may not be given to any one who begins things and never finishes them, or to any one who writes bad poetry. On the other hand, these things may not influence in the slightest my decision or Dandy's decision. And of course if the matter is to be decided by lot, it doesn't matter what you do or don't do. And finally it may go to somebody who doesn't live on the Island at all. Now, you know as much about it as you're going to know."

Aunt Becky sank back on her pillows and enjoyed their expressions. Nobody dared say anything but how they thought! And looking at each other as if to say,

"Well, *you* don't have much chance. You heard what she said."

All the old bachelors and old maids reflected that they were practically out of it. Titus Dark and Drowned John were marked men because they swore. Chris Penhallow, a queer widower who lived by himself and played the violin when he should have been carpentering, wondered if he could live nearly a year and a half without touching it. Tom Dark, who had stolen a pot of jam from his aunt's pantry when he was a boy, wondered if Aunt Becky meant him when she spoke of dishonest people. Gosh, how hard it was to live some things down. Abel Dark, who had put a staging up to paint his house four years ago but had painted only a small patch and left the staging there, reflected that he really must get down to that job right away. Sim Dark wondered uneasily if Aunt Becky had or had not looked at him when she spoke of untruthful persons. She always seemed able to instil such venom into what she said. As for Penny Dark, the idea struck him then and there that it was time he got married.

Homer Penhallow and Palmer Dark wondered if they hadn't better forswear their ancient grudge. They had always been bad friends, ever since the day in school when a band of boys, headed and incited by Homer Penhallow, had taken the pants off little Palmer Dark and made him walk a mile home in his shirttail. Still, though this rankled for years, they had not been open enemies till the affair of the kittens. Homer Penhallow's cat went down to Palmer Dark's barn and had three kittens which were not discovered until they were old enough to run around. Palmer Dark, who was out of cats just then, claimed them as his. Born in his barn and nourished on his premises. Homer wanted the kittens but Palmer, secure in possession, snapped contemptuous fingers at him. Then Homer's cat did an ungrateful thing. She went home and took the kittens with her. Homer was openly triumphant. What a joke on Palmer! Palmer bided his time in an ominous calm. One Sunday when Homer and his family were all in church, Palmer sneaked up to Homer's barn, caught the kittens and carried them home in a bag. Homer's cat came down the next day and succeeded in retrieving one. The other two Palmer kept shut securely up until she had forgotten them. So Palmer thought he had come off best. He had the two handsome striped toms while Homer had only an ugly little spotted tabby, afflicted with a cough. Palmer told the story around the clan, and after that he and Homer were at open feud. This had lasted for years, although all the cats concerned had long since gone where good cats go.

"Now you've found out all you're going to find out, so you can go," said Aunt Becky. "Be sure to think nice thoughts. I leave you all my forgiveness. I've had an amusing afternoon. Heaven will be kind of tame after this, there's no manner of doubt. Speaking of heaven, would any of you like me to do any errands there for you?"

What a question! Nobody answered, although Drowned John would have liked to send word to Toynbee Dark that he had never repaid him the three dollars he had borrowed of him before his death. But as Aunt Becky had never spoken to Toynbee on earth, it was not likely she would do it in heaven, so it would be a waste of breath to ask her. Anyway, it was too late. Aunt Becky was saying.

"Ambrosine, shut the doors."

Ambrosine closed the sliding doors, shutting the table with the jug in with Aunt Becky. Tongues were loosed, though they still talked in undertones. They said all, or most, of the things they had been thinking. There was great dissatisfaction. The Darks felt that they had been slighted; the Penhallows thought the Darks had got everything. The idea of giving old Ambrosine Winkworth the diamond ring!

XII

Drowned John rose and stalked out. There was one thing he could do, and he did it thoroughly. He banged the door.

"Let's leave the females to fight it out," he said. But the men, as soon as they got outside, had plenty to say.

"Would you believe it?" demanded William Y., looking around him as if appealing to the world.

"Nobody got much change out of Aunt Becky, did they?" chuckled Murray Dark.

Dandy Dark was puffing himself out. He had never in all his life been of any importance, save what little accrued from the fact that he was the only man in the countryside who kept a bulldog. And now he had, in a wink, become the most important person in the clan.

"All the weemen will be wishing I was single," he chuckled. But his face was inscrutable—purposely so. No fear of his giving away the secret.

"Too mean to give anything away, even a secret," muttered Artemas Dark.

"The heathen are raging already," said Stanton Grundy to Uncle Pippin. "If that jug doesn't set everybody on ears in a month's time, may I fight with Irishmen to the end of my life. Keep your eyes buttoned back for sights, Pippin."

"Oh, take in the slack of your jaw," said Uncle Pippin snappishly.

"Well, a nice lot of family skeletons have had a good airing," said Palmer Dark.

"I haven't had as much fun since the dog-fight in church," said Artemas Dark.

"Aunt Becky never liked any of us, you know," said Hugh. "She's bound to get all the rises she can out of us."

"She isn't like any other woman" growled Drowned John.

"Nobody is," said Grundy.

"You don't know much about women, John," said Sim Dark.

No man can endure being told he knows nothing about women—especially if he has coffined two wives. Drowned John went into an icy rage.

"Well, I know something about *you*, Sim Dark, and if you don't stop circulating lies about me as you've been doing for years, you'll have to reckon with me."

"But surely you don't want me to tell the *truth* about you," said Sim in bland amazement.

Drowned John did not reply in words—could not—since he dared not swear so near Aunt Becky. He simply spat.

"It's an outrageous way to leave the jug," growled William Y.

"You should be thankful she didn't make it a condition that everybody should turn a somersault in the church aisle," said Artemas. "She would if she'd thought of it."

"*You* would have liked that, I don't doubt," retorted William Y. "Grinning like a chessy cat over the very thought of it."

Oswald Dark turned around and surveyed the irritated William Y.

"Look at the moon," he said softly, waving his hand at a pale, silver bubble floating over the seaward valley. "Look at the moon," he repeated insistently, laying a long thin hand on the arm of William Y.

"Heavens, I've seen moons before—hundreds of them!" snorted William Y. peevishly.

"But can one see a thing of perfect beauty—like the moon—too often?" inquired Oswald, fixing his large agate eyes questioningly on William Y., who jerked his arm away and turned his back both on Oswald and his moon.

"That jug shouldn't be in a house where there is no responsible woman," said Denzil Penhallow sourly. Everybody knew that Mrs. Dandy was as mad as a November partridge by spells.

"If anyone has anything to say against my wife he'd better not let me hear him saying it," retorted Dandy ominously. "I'll smash his face for him."

"Any time and any place," said Denzil obligingly.

"Come, come, let us preserve decorum," implored Uncle Pippin nervously.

"Pippin, go home and soak your head in turpentine for three days," boomed Drowned John.

Uncle Pippin subsided. This, he reflected, was what came of Aunt Becky's not giving them anything to eat.

"Devil take the jug," he muttered.

"I doubt if the devil will be so obliging," said the irrepressible Grundy.

The women were coming out now and the men went off to get car or horse, according to purse or age. Tempest Dark, who was walking, sauntered out of the gate, reflecting that he wanted to see this comedy played out. He would live long enough to see who got the jug.

Titus Dark on the way home was importuned by a tearful wife to give up swearing.

"Damn it, I can't," groaned Titus. "And I ain't the only one in the tribe that swears. Take Drowned John."

"Drowned John knows when and when not to swear and you don't," sobbed Mrs. Titus. "It's only for a year and a quarter, Titus. You *must*. Dandy'll never give us the jug if you don't."

"I don't believe Dandy'll have a thing to say about it. Aunt Becky wouldn't let any one else decide that," said Titus. "I'd just go for months in misery and not get a da—not get a blessed thing out of it. Besides, Mary, how is anyone going to live with me if I can't swear? When I swear for ten minutes on end a child could eat out of my hand. Isn't that better than bottling it up and thinking murder? Take this horse now. I've just gotter swear at him or he'd never travel. If I talked anything else to him he wouldn't understand what I was saying."

However, Titus had to promise to try. It would, he reflected, be damned hard. These women were so damned unreasonable. But he'd have a go at it, damned if he wouldn't. The race for the jug was on and devil take the hindmost.

Gay slipped away alone. She knew a certain little ferny corner down the side road where she meant to stop and read Noel's letter. She looked so happy that the Moon Man shook his head at her.

"Take care," he whispered warningly. "It's dangerous to be too happy—those that sit in the high places don't like it. Look how they hide my Lady from me so much of the time."

But Gay only laughed at him and ran on down the side path and out by the side gate under the apple blossoms. Gay loved apple blossoms. It always hurt her that they lasted such a little while—such milky, wonderful things with hearts of love's own hue. To be sure, the roses came afterwards. But if one could only have the apple blossoms and the roses, too. Gay felt greedy of beauty. She wanted every kind all at once, now when life itself seemed just on the point of breaking into some marvelous blossom and all the coming days were in a hurry to be born. Youth is like that. It wants everything at once, not realising that something must be saved for autumn days. Save? Nonsense! Pour it all out now, a libation to the approaching god. Gay did not think this—she only felt it, hurrying down the road, as sweet and virginal as the apple blossoms.

"A nice little cuddler that, if you ask me," chuckled Stanton Grundy admiringly, giving Uncle Pippin a dig in the ribs.

"I'm not asking you," said Uncle Pippin irritably. *He* had a sense of the fitness of things. Poke fun at old maids and fat married women if you like, but leave young things like Gay alone. Grundy's vulgar chuckle seemed to debase everything. Hadn't that man *any* reverence for anything? And why didn't he read a few halitosis advertisements? Heaven knew the magazines were full of them.

Gay read her letter in her ferny corner and kissed it and put it back in her bosom. There was only one terrible thing in it. Noel said he could not come out till Saturday. They were going to be extra busy in the bank. Had she to live three whole days without seeing him? Could she? A little cluster of silver daisies growing by a lichened old stone nodded at her. She picked one of them—witch daisies that knew whether your sweetheart loved you or not. Too-wise daisies. Gay pulled away the tiny ivory petals one by one—he loves me—he loves me not—he loves me. Gay took out the letter again and kissed it and put the torn daisy petals into it. She was young and pretty and very much in love. And he loved her. The daisies said so. What a world! The poor Moon Man! As if one could be too happy! As if God didn't like to see you happy! Why, people were made for happiness. And wasn't it the most miraculous thing that out of all the world she and Noel should have met and loved! When there were so many other girls he might have fancied. She seemed to be at the very heart of some exquisite magic that had changed everything in life for her.

XIII

Donna came out beside Virginia. She had begun to collect her wits, but she did not quite know yet exactly what had taken place. She knew Peter was sitting on the railing, and she meant to sweep past him haughtily in all her dark dignity of widowhood, with lids cast down. But as she passed him she had to look up. They had another momentary unforgettable exchange of eyes. Virginia saw it this time and was vaguely disturbed by it. It did not look like a glance of hatred. She clutched Donna's arm as they went down the steps.

"Donna, I believe that pig of a Peter is falling in love with you."

"Oh—do you think so—*do* you really think so?" said Donna. Virginia could not understand her tone at all. But it *must* be a horrified one.

"I'm afraid so. Wouldn't it be terrible for you? What a blessing he's leaving for South America tonight. Just *think* what it would be like to have him trying to make love to you."

Donna *did* think of it. A strange shiver of terror and delight went over her from head to foot. She felt thankful that Drowned John bellowed to her that instant to hurry up. She fled to his car, leaving a puzzled and somewhat alarmed Virginia on the steps. *What* had come over Donna?

Mrs. Foster Dark went home and ate her supper under Happy's fiddle hanging on the wall. Murray Dark went home and thought about Thora. Artemas Dark reflected dismally that it wouldn't do for him to get drunk for over a year. Crosby Penhallow and Erasmus spent the evening

with their flutes—on the whole happily, although Crosby
had to put up with some sly digs from Erasmus about old
Becky's being in love with him. Peter Penhallow went
home and unpacked his trunk. He had searched the world
over for the meaning of life's great secret and now he had
found it in one look from Donna Dark's eyes. Was he a
fool? Then welcome folly.

Big and Little Sam went home across windy seafields,
and on the way home Little Sam bought a ticket from little
Mosey Gautier for the raffle Father Sullivan was getting up
down at Chapel Point to raise funds for the Old Sailors'
Home. Big Sam wouldn't buy a ticket. *He* wasn't going to
have no truck with Catholics and their doings, and he
thought Little Sam might have expended his quarter to far
better advantage. They had the heathen to think of.

"No good's going to come of it," he remarked sourly.

Little Sam went home and, dismissing the old Dark jug
from his mind, sat down to read his favourite volume,
Fox's Book of Martyrs, with the salt wind that even his
battered and unromantic heart loved, blowing in at his
window. Big Sam went down to the rocks and solaced
himself by repeating the first canto of his epic to the gulf.

XIV

Denzil Penhallow told Margaret she must walk home—
he and the wife were going down to have tea with the
William Y.'s. Margaret was secretly well pleased. It was
only a mile and the month was June. Besides, it would give
her a chance to stop and see Whispering Winds.

Whispering Winds was the small secret which made
poor Margaret's life endurable. It wound in and out of her
drab life like a ribbon of rainbows. It was the little house
on the Bay Silver side road where Aunt Louisa Dark had
lived. At her death, two years ago, it had become the
property of her son Richard, who lived in Halifax. It was
for sale but nobody had ever wanted to buy it—nobody,
that is, except Margaret, who had no money to buy
anything and would have been hooted at if it were so
much as suspected that she wanted to buy a house. Hadn't

she a perfectly good, ungrudged home with her brother? What in the world would *she* want with a house?

Margaret did want it—terribly. She had always loved that little house of Aunt Louisa's. It was she who gave it the dear secret name of Whispering Winds, and dreamed all kinds of foolish, sweet dreams about it. As soon as she got to the Bay Silver side road, she turned down it and very soon was at the lane of her house—an old, old lane, grassy and deep-rutted, with bleached old grey "longer" fences hemming it in. There were clumps of birches all along it for a little way—then young spruces growing up thickly on either side—then just between them, at the end, the little house, once white, now as grey as the longers. There it was, basking in the late sun—smiling at her with its twinkling windows. Back of it was a steep hill where tossing young maples were whitening in the wind, and off to the right was a glimpse of purple valley. There was an old well in one corner, with an apple tree spilling blossoms over it. A little field off to the right was cool and inviting in the shadow of a spruce wood. The scent of its clover drifted across to Whispering Winds. The air was like a thin golden wine and the quiet was a benediction.

Margaret caught her breath with the delight of it.

Whispering Winds was one of those houses you loved the minute you saw them, without being in the least able to tell why—perhaps because its roof-line was so lovely against the green hill. She loved it so. She walked about the old garden, that was beginning to have such a look of neglect. She longed to prune it and weed it and dress it up. That delightful big bed of striped grass was encroaching on the path, those forget-me-nots were simply running wild. They and the house were just crying out for someone to take care of them. The house and the garden belonged together some way—you couldn't have separated them. The house seemed to grow out of the garden. The shrubs and vines reached up around it to hold it and caress it. If she could just have this house—with a baby in it—she would ask for nothing more. Not even Aunt Becky's jug. Margaret realised pathetically that she must give up writing poetry for a while, or she might have no chance of the jug. And she still hankered after it. Since she could never

have Whispering Winds she wanted the jug. Dandy Dark
had always been friendly to her. If it should rest with him
to give the jug, she stood a better chance than from Aunt
Becky. Cruel old Aunt Becky who had jeered at her and
her poor little poems and her old-maidenhood before all
the clan. Margaret knew that perhaps she *was* silly and
faded and childish and unimportant and undesired, but it
hurt to have it rubbed in so. She never harmed anyone.
Why couldn't they leave her alone? Denzil and Mrs.
Denzil were always giving her digs, too, about "single
blessedness," and her nieces and nephews openly laughed
at her. But here, in this remote shadowy little garden, she
forgot all about it. Things ceased to sting. If she could only
stay here forever, where the robins called to one another
at evening in the maple wood. Listen to them.

But it was soon time to go home. Mrs. Denzil would expect
her to get the supper for the family and help milk cows.
She bade good-bye regretfully to Whispering Winds and
went on to the square bare house in a treeless yard where
the Denzil Penhallows lived. She went up to her hideous
little room looking out on the hen-yard, which she had to
share with Gladys Penhallow. Gladys was there with some
of her friends, thinking at the top of their voices as usual.
It was always noisy. There were never any quiet moments.
Margaret's head ached. She wished she had not gone to
Aunt Becky's levee. It hadn't done any good. As for the
old *Pilgrim's Progress*, it could lie on in The Pinery attic
for all she cared.

How pretty Gay Penhallow had looked today! And so
young. What was it like to be eighteen? Margaret had
forgotten if she had ever really known. What had been the
trouble between Hugh and Joscelyn? And how dared
Thora Dark, who had a husband, be so attractive to other
men? What would it be like to have a man look at you the
way she had seen Murray looking at Thora—though of
course he had no business to be looking at another man's
wife like that. Poor Lawson! It was dreadful to see the
hunger in Naomi's eyes. How tickled Ambrosine was over
that ring! Margaret did not grudge her the ring. Perhaps
Ambrosine felt about it the way *she* felt about Whispering
Winds. Though of course poor old Ambrosine's hands *were*

too thin and knotty to wear rings. Margaret looked with considerable satisfaction at her own slender, shapely fingers. Nobody could say she hadn't a pretty hand. Roger Dark was a nice fellow. Why didn't he get a nice girl for a wife? They said he was crazy about Gay Penhallow, who wouldn't look at him. There you were again. Love going to waste all around you and you starving for a little. The idea suddenly struck Margaret that God wasn't fair. She shuddered and dismissed it as a blasphemy. It sounded like something that dreadful Grundy man would say. Poor Cousin Robina! Peter Penhallow, they said, was off on another of his explorations. He always seemed to live life with such gusto. But Margaret did not envy him. She never wanted to go away from home. What she wanted was a place where she could put down roots and grow old quietly. Margaret thought she would not mind growing old if she could be left to do it in peace. It was hard to grow old gracefully when you were always being laughed at because you were not young. But there was only one career for women in her clan. Of course you could be a nurse or a teacher or dressmaker, or something like that, to fill in the time before marriage, but the Darks and Penhallows did not take you seriously.

XV

"Tell Joscelyn Dark I want to see her before she goes home, Ambrosine," ordered Aunt Becky.

Joscelyn had walked the short distance up from Bay Silver and intended to walk back. Palmer Dark had taken her mother and her Aunt Rachel home in his car. She felt that she had about enough of Aunt Becky for one day, but she went back to the bedroom readily enough. After all, the poor old soul was not long for this world.

Aunt Becky was lying back on her pillows. She was gazing earnestly on a little old tintype hanging on the wall near her bed. The picture was not decorative. At least so Joscelyn thought. But then she did not see it with Aunt Becky's eyes. Joscelyn saw only a tubby pompous old man, with a fringe of whisker around his face, and a thin, scrawny little woman in a preposterous dress. Aunt Becky saw a big, hearty, high-coloured man whose abounding vitality brought a gust of life into every existence and a vivid-eyed girl whose wit and sly mirth had been the spice of every company she was in and whose love affairs were stimulating and piquant. Aunt Becky sighed as she turned to Joscelyn. The fire had gone out of her eyes, the sting out of her voice. She looked exactly what she was—a very old, very ill, very tired woman.

"Sit down, Joscelyn. You now, I've been lying here thinking how many people will be glad when I'm dead? And not one to be sorry. And it seems to me that I wish I'd lived a bit differently, Joscelyn. I've always taken my fun out of them—I haven't spared them—they're all afraid of me. I'm just an ogress to them. It *was* fun watching them squirming. But now—I don't know. I've a devilish sort of feeling that I wish I'd been a kind, gentle, stingless creature like—well, like Annette Dark, for instance. Everybody was sorry when she died—though she never said a clever thing in her life. But she was smart enough to die before she got too old. Women should, Joscelyn. I've sat up too late. Nobody will miss me."

Joscelyn looked levelly at Aunt Becky. She knew that what Aunt Becky said was true enough in a way. And she sensed the secret bitterness in the old woman's soul behind all her satire and bravado. She wanted to comfort her without telling a lie. Joscelyn could neither tell nor live a lie—which was what had made a clan existence hard for her.

"I think, Aunt Becky, that every one of us will miss you a great deal more than you suppose we will—a great deal more than we imagine ourselves. You're like—like mustard. Sometimes you bite—and a big dose of you *is* rather awful—"

"As today, for example," interjected aunt Becky with a faint grin.

"But you *do* give a tang to things. They'd be flat without you. And you seem like—I don't know how to put it—the very essence of Dark and Penhallow. We won't be half so much a clan when you're gone. You've always made history for us somehow. If this had been an ordinary afternoon— if we'd come here and you'd been nice to us—"

"And fed you—"

"We'd have all gone away and forgotten the afternoon. There'd be nothing in it to remember. But this afternoon *will* be remembered—and talked about. When the girls are old women they'll tell their grandchildren about it— you'll live by it fifty years after you're in your grave, Aunt Becky."

"I *have* often thought it would be a frightfully dull world if everybody were perfectly good and sweet," conceded Aunt Becky. "I guess it's only because I'm tired that I'm wishing I'd been more like Annette. She was as sweet and good and unexciting as they make 'em. She never said a naughty word in her life. And I was far handsomer than she was, mind you. But Crosby loved *her*. Now, Joscelyn, here's a queer thing. You heard what I said today. There was a time I'd have given my soul if Crosby had loved me—I'd have given and done anything—except be like Annette. Not even for Crosby would I have been willing to be like Annette—even though now I'm getting childish and wishing I had been. I'd rather sting people than bore them, after all. But—"

Aunt Becky paused and looked earnestly at Joscelyn. Joscelyn had held her own well. She was very good-looking. The evening light, falling through the window behind her, made a tremendous primrose nimbus around her shapely head. But her eyes—Aunt Becky wanted to solve the haunting mystery of Joscelyn's eyes.

"I didn't keep you here to talk about my own feelings. I'm going to die. And I'm not afraid of death. Isn't it strange? I was once so afraid of it. But before I die I want to ask you something. I've never asked you before—do me that justice. What went wrong between you and Hugh?"

Joscelyn started—flushed—paled—almost rose from her chair.

"No—-sit down. I'm not going to try to make you tell if you don't want to. It isn't curiosity, Joscelyn. I'm done with that. I feel I'd just like to know the truth before I die. I remember your wedding. Hugh was the happiest-looking groom I ever saw. And you seemed very well pleased with yourself, too—when you came in first, at least. I remember thinking you were made for each other—the sort of people who should marry—and found a home—and have children. And I *would* like to know what wrecked it all."

Joscelyn sat silent a few minutes longer. Oddly enough, she was conscious of a strange desire to tell Aunt Becky everything. Aunt Becky would understand—she was sure Aunt Becky would understand. For ten years she had lived in an atmosphere of misunderstanding and disapproval and suspicion. She had not minded it, she thought— the inner flame which irradiated life had been her protection. But today she felt oddly that she *had*, after all, minded it more than she had supposed. There was a soreness in her spirit that seemed old, not new. She *would* tell Aunt Becky. No one else would ever know. It was a confidence to the grave itself. And it might help her—heal her. She bent forward and began to speak in a low, intense voice. Aunt Becky lay and listened movelessly until Joscelyn had finished it.

"So that was it," she said, when the passionate voice had ceased. "Something none of us ever thought of. I never thought of it. I thought perhaps it was something quite small. So many of the tragedies of life come from little, silly, ridiculous things. Nobody ever knew why Roger Penhallow hanged himself forty years ago—nobody but me. He did it because he was eighteen years old and his father *spanked* him. Ah, the things I know of this clan! All the things I said today were things every one knows. But I didn't say a word about scores of things nobody dreams I know. But weren't you very cruel, Joscelyn?"

"What else could I have done?" said Joscelyn. "I *couldn't* have done anything else."

"Not with that Spanish blood in you, I suppose. At least we'll blame it on the Spanish blood. Everything that isn't right in your branch of the Penhallows is laid at the door of that Spanish blood. Peter Penhallow and his hurry to be born, for instance. It must be the Spanish blood that makes you all fall in love with such terrible suddenness. Most of Captain Martin's descendants have been lovers at sight or not at all. I thought you'd escaped *that* curse— Hugh took so long courting you. Have you ever felt sorry you did it, Joscelyn?"

"No—no—no," cried Joscelyn.

"Two 'no's' too many," said Aunt Becky.

"I want to tell you the exact truth," said Joscelyn slowly. "It is quite true—I've never been sorry I *did* do it. You can't be sorry you did a thing you *have* to do. But I have been sorry—not many times but all the time—that I *had* to do it. I didn't want to do it. I didn't want to hurt Hugh like that—and I *did* want to have Treewoofe. I want it yet—you don't know how much I want Treewoofe—and all the lovely life I had planned to have there. It was dreadful to have to give it up. But I couldn't do anything else, Aunt Becky—I *couldn't*."

"Well, God bless you, child. The less we say about it the better. You'll probably hate me tonight because you've told me this. You'll feel I tricked you into it by being old and pitiful."

"No, you didn't trick me. I wanted to tell you. I don't know why—but I wanted to. And I'm glad you don't blame me too much, Aunt Becky."

"I don't blame you at all. I might even believe you were right if I were young enough to believe it. God save us all, what a world it is! The things that happen to people— things without rhyme or reason! Frank has never married, has he? Do you think it happened to him, too?"

Joscelyn's face crimsoned.

"I don't know. He went away the next morning, you know. Sometimes I think it might have—because—when I looked at him—oh, Aunt Becky, you remember that absurd thing Virginia Penhallow said about the first time she met Ned Powell. The whole clan has laughed over it. 'The moment I looked into his eyes I knew he was my predestined mate.' Of course it *was* ridiculous. But, Aunt Becky, that was just the way I felt, too."

"Of course." Aunt Becky nodded understandingly. "We all *feel* those things. They're not ridiculous when we feel them. It's only when we put them into words that they're ridiculous. They're not meant to be put in words. Well, when *I* couldn't get the man I wanted, I just decided to want the man I could get. That was Craig Penhallow's way of looking at it, too. Ever hear the story of Craig Penhallow and the trees in Treewoofe lane, Joscelyn?"

"No."

"Well, you've noticed—haven't you—something odd about the spruce trees up and down that lane? There's a gap in them every once in so long."

Joscelyn nodded. Aunt Becky could not tell her much she didn't know about the appearance of the trees in Treewoofe lane.

"Thirty years ago old Cornelius Treverne owned Treewoofe. Craig was courting his daughter Clara. And one night Clara turned him down. Hard. Craig was furious. He flung himself out of the house and stormed down the lane. Poor old Cornelius had spent that whole day setting out a hedge of little spruce trees all along both sides of that long lane. A hard day's work, mind you. And what do you think Craig did by way of relieving his feelings? As he stalked along he would tear up a handful of old Cornelius' trees on the right hand—a few steps more—up would come a bunch on the left. He kept that up all the way down the lane. You can imagine what it looked like when he got to the end of it. And you can imagine what old Cornelius felt when he saw it next morning. He never got time to replant the trees—Cornelius was a great hand to put things off. He was a good man—painfully good. It was a blessing he hadn't sons, or they'd certainly have gone to the bad by way of keeping up the family average. But he was no hustler. So the trees that were left grew up as they were. As for Criag, by the time he had finished with the lane he felt a lot better. There were as good fish in the sea as ever came out of it—Maggie Penhallow was just as handsome as Clara Treverne. Or at least she managed her eyes and hands so well, she passed for handsome. You see, Craig was like me. He decided to be sensible. Perhaps your way is wiser, Joscelyn—and perhaps we're all fools together with the Moon Man's high-seated gods laughing at us. Joscelyn—I don't know whether I should tell you this—but I think I should, for I don't think you know, and the things we don't know sometimes hurt us horribly, in spite of the old proverb. All Hugh's family are at him to go to the States and get a divorce. It's been done several times, you know. People brag that Prince Edward Island hasn't had but one divorce since Confederation. Stuff and nonsense! It's had a dozen."

"But—but—they're not really legal—here, are they?" stammered Joscelyn.

"Legal enough. They're winked at, anyhow. Mind, I don't say Hugh is going to do it. But they're at him— they're at him. Times have changed a bit these last ten years. No easy divorce for us—but in Hugh's case they'd condone it. Mrs. Jim Trent is the moving spirit behind it, I understand. She lived so long in the States she got their view-point. And she and Pauline Dark are as friendly just now as two cats lapping from the same saucer. Pauline's as much in love with Hugh as she ever was, you know."

"It matters nothing to me," said Joscelyn stiffly, rising to go. She bade Aunt Becky good-bye rather shortly. Aunt Becky smiled cryptically after Joscelyn had gone out.

"I've made Joscelyn Dark tell one fib in her life, if she never tells another," she thought. "Poor little romantic splendid fool. I don't know whether I feel envy or contempt. Yet I remember when I took myself almost as seriously as that. Lord, what *does* get into girls? Old Cy Dark's son!"

XVI

Joscelyn went home slowly through the glamour and perfume of the June evening. Slowly, because she was in no hurry to get home where her mother and her Aunt Rachel would be talking the afternoon over indignantly and expecting her to be as indignant as they were. Slowly, because some unwelcome shadow of imminent change seemed to go with her as she walked. Slowly, because she was living over again the story she had told Aunt Becky.

She had been very sure she loved Hugh when she had finally promised to marry him. She had been happy in their brief engagement. Everybody had been happy— everybody well enough pleased about it, except Hugh's mother, Mrs. Conrad Dark, and his second cousin, Pauline Dark. Joscelyn did not care whether Pauline was pleased or not, but she was sorry Mrs. Conrad wasn't. Mrs. Conrad did not like her—never had liked her. Joscelyn had never been able to imagine why—until this very afternoon, when Aunt Becky had illuminated the mystery by her reference to Alec. Joscelyn had known Mrs. Conrad detested her from their first meeting, when Mrs. Conrad had told her that her petticoat was below her dress. Now, in the days of petticoats, there were three different ways you could tell a girl that her petticoat was below her dress. You could tell it as a kindly friend who felt it a duty to help get matters righted as soon as possible before any one else noticed it, but who felt a sympathy with her as the victim of an accident which might happen at any time to yourself. You could tell it as a disinterested onlooker who had no real concern with the affair but wanted to do as you would be done by. Or you could tell it with a certain suppressed venom and triumph, as if you rather delighted in catching her in such a scrape and wanted her to know you saw the fatal garment and had your own opinion of any girl who could be so careless.

The last way had been Mrs. Conrad Dark's, and Joscelyn knew her for an enemy. But this did not disturb to any extent the happiness of her engagement. Joscelyn had a good deal of Peter Penhallow's power of detachment from the influence of anyone else's opinion. As long as Hugh loved her it did not matter what Mrs. Conrad thought; and Joscelyn knew how Hugh loved her.

Soon after their engagement Treewoofe Farm at Three Hills came into the market. Treewoofe had been so named from some old place in Cornwall whence the Trevernes had come. The house was built on a hill overlooking the valley of Bay Silver, and Hugh bought the farm because of its magnificent view. Most of the clan thought the idea of buying a farm because it was beautiful very amusing and suspected Joscelyn of putting him up to it. Luckily, they thought, the soil was good, though run down, and the house practically new. Hugh had not made such a bad purchase, if the winter winds didn't make him wish he'd picked a more sheltered home. As for the view, of course it was very fine. None of the Darks or Penhallows were so insensitive to beauty as not to admit that. There was no doubt old Cornelius had tacked another hundred on his price because of that view. But it was a lonely spot and

rather out of the world, and most of them thought Hugh
had made a mistake.

Hugh and Joscelyn had no qualms about it. They both
loved Treewoofe. The splendour of many sunsets had
flooded that hill and the shadows of great clouds rolled
over it. One evening after he had bought it, he and
Joscelyn walked up to see it, going to it, not by the road
but by a little crooked, ferny path through the Treewoofe
beech woods, full of the surprises no straight path can
ever give. They had run all over the house and orchard
like children and then stood together at their front door
and looked down—down—down—over the hill itself—over
the farmsteads and groves in the valley below—over her
own home, looking like a doll's house at that distance—
over the mirror-like beauty of Bay Silver—over the harbour
bar—out—out—out—to the great gulf—a grey sea, this
evening, with streaks of silver—Joscelyn had drawn a
breath of rapture. To live every day looking at that! And to
know that glorious wind ever day—sweeping up over the
harbour, over the sheltered homesteads that hid from
it—up—up—up—to their glorious free crest that wel-
comed it. And oh, what would dawn over those seaside
meadows far below be like?

"We'll have three good neighbours up here," said Joscelyn.
"The wind—and the rain—and the stars. They can come
close to us here. All my life, Hugh, I've longed to live on a
hill. I can't breathe in the valley."

Turning round she could see, past the other end of the
hall that ran right through the house, the lovely old-
fashioned garden behind—and behind it again the orchard
in bloom. Their home, haunted by no ghosts of the
past—only by wraiths of the future. Unborn eyes would
look out of its windows—unborn voices sing in its rooms—
unborn feet run lightly in the old orchard. Beautiful
tomorrows—unknown lovely years were waiting there for
them. Friends would come to them—hands of comrades
would knock at their door—silken gowns would rustle
through their chambers—there would be companionship
and good smacking jests such as their clan loved. What a
home they would make of Treewoofe! All the richness and
ripeness of life would be theirs.

Joscelyn saw their faces reflected in the long mirror that was hanging over the fireplace in the corner. A mirror with an intriguing black cat a-top of it which had been brought out from Cornwall and sold with the house. Young, happy, merry faces against a background of blue sky and crystal air. Hugh put his arm about her neck and drew her cheek close to his.

"That's an old looking-glass, honey. It has reflected many a woman's face. But never, never one so beautiful as my queen's."

The wedding was in September. Milly, Joscelyn's harum-scarum younger sister, was bridesmaid. Frank Dark was best man. Joscelyn had never seen Frank Dark. He lived in Saskatchewan, where his father, Cyrus Dark, had gone when his family were small, and where Frank and Hugh had been cronies during the years Hugh had spent in the west. But he came east for the wedding, arriving there only on the afternoon of the day itself. Joscelyn saw him for the first time when her Uncle Jeff swept in with her and left her standing by the side of her waiting groom. Joscelyn raised her eyes to look at Hugh—and instead found herself looking past him straight into Frank Dark's eyes as he gazed with open curiosity at this bride of Hugh's.

Frank Dark was "dark by name and dark by nature" as the clan said. He had black, satiny hair, a thin olive-hued face and dark liquid eyes. A very handsome fellow, Frank Dark. Beside him, Hugh looked rather overgrown and raw-boned and unfinished. And at that moment Joscelyn Penhallow knew that she had never loved Hugh Dark, save with the affection of a good comrade. She loved Frank Dark, whom she had never seen until that minute.

The ceremony was well begun before Joscelyn realised what had happened. She always believed that if she had realised it a moment sooner she could have stopped the marriage somehow—anyhow—it did not matter how, so long as it was only stopped. But Hugh was saying, "I will" when she came to her senses—and Frank's shadow was on the floor before her as she said, "I will" herself, without knowing exactly what she was saying. Another moment and she was Hugh Dark's wife—Hugh Dark's wife in the

throes of a wild passionate love for another man. And
Hugh at that moment was making a vow in his heart that
no pain, no sorrow, no heartache should ever touch her
life if he could prevent it.

Joscelyn never knew how she got through the evening.
It always seemed a nightmare of remembrance. Hugh
kissed her on her lips—tenderly—possessively. The husband's kiss against which Joscelyn found herself suddenly
in wild rebellion. Milly gave her a tear-wet peck next and
then Frank Dark, easy, debonair Frank Dark, bent forward
with a smile and good-wishes for Hugh's wife on his lips
and kissed her lightly on the cheek. It was the first and
last time he ever touched her; but to-day, ten years after,
that kiss burned on Joscelyn's cheek as she thought of it.

There was an orgy of kissing after that. At Dark and
Penhallow weddings everybody kissed the bride and everybody else who could or would be kissed. Joscelyn,
bewildered and terrified, had yet one clear thought in her
mind—no one—*no one* must kiss the cheek where Frank's
kiss had fallen. She gave them her lips or her left cheek
blindly, but she kept the right to him. On and on they
came with their good wishes and their tears or laughter—
Joscelyn felt her mother's tears, she felt her bones almost
crack in Drowned John's grip, she heard old Uncle Erasmus
whisper one of the smutty little jokes he always got off at
weddings, she saw Mrs. Conrad's cold, venomous face—
no kiss from Mrs. Conrad—she saw Pauline Dark's pale,
quivering lips—Pauline's kiss was as cold as the grave—
she heard jolly old Aunt Charlotte whispering, "Tell him
he's wonderful at least once a week." It was all a dream—
she must wake presently.

The ordeal of well-wishing over, the ordeal of supper
came. Joscelyn was laughed at because she could not eat.
Uncle Erasmus made another smutty jest and was punished
by his wife's sharp elbow. After supper Hugh took his
bride home. The rest of the young folks, Frank Dark
among them, stayed at Bay Silver to dance the night away.
Joscelyn went out with only a cloak over her bridal finery.
Hugh had asked her to go home with him so.

The drive to Treewoofe had been very silent. Hugh
sensed that somehow she did not want to talk. He was so

happy he did not want to talk himself. Words might spoil it. At Treewoofe he lifted her from the buggy and led her by the hand—how cold the hand was. She was frightened, his little love—across the green before the house and over the threshold of his door. He turned to welcome her with the little verse of poetry he had composed for the occasion. Hugh had the knack of rhyme that flickered here and there in the clan, sometimes emerging in very unexpected brainpans. He had pictured himself doing this a hundred times—leading in a white-veiled, silk-clad bride—but not a bride with such white lips and such wide, horror-filled eyes. For the first time Hugh realised that here was something most terribly wrong. This was not the pretty shrinking and confusion of the happy bride.

They stood in the entrance-hall at Treewoofe and looked at each other. A fire was flickering in the fireplace—Hugh had lighted it with his own hands before he left and bade his hired boy to keep it alive—and the rosy flamelight bathed the hall and fell over his lovely golden bride—his no more.

"Joscelyn—my darling—what is wrong?"

She found her voice.

"I can't live with you, Hugh."

"Why not?"

She told him. She loved Frank Dark and loving him she could be wife to no other man. Now her eyes were no longer blue or green or grey, but a flame.

There was a terrible hour. In the end Hugh set open the door and looked at her, white anger falling over his face like a frost. One only word he said:

"Go."

Joscelyn had gone, wraithlike in her shimmer of satin and tulle, out into the cold September moonlight silvering over Treewoofe Hill. She had half walked, half run home to Bay Silver in a certain wild triumph. As she went past the graveyard, her own people buried there seemed to be reaching out after her to pluck her back. Not her father, though. He lay very quiet in his grave—quieter than he had ever lain in life. There had been Spanish blood in *him*. Mrs. Clifford Penhallow could have told you that. Her clan thought—she thought herself—that she had had a hard life with Clifford's vagaries. Though when she became a widow she found there were a good many harder things he had fended from her.

Joscelyn cherished no delusion. She was Hugh's wife in law and she could marry no other man. The thought of divorce never entered her head. But she was free to be true to her love—this wonderful passion which had so suddenly filled her soul and given it wings, so that she seemed rather to fly than walk over the road. Its dark enchantment lifted her above fear and shame; nothing could touch her, not even what she knew was to be faced. And in this rapt mood she came back to her mother's door and the dismayed dancers scattered to their homes as if a ghost had walked in among them. Joscelyn, as she went upstairs with the frost of the autumn night wet on her limp wedding-veil, wondered if Frank saw her and what he would think. But Frank was not there. Ten minutes after Hugh had taken his bride away a telegram had come for Frank Dark. Cyrus Dark was dying in Saskatchewan. Frank left at once to pack his scarcely unpacked trunk and catch the early boat-train, thereby perhaps escaping the horsewhipping a madman at Treewoofe was silently threatening to give him and which, it must be admitted, he did not in the least deserve.

Frank Dark returned to the west without ever knowing that his friend's bride had fallen in love with him. He hadn't the slightest wish that she should fall in love with him—though he thought her a dashed pretty girl. A bit of money, too. Hugh had always been a lucky beggar.

XVII

Joscelyn paused at the gate of her home and looked at it with some distaste. The old Clifford Penhallow house was prim, old-fashioned and undecorated, but it was considered to be very quaint by the summer tourists who came to Bay Silver, and a postcard had been made of it. The house was built on a little point running out into Bay Silver. On one side its roof sloped unbrokenly down to within a few feet of the ground. Its windows were high and narrow. A little green yard surrounded it, with nothing in it but green grass which Rachel Penhallow swept every day. To the right was a huddle of trees—a lombardy, a maple, and three apple trees, girt by a tidy stone dyke. On the left a neat gate opened into a neat pasture—oh, everything was so neat and bare—where there were some windy willows and where Mrs. Clifford kept her cow. Back of it was a straight blue line of harbour, a glimpse of pink sand-dunes and over them a hazy sunset.

For ten years this had been to Joscelyn merely a place to live her strange inner dream-life. She asked no more of it. But now she was suddenly conscious of this odd distaste for it. She had never cared very much for it. It lay too low—she wanted the wind and outlook of a hill. She did not want to go in. She could see her mother and Aunt Rachel at the living-room window. They seemed to be quarrelling as usual. Rather—bickering. They couldn't do anything as genuine and positive as quarrel. There was no Spanish blood in either of them. Joscelyn knew what was ahead of her if she went in—the whole afternoon would be threshed over and somehow they would make her feel that she was responsible for their not getting what they wanted. She could not endure that just now—so she walked around the pasture, as if she were going to the shore, and when she was out of their sight she slipped through the sweet-briar thicket, in at the kitchen door, and upstairs to her own room. With a sigh of relief and weariness she sank into a chair by the open window.

She suddenly felt tireder than she had ever felt in her life before. Was this to be her existence forever? She had not thought about the future for years—there was *no* future to think of—nothing but the strange present where her secret love burned like an altar flame she must tend forever, a devoted priestess. But now she thought of the future. A future lived with two old women who were always bickering—an aunt who was bitter and miserly, a mother who was always complaining of "slaving" and not being appreciated. Milly, gay, irresponsible Milly, was long since married and gone. Her going had been a relief to Joscelyn because Milly thought her a fool, but now she missed Milly's laughter. How still and quiet everything was. But up at Treewoofe there would be wind. There was always a wind there. She could see every dell and slope of Treewoofe Farm from where she sat, lying in the light of a queer red smoky sunset. Dear Treewoofe which seemed in some curious way to belong to her still, when she watched the moon sinking over its snowy hill on winter nights or the autumn stars burning over its misty harvest fields. Over it a cloud was drifting—a cloud like a woman with long, blowing, wet hair. She thought of Pauline Dark— Pauline who still loved Hugh. Could it be true that Hugh's family really wanted him to get a U. S. divorce? Would Pauline ever be mistress of Treewoofe? Pauline with her thin malicious smile. Demure as a cat, too. At the thought Joscelyn felt a wave of homesickness engulf her. Treewoofe was *hers*—hers, though she could never enter into her heritage. Hugh would never—could never—take another woman there in her place. It would be sacrilege. Joscelyn shivered again. She had a bitter realisation that her spring-time suddenly seemed far away. She was no longer young— and all she had had out of life was a certain cool indifferent kiss dropped ten years ago on a cheek that no lips had ever touched since. Yet for that kiss she had given her soul.

Aunt Rachel came in without the useless formality of a knock. She had been crying and the knobby tip of her long nose was very red. But she was not without her consolation. Mercy Penhallow hadn't got Aunt Becky's bottle of Jordan water, thank heaven. *She*, Rachel Penhallow, was now the only woman in the clan who had one. Penny Dark didn't count. Men had no real understanding about such sacred things.

"What did you think of the afternoon, Joscelyn?"

"Think—the afternoon—oh, it was funny," said Joscelyn.

Aunt Rachel stared. She thought the afternoon had been dreadful and scandalous but it would never have occurred to her to call it funny.

"*We* have no real chance for the jug, of course. I told your mother that before we went. And less than ever *now*. Dandy Dark and Mrs. Conrad are first cousins. If you had not been so crazy—Joscelyn—" Joscelyn winced. She always winced when Aunt Rachel gave her jabs about her behaviour. She hated Aunt Rachel. Always had hated her. It was always a comfort to reflect that if she chose she could humiliate Aunt Rachel to the dust. Aunt Rachel with her poor pitiful pride in the possession of that bottle of Jordan water, one of several which an itinerant missionary had once sold for the benefit of his cause. She and Theodore Dark had been the only ones in the clan to buy one. The bottle stood in the middle of the parlour mantelpiece. Aunt Rachel dusted it every day with reverent hands.

One day when Joscelyn had been a little girl, she had found herself alone in the parlour, and she had boldly climbed up on a chair and taken the sacred bottle in her hand. It was a pretty bottle with a faceted glass stopper, and Aunt Rachel had tied a bow of blue satin ribbon lovingly around its throat. Somehow Joscelyn had dropped it. Luckily it fell on the soft, velvety, padded roses of one of Mrs. Clifford's famous hooked rugs. So it did not break. But the stopper came out and before the horrified Joscelyn could leap down and rescue it, every drop of the priceless Jordan water had been spilled. At first Joscelyn was cold with horror. Even at ten she did not think there was anything special or sacred about that water. She had understood too well her father's satirical speeches about it. But she knew what Aunt Rachel would be like. Then an impish idea entered her mind. Luckily she was alone in the house. She went out and deliberately filled up the bottle from the kitchen water-pail. It looked exactly the same. Aunt Rachel never knew the difference.

Joscelyn had never told a soul—less for her own sake than for Aunt Rachel's. That bottle of supposed Jordan water was all that gave any meaning to Aunt Rachel's life. It was the only thing she really loved—her god, in truth, though she would have been horrified if such a suggestion had ever been made to her.

As for Joscelyn, she could never have stood Aunt Rachel and her martyr airs at all had it not been for the knowledge of how securely she had her in her power.

"Where did you put that bottle of St. Jacob's oil when you housecleaned the pantry?" Aunt Rachel was asking. "I want to rub my joints. There's rain coming. I shouldn't have put off my flannels. A body should wear flannel next the skin till the end of June."

Joscelyn went silently and got the St. Jacob's oil.

XVIII

Hugh Dark leaned over the gate at Treewoofe for a time before going in, looking at the house dead black on its hill against the dull red sky—the house where he had once thought Joscelyn Penhallow would be mistress. He thought it looked lonely—as if it expected nothing more from life. Yet it had nothing of the desolate peace of a house whose life has been lived. It had an unlived look about it; it had a defrauded defiant air; it had been robbed of its birthright.

Before his marriage Hugh had liked to stand so and look at his house when he came home, dreaming a young man's dreams. He imagined coming home to Joscelyn; he would stand awhile before going in, looking up at all its windows whence warm golden lights would be gleaming over winter snows or summer gardens or lovely, pale, clear autumn dusks. He would think of the significance of each window—the dining-room, where his supper would be laid, the kitchen, where Joscelyn was waiting for him, perhaps a dimly lighted window upstairs in a room where small creatures slept. "*She* is the light of my house," he would think. Pretty? The word was too cheap and tawdry for Joscelyn. She was beautiful, with the beauty of a warm pearl or a star or a golden flower. And she was his. He would sit with her by rose-red fires on stormy winter nights and wild wet fall evenings, shut in with her for secret happy hours, while the winds howled about Treewoofe. He would walk with her in the twilight orchard on summer nights, and kiss her hair in that soft blue darkness of shadows.

For years he had not looked at his house when he came home. In a sense he hated it. But tonight he was restless and unhappy. Only after seeing Joscelyn did he realise to the full how empty his life was. Empty like his house. It was always difficult to believe that the incidents of his wedding-night had been real. We can never believe that terrible things really have happened. Years after they *have* happened we are still incredulous. So it was with Hugh. It simply could not be so. Joscelyn *must* be in that house, waiting for him to come to her. If he stood here patiently by the gate he would see her at the door looking for him and see the garland gold of her hair shining like a crown in the light behind her.

Would he get the divorce his mother and sisters were always hinting at? No, he would not. He struck his clenched fist furiously on the gate-post. Frank would come home then and marry Joscelyn. He should never have her.

There was no light in the house. His old housekeeper must be away. Hugh went in sullenly, not by the front door, though it was nearest. He knew that it was locked. He had locked it behind Joscelyn on their wedding-night and it had never been opened since. He went in by the kitchen door and lit a lamp. He was restless. He went all over the house—the dusty ill-kept house. It *was* lonely and unsatisfied. The chairs wanted to be sat upon. The mirrors wanted to reflect charming faces. The rooms wanted children to go singing through them. The walls wanted to re-echo to laughter. There had been no laughter in this house since that wedding-night—no real laughter. A house without remembered laughter is a pitiful thing. He came finally to the square front hall where the ashes of the bridal fire were still in the grate. His housekeeper had her orders never to meddle with anything in the front hall. The dust lay thick over everything. The mirror was turned to the wall. He hated it because it had once reflected her face and would reflect it no more forever. The clock on the mantelpiece was not going. It had stopped that night and had never been wound again. So time had stopped for Hugh Dark when he had looked at Joscelyn and realised that she was no longer his.

On the mantelpiece, just before the clock, a wedding-ring and a small diamond ring were lying. They had been there ever since Joscelyn had stripped them from her fingers.

The moonlight was looking in through the glass of the front door like a white hopeless face. Hugh recalled an old saying he had heard or read somewhere—"God had made a fool of him."

Ay, verily God had made a fool of *him*.

He would go out and roam about in the night as he

often did to drive away haunting thoughts. In the house he could think of nothing but Joscelyn. Outside he could think of his plans for making money out of his farm and the possibilities that were looming up for him in local politics. But first he must feed his cat. The poor beast was hungry, crouched on the kitchen doorstep looking at him accusingly. It was not the cat he and Joscelyn were reputed to have quarrelled over.

"At least," thought Hugh bitterly, "a cat always knows its own mind."

XIX

So Aunt Becky's famous last "levee" was over with all its comedy and tragedy, its farce and humour, its jealousies and triumphs; and it may be concluded that very few people went home from it as happy as they went to it. The two Sams, perhaps, who were untroubled by love or ambition and had no suspicion of the dark clouds already lowering over their lives—Gay Penhallow—and maybe Peter, who was tearing the bowels out of his trunk. He had said to Nancy on the way home:

"Nancy—Nancy, I've fallen in love—I have—I have— and it's glorious. Why did I never fall in love before?"

Nancy caught her breath as Peter whirled around a corner on two wheels.

"What *do* you mean? And who is it?"

"Donna Dark."

"Donna Dark!" Nancy gasped again as Peter shaved old Spencer Howey's team by the merest fraction of an inch. "Why, Peter, I thought you always hated her."

"So did I. But, dearest of Nancys, have you never heard the proverb, 'Hate is only love that has missed its way'?"

2
WHEELS WITHIN WHEELS

▼

I

Most of the clan who were at The Pinery went home thinking it was all nonsense to talk of Aunt Becky's dying. Anybody as full of vim and devilment as she was would last for years. Roger must be mistaken.

But Roger had, as usual, made no mistake. Less than a week after the famous levee, Aunt Becky died—very quietly and unostentatiously. And tidily. Aunt Becky insisted on dying tidily. She made Ambrosine put on a smooth and spotless spread, tuck all the edges neatly in, and fold back the fresh sheet in unwrinkled purity.

"I've lived clean and I'll die clean," said Aunt Becky, folding her hands on the sheet. "And I'm glad I'm not dying in my sleep. Roger told me I might. I want to have all my wits about me when I die."

She was done with life. As she looked back in this last hour she saw how few things had really mattered. Her hates now seemed trivial and likewise many of her loves. Things she had once thought great seemed small and a few trifles loomed vastly. Grief and joy had alike ceased to worry her. But she was glad she had told Crosby Dark that she had loved him. Yes, that was a satisfaction. She closed her sunken old eyes and did not open them again.

Of course there was a clan funeral and everybody with one exception came, even Mrs. Allan Dark, who was dying of some chronic trouble but had determined—so it was reported—to live until she knew who got the Dark jug. The exception was Tom Dark, who was in bed with a dislocated shoulder. The night before, as he was sitting on his bed, studying if there were any way to wheedle the secret out of Dandy Dark, he had absently put both feet into one pajama leg. Then when he stood up he fell on the floor in what his terrified wife at first thought was a fit. Very few of the clan sympathised with him as to his resulting shoulder. They thought it served him right for wearing new-fangled duds. If he had had a proper nightshirt on it couldn't have happened.

Thekla Penhallow, who always looked as if her nose were cold, appeared at the funeral in heavy mourning. Some of the other women wondered uneasily if they shouldn't have, too. To be sure, Aunt Becky had hated mourning; she called it a "relic of barbarism." But who knew what Dandy thought about it?

Everything proceeded decently and in order—until just at the last. Aunt Becky, who had never cared for flowers in her life, had her casket heaped with them But her clan at least respected her wish as regards "made-up" flowers. There was nothing but clusters and bouquets gathered in old homestead gardens and breathing only of the things Aunt Becky had known—and perhaps loved—all her life.

Aunt Becky was sternly handsome in what some considered far too expensive a coffin, with her lace shawl draped about her and her cold white lips forever closed on all the clan secrets she knew—so handsome that her clan, who had thought of her for years only as a gaunt unlovely old woman, with straggling hair and wrinkled face, were surprised. Crosby Dark, who had felt ashamed at the levee when she told him she had loved him, now felt flattered. The love of that stately old queen was a compliment. For the rest, they looked at her with interest, respect, and more grief than any of them had expected to feel. With considerable awe as well. She looked as if she might open her eyes with that terrible inquisitorial look of hers and shoot some ghastly question at them. It would be like her.

Very few tears were shed. Mrs. Clifford cried; but then she shed gallons at everybody's funeral. And Grace Penhallow cried, which was so unusual that her husband whispered testily, "What are *you* crying for? You always hated her."

"That's why I'm crying," said Grace drearily. She could not explain how futile that old hate seemed to her now. And its futility made her feel sad and temporarily bereft of all things.

The Rev. Mr. Trackley conducted the service very fittingly and gracefully, most people considered. Though Uncle Pippin thought, "Oh, you are drawing it rather strong" at some of the phrases used in Mr. Trackley's eulogy of the departed. Aunt Becky had hardly been such a saint as *that*. And Drowned John thought shamelessly, when Mr. Trackley said the Lord had taken her, "He's welcome to her." William Y. was by no means so sure of it as the minister seemed to be. Aunt Becky, he reflected, had never been a member of the church. But then she was a Penhallow. A Penhallow couldn't go anywhere but to the right place, William Y. felt comfortingly.

The funeral procession from The Pinery to the grave yard at Rose River was, so Camilla proudly remarked to Ambrosine that night, the longest that had ever been known in the clan. It was a day of heavy clouds with outbursts of sunshine between them; an occasional grey mist of rain drifted over the spruce barrens down by the harbour, much to the comfort of the superstitious. Aunt Becky was buried in the Theodore Dark plot, beside her husband and children, under a drift of blooming spirea. The old graveyard was full of the pathos of forgotten graves. Men and women of the clan lay there—men and women who had been victorious, and men and women who had been defeated. Their follies and adventures, their gallantries and mistakes, their fortunes and misfortunes, were buried and forgotten with them. And now Aunt Becky had come to take her place among them. People did not hurry away after the grave service had been conclud-ed. A clan funeral was by way of being a bit of a social function as well as a funeral. They broke up into little groups and talked—with rather easier minds than they had brought to the funeral—for Camilla had told them that that dreadful obituary had simply been a hoax on Aunt Becky's part. She had wanted to give them one good final scare.

"Thank God," said William Y., who really hadn't slept anything to speak of since he had heard that obituary read.

Everybody looked at Dandy Dark with a new outward respect. People came up and spoke to him who did not ordinarily notice him unless they fell over him. He felt his importance, as the possessor of a dying trust, but did not presume on it too much. Folks felt sure he knew already who was going to get the jug. If Aunt Becky hadn't told him, no doubt he had steamed the letter open the night after the levee. Artemas Dark, while the burial service was going on, was speculating as to whether there were any chance of getting Dandy "lit up" and worming the secret out of him that way. He sadly concluded there wasn't. Dandy had never tasted liquor in his life. Too mean—and unadventurous, thought Artemas. Titus Dark wondered if it would be any good to try the Sams' ouija-board. It was said to do wonderful things. But—would that be tampering with the powers of darkness? He knew Mr. Trackley thought so.

Palmer Dark and Homer Penhallow nodded to each other shamefacedly. Young Jimmy Dark meowed very distinctly at this, but Palmer and Homer pretended not to have heard.

"Good thing they made up at last," said Uncle Pippin. "Never could see the sense of keeping up a mouldy old scrap like that."

"As for the sense of it, there's no sense in heaps of things we do," said Stanton Grundy. "Life would be tedious without a vendetta or two."

Everybody was on tiptoe. Abel Dark had already begun to finish painting his house and Miller Dark had actually commenced work on his clan history and had a genealogical table neatly made out. Chris Penhallow had never touched a violin. Drowned John and Titus Dark had not sworn for a week—at least nobody had heard them do it. Titus showed the strain but there was no shadow on Drowned John's brow as he strode across the graveyard, trampling on the graves, to look at Jennie's and Emmy's, and read his own epitaph. Ambrosine Winkworth wore her diamond ring—most unfitting, it was thought. Mrs. Toynbee Dark went faithfully to visit each husband's grave. People said Nan Penhallow might have left the lipstick off for a funeral.

"She's a flip piece," said Rachel Penhallow.

"She tries to flirt with every man—why, she even tries to flirt with Pa," said Mrs. William Y.

"Little Sam saw her digging clams down at the sea-run in her bathing-suit the other night," said Mercy Penhallow.

"Yes, and I warrant you she'd just as soon dig them with nothing at all on," said Mrs. Clifford bitterly. "Such an example for our girls! What did Little Sam think of it?"

"Well, you know how men are," said Mercy. "He said of course it was hardly a decorous garb but she'd have looked all right if she'd had a bit more meat on her legs."

"Dear me!" was all Mrs. Clifford could say; but she said it adequately.

Mrs. William Y. looked solemnly at Nan, who was wearing a dress Mrs. William Y. thought was a sheer impertinence.

"I would like," she said bitterly, "to ask that girl how she would like to meet her God with those bare knees."

"Naked and ashamed," quoted Mrs. Clifford vaguely.

"Oh, I think you exaggerate," said Stanton Grundy, passing by. "Naked and *not* ashamed."

"At any rate, she has *good* knees," said Mrs. William Y. majestically. Stanton Grundy was not going to be allowed to sneer unrebuked at any Penhallow.

The little perverse lock stuck up on Hugh's head when he took off his hat for prayer, and Joscelyn had the same irrational impulse to go and smooth it down. Later on she saw Pauline talking to him and looking up at Treewoofe as she talked. Joscelyn resented the latter fact more than the former. Then Sim Penhallow came up and told her he had heard Hugh was going to sell Treewoofe—looking at her to see how she took it. Joscelyn did not let him see the sick dismay which invaded her soul. She took the news impassively, and Sim revenged himself nastily.

"You made a sad mess of things there, my girl."

Joscelyn turned her back on him without a word. Sim went off, vowing Hugh was well rid of *that*, and Joscelyn stood looking at Treewoofe, dim and austere and lovely on its distant hill. Oh, surely, surely Hugh would not sell it. But hadn't Pauline once said she wouldn't live on a bleak hill like that for anything?

Exaggerated reports of the value of the jug had already got around and mythical collectors had offered Aunt Becky fabulous sums for it. Another rumor was that it was to be left to the most truthful person in the clan. A group of men standing near the grave discussed it.

"Have we got to live for a year without telling any lies?" said Uncle Pippin sadly, but with a glint of mischief in his young blue eyes.

"There won't be many of us left in that case," said Stanton Grundy.

"*Us!*" grunted Uncle Pippin resentfully to himself.

Penny Dark went as always to look at what he thought the handsomest stone in the graveyard, which had been put up by Stephen Dark to the memory of a wife he hated. The gravestone was considered one of the sights of Rose River. A high pedestal of white marble surmounted by the life-size figure of an angel with outstretched wings. It had cost Stephen Dark—who never gave his wife a cent he could help giving—a thousand dollars. It was much admired by those who had never seen it on a wet day. *Then* the water ran down the angel's nose and poured off in a stream.

Penny minced past Margaret Penhallow without even noticing her. She thought his bandy legs bandier than ever and she detested his curly eyebrows.

Adam Penhallow was gloomy and would not be sociable. His wife had had twins the previous day. Not that Adam had anything against the poor twins, but—"that finishes us for the jug. Aunt Becky hated twins," he thought sadly. Murray Dark contrived to visit a few graves with Thora and went home satisfied.

The Moon Man was there, wandering about the grave-yard, talking to the dead people in a gruesome way.

"Do you remember, Lisa, the first time I kissed you?" He said to the grave of a woman who had been dead for fifteen years. A group of young folks, overhearing him, giggled. To them the Moon Man had always been old and crazy. They could not conceive of him as young and sane, with eager eyes and seeking lips.

"What do you suppose they're thinking of down there?" he asked eerily of William Y., who had never supposed anything about it and shivered at the very idea. Oswald was entirely too friendly with dead people. They were standing by a gravestone on which was a notorious inscription. "She died of a broken heart." The girl whose broken heart was hidden in that neglected corner had been neither Dark nor Penhallow—for which mercy the clan were thankful. But the Moon Man looked at the old lichened stone gently. "If the truth were told, that line could be engraved on many another stone here," he said. "Your mother now—your mother, William Y.—wouldn't it be true on *her* stone, too?"

William Y. made off without a reply, and his place was filled by Gay Penhallow, who couldn't help looking pretty in a smart little hat of black velvet pulled down over her happy eyes, with tiny winglike things sticking up at the sides, as if black butterflies had alighted there. Entirely too smart a hat for a funeral, the matrons reflected. But the old Moon Man smiled at her.

"Don't stay too late at the dance tonight," he whispered. "They kept up a dance too late there once—and Satan entered."

His tone made Gay shiver a little. And how did he know she was going to the dance? She had kept it very secret, knowing many of the clan would disapprove of her going to a dance the night after a clan funeral. This queer old Moon Man knew everything.

The Moon Man turned to Amasa Tyler, who was standing near, and said:

"Have you thought out the pattern of your coffin yet? You'll be needing it soon."

Amasa, who was young and in the pink of health, smiled

contemptuously. But when Amasa was killed in a motor-car accident a month later, people recalled what the Moon Man had said and shook their heads. How did he know? Say what you like, there was something in this second-sight business.

Nobody, as usual, took any notice of little Brian Dark. He had asked his uncle to take him to the funeral. Duncan Dark had at first refused. But Mr. Conway interceded for him.

"Aw, take the kid," said Mr. Conway——"he doesn't have much fun."

So Duncan Dark, being in one of his rare good-humored moods, had taken him.

Brian knew nothing and cared nothing about Aunt Becky. But he wanted a chance to put a little bouquet of wild flowers on his mother's grave—he always did that when he could, because she had no headstone and nobody ever went near her grave. If she had had a stone the line about the broken heart might very well have been inscribed on it also, though Brian knew nothing about that. He only knew he had no father and that he was a disgrace and nobody loved him. Nobody spoke to him at the funeral—though this was not out of unkindness but simply because they did not think of him. If they had thought of it they would have spoken, for they all had forgotten poor Laura Dark's shame and in any case were not, with all their faults and prejudices, cruel enough to visit it on her child. Besides, Duncan Dark himself was very off colour, and the clan had little to do with him or his household. But Brian believed it was because he was a disgrace. He would have liked to join the group of boys but he saw in it big Marshall Tracy, who had once taken his scanty lunch from him in school and trampled on it. So he drew back. Anyway, the boys wouldn't welcome him, he knew. He was a shy, delicate, dreamy little creature and the other boys at school tormented him for this. So he had no playmates and was almost always lonely. Sometimes he wished wistfully that he had just one chum. He felt tears come into his eyes when he saw a sweet-looking woman come up to little Ted Penhallow and kiss him. Ted didn't like it, but Brian, who had never been kissed in his life that he could remember, envied him. He wished there was someone who cared enough to kiss him. There seemed to be so much love in the world and none of it for him.

"Everybody has some friends but me," he thought, his heart swelling under his shabby coat. On his way back from putting his little bouquet on his mother's grave, he passed Margaret Penhallow. Margaret would have spoken to him but Brian slipped by her before she could. He liked her looks—her eyes were kind and beautiful—but he was too shy and timid to linger. Margaret, who had once known and liked poor Laura Dark, thought it a pity her child was so sulky and unattractive. Sickly looking, too. But likely Alethea Duncan starved him.

II

Peter Penhallow was at the first clan funeral he had ever attended and had already been held up by indignant Mrs. Lawyer Dark of Summerside, who wanted to know why he hadn't come to her dinner Tuesday night.

"Your dinner—your dinner?" repeated Peter vaguely. "Why, I wasn't hungry." He had forgotten all about her confounded dinner. He had spent Tuesday evening wondering how he could get possession of Donna Dark. If he had been quite sure of her he would have simply gone to Drowned John and demanded her. But he must be quite sure before he could do that. So now he came boldly up to her at the funeral. She and Virginia were together of course. They had been together the evening before, too, because it had rained. Virginia and Donna had always made it a part of their ritual to spend every rainy evening together. They sat in what Virginia was pleased to call her "den," perfumed by burning incense—which Virginia defined as a "subtle suggestion of exotic romance." When Donna tried it once at home Drowned John fired the burner out of the window and told her never to let him smell that damned stink in his house again.

Donna was still trying to be faithful to Barry's memory. Aided by Virginia's sentimentalities she succeeded for an hour in forgetting Peter and remembering Barry. It was like a wind blowing over an almost dead fire and for a brief space fanning one lingering ember into a fitful flame. After she went home she had got out Barry's letters and re-read them for the thousandth time. But they were suddenly lifeless—a casket rifled of its jewels—a vase with the perfume gone—a lamp with its flame blown out. The pulsing, vivid personality that was Peter Penhallow had banished the pale phantom that Barry had become.

Virginia was very suspicious. How dared Peter speak to Donna? he was actually holding out his hand.

And Donna was taking it.

"I thought you were on your way to South America," said Donna.

"I've postponed my trip there," said Peter, staring at her. "I think I'll take it as a honeymoon."

"Oh," said Donna, looking at him, too. Eyes can say a great deal in a second—especially when they are like twin deep pools with a star in them, as Peter was thinking Donna's were. And what a delicious mouth she had. He knew now that what he had been seeking for all his life was just the chance to kiss that dimpled mouth. To be sure, her nose was slightly irregular—rather too much like Drowned John's. When all was said and done he had seen hundreds of prettier women. But there was a charm about this Donna—a mighty and potent charm. And her voice was such a sweet, throaty, summery drawl. What a voice for love-making! Peter trembled before this slip— Peter who had never known fear. If he had been quite sure of her he would have put his arm around her and walked her out of the graveyard. But he was not sure, and before he knew what had happened Virginia had whisked Donna off to see the Richard Dark family plot, where Barry should have been buried, even if he wasn't, and where there was a monument to his memory. In the next plot to it Ned Powell was buried. Virginia had already knelt there in silent prayer for ten minutes, her long black veil sweeping picturesquely about her.

"I woke up last night thinking I heard him calling my name," she murmured with tears in her voice. Virginia could infuse tears into her voice at will.

Donna was conscious of a new feeling of disgust and impatience. Was Virginia really any better than old Cousin Matilda Dark, who was always whining about her dear departed husband? When did grief cease to be beautiful and become ridiculous? Donna knew. When it became a second-hand grief—a mere ghost of grief. Yet she had loved Barry very truly. When the word came of his death, her agony had been so great that she had thought it must tear her in pieces. It had seemed the most natural thing in the world to resolve on a dedication of her whole life to his memory. *What* was Virginia reciting as she gazed mournfully at Barry's monument.

Oh, that old verse of Mrs. Browning's—

> *"Unless you can think when the song is done*
> *No other is soft in the rhythm,*
> *Unless you can feel when left by one*
> *That all other men go with him*
> *Unless you can dream that his faith is fast*
> *In behoving or unbehoving,*
> *Unless you can die when the dream is past*
> *Oh, never call it loving."*

"That's so true of us, isn't it,' Donna darling?" sobbed Virginia.

Donna felt still more impatient. Time was when she had thought that verse very beautiful and affecting. Well, it was so still. But not for her. Some mysterious hour of change had struck. All the melancholies and ecstasies of her young love belonged in a volume to which "finis" was at last written. With eyes suddenly made clear by what Donna, if she had ever heard the phrase, might have defined as "the expulsive power of a new affection," she saw Virginia and herself as they were. The dramatic lovers of grief—nothing else.

"After all, you know," she said coldly, "neither of us *did* die."

"No-o," admitted Virginia reluctantly. "But for weeks after Ned—died—I was tempted to drown myself. I never told you *that*."

Donna reflected that it must be the only thing Virginia had *not* told her. It suddenly seemed to her that for ten years she had heard of nothing but Virginia's feelings when Ned died. It was an old story and a very boring one. Donna wondered if she were becoming heartless. But really poor Virginia was tiresome. Donna felt thankful she had never talked much about her feelings in Barry's case. She had no silly outpourings to blush over now and she was fortunately ignorant of how many of Virginia's absurdities were imputed to her. She walked away abruptly. After all, Barry's grave was not there. It was foolish to stand, a figure of woe, beside a plot where only his grandfather and grandmother were buried. She didn't believe for a moment that Virginia had ever had the faintest notion of drowning herself. She had been enjoying her weeds and her romantic position as a young war widow—Donna felt herself growing more hateful and cynical every moment— far too much for that.

Aunty But came wandering along—an odd little figure in her rusty black and her queer old bonnet with its rampant spray of imitation osprey. Aunty But was seventy-five but she was, as she claimed, spry as a cricket and still busy most of her time helping babies into the clan. She looked at the headstone of Barry's grandmother and sighed.

"She was his second wife—but she was a very nice woman," she said. "And hasn't it been a lovely funeral, dears? But—don't you think—a little bit *too* cheerful."

"Aunt Becky wanted it cheerful," reminded Donna.

Aunty But shook her head. But what Aunty But would have said was never known. For at that moment the scandal took place and everybody swarmed to the gate, where there was a great commotion among a crowd of men. *Outside* the graveyard—oh, most providentially outside of it—two men were fighting each other—Percy Dark and David Dark, two hitherto peaceable friends. Going at each other, hatless and coatless, red-faced and furious. Nobody ever knew just what had started the fight except that it was something one of them had said about the jug. From verbal warfare they resorted to fists. Percy was heard to exclaim, "I'll take some of the conceit out of you!" and assaulted first. William Y. tried to stop them and for reward got a whack on the nose that made it bleed profusely and robbed him of his pomposity for a week. Mrs. David Dark fainted and Mrs. Percy was never to go

out anywhere the rest of the summer, so ashamed was she.
Though at the time she behaved very well. She neither
fainted nor had hysterics. Undismayed by William Y.'s fate
she got between the two mad creatures and dared David
to strike *her*. Before David could accept or refuse the
challenge, both he and Percy were caught from behind
and frog-marched to their respective cars. The fight was
finished but the scandal was not. Before night it was all
over the country that two of the Darks had fought at their
aunt's funeral over her property and had to be dragged
apart by their wives. It took years for them to live it down.

"Thank heaven, the minister was away before they
started," sobbed Mrs. Clifford.

Uncle Pippin pretended to be horrified, but in secret he
thought the fight made the funeral more interesting and
felt it a pity Aunt Becky wasn't alive to see the prayerful
David and the sanctimonious Percy pummeling each other
like that. Tempest Dark laughed for the first time since his
wife's death.

III

Donna and Virginia walked home together. Virginia
contrived to tell Donna some weird tales about Peter—
especially those years of his having "gone native" in the
East Indies and having several dozens of dark-skinned
wives. Donna didn't believe a word of them, but as yet
she did not dare to defend Peter. She was not at all sure
about him—especially about his attitude to her. Did she
really exist for him at all? Until she was certain of that she
was not going to commit herself. Let Virginia rave.

"I wonder if it's going to rain," said Virginia at Drowned
John's gate.

"No—no, I'm sure it isn't—it's going to be a lovely
evening. The moon will clear away the clouds," said
Donna positively. She really couldn't stand any more of
Virginia just then. Besides, she was dreadfully hungry and
Virginia, who cared nothing for eating, always contrived to
make the hearty Donna feel like a pig.

"I wish there was no moon tonight. I hate moonlight—
it always reminds me of things I want to forget," said

Virginia mournfully and inconsistently. For Virginia certainly did not want to forget things. But Virginia never allowed consistency to bother her when she got hold of what she thought a touching phrase. She floated off in her weeds uneasily. Certainly something had come over Donna. But it couldn't be Peter. It was absurd to suppose it could be Peter.

It *was* Peter. Donna knew that at last as she entered Drowned John's stodgy and comfortable home. She was in love with Peter Penhallow. And he, if eyes were to be believed, was in love with her. And what was to be done about it? Drowned John would raise the roof. Both he and Thekla were opposed to her marrying again—marrying anybody. But imagination faltered before the scenes they would make if she tried to marry Peter Penhallow. Well, Peter hadn't asked her to marry him. Perhaps he never would. Who in the world was laughing upstairs? Oh, that fool of a Thekla! Thekla was always trying some new health fad. Just now it was laughing for ten minutes every day. It got on Donna's nerves and she was raspy enough when she went to the supper table. Drowned John was in a bad temper, too. He had come home from the funeral to find his favourite pig sick and couldn't swear about it. Thekla tried to placate him and ordinarily this would have appeased him. He liked to feel that his women-folk felt the need of placating him. But why wasn't Donna doing it? Donna was sitting in an absent silence as if his good or bad temper were nothing to her. Drowned John took his annoyance out in abusing everybody who had been at the funeral—especially Peter Penhallow. He expressed himself forcibly regarding Peter Penhallow.

"How would you like him for a son-in-law?" asked Donna.

Drowned John thought Donna was trying to be funny. He barked out a laugh.

"I'd sooner have the devil," he said, banging the table. "Thekla, is this knife *ever* sharpened? Two women to run this house and a man can't get a decent bread-knife!"

Donna escaped after supper. She could not spend the evening in the house. She was restless and unhappy and lonely. What had Peter meant about taking a honeymoon in South America. Who was to be the bride? Oh, she was tired of everything. Even the very moon looked forlorn—a widow of the skies.

Donna walked along the winding drive by Rose River till she reached a little point running out into it. It was covered by an old orchard with an old ruined house in the middle of it. The Courting-House Uncle Pippin had named it, because spoony couples were in the habit of sitting on its steps; but there were none there when Donna reached it. She was just in time to meet Peter Penhallow, who had tied his boat to a bough and was coming up the old mossy path. They looked at each other, knowing it was Fate.

Peter had gone home from the funeral in a mood of black depression. What particular kind of an ass was he! Donna had deliberately turned her back on him and gone to weep at Barry's grave—or at least his gravestone. Her heart was still buried there. Peter had laughed when he had first heard Donna had said that. But he laughed no longer. It was now a tragedy.

In his despair he rushed to young Jeff's boat and began rowing down the river. He had some mad romantic notion of rowing down far enough to see Donna's light. Peter was so love-sick that there was no crazy juvenile thing he would not do. The day grew dimmer and dimmer. At first the river was of pale gold; then it was dim silver—then like a waiting woman in the darkness. Along its soft velvet shores home-lights twinkled out. He, Peter, had no home. No home except where Donna was. Where she was would always be home for him. And then he saw her coming up the winding drive.

When they came to their senses they were sitting side by side on the steps of the Courting-House between two white blooming spirea bushes. Peter had said, "Goodevening," when what he had wanted to say was, "Hail, goddess." Donna could never recall what she said.

About them was night—and faint starlight—and scented winds. A dog was taking the countryside into his confidence two farms away.

Donna knew now that Peter loved her. She would share the flame and wonder that was his life—she would know the lure in the thought of treading where no white wom-

an's foot had ever trod—they would gaze together on
virgin mountain tops climbing upward into sunset skies—
they would stand on peaks in Darien—they would spend
nights together in the jungle—hot, scented, spicy nights—
or under desert stars—didn't she hear the tinkling of
camel-bells?

"I think I've been drunk ever since I saw you at Aunt
Becky's levee—a week ago—a year ago—a lifetime ago,"
said Peter. "Drunk with the devilish magic of you, girl.
And to think I've been hating you all my life! *You!*"

Donna sighed with rapture. She must keep this moment
forever. Adventure—mystery—love—the three most significant words in any language—were to be hers again.
She was for the time being as perfectly, youngly, fearlessly
happy as if she had never learned the bitter lesson that joy
could die. She couldn't think of anything to say, but words
did not seem to be necessary. She knew she was very
beautiful—she had put on beauty like a garment. And the
night was beautiful—and the sunken old rotten steps were
beautiful—and the dog was beautiful. As for Peter—he
was just Peter.

"Isn't that a jolly wind?" said Peter, as it blew around
them from the river. "I hate an evening when there's no
wind. It seems so dead. I always feel ten times more alive
when there's a wind blowing."

"So do I," said Donna.

Then they spent some rapturous silent minutes reflecting
how wonderful it was that they should both love wind.

The moon came out from behind a cloud. Silver lights
and ebon shadows played all about the old orchard. Peter
had been silent so long that Donna had to ask him what he
was thinking of. Just for the sake of hearing his dear voice
again.

"Watch that dark cloud leaving the moon," said Peter,
who had no notion of making love in the common way.
"It's as good as an eclipse."

"How silvery it will be on the moon side," said Donna
dreamily. "It must be wonderful."

"When I get my aeroplane we'll fly up in it when there's
a cloud like that and see it from the moon side," said
Peter, who had never thought of getting an aeroplane

before but knew now he must have one and sweep in it with Donna through the skies of dawn. "And I'll get you the Southern Cross for a brooch. Or would you prefer the belt of Orion for a girdle?"

"Oh," said Donna. She stood up and held out her arms to the moon. Perhaps she knew she had very beautiful arms, shining like warm marble through the sleeves of her filmy black dress. "I wish I could fly up there now."

"With me?" Peter had risen, too, and snatched at the dark blossom of her loveliness. He kissed her again and again. Donna returned his kisses—shamelessly, Virginia would have said. But there was no thought of Virginia or Barry or old feuds. They were alone in their exquisite night of moonlight and shadow and glamour.

"With me?" asked Peter again.

"With you," answered Donna between kisses.

Peter laughed down into her eyes triumphantly.

"I'm the only man in the world you could ever love," he said arrogantly and truthfully. "How soon can we be married?"

"Tee hee—how very romantic!" tittered Mrs. Toynbee Dark, who had been standing for ten minutes at the corner of the old house watching them with sinister little black eyes.

"Ho, ho, my pet weasel, so you're there," said Peter. "Rejoice with me, widow of Toynbee, Donna has promised to marry me."

"So her heart has had a resurrection," said Mrs. Toynbee. "It's an interesting idea. But what will Drowned John say about it?"

IV

Peter and Donna were not the only pair whose troth was plighted that night. The phrase was Gay's —she thought it sounded much more wonderful than just getting engaged. Nan, who was to go to the dance with Gay and Noel, went home with her from the funeral and on the way told Gay that her mother had decided to stay on the island until the matter of the jug was settled.

"She says she won't go back to St. John till it's known who is to get it. Poor mums! She'll certainly go loco if *she* doesn't. Dad is to be in China most of the year on business, so he won't miss us. We're taking the rooms at The Pinery Aunt Becky had. To think when life is so short I must be buried here for a year. It's poisonous."

Gay felt a little dashed. She didn't know why it chilled her to hear that Nan was going to stay around, but it did. She did not talk much and was rather relieved when they reached Maywood. Maywood had been one of the show-places of the clan when Howard Penhallow was alive, but it had gone to seed since—the shingles curled up a bit—the verandah roof was sagging—it needed paint badly. The grounds had run wild. But it had beauty of a sort yet, nestled under its steep hill of dark spruces with the near shore in its sapphire of sky and wave, and Gay loved it. It hurt and angered her when Nan called it a picturesque old ruin.

But she forgot all about Nan and her prickles as she dressed for the dance. It was delightful to make herself beautiful for Noel. She would wear her dress of primrose silk and her new, high-heeled fairy slippers. She always felt she was beautiful when she put on that dress. To slip such a lovely golden gown over her head—give her bobbed hair shake like a daffodil tossing in the wind—and then look at the miracle.

All very fine till Nan slipped in and stood beside her—purposely perhaps. Nan in a wispy dress you could crumple in your hand—a shining, daring gown of red with a design of silver grapes all over it—hair with a fillet of silver-green leaves, starred with one red bud, around her sleek, ash-gold head. Gay felt momentarily quenched.

"I look *home-made* beside her, that's the miserable truth," she thought. "Pretty, oh, yes, but home-made."

And her eyebrows looked so black and heavy beside the narrower line over Nan's subtle eyes. But Gay plucked up heart—the faint rose of her cheeks under the dark stain of her lashes was not make-up and say what you might about smartness, that curl of Nan's in front of her ear looked exactly like a side-whisker. Gay forgot Nan again as she ran down to the gate in the back of the garden whence she could see the curve in the Charlottetown road around which Noel's car must come.

She saw Mercy Penhallow and her mother in the glass porch as she ran. And she knew that quite likely they were clapper-clawing Noel—Mercy, anyhow. When Gay had first begun to go about with Noel, her whole clan lifted their noses and keened. If people only wouldn't interfere so in one's life! The idea of them insinuating that Noel wasn't good enough for her—those inbred Darks and Penhallows! Don't dare marry outside of the Royal Family! Gay tossed her head in a fine scorn of them as she flitted through the garden on her slender and golden feet.

Mercy Penhallow had not yet begun on Noel. She and Mrs. Howard had been discussing the funeral in all its details. Now Mercy's pale watery eyes were fixed on Nan, who was on the front verandah smoking a cigarette to the scandal of all Rose River folks who happened to go by.

"She must think her back beautiful—she shows so much of it," said Mercy. "But then it's old-fashioned to be modest."

Mrs. Howard smiled tolerantly. Mrs. Howard, her clan thought, was too tolerant. That was why matters had gone so far between Gay and Noel Gibson.

"She's going to the dance at the Charlottetown Country Club with Gay and Noel. I would have preferred Gay not to have gone, the night after the funeral—but the young people of today don't feel as we used to do about such things."

"The whole world is dancing mad," snapped Mercy. "The young fry of today have neither manners nor morals. As for Nan, she's out to catch a man, they say. Boys on the brain—running after them all the time, I'm told."

"The girls of our time let the boys do the running," smiled Mrs. Howard. "It was more fun, I think—one could stop when one wanted to be caught."

Mercy, who had never been "caught," whether she wanted to be or not, sniffed.

"I suppose Gay is still crazy after Noel?" she said. "Why don't you put a stop to that, Lucilla?"

Mrs. Howard looked distressed.

"How can I? Gay knows I don't like him. But the child is

infatuated. Why, when I said something to her about his pedigree she said, 'Mother dear, Noel isn't a horse.'"

"And Roger just mad about her!" moaned Mercy. "A splendid fellow with gobs of money. He could give her *everything*—"

"Except happiness," said Mrs. Howard sadly. But she said it only in thought and Mercy prattled on.

"Noel hasn't a penny beyond his salary and I doubt if he'll ever have more. Besides, what are those Gibsons? Merely mushrooms. I wonder what her poor father would have thought of it."

Mrs. Howard sighed. She was not as worldly as some of her clan. She did not want Gay to marry Roger, when she did not love him, simply because he had money. And it was not one of her counts against Noel that he had none. His Gibsonness mattered more. Mrs. Howard knew her Gibsons as Gay could never know them. And she had, in spite of Gay's quip about the pedigree, an old-fashioned conviction about what was bred in the bone. The first time she had seen Noel she had thought, "A boy shouldn't know how to use his eyes like that. And he has the Gibson mouth."

But she couldn't bear to quarrel with Gay. Gay was all she had. Mercy didn't understand. It wasn't so simple "putting a stop" to things. Gay had a will of her own under all her youth and her sweetness, and Mrs. Howard couldn't bear to make her child unhappy.

"Maybe he's only flirting with her," was Mercy's response to the sigh. "The Gibsons are very fickle."

Mrs. Howard didn't like that either. It was unthinkable that a Gibson should be "only flirting" with a Penhallow. She resented the insinuation that Gay might be tossed aside.

"I'm afraid he's only too much in earnest and I think— I'm pretty sure—they're almost engaged already."

"Almost engaged. Lucilla dear, talk sense. Either people are engaged or they are not. And if Gay were *my* daughter—"

Mrs. Howard hid a smile. She couldn't help thinking that if Gay had been Mercy's daughter neither Noel nor any other boy might have bothered her much. Poor Mercy! She was so very plain. With that terrible dewlap! And a face in which the features all seemed afraid of each other. Mrs. Howard felt for her the complacent pity of a woman who had once been very pretty herself and was still agreeable to look upon.

Mrs. Howard was by all odds the most popular woman in the clan. Wherever she was she always seemed to be in the right place without making any fuss about it. She generally got the best of any argument because she never argued—she only smiled. She did not know anything about a great many things, but she knew a great deal about loving and cooking and a woman can go far on that. She was no paw-and-claw friend, giving a dig now and a pat then, as so many were; and there was something about her that made people want to tell her their secrets—their beautiful secrets. Aunt Becky had always flattered herself that she knew all the clan secrets before anybody else, but Mrs. Howard knew many things before Aunt Becky did.

Even Stanton Grundy, who seldom spoke well of a woman because he had a reputation for sardonic humour to keep up, had been heard to say of Mrs. Howard that for once God knew what He was about when He made a woman.

Some of the clan thought Mrs. Howard dressed too gay for a widow of her age, but Mrs. Howard only laughed at this.

"I always liked bright colours and I'll wear them till I die," she told them. "You can bury me in black if you want to, but as long as breath's in me I'll wear blue."

"Talking of Roger," said Mercy, "he's looking miserable of late. Thin as a lath. Is he worrying over Gay? Or overworking?"

"A little of both, I'm afraid. Mrs. Gateway died last week. No one on earth could have saved her, but Roger takes it terribly hard when he loses a patient."

"He's got more feeling than most doctors," said Mercy. "Gay's a blind little goose if she passes him over for Noel, that's all I've got to say."

It wasn't all Mercy had to say but Mrs. Howard deftly changed the unwelcome subject by switching to Aunt Becky's jug. Had Mercy heard? Two of Mrs. Adam Penhallow's boarders at Indian Spring, Gerald Elmslie and

Grosset Thompson, had quarrelled with each other over the jug and left. It was hard on Mrs. Adam, who found it hard enough to make both ends meet.

"But what on earth made Gerald and Grosset quarrel over the jug?" asked Mercy. "*They're* nothing to do with it."

"Oh, Gerald is keeping company with Vera Dark and Grosset is engaged to Sally Penhallow," was the sufficient explanation. But that would not fill Mrs. Adam's lean purse.

"It's my opinion that jug will drive somebody crazy yet," said Mercy.

Gay was watching for Noel at the gate, under an old spruce tree that was like a grim, black sorrowful priest. Evenings out of mind she had watched for him so. She could distinctly hear on the calm evening air Drowned John's Olympian laughter echoing along the shore down at Rose River and she resented it. When she came her to dream of Noel, only the loveliest of muted sounds should be heard—the faintest whisper of trees—the half-heard, half-felt moan of the surf—the airiest sigh of wind. It was the dearest half-hour of the whole day—this faint, gold, dusky one just before it got truly dark. She wanted to keep it wholly sacred to Noel—she was young and in love and it was spring, remember. So of course Drowned John had to be bellowing and Roger had to come stepping up behind her and stand beside her, looking down at her. Tall, grim, scarred Roger! At least Gay thought him grim, contrasting his thin face and mop of dark red hair with Noel's smoothness and sleekness. Yet she liked Roger very much and would have liked him more if her clan had not wanted her to marry him.

Roger looked at her—at the trim, shining, golden-brown head of her. Her fine black brows. Her fan-lashed, velvety eyes. That dimple just below the delightful red mouth of hers. That creamy throat above her golden dress. She was as shy and sweet and wilful as April, this little Gay. Who could help loving her? Her very look said, "Come and love me." What a soft, gentle little voice she had—one of the few women's voices he had ever heard with pleasure. He was very critical as regards women's voices, and very sensitive to them. Nothing hurt him quite so much as an unlovely voice—not even unloveliness of face.

She had something in her hand for him, if she would but open her hand and give it. He had ceased to hope she ever would. He knew the dream behind her lashes was not for him. He knew perfectly well that she was waiting there for another man, compared to whom he, Roger, was a mere shadow and puppet. Suddenly he realised that he had lived thirty-two years against Gay's eighteen.

Why on earth, he wondered, had he to love Gay when there were dozens of girls who would jump at him, as he knew perfectly well? But there it was. He did love her. And he wanted her to be happy. He was glad that in such a world anyone could be as happy as Gay was. If that Gibson boy didn't *keep* her happy!

"This old gate is still here. I thought your mother was going to have it taken away."

"I wouldn't let her," said Gay. "This is *my* gate. I love it."

"I like any gate," said Roger whimsically. "A gate is a luring thing—a promise. There may be something wonderful beyond and you are not shut out. A gate is a mystery—a symbol. What would we find, you and I, Gay, if we opened that gate and went through?"

"A little green sunset hollow of white violets," laughed Gay. "But we're not going through, Roger—there's a dew on the grass and I'd spoil my new slippers."

She looked at him as she laughed—only for a moment, but that was the moment Noel's car flashed around the curve and she missed it. When she went back to the house, leaving Roger at the unopened gate, she found Noel sitting beside Nan on the steps. They had never met before but already they seemed to have known each other all their lives. And Nan was looking up at Noel with the eyes that instantly melted men but were not quite so effective with women. A strange, icy, little ripple ran all over Gay.

"I've just been asking Noel if he waves his hair with the curling-tongs," said Nan in her lazy, impudent voice.

Gay forgot her shivers and all other unpleasant things as

she drifted through the dances. Noel said delicious things to her and looked things still more delicious; and when halfway through it she sat out a dance with Noel in a shadowy corner of the balcony her cup brimmed full. For Noel whispered a question and Gay, smiling, blushing, yet with a queer little catch in her throat, and eyes strangely near to tears, whispered her answer. They were no longer "almost" engaged.

For the rest of the evening Gay floated—or seemed to float—in a rosy mist of something too rare and exquisite even to be called by so common a name as happiness. They left Nan at The Pinery on their way back and drove on to Maywood alone. They lingered over saying good-bye. It was such a sweet pleasure because they would meet so soon again. They stood under the big, late-blooming apple tree at the turn of the walk, among the soft, trembling shadows of the moonlit leaves. All around and beyond was a delicate, unreal moonlit world. The night was full of mystery and wonder; there never had—there never could have been—such a night before. Gay wondered as she gave her lips, red as the Rose of Love itself, to Noel, how many lovers all over the world were standing thus entranced— how many vows were being whispered thus in the starlight. The old tree suddenly waved its boughs over them as if in blessing. So many lovers had stood beneath it—it had screened so many kisses. Many of the lips that had kissed were ashes now. But the miracle of love renewed itself every springtime.

In her room Gay undressed by moonlight. She shredded the petals of the white June roses she had worn into the little blue rose-jar on her table. Her father had given her the jar when she was a child and had told her to drop a handful of rose leaves in it for every perfectly happy day she had. The jar was almost full now. There was only room really for one more handful. Gay smiled. She would put that handful in it on her wedding-day and then seal it up forever as a symbol of her girlhood.

Of course she didn't sleep. It would be a pity to waste a moment of such a night sleeping. It was nicer to lie awake thinking of Noel. Even planning a little bit about her wedding. It was to be in the fall. Her wedding-dress—

satin as creamy as her own skin—"Your skin is like the petal of a white narcissus," Noel had told her—shimmering silk stockings—laces like sea-foam—one of those slender platinum wedding-rings—"the lovely Mrs. Noel Gibson"— "one of the season's most charming brides"—a little house somewhere—perhaps one of those darling new bungalows— with yellow curtains like sunshine on its windows and yellow plates like circles of sunshine on its breakfast-table. With Noel opposite.

"Little love." She could hear him as he said it under the apple tree, looking down into the pools of darkness that were her eyes. How wonderful and unbelievable it was that out of a whole world of beautiful girls, his for the asking, he should have chosen *her*.

Just once she thought of the old Moon Man's warning— "Don't be too happy." That poor old crazy Moon Man. As if one could be too happy! As if God didn't like to see you happy! Why, people were made for happiness.

"I'll always love this night," thought Gay. "The eighth of June—it will always be the dearest date of the year. I'll always celebrate it in some dear secret little way of my own."

And they would always be together—always. On rough paths and smooth. Dawns and twilights would be more beautiful because they would be together.

"If I were dead," thought Gay, "and Noel came and looked at me I'd live again."

Next day Nan rang Gay up on the telephone.

"I think I like your Noel," Nan said drawlingly "I think I'll take him from you."

Gay laughed triumphantly.

"You can't," she said.

V

Gay was not the only one of the clan who kept vigil that night. Neither Donna nor Peter slept. Mrs. David Dark and Mrs. Palmer Dark lay awake in their shame beside snoring spouses, wondering dumbly why life should be so hard for decent women who had always tried to do what was right. Virginia was awake worrying. Mrs. Toynbee

Dark was awake nursing her venom. Pauline Dark was awake wondering if Hugh would really get that divorce. Thora Dark waited anxiously for a drunken, abusive husband to come home. The Sams slept, although both, did they but know it, had cause to be wakeful. Hugh Dark and Roger Penhallow slept soundly. Even William Y. slept, with a poultice on his nose. On the whole, the men seemed to have the best of it, unless Aunt Becky, sleeping so dreamlessly in her grave in the trim Rose River churchyard, evened things up for the women.

Joscelyn was not sleeping either. She went to bed and tossed restlessly for hours. Finally she rose softly, dressed, and slipped out of the house to the shore. The hollows among the dunes were filled with moonlight. The cool wind nestled in the grasses on the red "capes," bringing whiffs of the faint, cold, sweet perfumes of night. There was a wash of gleaming ripples all along the shore and a mist mirage over the harbour. Far out she heard the heart-breaking call of the sea that had called for thousands of years.

She felt old and cold and silly and empty. Suppose Hugh really loved Pauline and wanted to be free. Very well, why not? Did not *she* love Frank Dark? Why could she not think philosophically, "Well, if Hugh gets a divorce *I* will be free, too, and perhaps Frank will come back"—no, she could not think that. Such a thought seemed to tarnish and cheapen the high flame of love she had nursed in her heart for years.

Dawn was breaking over the dunes and little shudders were running through the sand-hill grasses when she went back to the house. She had not dreamed of meeting any one at that early hour, but who should come trotting across Al Griscom's silent white pasture of morning dew but Aunty But, bent two-double, with her head wrapped in a grey shawl, out of which her bright little eyes peered curiously at Joscelyn. She seemed at once incredibly old and elfinly young.

"You're up early, Mrs. Dark."

Joscelyn hated to be called Mrs. Dark, just as she hated to take a letter out of the post-office addressed to "Mrs. Hugh Dark." Once when she had had to sign some legal document "Joscelyn Dark," she had thrown down the pen and risen with lips as white as snow. Aunty But was the only one of the clan who ever addressed her as "Mrs. Dark." And there was no use in snubbing Aunty But.

"And you, too, Aunty."

"Eh, but I've never been in bed at all. I've been up at Forest Myers' all night. A little girl there—a fine baby but got the Myers mouth, I'm afraid."

"And Alice?"

"Alice is fine but awful sorry for herself. Yet she didn't have a bad time at all. No caterwauling to speak of. It's a pleasure to help a woman like that to a baby. I might have done the same for you in that house up there"—Aunty But waved her hand at distant Treewoofe, taking shape in the pale grey light that was creeping over the hill—"if you hadn't behaved as you did. *I* brought babies into that house many a time—I was there when Clara Treverne was born. Such a time! Old Cornelius—but he was young Cornelius then—was crazy wild. You'd have thought nobody'd ever had a baby before. Finally I had to decoy him to the cellar and lock him up, or that child would never have got born. Poor Mrs. Cornelius couldn't rightly give her mind to it for the racket Cornelius was making. Clara was the last baby at Treewoofe. It's high time there was some more. But there may be. I'm hearing Hugh is going to get a Yankee divorce. If that's so Pauline won't let him slip through her fingers a second time. But she'll never have the babies you'd have had, Joscelyn. She hasn't the figger for it."

VI

Little Brian Dark had to walk home from the funeral because his Uncle Duncan took a notion to go on to town.

"Mind ye get the stones picked off the gore-field before milking," he told him.

Brian never had a day to play—never even half a day. He was very tired, for he had picked stones all the forenoon since early morning; and he was hungry. To be sure, he was always hungry; but the hunger in his heart was worse than any physical hunger. And there was no monument to his mother. Would he ever be able, when he grew up, to earn enough money to get one?

When he reached Duncan Dark's ugly yellow house among its lean trees, he took off his shabby "best suit," put on his ragged work-garb, and went out to the gore to pick stones. He picked stones until milking time, his back aching as well as his heart. Then he helped Mr. Conway milk the cows. Mr. Conway was the only hired man Brian had ever heard of who was called "Mr. " Mr. Conway said he wouldn't work for anyone who wouldn't call him "Mr." He was as good as any master, by gosh. Brian rather liked Mr. Conway, who looked more like a poet gone to seed than a hired man. He had a shock, of wavy, dark auburn hair, a drooping moustache and goatee, and round, brilliant, brown eyes. He was a stranger from Nova Scotia and called himself a Bluenose. Brian often wondered why, for Mr. Conway's nose was far from blue. Red in fact.

When milking was over, Aunt Alethea, a tall, fair, slatternly woman, with a general air of shrewishness about her, told him to go down to Little Friday Cove and see if he could get a codfish from one of the Sams.

"Be smart about it, too," she admonished him. "None of your dawdling, or the Moon Man will cotch you."

What the Moon Man would do when he "cotched" him she never specified, perhaps reasoning that the unknown was always more terrible than the known. Brian's private opinion was that he would boil him in oil and pick his bones. He was more afraid of the Moon Man now than of the devil. Somebody had told him that when a boy had no father, the devil was his father and would come along some night and carry him off. He had been sick with horror many a night after that. But Mr. Conway had told him there was no devil and emphasised it with so many "By goshes" that Brian believed him. He wanted to believe him. But Mr. Conway By-goshed heaven away, too, and that was not so good because it meant he would never see his mother again. Mr. Conway didn't go so far as to say there was no God. He even admitted there probably was. Somebody had to run things, though he was making a poor job of it.

"Likely a young God who hain't learned his business yet, by gosh," said Mr. Conway.

Brian was too young himself to be scandalised by this. He rather liked the idea of a young god. He had always thought of God as a stern, bearded Old Man.

If Brian had not been so tired he would have enjoyed the walk to Little Friday cove. He loved to watch the harbour lights blossoming out in the blue of the twilight. He loved to watch the mysterious ships sailing out beyond the dunes to who knew what enchanted shores. He picked one that was just going over the bar and went with it in fancy. When he reached Little Friday Cove he found Big Sam alone and rather low in his mind. Trouble was coming; various signs and portents had pointed to it for days. No longer could he be blind to them. Salt, the dog, had howled dismally all Monday of the preceeding week. On Tuesday Little Sam had smashed the looking-glass he had shaved by for forty years. On Wednesday Big Sam had failed to pick up a pin he had seen; on Thursday he had walked under Tom Appleby's ladder at the factory —and on Friday—Friday, mind you—Big and Little Sam between them had contrived to upset the salt at supper.

Big Sam was determined not to be superstitious. What did spilled salt and broken looking-glasses matter to good Presbyterians? But he did believe in dreams—having Biblical warrant for the same. And he had had a horrible one the night after Aunt Becky died—of seeing the full moon, one moment burning black, the next livid red, coming nearer and nearer the earth. He woke, just as it seemed near enough to be touched, with a howl of agony that shattered the stillness of the spring night at Little Friday Cove for yards around. Big Sam, who had kept a careful and copious diary of his dreams for forty years, looked them all over and concluded that none of them had been as awe-inspiring as this one.

Then there was that peculiar sound the gulf had been making of late. When the Old Lady of the Gulf skirled like a witch, somebody was going to sup sorrow.

"Little Sam sneaked off somewhere's after supper," he told Brian. "I kinder thought I'd go up to the run myself and dig some clams. But I didn't—felt a bit tired. I'm beginning to feel my years. But I've got the key of the fish-house and I'll get a cod out for you. They're all most too big for you to carry, though. Stay and have a saucer of clam chowder. There's some left. That man can make chowder, I'll admit."

Brian would have liked the chowder well enough, for his supper had been of the sketchiest description, but it was getting dark. He must get home before it got very dark— he was afraid. He was ashamed of his cowardice, but there it was. Sometimes he thought if any one really loved him he would not be afraid of so many things. He looked so small and wistful that Big Sam gave the poor little shrimp a nickel to buy a chocolate bar at the Widow Terlizzick's little store on the way home. But Brian did not stop at the store. He did not like the widow Terlizzick or the noisy crowd of loafers who were always in and around the store on summer nights. He hurried home with his heavy codfish and was told to clear off to bed—he would have to be up at four to help Mr. Conway take some calves to market. Brian would have liked to sit out under the big apple tree for a little while and play his jew's-harp. He liked the old apple tree. It seemed like a friend to him—a great, kindly fragrant, blooming creature stretching protecting arms over him. And he loved to play on his jew's-harp. Once he had played on his jew's-harp in the evening at a house where he was planting potatoes, and two young people—one of them a girl in a white dress— had danced to his playing in the moonlit orchard. It was one of the few memories of beauty in his life. When he played his jew's-harp now he saw them again—dancing— dancing—dancing. With the grace of wind-blown leaves— white and mystic and lovely—to his elfin tune.

But Aunt Alethea was inexorable and Brian climbed the ladder to the kitchen loft, where he always slept alone and which he hated. He was afraid of the rats that infested it. There was only one thing he liked about it—from its window he could get a glimpse of the sea and a misty blue headland beyond which were wonderful sunsets. To-night there was a lovely rose and gold afterlight and the sea was blackly-blue under it. And he could see the pink-shaded lamp in the window of the Dollar house on the other side of the road. He loved to watch it, making a great glowing spot of colour in the darkness. When it suddenly went out he felt terribly lonely. Tears came to his eyes. He was such a little creature, alone in a great, dim, hostile world. Brian looked up at the sky. How dark the night was! How fearfully bright the stars!

"Dear God," he said softly, "dear *Young* God, please don't forget me."

He lay down on his hard little mattress. He was glad there was no moonlight yet. Moonlit nights in the loft frightened him. The things hanging from the rafters took on such queer shapes. And that hole in the wall of the loft that opened into the unfloored attic of the main house—it was dreadful on moonlit nights, when it looked so black and menacing. Who knew what might pop out of a hole like that? When it was dark he could not see it. It was a long while before he fell asleep. But at last he did—just about the time that Little Sam came home to Little Friday Cove.

VII

Little Sam had heard at the funeral that the raffle for which he had bought the ticket from Mosey Gautier, was to be held that night. So after supper he thought he might as well saunter around to Chapel Point and see if he had any luck.

He had.

Big Sam was sound asleep in his bunk, with Mustard rolled up in a golden ball on his stomach. Little Sam unwrapped something from the parcel he was carrying, looked at it rather dubiously, shook his head, and tried the effect of it on the clock shelf. Something in him liked it. Something else was uneasy.

"She's got a real fine figger," he reflected, with a speculative glance at the unconscious Big Sam. "But I dunno what he'll think of her—I dunno. Nor the minister."

These considerations did not keep Little Sam awake. He fell asleep promptly and Aurora, goddess of the dawn, kept her vigil on the clock shelf through the hours of darkness, and was the first thing on which Big Sam's eyes rested when he opened them in the morning. There she stood, her lithe lovely form poised on tiptoe, smitten by a red-gold beam from the sun that was rising across the harbour.

"What the devil is that?" said Big Sam, thinking this was another dream. He flung himself out of his bunk, upsetting an indignant cat, and walked across the room.

"It ain't a dream," he said incredulously. "It's a statoo—a naked statoo."

Salt, who had been curled up at Little Sam's feet, bounded to the floor after Mustard. He liked Mustard well enough but he wasn't going to have her sitting there on the floor grinning at him. The resultant disturbance awoke Little Sam, who sat up drowsily and inquired what the row was about.

"Samuel Beelby Dark," said Big Sam ominously, "what's that up there?"

"Samuel Phemister Dark," returned little Sam mockingly, "that's an alabaster statooette—genuine alabaster. I drew it for fifth prize at the Chapel lottery last night. Pretty, ain't it?"

"Pretty?" Big Sam's voice boomed out. "Pretty! It's indecent and obscene, that's what *it* is. You take it right down and fire it out in the gulf as far as you can fire it."

If Big Sam had not thus flown off the handle it is probable that Little Sam would have done exactly that, being somewhat uneasy over the look of the thing generally and what Mr. Trackley might say about it. But he was not going to be bullied into it by that little runt of a Big Sam and he'd let him see it.

"Oh, I guess not," he retorted coolly. "I guess it's going to stay right there. Stop yelping now and let your hair curl."

Big Sam's scanty love-locks showed no signs of curling but his red beard fairly crackled with indignation. He began striding about the room in a fine rage, biting his right hand and then his left. Salt fled one way and Mustard another, leaving the Sams to fight it out.

"'Tain't right to have any kind of statoos, let alone naked ones. It's agin God's law. 'Thou shalt not make unto thee any graven immidge—'"

"Good gosh, I ain't made it and I ain't worshipping it—"

"That'll come—that'll come. And a Catholic geegaw at that. S'pose likely it's the Virgin Mary."

Little Sam looked doubtful. He had been bred up in a good old Presbyterian hatred of Catholics and all their ways and works, but somehow he didn't think even they would go so far as to represent the Virgin Mary entirely unclothed.

"No, 'tain't. I think her name's there at the bottom— Aurorer. Just a gal, that's all."

"Do you think the Apostle Paul ever carried anything like that around with him?" demanded Big Sam. "Or"— as an afterthought that might carry more weight with Little Sam—"poor dear old Aunt Becky, who isn't cold in her grave yet?"

"Not likely. St. Paul was kind of a woman-hater like yourself. As for Aunt Becky, we ain't in the running for her jug, so why worry? Now stop chewing your fists and pretend you're grown up even if you ain't, Sammy. See if you can dress yourself like a man."

"Thank you. Thank you." Big Sam became ominously calm. "I'm entirely satisfied to be classed with the Apostle Paul. My conscience guides *my* conduct, you ribald old thing!"

"Been making a meal of the dictionary, it seems," retorted Little Sam, yanking his pants off their nail, "and it don't seem to have agreed with your stomach. Better take a dose of sody. Your conscience, as you call it, hasn't nothing to do with it—only your prejurdices. Look at that writing man. Hain't he got half a dozen of them statoos in his summer shanty up the river?"

"If he's a fool—and wuss—is that any reason why you should be? Think of that and your immortal soul, Sam Dark."

"This ain't my day for thinking," retorted the imperturbable Little Sam. "Now that you've blown off your steam, just set the porridge pot on. You'll feel better when you've had your breakfast. Can't 'preciate works of art properly on an empty stomach, Sammy."

Big Sam glared at him. Then he grabbed the porridge pot, yanked open the door, and hurled the pot through it. The pot bounded and clattered and leaped down the rocks to the sandy cove below. Salt and Mustard fled out after it.

"Some day you'll drive me too far," said Little Sam darkly. "You're just a narrow-minded, small-souled old maid, that's what you are. If you hadn't a dirty mind you wouldn't be throwing a fit 'cause you see a stone woman's legs. Your own don't look so artistic, prancing around in that shirttail, let me tell you. You really ought to wear pajamas, Sammy."

"I fired your old pot out to show you I'm in earnest," roared Big Sam. "I tell you I won't have no naked hussy in this house, Sam Dark. I ain't oversqueamish but I draw the line at naked weemen."

"Yell louder, can't you? It's *my* house," said Little Sam.

"Oh, it is, is it? Very well. *Very* well. I'll tell you this right here and now. It ain't big enough for me and you and your Roarer."

"You ain't the first person that idee's occurred to," said Little Sam. "I've had too many tastes of your jaw of late."

Big Sam stopped prancing and tried to look as dignified as a man with nothing on but a shirt can look, as he laid down the ultimatum he never doubted would bring Little Sam to his senses.

"I've stood all I'm a-going to. I've stood them skulls of yours for years but I tell you right here and now, Sam Dark, I won't stand for that atrocity. If it's to remain—*I* leave."

"As for leaving or staying, suit yourself. Aurorer stays there on that clock shelf," retorted Little Sam, striding out and down the rocks to rescue his maltreated porridge pot.

Breakfast was a gloomy meal. Big Sam looked very determined, but Little Sam was not worried. They had had a worse row than this last week, when he had caught Big Sam stealing a piece of raisin pie he had put away for his own snack. But when the silent meal was over and Big Sam ostentatiously dragged an old, battered, bulging valise out from under his bunk and began packing his few chattels into it, Little Sam realised that the crisis was serious. Well, all right—all right. Big Sam needn't think he could bully *him* into giving up Aurorer. He had won her and he was going to keep her and Big Sam could go to Hades. Little Sam really thought Hades. He had picked up the word in his theological reading and thought it sounded more respectable than hell.

Little Sam watched Big Sam stealthily out of his pale woolly eyes as he washed up the dishes and fed Mustard, who came scratching at the window-pane. The morning's sunlit promise had been delusive and it was now, as Little Sam reflected testily, one of them still, dark, misty mornings calc'lated to dampen one's spirits. This was what came of ladders and looking-glasses.

Big Sam packed his picture of Laurier and the model of a ship, with crimson hull and white sails, that had long adorned the cater-cornered shelf above his bunk. These were indisputably his. But when it came to their small library there was difficulty.

"Which of these books am I to take?" he demanded frostily.

"Whichever you like," said Little Sam, getting out his baking-board. There were only two books in the lot he cared a hoot about, anyhow. *Fox's Book of Martyrs* and *The Horrible Confession and Execution of John Murdock (one of the Emigrants who lately left this country) who was hanged at Brockville (Upper Canada) on the 3rd day of September last for the inhuman Murder of His own brother.* When Little Sam saw Big Sam pack the latter in his valise, he had much ado to repress a grisly groan.

"I'm leaving you the Martyrs and all the dime novels," said Little Sam defensively. "What about the dog and cat?"

"You'd better take the cat," said Little Sam, measuring out flour. "It'll match your whiskers."

This suited Big Sam. Mustard was his favourite.

"And the weegee-board?"

"Take it. I don't hold no dealings with the devil."

Big Sam shut and strapped his valise, put the reluctant Mustard into a bag, and with the bag over his shoulder and his Sunday hat on his head he strode out of the house and down the road without even a glance at Little Sam, who was ostentatiously making raisin pie.

Little Sam watched him out of sight still incredulously. Then he looked at the white, beautiful cause of all the mischief exulting on the clock shelf.

"Well, he didn't get you out, my beauty, and I'm jiggered if he's ever going to. No, siree. I've said it and I'll stick to it. Anyhow, my ears won't have to ache any longer, listening to that old epic of his. And I can wear my earrings again."

Little Sam really thought Big Sam would come back when he had cooled down. But he underrated the strength of Big Sam's principles or his stubbornness. The first thing he heard was that Big Sam had rented Tom Wilkins' old shanty at Big Friday Cove and was living there. But not with Mustard. If Big Sam did not come back Mustard did. Mustard was scratching at the window three days after her ignominious departure in a bag. Little Sam let her in and fed her. It wasn't his fault if Big Sam couldn't keep his cat. He, Little Sam, wasn't going to see no dumb animal starve. Mustard stayed home until one Sunday when Big Sam, knowing Little Sam was safely in church, and remembering Homer Penhallow's tactics, came down to Little Friday Cove and got her. All to no purpose. Again Mustard came back—and yet again. After the third attempt Big Sam gave it up in bitterness of soul.

"Do I want his old yaller flannel cat?" he demanded of Stanton Grundy. "God knows I don't. What hurts my feelings is that he *knew* the critter would go back. That's why he offered her so free. The depth of that man! I hear he's going round circulating mean, false things about me and saying I'll soon be sick of living on salt codfish and glad to sneak back for a smell of good cooking. He'll see—he'll see. *I* ain't never made a god of my stomach as *he* does. You should have heard the riot he raised because I et a piece of mouldy old raisin pie he'd cached for himself, the greedy pig. And saying it'll be too lonesome at Big Friday for one of my gabby propensities. Yessir, he said them words. Me, lonesome! This place just suits me down to the ground. See the scenery. I'm a lover of nature, sir, my favourite being the moon. And them contented cows up on the Point pasture—I could gaze at 'em by the hour. *They*'re all the society I want, sir—present comp'ny always excepted. Not," added Big Sam feelingly, "but what Little Sam had his p'ints. The plum puddings that man could make! And them clam chowders of his stuck to the ribs better'n most things. But I had my soul to think of, hadn't I? And my morals?"

3
MIDSUMMER MADNESS

▼

I

Gay did not find the first few weeks of her engagement to Noel all sunshine. One could not in a clan like hers. Among the Darks and Penhallows an engagement was tribal property and every one claimed the right to comment and criticise, approve or disapprove, according to circumstances. In this instance disapproval was rampant, for none of the clan liked any Gibson and they did not spare Gay's feelings. It simply did not occur to them that a child of eighteen had any feelings to spare, so they dealt with her faithfully.

"Poor little fool, will she giggle as loud after she's been married to him for a couple of years?" said William Y., when he heard Gay's exquisite laugh as she and Noel whirled by in their car one night. To do him justice, William Y. would not have said it in Gay's hearing, but it was straightway carried to her. Gay only laughed again. And she laughed when Cousin Hannah from Summerside asked her if it could be true that she was going to marry "a certain young man." Cousin Hannah would not say "a Gibson." Her manner gave the impression that Gibsons did not really exist. They might imagine they did but they were mere emanations of the Evil One, to be resolutely disbelieved in by anyone of good principles and proper breeding. One did not speak openly of the devil. Neither did one speak of the Gibsons. Her contempt stung Gay a bit, in spite of her laughter. But a letter from Noel, simply crammed with darlings, soon removed the sting.

"Do you *really* love him?" asked Mrs. William Y. solemnly.

Gay wanted to say no because she detested Mrs. William Y. But she also wanted to show her and everyone just what Noel meant to her.

"He's the only man in the world for me, Aunty."

"H'm! That's's a large order out of about five hundred million men," said Mrs. William Y. sarcastically. "However, I remember I once felt that way, too."

This, although Mrs. William Y. was unaware of it, was the most dreadful thing Gay had heard yet. Mrs William Y. couldn't have thought William Y. the only man in the world. Of course she had married him—but she *couldn't*. Gay, with the egotism of youth, couldn't believe that *any* woman had ever been in love with William Y., not realising that when William Y. had been slender and hirsute, twenty-five years before, he had been quite a lady-killer.

"You could do better, you know," persisted Mrs. William Y.

"Oh, I suppose you mean Roger," cried Gay petulantly. "You all think there's nobody like Roger."

"Neither there is," said Mrs. William Y. with simple and sincere feeling. She loved Roger. Everybody loved him. If only Gay wasn't so silly and romantic. Just swept off her feet by Noel Gibson's eyes and hair.

"I suppose you think it's all fun being married," Mrs. Clifford said.

Gay didn't think it was "fun" at all. That wasn't how she regarded marriage. But Aunt Rhoda Dark was just as bad.

"Do you realise what an important event marriage is in anybody's life, Gay?"

Gay was driven into a flippant answer that made Aunt Rhoda shake her head over modern youth.

Rachel Penhallow remarked in Gay's hearing that kidney trouble "ran" in the Gibsons. Mrs. Clifford advised "not to let him feel too sure of you." Mrs. Denzil raked Noel's father over the coals.

"The only way to get him to do anything was to coax him to do the opposite. I was there the day he threw a plate at his wife. She dodged it but it made a dent on the mantel. You can see that dent there yet, Gay, if you don't believe me."

"What has all this got to do with me and Noel?" burst out Gay.

"These things are inherited. You can't get away from them."

But Aunt Kate Penhallow didn't think Noel was stubborn like his father. She thought Noel was the opposite—weak and easily swayed. She didn't like his chin; and Uncle Robert didn't like his eyes; and Cousin Amasa didn't like his ears—"They lie too close to his head. You never see such ears on a successful man," said Cousin Amasa, who had outstanding ears of his own but wasn't considered much of a success for all that.

"You would think they were the only people who ever got engaged in the world," said Mrs. Toynbee, who, having come through three engagements, naturally didn't think it the wonder Gay and Noel did.

"All the Gibsons are very fickle," said Mrs. Artemas Dark, who had been engaged to one herself before she married Artemas. He had treated her badly, but in her secret soul she sometimes thought she preferred him to Artemas still.

"You'd better wait until you're out of the cradle before you marry," growled Drowned John, who was having troubles of his own just then and was very touchy on the subject of engagements.

All this sort of thing only amused Gay. It didn't amount to anything. What did worry her was the subtle undercurrent of disapproval among those whose opinion she really valued. *Nobody* thought well of her engagement. Her mother cried bitterly over it and at first refused to give her consent at all.

"I can't stop you from marrying him, of course," she said, with what was great bitterness for the easygoing Mrs. Howard. "But I'll never say I'm willing—never. I've never approved of him, Gay."

"Why—*why?*" cried Gay piteously. She loved her mother and hated to go against her in anything. "*Why*, Mother? What can you say against him?"

"There's nothing in him," said Mrs. Howard feebly. She thought it rather a poor reason, not realising that she was actually uttering the most serious indictment in the world.

Altogether Gay had a hard time of it for a couple of weeks. Then Cousin Mahala swept down on the clan from her retreat up west—Cousin Mahala, who looked like a handsome old man with her short, crisp, virile grey hair and strong wise face. The eyes a little sunken. The mouth with a humourous quirk. The face of a woman who has *lived*.

"Let Gay marry him if she wants to," she told the harassed Mrs. Howard, "and learn the ups and downs of life for herself, the same as the rest of us did. None of us have had perfect men."

"Oh, Cousin Mahala, you're the only person in this whole clan with a heart," cried Gay.

Cousin Mahala looked at her with a twinkle in her eye.

"Oh, no, I'm not, Gay. We've all got hearts, more or less. And the rest of us want to save you from the troubles and mistakes we've had. *I* don't. Mistakes and trouble are bound to come. Better come our own way than someone else's way. You'll be a lovely little bride, Gay. So young. I *do* like a young bride."

"Aunt Mavis asked me if I thought marriage 'all fun.' Of course I don't think it's all 'fun'—"

"You bet it isn't," said Cousin Mahala—

"—But I don't think it's all vexation either—"

"You're right there, too," said Cousin Mahala—

"—And whatever it is, I want to try it with Noel and nobody else."

Mrs. Howard, thus attacked from the rear, surrendered. But only on one condition. Gay and Noel must wait a year before marrying. Eighteen was too young to marry. She couldn't give Gay up so soon. And Mrs. Howard had another reason. Dandy Dark hated the Gibsons. If Dandy had the bestowal of the jug and if Gay were actually married to a Gibson, Mrs. Howard felt she would have no chance of it at all. This secret thought stiffened her against all the pleading of Gay and the ardent Noel, to which she would probably have succumbed otherwise. Noel resigned himself sulkily to the condition. Gay, sweetly. After all, she was glad to purchase her mother's acquiescence by a little waiting. She couldn't bear to do anything against her mother's will. And being engaged was very delightful. There was a big hope chest to be filled. Of course she knew the clan hoped that in a year she would change her mind. As if anything could ever make her stop loving Noel. She kissed his ring in the dark that night before she went to sleep. Dear Cousin Mahala! If only she lived nearer. Gay wanted to have her about while she made ready to be married. She knew all the rest, although they had tacitly agreed to recognise the engagement and make the best of it, would rub all the bloom off her dear romance with their horrible practicalities and go on regretting all the time in their hearts that it wasn't Roger.

Roger had been lovely. He had wished her joy—in his dear caressing voice—Roger *had* such a nice voice—and told her he wanted every happiness to be hers.

"If I'd a black cat's wish-bone I'd give it to you, Gay," he said whimsically. "They tell me as long as you have a black cat's wish-bone you can get everything you want."

"But I've got everything I want, Roger," cried Gay. "Now that mother has come around so sweetly I haven't a thing left to wish for—except—except—that *you*— " Gay went crimson—"that *everybody* could be as happy as I am."

"I'm afraid it would take more than a black cat's wish-bone to bring *that* about," said Roger. But whether his "that" referred to the "you" or to the "everybody" Gay didn't know and dared not ask. She danced back to the house, flinging a smile over her shoulder to Roger as if she had thrown him a rose. Then she forgot all about him.

Roger overtook the Moon Man on the way home and asked him to take a lift. The Moon Man refused. He would never get in a car. But he looked piercingly at Roger.

"Why don't you set your love on my Lady Moon?" he said. "I would not be jealous. All men may love her but she loves no one. It doesn't hurt to love if you do not hope to be loved in return."

"I've never hoped to be loved in return—but it hurts damnably," said Roger.

II

The clan had its shock at Aunt Becky's levee and its sensation over the fight at the graveyard; but the affair of Peter and Donna burst upon it like a cyclone. It was, naturally, almost the death of Drowned John.

Peter and Donna would have liked to keep it a delightful secret until they had perfected their plans, but as soon as they saw Mrs. Toynbee they knew there was no hope of that. Donna went home in a state of uplift that lasted until three o'clock at night. Then the terrors and doubts that stalk around at that hour swooped down on her. What— oh, what would Drowned John say? Of course, there was nothing he could *do*. She had only to walk out of the door and go with Peter. But Donna hated the thought of eloping. It was simply not done among Darks and Penhallows. And if she eloped she would have no chance of the jug. Not that the jug was to be compared to Peter. But if she could only have Peter and the jug, too! Donna thought she had a good chance of it if it rested with Dandy. She had always been a pet of Dandy's. But she had once heard Dandy's comments on an eloping couple.

Then there was Virginia. Virginia would never forgive her. Not that Virginia mattered beside Peter either. But she was fond of Virginia; she was the only chum she had ever had. And she was afraid of the reproachful things Virginia would say. In the morning she wouldn't feel like this. But at three o'clock one did have qualms.

It was all just as dreadful as Donna feared it would be. Mrs. Toynbee saw Drowned John at the post-office the next day, and Drowned John came home in a truly Drowned Johnian condition—aggravated by his determination not to swear. But in other respects he gave tongue.

Donna was plucky. She owned up fearlessly that she had kissed Peter at the Courting-House, just as Mrs. Toynbee said.

"You see, Daddy, I'm going to marry him."

"You're mad!" said Drowned John.

"I think I am," sighed Donna. "But, oh, Daddy, it's such a nice madness."

Drowned John repented, as he had repented often

before, that he had ever let Donna have that year at the Kingsport Ladies' College in her teens. It was there she had learned to say those smart, flippant things which always knocked the wind out of him. He dared not swear but he banged the table and told Donna that she was never to speak to Peter Penhallow again. If she did—

"But I'll have to speak to him now and again, Daddy. One can't live on terms of absolute silence with one's husband, you know."

There it was again. But Donna, though flippant and seemingly fearless, was quaking inside. She knew her Drowned John. When Peter came down that afternoon Drowned John met him at the door and asked him his business.

"I've come to see Donna," Peter told him cheerfully. "I'm going to marry her, you know."

"My *dear* young man"—oh, the contempt Drowned John snorted into the phrase!—"you do yourself too much honour."

He went in and shut the door in Peter's face. Peter thought at first he would smash a window. But he knew Drowned John was quite capable of having him arrested for housebreaking. Where the devil was Donna! She might at least look out at him.

Donna, with a headache, was crying on her bed, quite ignorant of Peter's nearness. Thekla had been so nasty. Thekla had said that one husband, like one religion, should be enough for anybody. But then Thekla had always hated her for getting married at all. She had no friends—she was alone in a hostile, unfeeling clan world. But she *was* going to marry Peter.

It wasn't so easy. Peter, who would have made no bones of carrying off a bride from the Congo or Yucatan if he had happened to want one, found it a very different proposition to carry one off from the Darks and Penhallows. He couldn't even see Donna. Drowned John wouldn't let him in the house or let Donna out of it. Of course this couldn't have lasted. Drowned John couldn't keep Donna mewed up forever, and eventually Peter and she would have found a way to each other. But the stars in their course, so poor Donna thought, fought against them. One night she sneezed;

the next night her eyes were sore; the next night they had
Roger, who told Donna she was down with measles.

It would, of course, have been more romantic if she had
had consumption or brain fever or angina pectoris. But a
veracious chronicler can tell only the truth. Donna Dark
had measles and nearly died of them.

Once the rumour drifted to the distracted Peter that she
had died. And he couldn't even see her. When he tore
down to Rose River nobody answered his knock and the
doors were locked and the lower windows shuttered. Peter
thought of simply standing on the step and yelling until
somebody had to come; but he was afraid any excitement
might hurt Donna. Roger came along and tried to calm
him down.

"Donna's not dead. She's a very sick girl yet and needs
careful nursing, but I think she's out of danger. I was
afraid of pneumonia. Don't be an ass, Peter. Go home and
take things coolly till Donna recovers. Drowned John can't
prevent your marrying her, though he'll make everything
as unpleasant as he can, no doubt."

"Roger, were you ever in love with anyone?" groaned
Peter. "No, you couldn't have been. You wouldn't be such
a cold-blooded fish if you were. Besides, you'd have fallen
in love with Donna. I can't understand why everyone isn't
in love with Donna. Can you?"

"Easily," said Roger coolly.

"Oh, you like them buxom, I suppose," sneered Peter,
"like Sally William Y.—or just out of the cradle like Gay
Penhallow. Roger, you don't know what it's like to be in
love. It's hellish—and heavenly—and terrible—and exquisite. Oh, Roger, why don't you fall in love?"

Roger had never been in any danger of falling in love
with Donna Dark. As a matter of fact he only half liked
her and her poses, not realising that the latter were only a
pitiful device for filling an empty life. And he only half
liked Peter. But he was sorry for him.

"I'll take a message to Donna for you—"

"A letter—"

"No. She couldn't read it. Her eyes are very bad—"

"Look here, Roger. I've got to see Donna—by the
sacred baboon I've got to. Have a heart, Roger—smuggle

me in. They'll have to open the door for you, and once I'm inside the devil himself shan't get me out till I've seen Donna—that Thekla is quite capable of murdering her—the whole pack are worrying her—that fiend of a Virginia is with her night and day, I hear, poisoning her mind against me."

"Stop gibbering, Peter. Think what effect a fracas in the house would have on Donna. It would set her back weeks if it didn't kill her. Thekla is a capital nurse whatever else she is—and Donna's mind is too full of you to be poisoned by anybody—through all her delirium she raved about you—you should have seen Drowned John's face."

"Was she delirious—my poor darling? Oh, Roger Penhallow, are you keeping anything back from me? I met the Moon Man coming down. He looked at me strangely. They say the old dud has second sight—he knows when people are going to die. Pneumonia has always been fatal to that family—Donna's mother died of it. For God's sake, tell me the truth—"

"Peter Penhallow, if you don't clear out of this at once I'll kick you twice—once for myself and once for Drowned John. Donna is going to be all right. You act as if you were the only man in the world who was ever in love before."

"I am," said Peter. "*You* don't know a thing about love, Roger. They tell me you were in love with Gay Penhallow. Well, I'd never be a cradle-snatcher but if I were, Noel Gibson shouldn't have taken her from me—that tailor's mannequin. You're a white-livered hound, Roger, no blood in your veins."

"I've some sense in my noodle," said Roger drily.

"Which proves that you don't know anything about love," said Peter triumphantly. "Nobody's sensible if he's in love. It's a divine madness, Roger. Oh, Roger, I've never liked you over and above but I feel now as if I couldn't part from you. To think that you'll see Donna in a few minutes—oh, tell her—tell her—"

"Heaven grant me patience!" groaned Roger. "Peter, go out and get into my car and count up to five hundred slowly. I'll tell Donna anything you like and I'll bring back her message and then I'll take you home. It's not safe for you to be out alone—you damn' fool," concluded Roger under his breath.

"Roger—have you any idea how a man—"

"Tut—tut, Peter, you're not a man at all just now—you're only a state of mind."

Donna's convalescence was a tedious affair and not a very happy one. As soon as Drowned John suspected that Roger was fetching and carrying messages between Donna and Peter, he showed him to the door and sent for another doctor. Virginia haunted her pillow night and day and various relatives of the clique—a clan within a clan—came and went and "talked things over." Donna listened because she was too weak to argue. And all the talking-over in the world couldn't alter facts.

"You never loved Barry," sobbed Virginia. "It was only his uniform you loved."

"I did love Barry. But now I love Peter," said Donna.

" 'The mind has a thousand eyes,' " began Virginia—and finished the quotation. The trouble was she had quoted it so often before that it was rather stale to Donna.

"Love isn't done—for me. It's beginning all over again."

"I *don't* understand," said Virginia helplessly, "how you can be so fickle, Donna. It's a complete mystery to me. But *my* feelings have always been so very deep. I wonder you still keep poor Barry's picture over your dressing-table. Doesn't he look at you reproachfully?"

"No. Barry seems like a good old pal. He seems to say, 'I'm glad you've found someone to give you the happiness I can't now.' Virginia, we've been foolish and morbid—"

"I won't have you use such a word," sobbed Virginia. "I'm not morbid—I'm *true*. And you've broken our pact. Oh, Donna, how *can* you desert me? We've been through so many sad—and beautiful—and terrible things together. How *can* you break the bond?"

"Virginia, darling, I'm not breaking the bond. We can always be friends—dear friends—"

"Peter will take you away from me," sobbed Virginia. "He'll drag you all over the world—you'll never have any settled home, Donna—or any position in society."

"There'll be some adventure in marrying Peter," conceded Donna in a tone of satisfaction.

"And he'll never allow you to have any interest outside of him. He'll tell you what you are to think. He must possess exclusively."

"I don't want any interest outside of him," said Donna.

"You to say that—you who were Barry's wife—his *wife*. Why, to hear you talk—it might just as well have been someone else who was Barry's wife."

"Well, to be honest, Virginia, that's exactly the way I do feel about it. I'm *not* the girl who was married to Barry— I'm an entirely different creature. Perhaps I've drunk from some fairy pool of change, Virginia. I can't help it—and I don't want to help it. All I want just now is to have Peter come in and kiss me."

An aggravating sentence popped into Donna's head. She uttered it to annoy Virginia, who was annoying her.

"You've no idea how divinely Peter can kiss, Virginia."

"I've no doubt he has had plenty of practise," said Virginia bitterly. "As for me—*I* have my memories of Ned's kisses."

Donna permitted herself a pale smile. Ned Powell had had a little full red mouth with a little brown moustache above it. The very thought of being kissed by such a mouth had always made Donna shudder. She couldn't understand how Virginia could ever bear it.

"You can laugh," said Virginia coldly. "I suppose you can laugh now at everything we have held sacred. But *I* happen to know that Peter Penhallow said that you were a nice little thing and he could have you for the asking."

"I don't believe he said it," retorted Donna, "but if he did—why not? It's quite true, you know."

Virginia went away crying. She told Drowned John that it was useless for her to come again; *she* had no longer any influence over Donna.

"I knew that opal would bring me bad luck."

Drowned John banged a table and glared at her. Drowned John went about those days banging tables. Drowned John was in an atrocious humour with everything and everybody, and determined to make them feel it. Had a father no rights at all? This was all it came to—all your years of sacrifice and care. They flouted you—just flouted you. They thought they could marry any fool fellow they pleased.

Women were the very dickens. He had tamed his own two but the young ones were beyond him.

"She shall never marry him—never."

"She means to," said Virginia.

"She doesn't mean it—she only thinks she does," shouted Drowned John. Drowned John always thought that if he contradicted loud enough, people would come to believe him.

Bets were up in the clan about it. Some, like Stanton Grundy, thought it wouldn't last. "The hotter the fire the quicker it's over," said Stanton Grundy. Some thought Drowned John would never yield and some thought he'd likely crumple up at the last. And some thought it didn't matter a hoot whether he did or not. Peter Penhallow would take his own wherever he found it. To poor Donna, lying wearily in bed or reclining in an easy-chair, trying to endure the unfeeling way in which day followed day without Peter, they came with advice and innuendo and gossip. Peter had said, when Aunt But asked him how it was he was caught at last, "Oh, I just got tired of running." Peter, when a boy, had shot a pea at an elder in the church. Peter had flung a glass of water in his schoolmaster's face. Peter had taken a wasp's nest to prayer-meeting. Peter had set loose a trapped rat when the Sewing Circle met at his mother's house. They dragged up all the things they knew that Peter had done. And there were so many things he must have done that they knew nothing about.

"If you marry a rover like Peter what are you going to do with your family?" Mrs. William Y. wanted to know.

"Oh, we're only going to have two children. A boy first and then a girl for good measure," said Donna. "We can manage to tote that many about with us."

Mrs. William Y. was horrified. But Mrs. Artemas, who had come with her, only remarked calmly,

"I couldn't ever get them to come in order that way."

"If *I* was a widow-woman I wouldn't be fool enough to want to marry again," said Mrs. Sim Dark bitterly.

"That family of Penhallows are always doing such unexpected things and Peter is the worst of them," mourned Mrs. Wilbur Dark.

"But if your husband does unexpected things at least he

wouldn't bore you," said Donna." "I could endure any-thing but boredom."

Mrs. Wilbur did not know what Donna meant by her husband's boring her. Of course men were tiresome at times. She told her especial friends that she thought the measles had gone to Donna's brain. They did that some-times, she understood.

Dandy Dark came and asked her ominously how she thought Aunt Becky would have liked her taking a second helping after all her fine protestations.

"Aunt Becky liked consistency, that she did," said Dan-dy, who had a fondness for big words and used more of them than ever now that he was trustee of the jug.

This sounded like a threat. Donna pouted.

"Dandy," she coaxed, "you might tell *me* who's to get the jug—if you know. I wouldn't tell a soul."

Dandy chuckled.

"I've lost count how often that's been said to me the past month. No use, Donna. Nobody's going to know more about that jug than Aunt Becky told them until the time comes. A dying trust"—Dandy was very important and solemn—"is a sacred thing. But think twice before you marry Peter, Donna—think twice."

"Oh, Aunty Con, some days I just hate life," Donna told a relative for whom she had some love. "And then again some days I just love it."

"That's the way with us all," said plump Aunty Con placidly.

Donna stared at her in amazement. Surely Aunty Con could never either love or hate life.

"Oh, Aunty Con, I'm really miserable. I seem to get better so slowly. And Peter and I can't get a word to each other. Father is so unreasonable—he seems to smell brim-stone if anyone mentions Peter's name. Thekla is barely civil to me—though she *was* an angel when I was really ill—and Virginia is sulking. I—I get so blue and discouraged—"

"You ain't real well yet," said Aunty Con soothingly. "Don't you worry, Donna. As soon as you're real strong Peter Penhallow will find a way. Rest you with that."

Donna looked out of her open window over her right

shoulder into the July night. A little wet new moon was hanging over a curve of Rose River. There were sounds as if a car were dying in the yard. Nobody had told Donna that Peter came down to Drowned John's gate every night—where his father had hung the dog—and made all the weird noises possible with his claxon, but Donna suddenly felt he was very near her. She smiled. Yes, Peter would find a way.

III

Gay Penhallow could never quite remember when the first faint shadow fell across her happiness. It stole towards her so subtly. If you looked straight at it—it wasn't there. But turn away your eyes and out of the corners you could see it—a little nearer—still a little nearer—waiting to pounce.

Everything had been so wonderful at first. The weeks were not made up of days at all. Sunday was a flame, Monday a rainbow, Tuesday a perfume, Wednesday a bird-song, Thursday a wind-dance, Friday laughter, and Saturday—Noel always came Saturday night, whatever other night he missed—was something that was the soul of all the other six.

But now—the days were becoming just days again.

Nan and Noel were such friends. Well, why shouldn't they be? Weren't they going to be cousins! But still—there were moments when Gay felt like an outsider, as they talked to each other a patter she couldn't talk. Gay was not up-to-date in modern slang. They seemed to have so many mysterious catchwords and understandings—or perhaps Nan just made it appear so. Nan was an expert at that sort of thing—expert at catching and holding for herself the attention of any male creature, no matter what his affiliation might be. For Nan those affiliations didn't exist. She simply ignored them. Noel and Gay could not refuse to take her about with them—at least Gay couldn't and Noel didn't seem to want to. Nan continued to imply that she had no one to take her about—she was such a stranger. Gay felt it would be mean and catty to leave Nan out in the cold. But quite often—and oftener as the days went by—she felt as if it were she who was left out in the cold. And yet there was so little to take hold of—so little one could put into words or even into thoughts. She couldn't expect Noel to take no notice of anyone but herself. But she thought wistfully of the old untroubled days when there had been no Nan at Indian Spring.

There was that dreadful afternoon when she had heard Nan and Noel exchanging airy persiflage over the phone. Gay hadn't meant to listen. She had taken down the receiver to see if the line were free and she had heard Noel's voice. Who was he talking to? Nan! Gay stood and listened—Gay who had been brought up to think listening on the phone the meanest form of eavesdropping. She didn't realise she was listening—all she realised was that Nan and Noel were carrying on a gay, semi-confidential conversation. Well, what of it? After all, what was really in it? They didn't say a word the whole world mightn't have heard. But it was the suggestion of intimacy in it—of something from which everyone else was excluded. Why, Noel was talking to Nan as he should talk only to *her*.

When Gay hung up the receiver, after Nan had sent an impertinent kiss over the phone, she felt chilly and lost. For the first time she felt the sting of a bitter jealousy. And for the first time it occurred to her that she might not be happy all her life. But when Noel came that evening he was as dear and tender as ever and Gay went to bed laughing at herself. She was just a little fool to get worked up over nothing. It was only Nan's way. Even the kiss! Very likely Nan would have liked to make trouble between her and Noel. That was Nan's way, too. But she couldn't.

Gay was not so sure one evening two weeks later. Noel was to come that evening. Gay woke up in the morning expecting him. Her head lay in a warm pool of sunshine that spread itself over the pillow. She lay and stretched herself in it like a little lazy golden cat, sniffing delicately at the whiffs of heliotrope that blew in from the garden below. Noel would be out tonight. He had said so in his letter of the previous day. She had that to look forward to for a whole beautiful day. Perhaps they would go for a spin along the winding drive. Or perhaps they would go for a walk down to the shore? Or perhaps they would just linger at the side gate under the spruces and talk about themselves. There would be no Nan—Nan was away visiting friends in Summerside—she was sure of having Noel all to herself. She hadn't had him much to herself of late. Nan would be at Maywood or Noel would suggest that they go somewhere and pick her up—the poor kid was lonesome. Indian Spring was pretty quiet for a girl used to city life.

Gay lived the whole day in a mood of expectant happiness. A few weeks ago she had lived every day like that and she did not quite realise yet how different it had been lately. She dressed in the twilight especially for Noel. She had a new dress and she would wear it for him. Such a pretty dress. Powder-blue voile over a little slip of ivory silk. She wondered if Noel would like it and notice how the blue brought out the topaz tints of her hair and eyes and the creaminess of her slim throat. It was such delight to make herself beautiful for Noel. It seemed like a sacrament. To brush her hair till it shone—to touch the shadowy hollow of her throat with a drop of perfume—to make her nails shine softly like pink pearls—to fasten about her neck the little string of tiny golden beads— Noel's last gift.

"Every bead on it is a kiss,"he had whispered. "It's a rosary of our love, darling."

Then to look at herself and know he must find her fair and sweet. To know that she would see that little spark leap into his eyes as he looked at her.

Oh, Gay felt sorry for homely girls. How could they please their lovers? And she felt sorry for Donna Dark, who wasn't allowed to see *her* lover at all—though how could anybody care for that queer wild rover of a Peter Penhallow? And she felt sorry for Joscelyn, who had been so outrageously treated by her bridegroom—and she felt sorry for William Y.'s Sally, who was engaged to such an ugly, insignificant little man—and she felt sorry for Mercy Penhallow, who had never had a beau at all—and she felt sorry for poor Pauline Dark, who was hopelessly in love with Hugh—and for Naomi Dark, who was worse than widowed—even for poor silly Virginia Powell, who was so true and tiresome. In short, Gay felt sorry for almost every feminine creature she knew. Until late in the evening, when she was sorry only for herself.

Noel had not come. She had waited for him in the little green corner by the side gate, where Venus was shining over the dark trees, until ten o'clock and he had not come. Once she had got long-distance and called up his step-mother's house in town. But Noel was not there and his stepmother did not know where he was—or greatly care, her tone seemed to imply. Gay went back to her vigil by the gate. What had happened? Had his car acted up? But he could telephone. Suppose there had been an accident—a bad accident—suppose Noel had been hurt—killed? Or suppose he had just changed his mind? Had his good-bye kiss, three nights before, been just a little absent? And even his letter which had told her he was coming had begun with "dear" instead of "dearest" or "darling."

Once she thought she saw him coming through the garden. By the sudden uplift of heart and spirit she knew how terrible had been her dread that he would not come. Then she saw that it was only Roger. Roger must not see her. She knew she was going to cry and he must not see her. Blindly she plunged into the green spruce copse beyond the gate—ran through it sobbing—the boughs caught and tore her dress—it didn't matter—nothing mattered except that Noel had not come. She gained her room and locked her door and huddled herself into bed. Oh, what a long night was before her to live through. She remembered a pet phrase of Roger's—he was always saying, "Don't worry—there's always to-morrow."

"I don't want tomorrow," sobbed Gay. "I'm afraid of it."

It was the first night in her life she had cried herself chokingly to sleep.

In the morning Noel telephoned his excuses. He had a-plenty. Nan had called him on the long-distance from Summerside early in the evening and wanted him to run up and bring her home. He had thought he had plenty of time for it. But when he got to Summerside Nan's friends were having an impromptu party and she wanted to wait for it. He had tried to get Gay on long-distance but couldn't. It was late when he had brought Nan home—too late to go on to Maywood. He was frightfully sorry and he'd be up the very first evening he was free. They were confoundedly busy in the bank just now. He had to work till midnight, etc., etc., etc.

Gay believed him because she had to. And when her mother said to her that folks were beginning to talk about Nan and Noel, Gay was scornful and indifferent.

"They have to talk about something, Mumsy. I suppose they've got tired gossiping about poor Donna and Peter and have to begin on Noel and me. Never mind them."

"*I* don't mind them. But the Gibsons—they've always had a name for being fickle—"

"I won't hear a word against Noel," flashed Gay. "Am I to keep him in my pocket? Is he never to speak to a girl but me? A nice life for him. *I* know Noel. But you always hated him—you're glad to believe anything against him—"

"Oh, Gay, child—no—no. I don't hate him—it's your happiness I'm thinking of—"

"Then don't worry me with malicious gossip," cried Gay so stormily that Mrs. Howard dared not say another word on the subject. She switched to something safer.

"Have you written those chain letters yet, Gay?"

"No. And I'm not going to. Mumsy, you're really absurd."

"But, Gay—I don't know—no, I'm *not* superstitious—but you *know* it said if you broke the chain some misfortune would befall you—and it doesn't cost much—only six cents—"

"Mother, it *is* superstition. And I'm not going to be so foolish. Write the letters yourself, if you like—if it's worrying you."

"That wouldn't do any good. The letter was to you. It wouldn't take you long—"

"I'm not going to do it and that's all there is to it," said Gay, stubbornly. "You heard Roger on the subject, Mother."

"Oh, Roger—he's a good doctor but he doesn't know everything. There *are* things nobody understands—your father always laughed just as you do—but he was one of thirteen at a table just before he died. And say what you will, I knew a woman who wouldn't write the chain letters and she broke her knee-cap two weeks after she burned the one she got."

"Mrs. Sim Dark broke her arm last week, but I haven't

heard she burned any chain letters." Gay tried to laugh but she found it rather hard—she to whom laughter had always come so readily. There was such a strange, dreadful ache in her heart which she must hide from everyone. And she would *not* be jealous and hateful and suspicious. Nan was trying to weave her cobweb spells around Noel of course. But she had faith in Noel—oh, she must have faith in him.

Noel did come up four evenings later. And Nan came, too. The three of them sat on the verandah steps and laughed and chattered. At least Noel and Nan did. Gay was a little bit silent. Nobody noticed it. At last she got up and strolled away to the twilight garden, through the gay ranks of the hollyhocks and the old orchard full of mysterious moonlit delights—the place of places for lovers—to the side gate. She expected Noel would follow her. He had always done so—yet. She listened for his following footsteps. When she reached the side gate she turned and peeped back through the spruce boughs. Noel was still sitting on the steps beside Nan. She could not see them but she could hear them. She knew quite well that Nan was looking up at Noel with those slanting green eyes of hers—eyes that did something to men that Gay's laughing, gold-flecked ones could never do. And no doubt—Gay's lip curled in contempt—she was implying that he was the most wonderful fellow in the world. Gay had heard her do that before. Well—he *was!* But Nan had no right to think him so—or make him think she thought so. Gay clenched her hands.

She waited there for what seemed a very long time. There was a pale green sunset sky, and idle, merry laughter came from far across the fields on the crystal clear air. Somewhere there was a faint fragrance on the air, as of something hidden—unseen—sweet.

Gay remembered a great many things that she had almost forgotten. Little things that Nan had done in their childhood vacations when she had come over to the Island every summer. There was that day Gay had been quite broken-hearted at the Sunday-school picnic because she hadn't a cent to pay for the peep-show Hicksy Dark was running. And then she had found a cent on the road—and was going to see the peep-show—and Nan took the cent away from her and gave it to Hicksy and saw the show. Gay remembered how she had cried about that and how Nan had laughed.

The day when Nan had come in with a lovely big chocolate bar Uncle Pippin had given her. Chocolate bars were new things then.

"Oh, please give me a bite—just one bite," Gay had implored. She loved chocolate bars.

Nan had laughed and said,

"Maybe I'll give you the last one."

She sat down before Gay and ate the bar, slowly, deliberately, bite by bite. At last there was just one good bite left—a juicy, succulent bite, the lovely snowy filling oozing around a big Brazil-nut. And then Nan had laughed—and popped the bite into her own mouth—and laughed again at the tears that filled Gay's eyes.

"You cry so easy, Gay, that it's hardly any fun to make you cry," she said.

The day when Nan had snatched off Gay's new hair-bow, because it was bigger and crisper than her own, and slashed it to bits with the scissors. Mrs. Alpheus *had* whipped Nan for it, but that didn't restore the hair-bow and Gay had to wear her old shabby one.

The time when Gay was to sing at the missionary concert in the church and Nan had broken up the song and reduced Gay to the verge of hysterics by suddenly pointing her finger at Gay's slippered feet and calling out, "Mouse!"

Oh, there were dozens of memories like that. Nan had always been the same—as sleek and self-indulgent and cruel as a little tiger. Taking whatever she had a whim for without caring who suffered. But Gay had never believed she could take Noel.

Gay was not Dark and Penhallow for nothing. She did not go back to the steps. She went into the house by the sun-porch door and up to her room, though it seemed as if at every step she trod on her own heart. In her room she looked at herself in the mirror. It was as if her young face had grown old in an hour. Her cheeks were a stormy red, but her eyes were strange to her. Surely such eyes had never looked out of her face before. She shuddered with cold—with anger—

with sick longing—with incredulity. Then she blew out the lamp passionately and flung herself face downwards on her bed. The shadow had pounced at last. That other night she had cried herself to sleep—but she had slept. This was to be the first night of her life she could not sleep at all for pain.

IV

The quarrel and separation of the Sams had caused considerable sensation in the clan and for a time ousted Aunt Becky's jug, Gay Penhallow's engagement and Drowned John's tantrums over Peter and Donna as a topic of conversation in clan groups. Few thought it would last long. But the summer had passed without a reconciliation and folks gave up expecting it. That family of Darks had always been a stubborn gang. Neither of the Sams made any pretence of dignified reserve regarding their mutual wrongs. When they met, as they occasionally did, they glared at each other and passed on in silence. But each was forever waylaying neighbours and clansmen to tell his side of the story.

"I hear he's going about telling I kicked the dog in the abdomen," Little Sam would snort. "What's abdomen, anyhow?"

"Belly," said Stanton Grundy bluntly.

"Look at that now. I knew he was lying. I never kicked no dog in the belly. Touched his ribs with the toe of my boot once, that's all—for good and sufficient cause. Says I lured his cat back. What do I want of his old Persian Lamb cat? Always bringing dead rats in and leaving them lying around. And determined to sleep on *my* abdomen at nights. If he'd fed his cat properly she wouldn't have left him, but I ain't going to turn no broken-hearted, ill-used beast out of *my* door. I hear he's raving round about moons and contented cows. The only use that man has for moons is to predict the weather and as for contented cows or discontented cows, it's all one to him. But I'm glad he's happy. So am I. I can sing all I want to now without having some one sarcastically saying, 'A good voice for chawing turnips' or, 'Hark from the tombs a doleful sound,' or maddening things like that. I had to endure that for years.

But did I make a fuss about it? Or about his yelping that old epic of his half the night—cackling and chortling and guffawing and gurgling and yapping and yammering. You never heard such ungodly caterwauling as that poor creature could make. 'Chanting,' *he* called it. Till I felt as if I'd been run through a meat-chopper? Did I mind his always conterdicting me? No; it kept life from being too tejus. Did I mind his being a fundamentalist? No; I respected his principles. Did I mind his getting up at unearthly hours Sunday mornings to pray? I did not. Some people might have said his method of praying was irreverent— talking to God same as he would to me or you. I didn't mind irreverence, but what I didn't like was his habit of swinging round right in the middle of a prayer and giving the devil a licking. Still, did I make a fuss over it? No; I overlooked all them things, and yet when I brings home a beautiful statooette like Aurorer there Big Sam up and throws three different kinds. Well, I'd rather have Aurorer than him any day and you can tell him so. She's easier to look at, for one thing, and she don't sneak into the pantry unbeknownst to me and eat up my private snacks for another. I ain't' said much about the affair—I've let Big Sam do the talking—but some day when I git time I'm going to talk an awful lot, Grundy."

"I'm told that poor ass of a Little Sam spends most of his spare time imagining he's strewin' flowers on my grave." Big Sam told Mr. Trackley. "And I hear he's been making fun of my prayers. Will you believe it, he had the impidence to tell me once I had to make my prayers shorter 'cause they interfered with his mornin' nap? Did I shorten 'em? Not by a jugful. Spun 'em out twice as long. What I put up with from that man! His dog nigh about chewed up my Victory bond, but did *I* complain? God knows I didn't. But when my cat had kittens on his sheet he tore up the turf. Talking of the cat, I hear she has kittens again. You'd think Little Sam might have sent me one. I hear there's three. And I haven't a thing except them two ducks I bought of Peter Gautier. They're company—but knowing you have to eat 'em up some day spoils things. Look a' here, Mr. Trackley. Why did Jacob let out a howl and weep when he kissed Rachel?"

Mr. Trackley didn't know, or if he did he kept it to himself. Some Rose Riverites thought Mr. Trackley was too fond of drawing the Sams out.

"Because he found it wasn't what it was cracked up to be," chuckled Big Sam. He was happy all day because he had put one over on the minister.

But Big Sam was soon in no mood for joking about kisses, ancient or modern. He nearly had an apoplectic fit when he heard that some of the summer boarders up the river had gone to Little Sam under the mistaken impression that *he* was the poet, and asked him to recite his epic. The awful thing was that Little Sam *did*. Went through it from start to finish and never let on he wasn't the true author.

"From worshipping imidges to stealing poetry is only what you'd expect. You can see how that man's character's degen'rating," said Big Sam passionately.

V

Peter Penhallow was growing so lean and haggard that Nancy began to feel frightened about him. She tried to induce him to take some iron pills and got sworn at for her pains. A serious symptom, for Peter was not addicted to profanity. Nancy excused him, for she thought he was not getting a square deal, either from Drowned John or Providence. The very day Donna Dark was to be permitted to come downstairs she took tonsilitis. This meant three more weeks of seclusion. Peter sounded his horn at the enchanted portal every night or, in modern language, Drowned John's east land gate—but that was all he could do. Drowned John, so it was reported, had sworn he would shoot Peter at sight and the clan waited daily in horrified expectancy, not knowing that Thekla had hidden Drowned John's gun under the spare-room bed. Drowned John, not being able to find it, ignored Peter and his caterwauling and took it out on poor sick Donna, who was by this time almost ready to die of misery. Sick in bed for weeks and weeks, staring at that horrible wallpaper Drowned John had selected and which she hated. Horrible greenish-blue paper with gilt stars on it, which Drowned John thought the last word in elegance.

She had lost all her good looks, she told herself. She cried and said she didn't want to get better. Peter couldn't love her any more—this pallid, washed-out skeleton she saw in her mirror when she got up after tonsilitis. The doctor said she must have her tonsils out as soon as she was strong enough for the ordeal. This was reported to Peter and drove him still further on what all his friends now believed was the road to madness. He didn't believe in operations. He wasn't going to have pieces of his darling Donna cut out. They were all trying to murder her, that was what they were doing—the whole darn tribe of them. He cursed Mrs. Toynbee Dark a dozen times a day. Had it not been for her, Drowned John wouldn't have known of Donna's engagement, he wouldn't have kept such watch and ward—Peter would have been able to snatch her away, measles and tonsilitis to the contrary notwithstanding— and then a fig for your germs. But now—

"What am I to do?"groaned Peter to Nancy. "Nancy, tell a fellow what to do. I'm dying by inches—and they're going to carve Donna up."

Nancy could only reply soothingly that lots of people had had their tonsils out and there was nothing to do but wait patiently. Drowned John couldn't keep Donna shut up forever.

"You don't know him," said Peter darkly. "There's a plot. I believe Virginia Powell deliberately carried the tonsilitis germ to Donna. That woman would do anything to keep me and Donna apart. Next time it will be inflammatory rheumatism. They'll stick at nothing."

"Oh, Peter, don't be silly."

"Silly! Is it any wonder if I'm silly? The wonder is I'm not a blithering idiot."

"Some people think you are," said Nancy candidly.

"Nancy, it's eight weeks since I've see Donna—eight hellish weeks."

"Well, you lived a good many years without seeing her at all."

"No—I merely existed."

"Cheer up—- 'It may be for years but it can't be forever,'" quoted Nancy flippantly. "I did hear Donna was going to be out in Rose River Church next Sunday."

"Church! What can I do in church? Drowned John will be on one side of her and Thekla on the other. Virginia Powell will bring up the rear and Mrs. Toynbee will watch everything. The only thing to do will be to sail in, hit Drowned John a wallop on the point of the jaw, snatch up Donna and rush out with her."

"Oh, Peter, don't make a scene in church—not in church," implored Nancy, wishing she hadn't told him.

She lived in misery until Sunday. Peter did make a bit of a scene but not so bad as she feared. He was sitting in a pew under the gallery when the Drowned John's party came in—Drowned John first, Donna next, then Thekla— "I knew it would be like that," groaned Peter—then old Jonas Swan, the hired man—who had family privileges, being really a distant relative—then two visiting cousins. Peter ate Donna up with his eyes all through the service. They had nearly killed her, his poor darling. But she was more beautiful, more alluring than ever, with those great mauve shadows under her eyes and her thick creamy lids still heavy with the languor of illness. Peter thought the service would never end. Did Trackley preach as long as this every Sunday and if so, why didn't they lynch him. Did that idiot who was yowling a solo in the choir imagine she could sing? People like that ought to be drowned young, like kittens. Would they never be done taking up the collection? There were *six* verses in the last hymn!

Peter shot up the aisle before the rest of the congregation had lifted their heads from the benediction. Drowned John had stepped out of his pew to speak to Elder MacPhee across the aisle. Thekla was talking unsuspiciously to Mrs. Howard Penhallow in the pew ahead. Nobody was watching Donna just then, not dreaming that Peter would be in Rose River Church. None of his clique had ever darkened the door of Rose River Church since the sheepfight. They went to Bay Silver.

Donna had turned and her large mournful eyes were roving listlessly over the rising assemblage. Then she saw Peter. He was in the pew behind her, having put his hands on either side of little Mrs. Denby's plump waist and lifted her bodily out into the aisle to make way for him.

Mrs. Denby got the scare of her life. She talked about it breathlessly for years.

Peter and Donna had only a moment but it sufficed. He had planned exactly what to do and say. First he kissed Donna—kissed her before the whole churchful, under the minister's very eyes. Then he whispered:

"Be at your west lane gate at eleven o'clock tomorrow night. I'll come with a car. Can you?"

Donna hated the thought of eloping, but she knew there was nothing else to be done. If she shook her head Peter might simply vanish out of her life. Dear knows what he already thought of her for never sending him word or line. He couldn't know just how they watched her. It was now or never. So she nodded just as Drowned John turned to see what MacPhee was staring at. He saw Peter kiss Donna for a second time, vault airily over the central division of the pews and vanish through the side door by the pulpit. Drowned John started to say "damn" but caught himself in time. Dandy Dark's pew was next to his and Dandy had taken to attending church very regularly since the affair of the jug. People knew he went to keep tabs on them. Dandy had a pew in both Rose River and Bay Silver Churches and said shamelessly that he kept them because when he wasn't in one church he would get the credit of being in the other. The attendance at both churches had gone up with a rush since Aunt Becky's levee. Mr. Trackley believed his sermons were making an impression at last and took heart of grace anew.

Dandy gave Donna a little facetious poke in the ribs as he went past her and whispered:

"Don't go and do anything silly, Donna."

By which Donna understood that it really would injure her chances for the jug if she ran away with Peter. Even Uncle Pippin shook his head disapprovingly at her. As he said, when he left the church, their love-making was entirely too public.

Donna heard something from her father when she got home. It was a wonder they *did* get home, for Drowned John drove so recklessly that he almost ran over a few foolish pedestrians and just missed two collisions. Thekla had her say, too. The visiting cousins giggled, but old

Jonas went out stolidly to feed the pigs. Donna listened like a woman in a trance. Drowned John wasn't sure she even heard him. Then she went to her room to think things over.

She was committed to eloping the next night. It was not exactly a nice idea to a girl who had been brought up in the true Dark tradition—darker than the very Darkest. She thought of all the things the clan would say—of all the significant nods and winks. When Frank Penhallow and Lily Dark had eloped Aunt Becky had said to them on their return, "You were in a big hurry." Donna would hate to have any one say anything like that to her. But she and Peter would not be returning. That was the beauty of it. One thrust and the Gordian knot of their difficulties would be forever cut. Then freedom—and love—and escape from dull routine and stodginess—Thekla's jealousy and Drowned John's continual hectoring—and Virginia. Donna felt a pang of shame and self-reproach that there should be such relief in the thought of escaping from poor Virginia. But there it was. She couldn't *unfeel* it. Thirty-six hours and she must meet Peter at the west lane gate and the old scandal-mongers could go hang, jug and all. Luckily Thekla had gone back to her own room. Drowned John slept below. It would be easy to slip out. Had Peter thought she had gone off very terribly? Virginia said the tonsilitis had made her look ten years older. It was dreadful to have Peter kiss her before the whole congregation like that—dreadful but splendid. Poor Virginia's face!

Somehow or other, Sunday passed—and Monday morning—and Monday afternoon—though Donna had never spent such interminable hours in her life. She was glad that she was in such disgrace with her father and Thekla that they wouldn't speak to her. But that had begun to wear off by supper-time. Thekla looked at her curiously. Donna couldn't help an air of excitement that hung about her like an aura, and under the mauve shadows her cheeks were faintly hued with rose. A bit of amusement flickered in her sapphire eyes. She was wondering just what Thekla and Drowned John would say if they knew she was going to run away with Peter Penhallow that very night. Of course she couldn't eat—who could, under the circumstances?

"Donna," said Thekla sharply, "you haven't been putting on rouge?"

Drowned John snorted. He always had a fit of indignation when he caught a glimpse of Donna's dressing-table. Entirely too many fal-als for trying to be beautiful! Decent women didn't try to be beautiful. But if he had ever found or suspected any rouge about it, he would probably have thrown table and all out of the window.

"Of course not," said Donna.

"Well, your cheeks are red," said Thekla. "If you aren't painted you're feverish. You've got a relapse. I knew you would, going out so soon. You'll stay in bed tomorrow."

Donna grasped at the opportunity. She had been wondering if she and Peter could possibly get off the Island before Drowned John caught them. The Island was such a poor place to murder or elope. You were sure to be caught before you could get away from it. But by dinner-time next day they would be safely off, and then a fig for Drowned John.

"I—I think I will. For the forenoon, anyway. You can call me for dinner. I'm sure I haven't any relapse—but I'm tired."

Really, Providence at last seemed to be on her side.

Everybody in Drowned John's household went to bed early. At nine the lights were out and the door locked. This did not worry Donna. She knew quite well where Thekla hid the key, sly as she thought herself about it. She was ready at half-past ten, with a small suitcase packed. She opened her door and peered out. Everything was silent. Thekla's door was shut tight. Down the hall old Jonas was snoring. Fancy anyone snoring on this wonderful night. Would the stairs creak? They did, of course, but nobody seemed to hear. What would happen if she sneezed? Drowned John slept in the little cubby-hole off the dining-room and the key was in the blue vase on the clock shelf. Drowned John was snoring, too. Donna shuddered. She hoped Peter didn't snore. She unlocked the door, stepped out, and closed it behind her. Really, eloping was ridiculously easy.

Donna fled through the orchard to the west lane gate. She had nearly half an hour to wait. The tall black firs about the gate came out against the starlit sky. There were dancing northern lights over the dark harbour. The white birches down the west lane seemed to shine with a silvery light of their own. The night was full of wonder and delight and a subtle beauty that was not lost even on the excited Donna, who had inherited from her silent little mother a love and understanding for such things which sometimes amused and sometimes exasperated Drowned John, who would have thought it all of a piece with Virginia's maunderings if he could have realised the happiness Donna felt over a sunlight-patterned river—a silver shimmer on the harbour—starlight over fir trees—a blue dawn on dark hills—daisies like a froth of silver on seaside meadows.

Donna waited, enjoying the night for a time. If Peter had only come when she was in that mood all would have gone well. Then she began to shiver in the cool shrewish wind of September darkness. The trees whispered eerily over her. There were strange rustlings and shadows in the orchard. William Y.'s dog was exchanging opinions with Adam Dark's dog across the river. A roar swooped out of nothing—passed into nothing—a car had gone by. Donna shrank back into the shadow of the firs. Had they seen her? Oh, why didn't Peter come? Would she ever get warm again. She would catch her death of cold. She should have put on a heavier coat. It had been summer when she became ill. She hadn't realised that summer was gone and autumn here. Her courage and excitement ebbed with her temperature. Surely it must be eleven now. He had said eleven. If he didn't care enough for her to be on time—to avoid keeping her here in the cold half the night! Waiting—waiting. Donna knew how long time always seemed to one who was waiting. But even allowing for that, she was sure it must be nearer twelve than eleven. If he didn't come soon she would go back to bed—and then let Peter Penhallow propose eloping to *her* again!

Then she saw his lights—and everything was changed. There was his car coming up the west lane, with her destiny in it. If Thekla woke up she would see the lights from her window. God send she didn't wake up!

Peter caught her in his arms, exultantly.

"I've had the most devilish luck. Two flat tires and something wrong with the carburetor. I was afraid you'd have gone back—afraid you wouldn't be able to get out at all. But it's all right now. We've heaps of time. I allowed for delays. Listen—my plan is this: We'll motor to Broden and catch the boat. And we'll stop at the Kirtland manse and get Charlie Blackford to marry us. I've had the licence for days. Charlie's a good sort—I know him well. He'll marry us like a shot and make no bones if it is a few minutes before six. Once we're on the mainland—heigh-ho for New York in our own car—and we'll sail for South America from there. Girl of my heart, do you love me as much as ever? Lord, I could eat you. I feel famished. You're as lovely as dark moonlight. Donna—Donna—"

"Oh, Peter, don't smother me," gasped Donna. "Wait—wait—let us get away. I'm so afraid Father will come out. Oh, it seems I've been here for *years*."

"Don't worry. I'll settle him in a jiffy, now that I've got you out of the house. Donna, if you knew what I've been through—"

"Peter, stop! Let us get away."

Peter stopped, a bit sulkily. He thought Donna a trifle cool after such an agonising separation. Surely she needn't grudge him a few kisses. He didn't realise how cold and frightened she really was or how endless had seemed her waiting.

"We can't get away for a minute or two. When I passed your Aunt Eudora's over there, young Eudora was in the yard saying good-bye to Mac Penhallow. We've got to wait till he's gone. Darling, you're shivering. Get into the car. It'll be warm there, out of this beastly wind."

"Put out your lights—if Thekla sees your lights—oh, Peter, it's rather awful running away like this. We've never done such things."

"If you are sorry it's not too late yet," said Peter in a changed, ominous voice.

"Don't be ridiculous, Peter." Donna was still cold and frightened and her nerves were bad after all she'd been through. She thought Peter might be a *little* more considerate. Instead, here he was being deliberately devilish.

"Of course I'm not sorry. I'm only sorry it had to be like this. It's so—so *sneaky*."

"Well," said Peter, who had also been through something, especially with those fiendish tires, and had a good deal yet to learn about women, "what else do you propose?"

"Peter, you're horrid! Of course I know we must go through with it—"

"Go through with it. Is *that* how you look at it?"

Donna felt suddenly that Peter was a stranger.

"I don't know what you want me to say. I can't pick and choose words when I'm half frozen. And that isn't all—"

"I didn't think it would be," said Peter.

"You've been saying some funny things yourself—oh, I've heard—"

"Evidently. And listened, too."

"Well, I'm not deaf. You told Aunty But that—that—you let yourself be caught because you were tired of running."

"Good heavens, woman, I only said that to choke Aunty But off. Was I going to tell that old gossip I worshipped you?"

Donna had never really believed that he had said it at all. Now she felt as if she almost hated him for saying a thing like that in a clan like hers.

"As if I'd been *chasing* you—my friends have been telling me right along I was a fool."

If Donna had but known it, she was nearer having her ears boxed at that moment than ever in her life before. But Peter folded his arms and stared grimly ahead of him. What use was there in talking? Would that love-sick fool of a Mac ever get through making his farewells and clear out? Once they were on a clear road at fifty an hour Donna would be more reasonable.

"They'll think I was in such a hurry to run away like this—I know Dandy Dark will never give *me* the jug now—Aunt Becky always thought eloping was vulgar—"

The Spanish blood suddenly claimed right of way—or else the Penhallow temper.

"If you do get that filthy jug," said Peter between his teeth, "I'll smash it into forty thousand pieces."

That finished it. If it hadn't been for the jug this sudden tempest in a teapot might have blown off harmlessly, especially as Mac Penhallow's old Lizzie went clattering down the road at last. Donna opened the car door and sprang out, her eyes blazing in the pale starlight.

"Peter Penhallow—I deserve this—but—"

"You deserve a damn' good spanking," said Peter.

Donna had never sworn in her life before. But she was not Drowned John's daughter for nothing.

"Go to hell," she said.

Peter committed the only sin a woman cannot forgive. He took her at her word.

"All right," he said—and went.

Donna picked up the suitcase, which was lying where she had first set it down, and marched back through the orchard and into the house. She relocked the door and put the key in the blue vase. Drowned John was still snoring—so was old Jonas. She got into her own room and into her own bed. She was no longer cold—she was burning hot with righteous anger. What an escape! To think she had been on the point of running away with a creature who could say such beastly things to her. But of course one couldn't expect the Bay Silver Penhallows to have any manners. It served her right for forgetting she had always hated him. Virginia had been right— poor dear ill-used Virginia. But from henceforth forevermore she, Donna, would be a widow indeed. Oh, how she hated Peter! As she hated everybody and everything. Hate, Donna reflected for her comforting, was a good lasting passion. You got over loving but you never got over hating. She thought of a score of stinging things she could have said to Peter. And now she would never have a chance to say them. The pity of it!

Peter tore across the country all night and caught the boat. So she had Drowned John's temper as well as his nose! He was well out of *that*—by the sacred baboon he was! He had no use for women who swore—not knowing how lucky he had been that Donna hadn't gone into hysterics instead of swearing. Serve him right for taking up with that family at all. Well, madness was finished and hurrah for sanity! Thank heaven, he was his own man again—free to wander the world over, with no clog of a woman tied round his neck. No more love for him—he was through with love.

VI

Donna was not the only woman of the clan to be out that night. Gay Penhallow was lying among the ferns in the birch grove behind Maywood, weeping her heart out at midnight.

There was a dance at the Silver Slipper that evening— the closing dance of the summer season, before the last of the guests left the big hotel down by the harbour's mouth. Noel had promised to come for Gay. Of late a little hope had sprung up in Gay's heart that everything was coming right between her and Noel again. They had had a little quarrel after that night when Gay had left Noel and Nan on the steps. Gay found herself put in the wrong. Noel was very angry over the way she had acted. A nice position she had put him in. Gay, all her little bit of pride now worn down by suffering, had apologised humbly and been grudgingly forgiven. She even felt a little happy again

But only a little. Her pretty, dewy visions were gone never to return. There was always a little cold fear lurking deep down in her heart now. Day by day Noel seemed to drift further away from her. He wrote oftener than he came—and his letters had got so thin. When she hungered for the touch of his hand and the sound of his voice, with a hunger and longing that devoured her soul, came only one of those thin letters of excuse—from Noel, who only a few weeks ago had vowed he could *not* go on living ten miles away from her.

But she could not believe he meant to jilt her—her, Gay Penhallow of the proud Penhallows. Gay knew girls had been jilted—even Penhallow girls. But not so soon—so suddenly. Not in a few weeks after your lover had asked you to marry him. Surely the process of cooling off should take longer.

After she dressed for the dance that night she did a certain thing in secret. She hunted that old chain letter out of her desk and wrote three neat, careful little copies of it. Enveloped and addressed and stamped them. And flung on her coat and slipped down to the post-office in the cool windy September twilight to post them. Who knew? After all—there *might* be something in it.

When she got back long-distance was calling. Noel couldn't come after all. He had to work in the bank that night.

Gay went out and sat down on the steps, huddled in her grey coat. Her little face with its piteous eyes rose whitely over her soft fur collar. Roger found her there when he dropped in on his return from a sick-call.

"I thought you'd be at the Silver Slipper to-night," said Roger—who knew and was furious and helpless over certain things—more things than Gay knew. He looked down at her—this lovely, sensitive little thing who must be suffering as only such a sensitive thing could—with clenched hands. But he avoided her eyes. He could not bear the thought of looking into her eyes and seeing no laughter in them.

"Noel couldn't come," said Gay lightly. Roger was not to know—to suspect. "He has to work tonight. It's rather a shame, isn't it? Here I am 'all dressed up and nowhere to go.' Roger,"—she bent forward suddenly—"will you run me down to the Silver Slipper? It's only a mile—it won't take you long—I can come home with Sally William Y."

Roger hesitated.

"Do you really want to go, Gay?"

"Of course." Gay pouted charmingly. "A dance is a dance, isn't it—even if your best beau can't be there? Don't you think it would be a shame to waste these lovely slippers, Roger?"

She poked out a slender little golden foot in a cobweb of a stocking. Gay knew she had the daintiest ankles in the clan. But she was thinking wildly—desperately—she must be *sure*—sure that Noel had not lied to her.

Roger yielded. He did not know what Gay might find at the Silver Slipper but whatever it was she had better know it, hard as it might be. After all, it might not be Noel's car he had passed where the road turned down to the dunes.

Gay thanked Roger prettily at the door of the dance-hall and would not let him wait—or come in. She ran along the

verandah with laughing greetings to folks she knew, her
eyes darting hither and thither from one canoodling pair
to another in shadowy corners. Across the hall to the
dance-room, with its rustic seats and its red lanterns. It
was full of whirling couples, and Gay felt her head go
around. She steadied herself against the door-post and
looked about the room. Her head grew steadier, her lips
ceased to tremble. There was no sign of Noel—or Nan.
Perhaps—after all—but there was a little room off the
dance-room—she must see who was in there. She slipped
down the hall and stepped in. There had been laughter in
it before her entrance—laughter that ceased abruptly.
Several groups of young folks were in the room, but Gay
saw only Noel and Nan. They were perched on the edge of
the table where the punch-bowl was, eating sandwiches.
To speak the strict truth, *one* sandwich, taking bites from
it turn about. Nan, laughing shrilly in a daring new frock
of orchid and mauve tulle—a frock that was almost backless—
was holding it up to Noel's mouth when the general hush
that followed Gay's entrance made her look around. A
malicious, triumphant sparkle flashed into her eyes.

"Just in time for the last bite, Gay darling." She tossed it
insultingly at Gay—but Gay was gone, sick and cold with
agony to the depths of her being. Through the hall—over
the verandah—down the steps. Out into the night where
she could be alone. If she could just get away where it was
dark and cool and quiet—no lights—no laughter—oh, no
laughter! She thought everybody was laughing at her—at
her, Gay Penhallow, who had been jilted. Unconsciously
she clutched at the little gold bead necklace around her
neck as she ran—Noel's gift—and broke it. The gold beads
rolled like tiny stars over the dusty road in the pale
autumn moonlight, but she never thought of stopping to
pick them up. She knew if she ceased for a moment to run
she would shriek aloud with anguish and not be able to
stop. Some late-coming cars drenched the distraught little
figure with their radiance and one narrowly escaped running her down. Gay wished it had. Would she never get
away somewhere where no one could see her? The road
seemed endless—endless—she must keep running like
this forever—if she stopped her heart would break.

Eventually she did get to Maywood. There was a light in the living-room. Her mother was there still. Gay couldn't face her. She couldn't face anyone then. She was breathless and sobbing. Her pretty honey-hued gown hung about her in shreds, limp with dew, torn by the wild shrubs along the dune road. But that didn't matter. Dresses would never matter again. Nothing would matter. Gay found her tear-blinded way to a little ferny corner in the birch grove and flung herself down in it in a dreadful little huddle of misery. All the bitterness of all betrayed women was distilled in her young heart. The world had ended for her. There was nothing beyond—nothing. Nobody ever had suffered like this before—nobody ever would suffer like this again. How could she go on living? Nobody could suffer like this and live.

And it was all the fault of that horrible jug. Aunt Becky seemed to be laughing derisively at her from her grave. As all the world would soon be laughing—with the William Y. brand of laughter.

VII

Pennycuik Dark had decided that he must get married. Not without long and painful cogitations on the subject. For years Penny had believed he would always remain a bachelor. In his youth he had rather prided himself on being a bit of a lady-killer. He had then every intention of being married sometime. But—somehow—while he was making up his mind the lady always got engaged to somebody else. Before he realised it he had drifted into the doldrums of matrimonial prospects. The young girls began to think him one of the old folks and all the desirable maids of his own generation were wedded wives. The clan began to count Penny among its confirmed old bachelors. At first Penny had resented this. But of late years he had been well content. Marriage, he said, had no charms for *him*. He had enough money to live on without working, a comfortable little house at Bay Silver and a fairly good housekeeper in old Aunty Ruth Penhallow, a smart little car to coast about in, and two magnificent cats forever at his heels. First Peter and Second Peter, who slept at the foot of his bed and ate at his table. What more could matrimony offer him? He compared his lot complacently with most of the married men he knew. He wouldn't, he vowed, take any of their wives as a gift. As for a family—well, there were enough Darks and Penhallows in the world without his contributing any more. "Better let the cursed breed die out," Penny had growled irritably when Uncle Pippin rallied him about not being married. He liked to sit in church and pity Charlie Penhallow in the pew ahead, who had to buy dresses for seven foolish daughters and looked it. Penny's pity had a special flavour for him by reason of the fact that Mrs. Charlie had been the only girl he had ever seriously considered marrying. But before he could make up his mind positively that he wanted her she had married Charlie. Penny told himself he didn't care, but when now, in his mellow fifties, he sat and recalled his old flames, like a dog remembering how many bones he has buried, he did not linger on the recollection of Amy Dark. Which meant that the thought of her held a sting for him. Amy had been a pretty girl and was a pretty woman still, in spite of seven daughters and two sons, and sometimes when Penny looked at her in church he felt a vague regret that she hadn't waited until he had decided whether he wanted her or not.

But on the whole, Penny's bachelor existence suited him very well. He was fond of saying he had "kept the boy's heart," and had no suspicion that the younger folks thought him a comic valentine. He thought he was quite a dandy still, admired by all his clan. He could come and go as he liked; he had no responsibilities and few duties.

Nevertheless, now and then of late years, a doubt of his wisdom in remaining unmarried crept into his mind. Aunt Ruth was growing old and, with her heart, might drop off any time. What in thunder would he do for a housekeeper then? He began to feel rheumatic twinges in his legs and remembered that his grandfather, Roland Penhallow, had been a cripple for years. If he, Penny, went like that, who would wait on him? And if the rheumatism went to his heart, as it had gone to Uncle Alec's, and he had no housekeeper, he might die in the night and nobody know of it for weeks. The gruesome thought of himself lying there alone dead for weeks was more that Penny could endure. Perhaps, after all, he had better marry before it was too late. But these fleeting fears might not have stirred him to action had it not been for Aunt Becky and her jug. Penny wanted that jug. Not because he cared a hang for the dingus itself but as a question of right. His father was Theodore Dark's oldest brother and his family ought to have it. And he felt sure he would have no chance of it if he remained unwedded. Aunt Becky had as good as said so. This tipped the balance in favour of matrimony, and Penny, with a long sigh of regret for the carefree and light-hearted existence he was giving up, made up his mind that he would marry if it killed him.

VIII

It remained to decide on the lady. This was no easy matter. It should have been easier than it had been thirty years before. There was not such a wide range of choice, as Penny ruefully admitted to himself. He had no idea of marrying out of the clan. At twenty-five he had liked to toy with such a daring idea but at fifty-three a sensible man does not take such a risk. But which of the old maids and widows should be Mrs. Penny Dark? For old maid or widow it must be, Penny decided with another sigh. Penny was not quite a fool, in spite of his juvenile pretences, and he knew quite well no young girl would look at him. He had not, he said cynically, enough money for *that*. He balanced the abstract allurements of old maids and widows. Somehow, an old maid did not appeal to him. He hated the thought of marrying a woman no other man had ever wanted. But then—a widow! Too experienced in managing men. Better a grateful spinster who would always bear in mind what he had rescued her from.

Still, he would consider them all.

For several Sundays after he had made up his mind he went to both Rose River and Bay Silver Churches and looked all the possibilities over. It was an interesting experience. Much more fun than trying to count the beads on Mrs. William Y.'s dress, which was how he had contrived for several Sundays to endure the tedium of the sermon. Penny felt quite youthful and exhilarated over it. He wondered slyly what Mr. Trackley would think about it if he knew. And what excitement there would be among all the aforesaid possibilities if they dreamed what was hanging in the balance. Would Hester Penhallow in the choir look so sanctimonious and other-worldly if she knew that her chances of being Mrs. Pennycuik Dark were being debated down in the pew? Not that Hester had much of a chance. Marry that terrible beak of a nose! Never! Not for forty jugs.

"I can't marry an ugly woman, you know," thought Penny plaintively. The rest of the old cats in the choir he dismissed without a second thought.

Edna Dark was ladylike but her face was too tame. Charlotte Penhallow was too dowdy and her mouth too wide. Violet Dark was handsome enough still—a high-coloured woman with small, light brown eyes and a nasal voice. Handsome but charmless. Penny felt that he could do without beauty and style but charm he must have. Besides, in the back of his mind was an unacknowledged doubt if she would take him.

Bertha Dark's face was presentable, but where did she get such thick legs? Penny did not think he could stand a pair of legs like that waddling up the church aisle after him every Sunday. Elva Penhallow had slim, dainty legs but Penny decided she was "too devout" for him. Religion was all very well—a certain amount became a woman— but Elva really had too much to make a comfortable wife. Wasn't there a story that she was so conscientious that she used to write down in her diary every night the time she had spent in idleness that day, and pray over it? Too strenuous—by far too strenuous.

Penny wondered how old Lorella Dark really was. Nobody ever seemed to know, beyond the idea that she was kind of thirtyish. She was a plump and juicy little person, and he would have picked her in a second if he had not been afraid that she was not yet old enough to have given up hope of any man except an old bachelor. Penny did not mean to run any risk of a refusal.

Jessie Dark might have done. But he had heard her say she liked cats "in their place." She would never believe their place was on the marriage-bed, of that Penny felt sure. First and Second Peter would forbid those banns.

Bessie Penhallow—no, quite out of the question. He couldn't endure the big mole with three long hairs on it she had on her chin. Besides, she was as religious in her way as Elva. She was—to quote Penny's phrase—a foreign-mission crank. The last time he had been talking with her she had told him that interest in Christian literature was increasing in China and had been peeved because he didn't get excited over it.

Mildred Dark, who was a stenographer in a law office in town and came home for the week-ends, was stylish and up-to-date. But what a terrible complexion of moth patches. It was very well to say all women were sisters under their skins—Penny wasn't quite sure whether that was in Shake-speare or in the Bible—but the skin made a difference, confound it.

As for her sister Harriet, who "went in" for spiritualism and declared she had a "spirit lover" on "the other side," let her continue to love spiritually. Penny had no intention of being her love on *this* side. No spooky rivals for *him*.

Betty Moore would really have been his choice if she had been Dark or Penhallow. But one took too many chances in marrying a Moore. Emilia Trask had money but she had a temperish look. No, no, Dark or Penhallow it must be. Marriage was a risk at best, but better the devil you know than the devil you don't know.

There was Margaret Penhallow. She had been pretty and her eyes were still pretty. Mr. Trackley said she had a beautiful soul. That was probably true—but her body was so confoundedly lean. Mrs. Clarence Dark, now—ah, there was a fine armful of a woman for you! But she was a widow and there was a legend that she had once slapped her husband's face at prayer-meeting. And though Uncle Pippin had said that he would rather be slapped than kissed in public—as Andy Penhallow was—Penny could not see the necessity of either. After all, Margaret's figure was the more fashionable. All the young girls were skinny nowadays. None of the plump morsels he remembered in his youth. Where were the girls of yesteryear? Girls that *were* girls—ah! But Margaret was ladylike and gentle and would of course give up writing her silly poems when she had a husband. By the time Mr. Trackleys' sermon was finished Penny had decided that he would marry Margaret. He went out into the crisp sunshine of the October afternoon feeling himself already roped in and fettered. When all was said and done he would have liked a little more—well—romance. Penny sighed. He wished he had got married years ago. He would have been used to it by now.

IX

Big Sam was not particularly happy. Summer had passed; autumn was coming in; winter loomed ominously near. The Wilkins shanty was draughty and Big Friday Cove was a dod-gasted lonesome place. He was getting indigestion from eating his own cooking. Various clan housewives invited him frequently to meals, but he did not care to go because he felt that they were on Little Sam's side. Even the Darks and Penhallows were getting lax and modern, Big Sam reflected gloomily. They would tolerate anything.

But when Big Sam heard that Little Sam was going to see the Widow Terlizzick on Sunday nights, he was struck dumb for a time; then he turned himself loose on the subject to all who would listen.

"Wants to work another wife to death, I s'pose. I really would have thought Little Sam had more sense. But you can't trust a man who's been married once—though you'd think he'd be the very one to know better. And him the ugliest man in the clan! Not that the fair Terlizzick is any beauty, what with all them moles and her sloppy ankles. I'd say she looked like a dog-fight. And fat! If he had to buy her by the pound he'd think it over. She's been married twice already. Some folks never know when to stop. I'm sorry for Little Sam but it's certainly coming to him. I hear he waddles home from church with her. Next thing he'll be serenading her. Did I ever tell you Little Sam imagines he can sing? Once I says to him, says I, 'D'ye call that ungodly caterwauling music?' But the Terlizzicks never had any ear. Well, she'll have her troubles. I could tell a few things if I wanted to."

None of the clan approved of the hinted courtship. To be sure, they had all long ago tacitly agreed that the Sams were in a class by themselves and not to be judged by the regular clan standards. Still, the Terlizzicks were a little *too* rank. But none of them took Little Sam's supposed matrimonial designs to heart as much as Big Sam. When he was observed standing on a rock, waving his short arms wildly in the air, it was a safe bet that he was *not*, as heretofore, shouting his epic out to waves and stars, but abusing the Widow Terlizzick. She was, he told the world, a hooded cobra, a bit fat slob, a rapacious female animal and a tigress. He professed profound pity for Little Sam. The poor fellow little dreamed what he was in for. He oughter have more sense! Taking two men's leavings! Huh! But them widows did bamboozle people so. And the Terlizzick had so much experience. Two husbands done in.

All these compliments being duly reported to Little Sam and Mrs. Terlizzick may or may not have pleased them. Little Sam kept his own counsel and brought up Mustard's three kittens ostentatiously. The white goddess of the morning still stood on the clock shelf but the dust had gathered on her shapely legs. When Father Sullivan started up another lottery at Chapel Point Little Sam said it oughter be stopped by law and what were the Protestants thinking of?

4
THE MOVING FINGER

▼

I

The sudden arrival "home" of Frank Dark and his sister Edna fell on the clan like a mild bombshell. Frank announced that Edna thought she had as good a right to the jug as anybody and had given him no peace until he consented to come. Dandy was his uncle and who knew? They would be in at the killing, anyhow. And he was about sick of the west. Guessed he'd sell out there and buy on the Island. Settle down for the rest of his life among his own folks.

"And marry a little Island girl," said Uncle Pippin.

"Sure," laughed Frank. "They're hard to beat."

But after he had left the store amused smiles were exchanged.

"Doesn't look any too prosperous," was the comment.

"He's gone to seed. They say he's been going the pace," said William Y. "Drank up everything he made a little faster than he made it."

"Too handsome to be any good when he was young. That always spoils a man," growled Sim Dark, who had certainly never been spoiled for that reason.

Joscelyn heard he was home the next evening just as she was starting for church. Aunt Rachel mentioned it casually to Mrs. Clifford—"They say Frank Dark's home again"—and Joscelyn's head reeled and her universe whirled about her. For a moment she thought she was going to faint, and clutched wildly at the table to steady herself. Frank home—Frank! For a moment ten years folded themselves back like a leaf that is turned in a book and she saw herself, mist-veiled, looking into Frank Dark's handsome eyes.

"Ain't you ready yet, Joscelyn?" said Aunt Rachel fretfully. "We're going to be late. And if we are we won't get a seat. Everybody will be there to hear Joseph."

The Rev. Joseph Dark of Montreal was to preach in Bay Silver Church that night and naturally almost every Dark and every Penhallow would be be there. They were very proud of Joe. He was the highest salaried minister in Canada—little Joe Dark who used to run around Bay Silver barefooted and work in the holidays for his wealthier relatives. They hadn't bothered their heads much about him then, but now his occasional visits home were events and when he preached in Bay Silver Church they had to put chairs in the aisles.

Joscelyn walked to the church with her aunt. It was on an October evening as warm as June. A frolicsome little wind was stripping all the gold from the maple trees. The western sky was like a great smoky chrysanthemum over hills that were soft violet and brown. A few early autumnal stars were burning over the misty, shorn harvest fields. A great orange moon was rising over Treewoofe Hill, bringing out a remote, austere quality in its beauty. There was a pleasant smell of damp mould from red ploughed fields. Everybody was ploughing now. Hugh had been ploughing on the big hill field up at Treewoofe all day. Joscelyn knew that he had always loved to plough that hill field. She had seen him from her window and wondered again if he were really going to sell Treewoofe. Every few weeks the rumour revived. Aunt Rachel had mentioned it again that day and it had fretted Joscelyn like a grumbling toothache. But everything was forgotten now in the shock of what she had just heard. She walked as one in a dream. She did not know whether she felt glad or sorry or exultant or—or—

afraid. Ay, she *did* know. She was afraid. Suddenly and horribly afraid. Of seeing Frank.

She did not think there was any danger of seeing him that evening. He would be stopping with his brother Burton at Indian Spring and Burton never came to hear Joseph Dark preach. Joe Dark had married the girl Burt wanted and Burt always ascribed Joe's success in the ministry to the fact that he knew how to flatter the women. Besides, Burt always averred in his characteristic way that that old church at Bay Silver was lousy with fleas. As Uncle Pippin had once said, Burt Dark was a realistic sort of cuss.

But Joscelyn knew she would meet Frank somewhere and soon. And she was mortally afraid, with a sick, cold, dreadful fear.

They were late; when they reached the church the Reverend Joseph was praying and they waited in the porch that was full of other late-comers. The inner doors were tightly shut and only a sonorous murmur penetrated outwards. Joseph Dark had a beautiful voice and there was something in the faint, unworded rhythm of his prayer that soothed Joscelyn. She rather liked standing there in the porch, listening to it. One could fit one's own words, one's own needs, one's own desires to it.

She did not see Hugh at first. He was standing just behind her, gazing at her with smouldering eyes. Palmer Dark and Homer Penhallow were in the porch also. They had nodded amicably and mentioned the weather. Then they stood hating each other while Joseph prayed. The truce of the jug still held but underneath it the old dear feud rankled. Ambrosine Winkworth sailed in past them and streamed up the aisle, her head held high, her diamond ring on her ungloved hand. Ambrosine had no intention of waiting in the draughty porch until little Joe Dark, whom she had spanked in years gone by, had finished praying. He always prayed too proudly, anyway, Ambrosine thought. Ambrosine never wore gloves now, and she was the happiest woman in the church that night. Envious people said that the airs Ambrosine put on over that ring were simply ridiculous.

"Ain't she the fine lady now?" whispered Uncle Pippin,

sitting on the third step of the gallery stair beside Big Sam, who had come to find out if there were any truth in the story that Little Sam came to Bay Silver Church every Sunday night to walk home with the Widow Terlizzick.

"What a long tail our cat has," whispered Big Sam in return.

Back in the shadowy corner Stanton Grundy loomed, lean and tactiturn. He had never been able to hear Joe Dark preach before. Something had always prevented. But now his chance had come to see the man his Robina had secretly loved all her life. Robina, who was now a handful of ashes in an urn in the churchyard outside—all ashes, even to the heart that had belonged to Joseph Dark instead of to its lawful owner, Stanton Grundy. Donna Dark and her father were there, although Drowned John was never over-anxious to hear Joe preach. Not that he had anything against Joe. But he thought it might give him a swelled head if too many of his own clan went to hear him. However, Donna was set on coming and Drowned John gave in. Drowned John was by way of getting into the habit of giving in now and then to Donna. It eased things up a bit. In the month that had passed, gossip about Peter and Donna had died down. There had been a good deal of it at first and much wonderment as to why everything had stopped so suddenly. Drowned John did not vex himself wondering why. It was very simple. He had ordered Donna to discard the fellow and she had of course obeyed. Some thought Peter's behaviour that notable Sunday had disgusted Donna. Virginia thought that dear Donna's higher nature had reasserted itself. Though Virginia did not get a great deal of comfort out of that. Dear Donna was frightfully changed, there was no doubt about it. So cynical. She laughed at Virginia's sentimental memories. She said that if Barry had lived they would probably have fought like cat and dog, half the time. At home Donna's behaviour was rather like that of a ladylike tigress by times. Then Drowned John was driven to the relection that life might have been more comfortable if he had let Peter have her. And there was no longer any fun in her. There had used to be a good bit when Virginia wasn't around. In short, she would, he confided to his pigs, neither gee nor haw.

Kate Muir was there, buxom and rosy and overdressed as usual with the three little black curls everyone made fun of lying sleekly and flatly on her forehead. Murray Dark was there, waiting impatiently for Joe to get through, that he might go in and look at Thora for an hour. Percy Dark and David Dark were there, but they glowered gloomily past each other. They had never "spoken" since their fight at the funeral and by heck, they never would speak, jug or no jug. Tempest Dark was there because he had been a crony of Joe's in boyhood and still liked the beggar in spite of his priestly ways.

All in all, it was an odd mélange of passions—hates and hopes and fears—that waited in the old church porch at Bay Silver for Joseph Dark to finish his seemingly interminable prayer.

Joscelyn had a love for Bay Silver Church—a tranquil old grey church among its sunken graves and mossy gravestones. She was glad the graveyard had never been ironed out and standardised like the one at Rose River.

Outside, the moon was shining calmly on the tombstones and the Moon Man was wandering about among them. Occasionally he stopped and told a dead crony something. Occasionally he bowed to the moon. Occasionally he would come to the porch door or a church window and peer in. Later on when the congregation sang he would sing, too. But he would never enter a church door.

"What's Joe so damn' long about?" thought Drowned John impatiently. He dared not swear in words but, thank God, thought was still free.

Frank Dark was in the porch, standing under the little hanging lamp, before Joscelyn saw him. He stood there, beaming rather fatuously around him. Joscelyn stared at him with eyes in which dawning horror struggled with amazement. *This* could not be Frank Dark—oh, *this* could never be the slim, gallant stripling to whom she had so suddenly lost her heart on her wedding-night. *This* could not be the man she had loved in secret for ten years. *This!* Fat; half-bald; nose red; eyes puffy and bloodshot; sallow jowls; shabby. With failure written all over him. She saw him as he was; worse—as he had always been under all the charm of his vanished youth. Paltry—crude—cheap. She gazed at him in the stubborn incredulity with which we face the fact of a sudden death. It could not be! It could not be for *this* that she had torn Hugh's life in shreds and lost Treewoofe forever? Joscelyn wondered if it were she who was laughing—certainly someone was laughing. It was Hugh, behind her. A strange little laugh with nothing of mirth in it. So Hugh saw what she was seeing. Joscelyn wondered if there were any deeper depths of shame to which she could descend.

Hugh's laugh drew Frank's attention to them. He smiled broadly and came forward with outstretched hand, effusive and gushing.

"Hugh—and Joscelyn! How *do* you do! How *do* you do! My, it's good to see all you folks again. You don't look a day older, Joscelyn—handsomer than ever. It don't seem possible it's ten years since I danced at your wedding. How time does fly!"

Joscelyn felt sure she was in a nightmare. She must wake up. This ridiculous, hideous situation couldn't be real. She saw Hugh shaking hands with Frank—Frank whom he had vowed to thrash if he ever set eyes on him again. Now he would disdain to do it. Joscelyn saw the disdain in his eyes—in his bitter mouth. Thrash this poor creature for whom his bride had thrown him over. The idea was farcical.

"And how's the family?" said Frank with a sly wink.

Something in the electric silence that followed gave Frank to think. There was a titter from some ill-bred young cub by the door. Frank had never heard the sequel to the wedding at which he had danced. But he felt he had put his foot in it somehow. Probably they had no family and were sensitive about it. His tongue was always getting him into trouble. But hang it, if they hadn't a family they ought to have. Hugh needn't glower like that. As for Joscelyn, she had always been a high and mighty piece of goods. But she needn't be looking at him as if he were some kind of a new and fancy worm. The airs some people gave themselves made him tired.

The Reverend Joseph had concluded his prayer and

with a sigh of relief the waiting group passed into the church. Joscelyn, who only wanted to run—and run—and run, had to follow Aunt Rachel in and sit quietly through a sermon of which she heard not one word. She felt as if she had been stripped naked to the gaze of a world that was laughing at her shame. It was of no avail to tell herself that no one but Hugh ever knew or suspected that she had loved Frank Dark—or something she had believed Frank Dark to be. The feeling of naked humiliation persisted. How Hugh must be mocking her! "You flouted me for this! What do you think of your bargain?"

Hugh was not thinking anything of the sort. He thought Frank Dark a pretty poor specimen of a man—not worth all the hatred he had lavished on him—but he did not know that Joscelyn saw what he did. After all, Frank was still handsome in a florid way and women's tastes were odd enough. Hugh was another who did not hear much of Joseph Dark's sermon. All the old bitterness and anger of his wedding-night was surging up in his soul again. What a mess had been made of his life—through no fault of his own. There were a dozen girls he might have had; some of them were in the church that night. He looked at them all and decided that, after all, he'd rather have Joscelyn. Just as things were—Joscelyn with that glorious sweep of red-gold hair over her pale, proud face. If she were not his, at least she was no other man's. Nor could be. *She* could never divorce *him*. Hugh ground his teeth in savage triumph. Frank Dark should never get her—never!

Big Sam, with Little Sam sitting across from him, gazing at the buxom Widow Terlizzick like, Big Sam vowed to himself, an intoxicated dog, did not hear much of the sermon either. Which was a pity because it was a remarkably good sermon—brilliant, eloquent, scholarly. Joseph Dark's listeners sat spellbound. He played skilfully on their emotions—perhaps a shade too skilfully—and they responded as a harp responds to the wind. They felt caught away from sordid things to hill-tops of vision and splendour; life, for the time being at least, became a thing of beauty to be beautifully lived; and few there were who did not feel a throb of glad conviction when the speaker,

leaning earnestly over the desk and addressing individual-
ly every member of his audience, said thrillingly:

"And never, even in your darkest and most terrible
moments, forget that the world belongs to God," closing
the Bible, as he spoke, with a thunderclap of victory.

Of the few was Stanton Grundy. He smiled sardonically
as he went out.

"The devil has a corner or two yet," he said to Uncle
Pippin.

"Gosh, but that was a sermon though," said Uncle
Pippin admiringly.

"He can preach," conceded Grundy grudgingly. "I wonder how much of it he believes himself."

Which was unfair to Joseph Dark, who believed every
word he preached—while he was preaching it, at all
events—and surely could not be justly blamed because
Robina Dark had, all unasked, given him the heart that
should have belonged only to her liege lord, Stanton
Grundy.

"Frank Dark's got terrible fat," said Aunt Rachel as she
and Joscelyn walked home. "He's following in the footsteps of his father. *He* weighed three hundred and fifty-
two pounds afore he died. I mind him well."

Joscelyn writhed. Aunt Rachel had always possessed the
knack of making everything she mentioned supremely
ridiculous. Joscelyn's romantic love for Frank Dark was
dead—dead past any possibility of a resurrection. It had
died as suddenly as it had been born, there in the porch of
Bay Silver Church. But she could have wished, for her
own sake, to be able to look upon the corpse with some
reverence—some pity—some saving wish that it could
have been otherwise. It was dreadful to have to mock
herself over dead love—to hear others mocking. Dreadful
to think of having wasted on Frank Dark the years that
should have been given to bearing Hugh's children and
building a home for him and them at Treewoofe. Dreadful
to think that all the passion and devotion and high renunciation of those processional years had been squandered
on a man who had simply become a person likely to
"weigh three hundred and fifty-two pounds before he
died." Joscelyn would have laughed at herself except for

the fact that she knew if she began to laugh she would never be able to stop. All the world would laugh at her if it knew. Even the tall, wind-writhen lombardies against the moonlit clouds above William Y.'s place, seemed to be pointing derisive fingers at her. She hated the stars that twinkled at her—the chilly, foolish night-wind that whined mockingly—the round hill shoulders over the bay that were shaking with merriment. What was Aunt Rachel saying? Something about Penny Dark being more conceited than ever since he had got Aunt Becky's bottle of Jordan water.

"He needn't imagine he's got the only one in the clan."

Joscelyn felt that she wanted to do something very cruel. She wanted to make someone else feel a little of the pain and humiliation she was enduring.

"Oh, but he has, Aunt Rachel. I spilled your bottle of Jordan water long ago and filled it up with water from the barn pump. That's what you've been worshipping all these years!"

II

One grey November evening Gay carried home a letter from Noel. When the postmaster had handed it out to her, her heart had given a suffocating bound, as it would do, she thought, if she were buried underground and Noel walked by her grave. It was a long time since she had had a letter from him. A long time since she had seen him—not since that bitter night at the Silver Slipper. She did not even hear much about him—her clan were surprisingly considerate in regard to that. Almost too considerate. Their avoidance of all reference to Noel was too pointed. Gay knew what it meant when everybody stopped talking as she entered a room. It hurt her—or her pride. For she had still some pride left in which she tried pitifully to wrap herself from what she thought was the half-pitying, half-contemptuous gaze of her little world. She felt as if every one must be watching her to see how she took it—watching her around corners—behind window-blinds—across the church.

And she had still a tormenting secret hope that all

would come right yet. Noel *must* have loved her. It couldn't have been all pretence. He was just bewitched by Nan's daring and "differentness" and bold coquetry—by the way she could use her eyes. What if—Gay caught her breath as she hurried along—what if this letter were to tell her he had come to his senses—what if it were asking her to forgive him and take her back? Why else should he have written at all?

Gay flitted home like a little shadow through the melancholy moonlight of the late autumn night. The distant hills were cold and eerie in the chill radiance. The sea moaned hollowly down on the beach. A lonely wind was looking for something and moaning pitifully because it could not find it. It was a dead world—everything was dead—youth, hope and love were dead. But if Noel's letter only said what it might say there would be an immediate resurrection. Spring would come back even in grey November and her poor, cold, dead, little heart would beat again. If Noel would only come back to her. She did not care how much he had hurt her—how rottenly he had used her—if he would only come back. Her pride was only for the world. She had no pride as far as Noel was concerned. Only a dreadful longing to have him back.

She went to her room, when she reached Maywood, and laid the letter on the table. Then sat down and looked at it. She was afraid to open it. She dared not open it yet—she would let herself hope a little longer. She thought of that evening in June when she had gone from Aunt Becky's levee to read Noel's letter among the ferns in the shadowy hollow of that little wayside nook. There had been no fear then. How could a few short months have made such a difference in anybody's life? She wondered dumbly if she could possibly ever have been the happy girl of the lovely apple-blossom-time. Then a whole universe of wonder had been hers, with the Milky Way for a lover's path. Now it had shrunk to a little room where a pale girl sat staring with piteous dilated eyes at a letter she was afraid to open.

She recalled the first time she had got a letter from Noel—all the "first times." The first time they had met—the first time she had danced with him—the first time he had called her "Gay"—the first time his smooth, flushed cheek had rested against hers—the first time she had poked her finger through a little gold curl falling down on his forehead and saw it glistening on her hand like a ring of troth—the first time he had said, "I love you."

And then the first time she had doubted him—such a little, little doubt like a tiny stone thrown into a pool. The ripples had widened and widened until they touched the farthest shores of mistrust. And now she could not open her letter.

"I won't be such a coward any longer," said Gay passionately. She snatched it up and opened it. For a few minutes she looked at it. Then she laid it down and looked around her. The room was just the same. It seemed indecent that it should be just the same. She walked a little unsteadily to the open window and sat down on a chair.

Noel had asked her to release him from his engagement. He was "very sorry" but it would be foolish "to let a boyish mistake ruin three lives." He had "thought he loved her" but now he "realised that he had not known then what love was." There was a good deal more of this—Noel had so many apologies and excuses that Gay didn't bother to read them all. What did they matter? She knew what was in the letter now.

She sat at her window all night. She could not sleep and she did not want to sleep. It would be so terrible to awake and remember again. There was nothing in the world but cold, pale moonlight. Would she ever forget that dreadful white, unpitying moon above the waiting woods—the mournful sound of the wind rustling the dead leaves on the trees, this chilly November night? There was nothing left for her in life—nothing—nothing. It was just as the Moon Man had warned her—she had been too happy.

She thought the night would never end. Yet when the trees began to shiver in the wind of dawn she shrank from it. She could not bear this dawn—all other dawns she could bear but not this one. And it was such a wonderful dawn—a thing of crimson and gold and quivering splendour—of flames and wings and mystery—such a dawn as should break only over a happy world on a happy morning for happy people. It was an insult to her misery.

"I could live through this morning if there were to be no more mornings," thought Gay drearily. Those interminable mornings, stretching before her, year after year, year after year, till she was old and lean and faded and bitter like Mercy Penhallow. The very thought of them made Gay feel desperate. She shivered.

"Will I ever get used to pain?" she thought.

Gay told her mother quite calmly that afternoon that she had broken her engagement with Noel. Mrs. Howard wisely said very little and less wisely made Gay's favourite cake with spice frosting for supper. It did not heal Gay's broken heart; it only made Gay hate spice cake for the rest of her life.

Mercy recommeded fresh air and an iron tonic. William Y. said he hoped Noel Gibson would get enough of that little wasp of a Nan before she was through with him.

"Remember you're a Penhallow. They don't wear their hearts on their sleeves," cautioned Cousin Mahala kindly. Gay looked at her with sick eyes. She had gone on smiling, that day, before the clan until she could smile no more. But she did not mind Cousin Mahala seeing into her soul. Cousin Mahala *understood*.

"Cousin Mahala, *how* can I go on living? Just tell me how—that's all I want to know now. Because I *have* to live, it seems."

Cousin Mahala shook her head.

"I can't—nobody can. And you'd only think me heartless and unfeeling if I told you you'd get over this. But I will tell you something I've never told anyone before. Do you see that little field over there between Drowned John's farm and the shore road? Well, I lay there among the clover all night, thirty years ago, agonising because Dale Penhallow didn't want me. I didn't see how I was to go on living either. And now I never pass that field without thanking my lucky stars he didn't."

Gay shrank into herself. After all, Cousin Mahala didn't understand. Nobody understood.

Nobody but Roger. Roger came along that evening to find Gay huddled on the verandah steps in the twilight, feeling like some poor little cat freezing before a merciless locked door. She looked up at him with her terrible, tortured young eyes, over the fur collar as he sat down beside her, her face one little, white, pinched note of pain—the face that was meant for laughter.

"Gay—my poor little Gay," he cried. "What have they been doing to you?"

Gay laid her tired head down on his shoulder.

"Roger," she whispered, "will you take me for a drive in your car? A *fast* drive—I don't care how fast—a long drive—I don't care how long—right through the sunset if you like—and *don't talk to me*."

They had their long and fast drive—so fast that they nearly ran over Uncle Pippin at the turn of the Indian Spring road. He skipped nimbly out of their way and looked after them, chuckling.

"So Roger's out for the rebound," he said. "He always was a cool sort of devil. Knew how to wait."

But Uncle Pippin didn't understand either. Roger just then was feeling that it would be a delightful sensation to find Noel Gibson's throat between his fingers. And Gay wasn't feeling anything. She was numb. But that was better than suffering. She seemed to leave pain behind her as she swooped along the road, the lights flashing on dark woods and tossing trees and frosted ferns and alluring dunes—on—on—on through the night—across the world— not having to talk—not having to smile—conscious only of the sweep of free, cold wind in her face and Roger's dark strength beside her at the wheel. This big, quiet, gentle Roger, with his softly luminous eyes and his slim brown hands. It seemed the most natural thing in the world that he should be there beside her. When they went back— when they stopped—pain would run to meet her again. But this relief was blessed. If only they need never stop—if they could go on and on like this forever—over the hills—down into the valleys of night—along the windy shores of starlit rivers—past the curls of foam on long, shadowy beaches, in the beautiful darkness that was like a cool draught for a fevered soul to drink! If only they need never turn back!

III

Pennycuik Dark was on his way to propose to Margaret Penhallow. Though he had made up his mind to do it in September, it was not done yet. Every morning Penny thought he would go up to Denzil's that evening and have done with it. But every evening he found an excuse to defer it. He might never have gone at all had it not been for the gravy stains on the tablecloth. Penny, who was as neat as one of his own cats, could not endure a mussy tablecloth. Old Aunt Ruth was getting inexcusably careless. It was high time the house had a proper mistress.

"I'll go this evening and get it over," said Penny desperately.

He dressed and shaved as for a solemn rite, wondering uneasily what it would be like to have some one there in the room, watching him shave.

"It may be all right when a fellow gets used to it," signed poor Penny.

He walked up to Denzil's—no use wasting gas on a two-mile errand—wondering what the people he met would say if they knew what he was out for. Mrs Jim Penhallow's great flock of snowy geese in a dun, wet November field—white as snow in the autumnal twilight—hissed at him as he passed. Penny reflected that he might as well buy a goose for the wedding-supper from Mrs. Jim as not. She might let him have it a bit cheaper, since they were first cousins.

At Denzil's gate he paused. It was not too late yet to back out. He might still return home a free man. But the gravy stains! And the jug! Penny lifted the gate latch firmly. The Rubicon was crossed.

"By ginger, this makes me feel queer," thought Penny. He found he was perspiring.

The amazing, the ununderstandable thing was that Margaret did not jump at him. When she had finally disentangled his meaning—for Penny went all to pieces at the crucial moment—forgot every word of the speech he had so carefully composed and rehearsed and floundered terribly—realising that Pennycuik Dark was actually proposing marriage to her, she asked rather primly for time to consider it. This flabbergasted Penny. He, who had not had the least doubt that he would go home an engaged man, found himself going home nothing of the sort. He was so indignant that he wished he had never mentioned the matter to her. Gracious Peter, suppose she wouldn't have him after all! Ridicule would be his portion all the rest of his life. And she had wanted a week to make up her mind—to make up her mind whether or no to marry *him*, Pennycuik Dark! Did any one ever know the like?

Margaret really passed as disagreeable a week as Penny did. One day she thought she would marry Penny; the next she thought she couldn't. In spite of her desire for marriage in the abstract she found that in the concrete, as represented by little dapper Penny Dark, it was not wholly desirable. It would have amazed Penny, who had no small opinion of his own good looks, had he known that Margaret thought his bodily presence contemptible and his chubby pimply little face positively ugly—and worse than ugly, rather ridiculous. To wake up every morning and see that face beside you. To listen to his funny vulgar stories and his great haw-haws over them! To hear him yelling to Baal if he had a hangnail. To think it a joke, as he still did, when he stuck out his foot and tripped somebody up. To be always called "Marg'ret."

Then she didn't like his fussy, lace-trimmed house. Too many jigarees on it. So different from little gray Whispering Winds, veiled in trees. Margaret felt positive anguish when she realised that marriage meant the surrender of all the mystery and music and magic that was Whispering Winds. She would be too far away from it even for occasional visits. She could never again nourish a dear, absurd little hope that it might sometime be hers.

And she must give up certain imaginary love affairs with imaginary lovers, such as she had been fond of dreaming. She felt that it would be wrong, when she was married, to dream those romantic love-affairs. She must "keep her only" to Penny then. And she knew he would never consent to her adopting a baby. He detested children.

But there were certain advantages. She would be a wedded wife with a home and social standing such as she had never possessed. Nobody would ever say to her again, "Not married yet—well—well?" She would have a car of her own to ride in—or her husband's own. Margaret reminded herself very sensibly that she could not expect to have a man made for her. She knew most of the clan would think she was in luck to get Penny. Yet, as she worked all that week at Sally Y.'s nasturtium-colored chiffon dress, watching it grow to a thing of flame and loveliness under her fingers, she "swithered," as she expressed it. She just couldn't make up her mind to marry Penny, somehow. Finally she remembered that she would certainly have no chance of Aunt Becky's jug if she stayed an old maid. That tipped the balance. She sat down and wrote a note to Penny. Determined to infuse a little sentiment into her acceptance, she merely sent him a copy of some Bible verse—Ruth's immortal reply to Naomi. At first Penny didn't know what the deuce it meant. Then he concluded that she had accepted him. He and Second Peter looked at each other with an air of making up their minds to the inevitable.

He went up to see Margaret, trying to feel that it was the happiest day of his life. He thought it his duty to kiss her and he did. Neither enjoyed it.

"I'spose there isn't any particular hurry about getting married," he said. "It's a cold time of year. Better wait till spring."

Margaret agreed almost too willingly. She had had her white night after she had mailed her letter to Penny. She went to Whispering Winds and walked about it until midnight to recover her serenity. But she was now resigned to being Mrs. Pennycuik Dark. And she could have the winter to plan her trousseau. She would have a nice one. She had never had pretty clothes. Life, as far back as she could look, had been as dull and colourless in clothes as in everything else. She would have a wedding-dress of frost-grey silk with silvery stockings. She had never had a pair of silk stockings in her life.

Altogether Margaret was much more contented than Penny, who when he went home had to brew himself a jorum of hot, bitter tea before he could look his position squarely in the face. Sadly he admitted that he was not as happy as he ought to be.

"Things," Penny gloomily told the two Peters, "will never be the same again."

The affair surprised the clan but was generally approved. "The jug's responsible for that," said Dandy Dark when he heard of it.

Margaret suddenly found herself of considerable importance. Penny was well-off; she was doing well for herself. She rather enjoyed this in a shy way but Penny writhed when people congratulated him. He thought they had their tongues in their cheeks. The story went that when Stanton Grundy said to Penny, "I hear you're engaged," Penny had turned all colours and said feebly, "Well, it's not—not an engagement exactly—more like—like an experiment." But nobody knows to this day whether Penny really said it or not. The general opinion is that Stanton Grundy made it up.

The affair made less of a sensation than it might have, had it not coincided with Gresham Dark's discovery that his wife, after eighteen childless years, was going to present him with an heir. Gresham, who belonged to the excitable Spanish branch, quite lost his head over it. He rushed around, buttonholing people at church and auctions to tell them about it. The women of the clan could have killed him but the men chuckled.

"I suppose you can't blame *that* on the jug," said Uncle Pippin.

IV

Early in December Frank Dark's engagement to Mrs. Katherine Muir was announced in the local papers. It surprised nobody; all had seen in what quarter the wind was setting from the first week after Frank's arrival home. Frank, they thought, had feathered his nest well. Kate was a cut or two socially above what he had any right to expect. Her face was rather the worse for wear and she was a bit bossy. But she had the cash. That was what Frank was after. Of Kate's wisdom they had a poorer opinion. She was, it was thought, taking a risk. But Frank was not going west again. He was going to buy a farm—with Kate's money?—and settle down among his clan. He would likely go pretty straight, surrounded by such a cloud of witnesses. To be sure, on the day he married his plump widow, it was easy to see he was three sheets in the wind. But public opinion excused him. A man must have some courage even if it were only Dutch courage, to tackle Kate.

It was reported that he was trying to get Treewoofe. Some said Hugh refused to sell and had snubbed Frank cruelly; others had it that he was considering the offer. Kate had always had a fancy for Treewoofe.

Joscelyn heard all the rumours with many others. She had not seen Frank since that night in Bay Silver Church but gossip soon informed her that he was after Kate. Well, what did it matter? She had all ways despised Kate Muir. It was nothing to her whom this new Frank, red-nosed and puffy-eyed, married. But when she heard that he was going to buy Treewoofe a fresh agony possessed her. Frank at Treewoofe! Black, moustached little Kate mistress of Treewoofe! Joscelyn fled to her room to face the thought and found it could not be faced.

It had been a hard day for her. Her mother and Aunt Rachel had bickered almost continually, owing to Aunt Rachel's having upset her stomach eating something she should not. Aunt Rachel had been "on a diet" ever since the night Joscelyn had told her about the Jordan water. She had fretted so over it that she grew ill and Roger had been called in. Joscelyn hated herself for having told Aunt Rachel—poor Aunt Rachel who had so little to make life worth living. She would have bitten her tongue out if that would have unsaid the fatal words. Nothing could unsay them; stricken Aunt Rachel took the bottle off the parlour mantel and buried it in the garden; then she proceeded to develop "stomach trouble," and Joscelyn soon had plenty of other reasons for wishing she had held her tongue. Aunt Rachel's stomach became the pivot about which all the meals revolved; they could not have this and they could not have that because "poor Rachel" could not eat it. If they had it "poor Rachel" could not resist the temptation and calamity followed. The previous evening company had come to tea and something extra had to be provided. Mrs. Clifford had warned Rachel that the cheese soufflé would not agree with her stomach and Rachel had responded pettishly that she guessed it was her own stomach. Today was the consequence and Joscelyn had to set her teeth to endure it—as a sort of penance because it was all her fault. But this news about Treewoofe was unbearable.

She looked up at it, lying in its mysterious silence of moonlit snow fields, with flying shadows from the passing clouds of the windy night sweeping over it, so that it now became almost invisible in the silver loveliness of the winter landscape, and again loomed suddenly forth at her on its white eerie hill in that cold ghostly moonlight. Was Hugh there? Was he going to sell Treewoofe? Was he going to get a divorce and marry Pauline Dark? The silence around her seemed verily to shriek these questions at her. And there was no answer.

It had been a hard autumn and winter for Joscelyn. She felt indescribably poorer. Life had tricked her—betrayed her—mocked her. And when her romantic infatuation, as she now bitterly saw it, had vanished, her old feeling for Hugh had come back. All at once he was dear—so dear. Not that she held any hope that matters could ever be put right between them. Hugh, she was sure, hated her now, if he did not actually despise her. Besides, he was going to go to the States for a divorce and would marry Pauline. Everybody said so.

Joscelyn was racked with jealousy. She hated the very sight of Pauline. She felt that Pauline already pictured herself as Hugh's wife and mistress of Treewoofe. She remembered how she had seen Hugh and Pauline talking together at Aunt Becky's funeral and looking up at Treewoofe. But it was still more dreadful to think of Frank and Kate being there. That was desecration. As long as Hugh was at Treewoofe, even with Pauline, Joscelyn would not feel so helplessly bereft. Every day and night she looked up at Treewoofe, loving and craving it the more intensely that she dared not let herself love and crave Hugh. She saw it on stormy days, with swirls of snow blowing around it—under frosty sunsets when its lights burned like jewels over the rose tints of the snowy fields—on mild afternoons when the grey rain wrapped it like a cloak—in the pale gold and misty silver of early, windless mornings. Always it was there, her home—her real and only home—luring, repellent, scornful, desirable by turns. Her home from which she must always be an exile through her own folly. Pauline would be there—or fat, giggling Kate. Joscelyn gritted her strong white teeth. A mad impulse assailed her. Suppose she went to Hugh—now—when he was sitting alone in that lonely house with the winter wind blowing around it—and flung herself at his feet—asked him to forgive her—to take her back—humiliated herself in the very dust? No, she could never do that. She might if she had any hope he still cared. But she knew he didn't. He was in love with Pauline now—everybody said so— Pauline with her slim darkness and her long velvety eyes. She, Joscelyn, was a woman without love—without a home—without roots. She must spend the rest of her life forever beating with futile hands at closed doors. An old line of poetry, read long ago and forgotten for years, flickered back into memory:

> "*Exceeding comfortless and worn and old
> For a dream's sake.*"

Yes, that had been written for her. "For a dream's sake." And now the dream was over.

"Joscelyn," wailed Aunt Rachel from the hall, "I wish you'd fill the hot-water bottle and bring it up and lay it acrost my stomach. If that don't help you'll have to phone for Roger. And I suppose he'll be off joy-riding with Gay Penhallow. It's off with the old love and on with the new mighty easy nowadays. People don't seem to have any deep feelings any more. Aunty But's just been in on her way to Gresham's. They've sent for her three times already on false alarms, but she guesses this is genuine. She says Gresham was yelling over the phone as if 'twas him was having the baby 'stead of his wife. She says she knows for a fact that Aunt Becky's jug is to be raffled off. Dandy got stewed at Billy Dark's silver wedding and let it out. Raffling's immoral and oughter be stopped by law."

"Dandy didn't get drunk at the wedding," said Joscelyn wearily. "He took an overdose of pain-killer to cure a stomach-ache before he went and it made him act very queerly; but he kept fast hold on his secrets, Aunt Rachel."

"It's awful what stories get around," sighed Aunt Rachel. "And Aunty But says Mar'gret Penhallow's getting a lot of silly, fashionable clo'es to be married in. Mar'gret wants taking down a peg or two, and if my stomach was what it used to be"—Aunt Rachel gave a hollow groan—"I'd go and do it. But somehow I can't get up much pep nowadays—living on slops."

V

Likely Gay was "joy-riding" with Roger the night Aunt Rachel's stomach was acting up. If not, it was a safe wager that Roger was talking to her in the living-room at Maywood, with a driftwood fire dreaming dreams of fairy colours in the grate and a maddeningly complacent mother painstakingly effacing herself as soon as he came. Gay, who couldn't bear to be alone with herself, did not know what she would have done through that terrible autumn and winter without Roger.

By night she was still given over to torture but by day she had achieved self-command. The clan had decided that she hadn't cared so much for Noel Gibson after all. They thought she had taken it pretty well. Gay knew they were watching her to see how she did take it and she held her head up before the world. She would not give all those heartless gossippers food for talk. She would not let them think she knew of their whispers and their curious eyes. She did not laugh very much—she who had always been a girl of the merriest silver laughter—and Stanton Grundy said to himself, as he looked at her in church, "The bloom's gone," and, old cynic though he was, thought he would enjoy "booting" Noel Gibson. Some of the clan thought Gay was "improved" since certain little airs and graces had been dropped. All in all, they did not talk or think about her nearly as much as sensitive little Gay thought they were doing. They had their own lives to live and their own loves and hates and ambitions to suffer and scheme and plan for. And, anyway, Roger could be trusted to handle the situation.

At first, when they went riding, Gay wanted to go in

silence—silence in which a hurt heart could find some strength to bear its pain. But one night she said suddenly,

"Talk to me, Roger. Don't ask me to talk—I can't—but just talk to me."

Roger, to his own surprise, found that he could. He had never talked much to Gay before. He had always felt that he could talk of nothing that would interest her. There had been such a gap between her youth and his maturity. But the gap had disappeared. Roger found himself telling her things he had never told anybody. He had never talked of his experiences overseas to any one but he found himself relating them to Gay. At first Gay only listened; then, insensibly, she began to talk, too. She took to reading the newspapers—which worried Mrs. Howard, who was afraid Gay was getting "strong-minded." But Gay only wanted to learn more about the things Roger talked of, so that he would not think her an empty-headed goose. She had, without realising it, come a long, long way from the tortured little creature who had lain under the birches, that September night, and cried her heart out. No longer an isolated, selfish unit, she had become one with her kind. She had realised what some one had called "the infinite sadness of living" and the realisation had made a woman of her. Her April days were ended.

There was a sad peace in knowing nothing could ever happen to her again—that life held nothing for her but Roger's friendship. But she would always have that; and with it she could face existence. How splendid Roger was! She had never half appreciated him before. Tender—strong—unselfish. Seeing the best in everybody. He told her things about the clan she had never known before—not the petty gossip everybody knew or the secret scandals Aunt Becky and her ilk knew—but noble things and kindly things and simple, wholesome things that made Gay feel she came of a pretty decent stock, after all, and must live up to the traditions of it. It was amazing how good people really were. Even her own Darks and Penhallows whom she had laughed at or disliked. Who would have supposed that Mercy Penhallow, malicious Mercy who was afraid to be out after dark—perhaps for fear of the ghosts of reputations she had slain—could have been a perfect heroine during the terrible Spanish flu epidemic? Or that William Y., who held the mortgage on Leonard Stanley's farm, should, when Leonard died, leaving a wife and eight children, have gone to Mrs. Leonard—pompously, because William Y. couldn't help being pompous—and torn the mortgage to pieces before her eyes? Or that shrinking little Mrs. Artemas Dark, seeing that big bully of a Rob Griscom at the harbour cruelly beating his dog one day, had flown through the gate, snatched the whip from the thunderstruck Griscom, and whipped him around and around his own house until he had fallen on his knees before her and begged for mercy?

And—Gay thought it suddenly one evening before the driftwood fire—what nice dimples Roger had in his thin cheeks when he smiled!

Still, Gay had her bad hours—hours when her heart ached fiercely for her lost happiness—hours when she wanted nothing but Noel. If she could only wake and find it all a dream—if she could only feel his arms about her again and find it all a dream—if she could only feel his arms about her again and hear him saying he loved her and her only! She wanted to be happy again. Not just this dull resignation with the moonlight of friendship to show the narrow path of life. She wanted love and full sunshine and—Noel. Everything was summed up in Noel. And Noel was with Nan.

Gay saw nothing of Nan now. Mrs. Alpheus had found herself no longer able to endure the dullness of Indian Spring and had taken an apartment in town. She never saw Noel either. She wondered when he and Nan would be married and how she could get out of going to the wedding. Nan would invite her, she was sure of that. Nan who had told her so confidently that she was going to take Noel from her. And Gay had been so sure she couldn't. Oh, poor little fool!

"Life isn't fair," said Gay, her lips quivering. For an hour she would be nothing but little, jilted, heartbroken Gay again, only wanting Noel. If he would only come back to her! If he would only find out how selfish and vain and—and—empty Nan was! Nan couldn't love anybody—not really. Of course she loved Noel after a fashion—

nobody could help loving Noel—but never, never as Gay loved him.

There came an evening at the end of a blustery March day when Mercy Penhallow told Mrs. Howard that Mrs. Alpheus had told her that Noel and Nan would be married in June. There was to be a clan church wedding with bridesmaids in mauve taffeta, tulle hats of mauve and pink, and corsage bouquets of pink sweet peas. Nan had everything planned out to the smallest detail. Also her house. She was even, so Mercy said, going to have sheets in her guest-room to match her guests' hair—nile-green for red hair, orchid for brunettes, pale blue for golden hair. And all the furniture was to be extremely modern.

"I expect she's even got the nursery planned out," said Mercy sarcastically.

Mrs. Howard did not tell Gay about the nile-green and orchid sheets or the mauve and pink bridesmaids but she did tell her of the wedding. Gay took it quietly, her eyes growing a little larger in her small white face. Then she went up to her room and shut the door.

Why had she kept hoping—hoping? She must have been hoping, else this would not twist her heart-strings so. She took a bundle of Noel's letters out of her desk. She had never been able to burn them before but she must do it now. Here they all were—the ones he had written her first on top—fat, bulging letters. They grew thinner and thinner. The later ones were pitifully thin. Still, they were from Noel. Something of his dear personality was in them. *Could* she burn them? An old verse came into her head—a verse from a sentimental poem in an old faded scrapbook of her mother's. There had been a time when Gay had thought it so lovely and sweet and sad. She quoted it now about Noel's letters, feeling that it was very appropriate.

"Yes—yes," said poor Gay trembling,

> "Yes, the flames the link shall sever
> Their red tongues will never tell,
> When I've crossed the mystic river
> They will keep my secret well."

She laid Noel's first letter in the grate and held a lighted match to it. The little flames began to eat it greedily. Gay dropped the match and covered her face. She couldn't bear to look at it. She *couldn't* burn those dear letters. It was too much to ask of herself. She snatched up the rest of them, her body racked by painful little sobs, and hurried them back into her desk. They were all she had left. Nobody could blame her for keeping them.

She sat at her window for awhile before she went to bed. A red, red sun was sinking between two young spruces in Drowned John's hill pasture. After it disappeared there came the unearthly loveliness of a calm blue winter twilight over snow. A weird moon with a cloud-ribbed face was rising over the sad, dark harbour. Winter birches with stars in their hair were tossing all around the house. There was a strange charm about the evening. She wished Roger could see it with her. He loved evenings like this. There had been a little snow that day, following on the heels of the mad galloping March wind, and the hedge of young firs to the left of the house was white with it. Something about them made her think of the apple blossoms on the day of Aunt Becky's levee. How happy she had been then. And it had all gone with the apple blossoms.

"I feel so old," said Gay, looking particularly young and piteous.

VI

Little Brian Dark was alone in his kitchen loft one night in late March, looking out on a landscape that was black and ugly in the ugliest time of year—when the winter whiteness has gone, leaving only the bare bones of the world exposed to view. There was a cold, yellow strip of sky in the west under a sullen, cloudy sky, hanging over frozen fields. The trees looked as if they could never live again.

Brian, as usual, was lonely and hungry and tired. As long as the light lasted he had consoled himself by looking at the gorgeous pictures of good things to eat in the advertising pages of a pile of old magazines under the eaves. What curly, delicious strips of bacon—what tempting muffins—what mouth-melting cakes with icing! Were

there really people in the world—perhaps little boys—
who ate such delicious things?

The lamp in the Dollar living-room was out but a light
burned in the little room upstairs looking out on the
kitchen roof. Brian knew that Lennie Dollar slept there;
he had envied Lennie all winter because he had such a
warm cosy little room to sleep in. Often during the past
winter Brian had wished he could snuggle in there, too.
The loft was always cold, but it had been colder this
winter than ever because in the preceding autumn Brian
had accidentally broken one of the window panes and
Uncle Duncan and Aunt Alethea were so angry with him
because of his carelessness that they would not replace it.
Brian had stuffed an old sweater in it but that did not keep
all the extra cold out.

Yet Brian was not so entirely friendless as he had been.
There was Cricket. One little white blossom of love had
begun to bloom in the arid desert of his unwelcome
existence. Cricket would soon come now. He pulled out
the old sweater before he lay down on his bed, so that
Cricket could get in.

He lay there expectantly, listening to the eerie sounds
the spruce trees made outside in the dark. It was time
Cricket came. Surely Cricket would come. Surely nothing
had happened to Cricket. Brian lived in daily terror that
something would happen to Cricket.

Cricket had been coming every night for three weeks.
He had been there alone one night, very lonely and
unhappy as usual. Aunt Alethea had been angry with him
and had sent him supperless to bed. He looked out of the
window. The sky was sharp and brilliant, the stars cold and
bright. He was such a little fellow to be all alone in a
great, lonely world. He had prayed to his dead mother in
heaven for food and comfort. He was afraid that God, even
a young God, might be too busy looking after more
important things to bother about him, but Mother would
have time. Brian knew a little about his mother now. One
day he had met the old Moon Man on his ceaseless quest
and the Moon Man had stopped and beckoned to him.
Brian's knees knocked together as he obeyed. He did not
dare disobey, although he went in such terror of the Moon

Man. And then he found the Moon Man was looking down at him with gentle, kind eyes.

"Little Brian Dark, why are you so frightened of me?" asked the Moon Man. "Have they been telling you false, cruel things about me?"

Brian nodded. He could not speak but he knew now the things *were* false.

"Don't believe them any longer," said the Moon Man. "I would hurt nothing, much less a child. Laura Dark's little child. I knew your mother well. She was a sweet thing and life hurt her terribly. Life is cruel to us all but it was doubly cruel to her. She loved you so much, Brian."

Brian's heart swelled. This was wonderful. He had often wondered if his mother had loved him. He had been afraid she couldn't, when he was such a disgrace to her.

"She loved you," went on the Moon Man dreamily. "She used to kiss your little face and your little feet and your little hands when nobody saw her—nobody but the poor crazy old Moon Man. And she took such good care of you. There wasn't any baby taken such good care of, not even the rich folks' babies that came through a golden ring."

"But I hadn't any right to be born," said Brian. He had heard that so often.

The Moon Man looked at him curiously.

"Who knows? *I* don't think Edgely Dark had any right to be born when his mother hated and despised his father. But the clan thinks that is all right. It's a strange world, Brian. Good-night. I cannot stay longer. I have a tryst to keep—she's rising yonder over that dark hill, my beautiful Queen Moon. We all must have something to love. I have the best thing of all—the silver lady of the skies. Margaret Penhallow has a little grey house down yonder—foolish Margaret who is going to marry and desert her dream. Chris Penhallow loves his violin. He's given it up just now for the sake of an old shard but he'll go back to it. Roger Dark and Murray Dark, foolisher still, loving mortal women, disdaining the wisdom of the moon. But not so foolish as if they didn't love anything. What have you to love, Brian?"

"Nothing." Brian felt the tears coming into his eyes.

The Moon Man shook his head.

"Bad—very bad. Get something to love quick—or the devil will get hold of you."

"Mr. Conway says there isn't any devil,"said Brian.

"Not the devil of the Darks and Penhallows—no, there's no such devil as that. You needn't be afraid of the clan devil, Brian. But get something to love, child, or else God help you. Good-night. I'm glad I've met you."

Brian was glad, too, although he didn't understand more than half the Moon Man had said. Not only because one fear, at least, had gone out of his. life but because he knew that his mother had loved him—and had taken good care of him. That seemed wonderful to Brian, who could not remember any one taking care of him in his life. It must be very sweet to be taken care of.

So he had prayed to his mother, thinking that perhaps she might be able to take a little care of him yet if she knew he needed it so much. Then he had lain down on his poor bed, forgetting to stuff the sweater in the window. Presently there was a little scramble on the roof of the porch outside the loft, a dark little body and two moon-like eyes for a moment poised on the sill against the dim starlight—then a leap to the floor—the pad of tiny paws—a soft furry thing nestling to him—a silken tongue licking his cheek—a little body purring like a small dynamo. Cricket had come.

Brian gathered the little creature in his arms in rapture. He loved cats and Aunt Alethea would not have one around the place. Now he had a kitten of his own—a dear striped grey thing after his own heart, as he discovered when the dawn came. The kitten stayed with him all night but at the first hint of daylight it was off. Brian thought sadly he would never see it again. But every night since then it had come. Brian had no idea where it came from. It did not belong to the Dollars and there was no other house near. He believed his mother had sent it. She was still taking care of him.

Brian loved the little cat passionately and knew it loved him. It purred so ecstatically when he petted it. What comfort and companionship he found in it! He was no longer afraid of the rats. They never dared come out when

Cricket was there. And he was no longer lonely. He saved bits from his own scanty rations for Cricket, who was thin and evidently got none too much food, although occasionally he would bring a mouse in his own little jaws and eat it daintily on the loft floor. How Cricket enjoyed those morsels and how Brian enjoyed seeing him enjoy them, licking his small chops after them as if to salvage every ghost of flavour. Brian was desperately afraid his aunt would find out about Cricket. Suppose Cricket were to come in the day? But Cricket never came by day. Just at night he came to bring a message of love to a lonely child who had no friends.

And this night, too, Cricket came, just as Brian was beginning to feel really frightened that he was not coming. "Darling Cricket." Brian reached under his flat chaff pillow and drew out the bit of meat he had saved from his dinner. Hungry as he was himself, he never thought of eating it. He listened with a heart full of happiness to Cricket crunching it in the darkness and fell asleep with the kitten cuddled on his breast.

VII

It was spring again and Gay Penhallow was walking over a road she had walked with Noel a year ago—and remembering it. Calmly remembering it! Gay had reached the stage where she remembered these things calmly, as things that had happened long ago to somebody who was a quite different person. Some of the old sweetness had come back into life. One couldn't be altogether hopeless in spring. She was actually enjoying the charm of the May evening; she was conscious of the fact that she had on a very becoming new dress of young-leaf green with a little scarlet sweater. She wondered if Roger would like it.

All the familiar things that had once made life sweet wore beginning to make it sweet again. Yet there was always that little heartache under it all. A year ago she and Noel had walked down this road on just such an evening. There had been a misty new moon, just as to night; there had been the same gay little wind in the tree-tops and the same little smoky shadows under the young, white, wild cherry trees. And their steps and hearts had beaten time together and Gay had been thrilled with a rapture she would know no more.

She saw old Erasmus Dark whitewashing the trunks of his apple trees as she passed by his orchard, and envied him a little—done with all passions of life. Drowned John, Uncle Pippin and Stanton Grundy were talking at the latter's gate as she went by. Gay smiled at Uncle Pippin, whom she liked, and the radiance of it fell alike over Drowned John, whom she liked only moderately, and on Stanton Grundy, whom she did not like at all because he always seemed to be so cynically sceptical of the existence of things that were pure and lovely and of good report. She did not know that Grundy's glance followed her admiringly.

"An eyeful, eh—an eyeful," he remarked, nudging Uncle Pippin.

Drowned John nodded agreement. A thoroughbred, every inch of her. Showed her knees too much, of course. But at any rate knees that could be shown. Not like Virginia Powell's knees—knocks that affronted the daylight.

When Roger's car flashed past them and picked up Gay at the curve of the road, the three weather-beaten old farmers smiled quite sympathetically.

"Looks as if that would be a match yet," said Grundy.

"Fine—fine—except—isn't he a *little* too old for her?" asked Uncle Pippin anxiously.

"A husband older than herself would be a good thing for Gay," said Drowned John.

"If she marries Roger, will it be for love or loneliness?" queried Grundy drily.

"Love," said Drowned John, with an air of knowing all about it. "She's in love with Roger now, whether she knows it or not."

"I reckon she *can* love," said Grundy. "Some women can love and some can't, you know—just as some can cook and some can't."

"Well, it's a good thing kissing never goes out of fashion," said Uncle Pippin.

Roger thought Gay looked like a slim green dryad as she stood against the trees at the curve in the road. In spite of

the new moon and the shadows and the faint stars, she
made him think of morning. There was always something
of the dawn about her; her very hair seemed to laugh; the
little rosy lobes of her ears looked like unfolded apple
blossoms. And she was gazing at him with just the very
eyes a dryad should have.

"Hop in, Gay," he ordered laconically. Gay hopped,
thinking what a delightful voice Roger had, even when he
spoke curtly.

"Going anywhere in particular?"

"No. I just came out for a walk to escape Mrs. Toynbee.
She was at Maywood for supper and I nearly died of her."

"It's only female mosquitoes that bite," said Roger
cheerfully. "Where'll we go?"

"The shore road and step on the juice," laughed Gay.

The shore road. Had Gay forgotten the last time they
went along it? They whirled past the blueberry barrens
and the maple clearings, past the Silver Slipper and the
big empty hotel, on down to where the dunes lay, darkly
soft against a silvery sea. Roger stopped his car and they
sat in silence for awhile—one of those silences Gay loved.
It was so easy to be silent with Roger. There had never
been any silence with Noel—Noel was too much of a
talker to like silence.

The moon had gone down and the world lay in the
starlight. Starlight is a strange thing and not to be taken as
a matter of course. Roger suddenly fell under its magic
and did something he hadn't seen himself doing for a long
time yet.

"Gay," he said coolly, "I always do one wild thing every
spring. I'm going to do this spring's tonight. I'm going to
ask you to marry me."

Gay flushed beautifully—then turned very white.

"Oh, Roger—must you?" she said.

"Yes. I must. I can't stand this any longer. Either you've
got to marry me, Gay—or we must stop—all this."

"All this." All their jolly drives and talks together. All the
vivid companionship that had helped her through the
otherwise unbearable months behind. Gay felt desperately
that she could not lose it. She was so afraid of life. It is
dreadful and unnatural to be afraid of life in youth. But it

had played her such a trick. She must have some one to help her face it again. She didn't want to marry anyone, but if she had to, it might as well be Roger. He needed someone to take care of him—he worked so hard.

"You know I don't—love you, Roger," she whispered. "Not in *that* way."

"Yes, I know. That makes no difference," said Roger mendaciously.

"Then—" Gay drew a long sigh—"then I'll marry you, Roger—whenever you please."

"Thank you, dear," said Roger in a strangely quiet voice. Inside he was a seething volcano of joy and exultation. She would be his—his at last. He'd soon teach her to forget that popinjay. Love him. She'd love him fast enough—he'd see to that when the time came. Gay, darling adorable little Gay was his, with her wind-blown curls and her marigold eyes and the slim little feet that were made for dancing. Roger could have knelt and kissed those little feet. But he did not even kiss her lips. Only her little hands when he lifted her from the car at the end of their drive. Roger was wise—the time for kisses had not come yet. Gay was glad he did not kiss her. Even yet her lips seemed to belong to Noel. She went up to her room very quietly and sat for a long time behind her white curtains. She felt a little tired but content. Only she wished she could just find herself married to Roger without any preliminaries. The clan would be so odiously pleased. Their complacency would be hard to bear. What was it Mercy had said to her one day lately—"You'll find Roger will be the best for keeps"? No doubt he would be, but Gay knew if Roger and Noel were standing there before her, hers for the taking, to which one she would turn. Yet Roger, knowing this, still wanted to marry her.

Gay did one foolish secret thing before she went to sleep. She took the little rose-bowl, where the last rose leaves had been dropped on the night she was engaged to Noel, and went down with it to the gate at the side of the garden. The field before her was Artemas Dark's and the garden behind her was her mother's. But this wee green corner was *hers*; she dug out a hole under the trees with a trowel and buried the little rose-jar, patting the earth on the grave tenderly. All her childhood and girlhood were in it—all the happiness she had ever known. No matter what life held for her with Roger, there would be no more rose leaves for the little Wedgwood jar. It was sacred to something that was dead.

VIII

Penny and Margaret were not married yet. It was to have been in the spring; but when spring came Penny thought they'd better put it off to the fall. There were some alterations to make in the house; a new porch would be built and a hardwood floor laid in the dining-room. Margaret was very willing. She was no more eager for the happy day than Penny was.

In reality Penny was a rather miserable man. At times he fairly oozed dejection.

"Dash it," he informed the two Peters gloomily, "I've lost my enthusiasm."

He didn't want to break up his old habits—his comfortable ways of life. As for Aunt Ruth, certainly she had her faults. But he was used to them; it would be easier to put up with them than to get used to Margaret's new virtues. There wasn't really any danger of his dying in the night. He was good for twenty years yet.

He began to have horrible nightmares, in which he really found himself married—sewed up fast and hopelessly. It was an infernal sensation. He began to lose weight and a hunted look came into his eyes. Margaret was quite unconscious of this but the clan at large were not so blind, and bets were exchanged at the blacksmith's forge as to whether Penny's affair would ever come to a climax or not. The odds were against it, the general opinion being that Penny was simply stringing Margaret along until the matter of the jug should be decided.

"*Then* he'll squirm out of it some way, slick and clever," said Stanton Grundy. "Penny's nobody's fool."

Penny, however, felt like a fool. And when the incident of the merry-go-round occurred he felt more keenly than ever that Margaret would never do for a wife.

The merry-go-round affair did make considerable of a

stir. More people than Penny were scandalised. It was certainly an odd thing for a woman of Margaret's age to do. Had she no dignity? No sense of the fitness of things? No realisation that she was a Penhallow?

The merry-go-round was in the park in town. Margaret found herself looking wistfully at it one evening when Penny had taken her in for a drive and had gone to park his car before they settled down to listen to the band concert. Neither he nor Margaret cared for band concerts but hang it, a fellow had to do something to pass the time when he took his girl out.

Margaret had hankered all her life for a ride on the merry-go-round. There was something about it that fascinated her. She thought it would be delightful to mount one of those gay little horses and spin madly round and round. But she had never really thought of doing it. It was only a bright impossible dream.

Then she saw little Brian Dark looking at it longingly. Mr. Conway had brought Brian in and had gone off and left him. He did not mind giving the kid a drive but he had no money to waste on him, by gosh. Brian thought it would be a wonderful thing to have a ride on the merry-go-round. His little face was so wistful that Margaret smiled at him and said,

"Would you like a ride, Brian?"

"Oh, yes," whispered Brian. "But I haven't any money."

"Here's the dime," said Margaret. "Take it and have a good ride."

For a moment Brian was radiant. Then his face clouded over.

"Thank you," he stammered, "but—I guess—I don't know—I guess I'm a little scared to go alone," he concluded desperately.

Margaret could never quite understand and explain just what did come over her. The inhibitions of years fell away.

"Come with me. I'll go with you," she said.

And that was how Penny, returning a moment later, saw a sight that paralysed him with horror. Margaret—*his* Margaret—spinning furiously about on the merry-go-round—up and down—round and round—riding for dear life and *riding astride*. Her hat had fallen off and her loosened hair blew wildly round her face. Penny gave an agonised yelp but Margaret neither heard nor heeded. She was having the time of her life—she was—why, she was drunk or exactly like it, Penny thought in disgust. Her eyes were shining, her face was flushed. When the ride was ended Margaret wouldn't get off. She paid for herself and Brian for another ride—and then another. At the end of the third her senses returned to her and she got off dazedly. It did not need Penny's expression to make her thoroughly ashamed of herself.

"Oh, Penny—I'm sorry—I don't know what got into me," she gasped.

"You made a nice exhibition of yourself,"said Penny coldly.

"I know—I know—but oh—" for a moment that graceless exultation swept over Margaret again—"Oh, Penny, it was glorious. Why don't you try it yourself?"

"No, thank you." Penny was very dignified all the rest of the evening, and he snubbed Margaret on the way home. Margaret took it meekly, recognising his right and his just grievance. But she was not so meek when Mrs. Denzil tackled her a few days later about it. They had an actual fight over it. Margaret was by no means as unassertive as she used to be. Sometimes she spoke her mind with astonishing vim. Getting engaged, Mrs. Denzil told her, seemed to have gone to her head. Denzil soon settled them. He wasn't going to have any ructions among his womenfolk. He told Margaret she'd better mind her P's and Q's or she wouldn't get Penny after all. This did not alarm Margaret quite as much as Denzil expected. There were times when Margaret, in spite of her trousseau dresses and silk stockings, and the glamour of being Mrs., almost wished she had never promised to marry Penny— times when she wondered if it were not possible somehow to escape marrying him. She always concluded rather sadly that it wasn't. Nobody would believe anything but that Penny had thrown her over and Margaret couldn't face *that*. It would be too humiliating. She must go through with it.

Penny, however, had made up his mind after the merry-go-round that Margaret would never suit him—not with

that wild strain in her. Where on earth did she get it?
There was no Spanish blood in *her*. But how to get out of
it? *That* was the difficulty. The whole clan would cry
shame on him if he threw Margaret over. And Dandy
would never give him the jug. If he could only induce
Margaret to throw *him* over. Ah, there was an idea now!
But it would be no easy matter—no easy matter. Penny
had what he considered a veritable inspiration. He would
get drunk—ay, that was it. He would get drunk and go
drunk to the church garden-party at Bay Silver. Margaret
would be so disgusted that she would turn him down. He
knew her strict temperance principles. Hadn't he heard
her recite at a concert long ago, "Lips that touch liquor
shall never touch mine"? He would shock her till she was
blue round the gills, by gad he would. Of course there
would be a bit of scandal but he could soon live it down.
Lots of other men in the clan got stewed now and then.
He did not think it would seriously impair his chances for
the jug. Aunt Becky had said "addicted to drinking." You
couldn't be thought an addict on the ground of one spree.
It was over twenty-five years since he had been drunk
before and an election had been to blame for that. He had
been pretty offensive on that occasion. A prim old maid
like Margaret wouldn't stand for it. Penny chuckled. He
was as good as free.

Everybody was at the garden-party when Penny arrived
there. Nan and Noel were there; their wedding, which
was to have been in June, had been put off till September.
Gay and Roger were there. You had to go to your own
church garden-party, even though you would much rather
be away for a long moonlit spin together. Gay achieved a
careless, impudent little nod for Nan and Noel, though
her heart seemed to turn over in her breast at sight of
them. Joscelyn was there—and Hugh. Frank and Kate
were there, though the women thought Kate would be
better at home in her condition. But people had no shame
nowadays. The two Sams were there, carefully avoiding
each other. Big Sam came to get a square feed, but when
he saw Little Sam treating the Widow Terlizzick to hot-
dogs and ice-cream it spoiled the party for him.

A cog had slipped in Penny's plans. Most of the clan

perceived with a tolerant smile that Penny was more or
less lit up, but he was not actually drunk. He had only got
as far as the sentimental stage when it was suddenly
revealed to him that he was really desperately in love with
Margaret. By gad, she was a fine little woman—and he
was mad about her. He would go and tell her so. Had he
ever thought of jilting her? Never! He hunted out some
cloves and set out for Bay Silver, the ardent lover at last.

Margaret had visited Whispering Winds before coming
to the party. She went there as often as she could now,
because she knew that she would never see it again once
she was married to Penny. That night she had hung an old
iron pot on a tree and filled it with water for the birds.
The little garden was very sweet, with the perfume of
young wild ferns growing along the sagging fence. The
peace and dignity and beauty of it seemed to envelop her
like a charm. She wanted to stay there forever, alone with
the happy thoughts that came to her among its flowers and
grasses. Tears came into her eyes. She loathed the sparkle
of Penny's ring on her hand. It was a diamond—Penny
liked to do things handsomely and he was not mean—and
Margaret had once thought it would be a wonderful thing
to have a diamond engagement-ring. But now it was only a
fetter.

Margaret was surprised when Penny rushed to meet her
on the church grounds. She had a dreadful feeling that he
was going to kiss her right there before everybody; and
although he did not actually do it, it was certain she had a
narrow escape. Margaret was so innocent that she really
never suspected Penny's condition; but she was sure something queer had come over him. He was squeezing her
hand—he was gazing at her adoringly—he was—yes, he
was actually calling her "Little One."

"Little One," he was saying, "I had begun to think you
were never coming."

Margaret let Penny carry her off for a walk through the
graveyard. He insisted on walking with his arm around her
waist, which made her feel terribly self-conscious. From
the bottom of the graveyard there was a very fine view of
the gulf and the Rose River valley with the moon rising
over it.

"What a lovely moon," said Margaret desperately, because she had to say something. What *had* got into Penny?

"Oh, damn the moon," said Penny, aggrieved because Margaret was not so responsive as he thought she ought to be.

Margaret was shocked. She knew men swore but surely not in the presence of ladies they were engaged to. Penny might at least wait until they were married.

Penny made haste to apologise.

"I never could see much sense in admiring the moon," he explained, "but I only said that because I want you to think about *me* and not about the moon. Forgive me, Little One. I won't say naughty words again before my own sweetest."

"We—we ought to get back to the grounds," said Margaret confusedly. Really, this love-making which was so attractive in fancy, was nothing more or less than dreadful in reality. "We won't get a good seat if we are late."

"I don't care where I sit as long as I sit with you, my darling," said Penny.

Penny sat with his arm around Margaret all through the programme, oblivious to the giggles of the young fry and the amused grins of the oldsters. He squeezed Margaret's hand at all the sentimental passages in the songs, and he told her she had the finest pair of legs in the clan, by gad, she had!

Margaret, who had always secretly thought her slender, well-shaped legs rather nice, nevertheless belonged to a generation that did not discuss legs. She was embarrassed and tucked her legs blushingly out of sight under the plank she sat on, To turn the conversation into safer channels, she told Penny that Nigel Penhallow had called to see her on his recent visit from New York and had told her he wouldn't be surprised if that old *Pilgrim's Progress* Aunt Becky had given her turned out to be of some value. It was a very old edition and in fair condition. He had offered to find out just what it was worth. Margaret wondered if she hadn't better let him. Penny advised against selling it.

"I've enough for our comfort, Little One, and"—Penny was on the verge of tears by now—"when I'm gone,

Mar'gret, there'll be enough to keep you in decent widowhood."

Margaret had not yet accustomed herself to the thought of being Penny's wife. The idea of being his widow overcame her. She went home very unhappy. Penny had almost wept when he kissed her good-night. And, having heard someone ask her if her sore throat were better, he could not leave her until she had promised to tie a stocking round her throat when she went to bed. If he cared as much as this for her she must be faithful to him.

5
BLINDLY WISE

▼

I

"That damn' jug will be the death of some of us yet," said
Uncle Pippin viciously.

For it had come out that the reason Walter Dark's pig
was where it should not have been that particular afternoon, was because Walter was having a spat in his yard
with Palmer Penhallow about who should get the jug.
They were so hot about it that Walter did not notice
before it was too late that his pig had got out of its pen at
the barn and was scooting down the lane to the road.
When Walter did see it and started in pursuit, the pig was
already out on the King's Highway and before Walter
could even yell, the whole thing happened.

Young Prince Dark and Milton Granger were spinning
up the road in Prince's motor-cycle. Hugh Dark was
coming down the road in his car, on his way home from a
political convention where it had been as good as decided
that he was to be his party's candidate at the forthcoming
Provincial election. It had been one of Hugh's ambitions
for years but he felt no elation over its realisation. He was
not thinking of it at all as he drove moodily along through
the amber haze of the warm July afternoon, past sunny old
pastures and rose-sweet lanes, friendly gardens full of

wine-hued hollyhocks, misty river shores, old stone dykes under the dark magic of the spruce woods, and windy hills where the fir trees were blowing gaily and the tang of the sea met him. All the beauty of the world around him suggested only thoughts of Joscelyn. Suppose he were going home to Treewoofe to tell *her* of the honour that had come to him. Suppose when he got out at his gate Joscelyn were meeting him with the wind of the hill ruffling her red-gold curls, eager to know what had happened at the convention—ready to console or congratulate, as the event required. It would be worth while then. But now—dust and ashes.

At this moment everything happened at once. Walter Dark's pig had reached the road. Prince Dark, tearing onward at his usual headlong rate, struck it before he could turn or slow down. Prince and Granger were both thrown out by the impact, Prince flying clean across the ditch against the fence and Granger being hurled like a stone into the ditch itself. The pig lay calmly, too dead to tell what he thought about it, and the motor-cycle shot blindly across the road. Hugh swerved sharply to avoid it. His car skidded in a circle. Everything suddenly became doubly clear. All the colours of the landscape took on an incredible vividness and brilliancy. Also the whole affair seemed to take an interminable time, during which he lived over all the emotions of his life and loved and hated and despaired for an eternity. Then the car went over the edge of the little ravine that skirted the road, just as Walter's belated yell rent the air and the group of men before the blacksmith's forge awoke to the fact that a tragedy had been enacted before their eyes.

Wild confusion followed for a space. Uncle Pippin frantically implored them to keep their heads. The conscious Prince and the unconscious Granger were picked up and carried in, the latter with an ear almost sliced off. Hugh's car was upside down in the ditch with Hugh still clutching the wheel. When he was eventually extricated he gasped Joscelyn's name twice before relapsing into complete unconsciousness. By the time the three victims had been taken to the hospital and Walter Dark had sadly dragged his dead pig home on a stone boat, uneasily speculating whether Prince Dark could sue him for damages or whether he had a case against Prince for killing a valuable pig, the news of the accident had spread to Bay Silver in a garbled fashion that left everyone in doubt as to who was killed and who were maimed for life, and Joscelyn was walking up and down her room in a frenzy of suspense and dread. What really had happened? Was Hugh badly hurt or—she would not let herself even think the word. And she could not go to him. He would not want her. He had no need of her. She meant nothing to him—she who had once meant so much. She could not even telephone to find out the truth about the affair. Anyone—everyone else—could make inquiries but not she. Meanwhile she would go mad; she could not endure it; she had been a fool and an idiot, but even fools and idiots can suffer. Once she paused with clenched hands and looked at Treewoofe. The day had been cloudy by times but now the sun suddenly came out and performed its usual miracle. The hill swam in loveliness and Treewoofe—her home—her *home*—shone on it like a jewel. Was Hugh there—dead—suffering? And she could not go to him! Perhaps Pauline was there!

"If I think things like this I'll lose my senses," moaned Joscelyn. "Oh, God, dear God, I know I was a fool. But haven't You any pity for fools? There are so many of us."

Joscelyn had to endure as best she could until the evening. And yet, amid all her agony, she was conscious of an exultation that she had this to be in anguish over. Anguish was not so dreadful as the emptiness that had been her life of late. Then Uncle Pippin called and told them the truth. Things were not so bad after all. Prince and Hugh were not seriously hurt. Prince was already home, and Hugh was still in the hospital, suffering from slight concussion, but would be all right in a few days. Young Granger was the worst; he had nearly lost an ear and was still unconscious, but the doctors thought he would recover and meanwhile they had sewed on his ear.

"I hope it will cure Prince of that habit of reckless driving," said Uncle Pippin, shaking his head, "but I dunno's anything will do that. He was swearing dreadful when we picked him up; I rebuked him. I says. 'Any one that's been as near the pearly gates as you was two minutes ago hadn't ought to swear like that,' but he just kept on. He damned that poor pig up and down and the universe thrown in."

"I didn't like the way the wind sobbed last night," said Aunt Rachel, shaking her head. "I knew sorrow was a-coming. This proves it."

"But sorrow hasn't come—Hugh wasn't badly hurt," cried Joscelyn involuntarily. She was so suddenly light-hearted in her release from torture that she hardly knew what she was saying.

"What about poor young Granger in the hospital, with his ear off?" said Aunt Rachel reproachfully.

"And the pig?" said Uncle Pippin. "It was sorrow enough for the pig."

II

Joscelyn, coming home across lots from an errand to the harbour, paused for a moment at the little gate in Simon Dark's pasture that opened on the side road leading down to Bay Silver. It was a windy, dark grey night, cold for August, with more than a hint of nearing autumn in it. Between the gusts of wind the air was full of the low continuous thunder of the sea. Low in the west was a single strip of brilliant primrose against which the spire of a church stood up blackly. Above it was the dark sullen beauty of the heavy stormclouds. Everywhere, on the hills and along the roads, trees were tossing haglike in the wind. A group of them overhanging the gate was like a weird cluster of witches weaving unholy spells.

The summer—another summer—was almost over; asters and goldenrod were blooming along the red roads; goldfinches wore eating the cosmos and sunflower seeds in the gardens; and in a little over a month the matter of the jug would be decided. Clan interest was again being keenly worked up over it. Dandy had kept his mouth shut immovably and nobody knew anything more about it than at the start.

But Joscelyn cared nothing who got the jug. She was glad to be alone with the night—especially this kind of a night. It was in keeping with her own stormy mood. She liked to hear the wild night wind whistling in the reeds of the swamp in the corner of the pasture—she liked to hear its sweep in the trees above her.

She had been tempest-tossed all day. In such stress she was accustomed to think that peace was all she asked or desired. But now she faced the thought that she wanted much—much more. She wanted womanhood and wifehood—she wanted Hugh and Treewoofe—she wanted everything she had wanted before her madness came upon her.

Everything beautiful had gone out of her life. She had lived for years in a fool's paradise of consecration to a great passion. Now that she had been rudely made wise, life was so unbelievably poor—thin—barren—so bitterly empty. If Frank had never come home she could have gone on loving him. But she could not love the tubby, middle-aged husband of Kate and the prospective father of Kate's baby. Life, with all its fineness and vulgarity, its colour and drabness, its frenzy and its peace, seemed to have passed her by utterly and to be laughing at her over its shoulder.

Nothing was talked of in the clan just now but weddings—Nan and Noel, Gay and Roger, Penny and Margaret, Little Sam and the Widow Terlizzick—even Donna and Peter. For Peter was home again, and report said he had come for Donna and would have her in Drowned John's very teeth. As Uncle Pippin said, Cupid was busy. Amid all this chatter of marrying and giving in marriage, Joscelyn felt like a nonentity—and nobody, least of all a Penhallow with Spanish blood in her, likes to feel like a nonentity.

It was not quite dark yet—not too dark to see Treewoofe. The hill had been austere all that day, under the low, flying grey clouds. Now it was withdrawn and remote. One solitary light loomed on it through the stormy dusk. Was Hugh there—alone? Suppose he did really love Pauline and wanted to be free? The thought of Pauline was like a poison. Pauline had gone to see him when he was in the hospital. But so had every other Dark and Penhallow in the clan—except Joscelyn and her mother and aunt.

Sometimes, as now, Joscelyn felt that if she could not discover the answer to certain questions that tortured her she would go wholly mad.

She did not see Mrs. Conrad Dark until they were fairly

face to face over the gate. Joscelyn started a little as she
recognised the tall, dark, forbidding woman before her.
Then she stood very still. She had not seen Mrs. Conrad
for a long while. Now, even in the gloom, she could
recognise that hooded look of hers as she brooded her
venom.

"So?" said Mrs. Conrad tragically. Stanton Grundy had
once said that Mrs. Conrad always spoke tragically, even if
she only asked you to pass the pepper. But now she had a
fitting setting for her tragic tone and a fitting object. She
leaned across the gate and peered into Joscelyn's face.
They were both tall women—Joscelyn a little the taller. People had once said that the main reason Mrs. Conrad didn't
like Joscelyn was that she didn't want a daughter-in-law
she would have to look up to.

"So it's you—Joscelyn Penhallow. H'm—very sleek—very
handsome—not quite so young as you once were."

Convention fell away from Joscelyn. She felt as if she
and Mrs. Conrad were alone in some strange world where
nothing but realities mattered.

"Mrs. Dark," she said slowly, "why have you always
hated me—not just since—since—since I married Hugh—
but before it?"

"Because I knew you didn't love Hugh enough," answered
Mrs. Conrad fiercely. "I hated you on your wedding-night
because you didn't deserve your happiness. I knew you
would play fast and loose with him in some way. Do you
know there hasn't been a night since your wedding that I
haven't prayed for evil to come on you. And yet—if you'd
go back to him and make him happy—I'd—I'd forgive you.
Even you."

"Go back to him. But does he want me back? Doesn't
he—doesn't he love Pauline?"

"Pauline! I wish he did. *She* wouldn't have broken his
heart—she wouldn't have made him a laughingstock. I
used to pray he would love her. But she wasn't pretty
enough. Men have such a cursed hankering for good looks.
You had him fast—snared in the gold of your hair. Even
yet—even yet. When he was fainting on the road down
there, after the accident that might have killed him—he

called for you—you who had left him and shamed him—it was you he wanted when he thought he was dying."

A fierce pang of joy stabbed through Joscelyn. But she would not let Mrs. Conrad suspect it.

"Isn't he going to sell Treewoofe?"

"Sell Treewoofe! Sometimes I'm afraid he will—and go God knows where—my dearest son."

Something gave way in Mrs. Conrad. Joscelyn's apparent immobility maddened her. She let loose all the suppressed hatred of years. She shouted—she cried—she raved—she leaned across the gate and tried to shake Joscelyn. In short she made such a show of herself that all the rest of her life she went meekly and humbly before Joscelyn, remembering it. Uncle Pippin, ambling along the side road from a neighbourly call, heard her and paused in dismay. Two women fighting—two women of the clan—they must be of the clan, for nobody but Darks and Penhallows lived just around there. It must be Mrs. Sim Dark and Mrs. Junius Penhallow. They were always bickering, though he could not recollect that they had ever made such a violent scene as this in public before. What if Stanton Grundy should hear of it? It must be put a stop to. Little Uncle Pippin valiantly trotted up to the gate and attempted to put a stop to it.

"Now, now," he said. "This is most unseemly!"

Just then he discovered that it was Joscelyn Dark and her mother-in-law. Uncle Pippin felt that he had rushed in where both angels and fools might fear to tread.

"I—I beg your pardon," he said feebly, "I just thought it was someone fighting over Aunt Becky's jug again."

It was quite unthinkable that Joscelyn and Mrs. Conrad could be rowing over the jug. Since it couldn't be the jug it must be Hugh, and Uncle Pippin, who was not lacking in sense of a kind—as he put it himself, he knew how many beans made five—understood that this was no place for a nice man.

"Pippin," said Mrs. Conrad, rather breathlessly but still very tragically, "go home and thank the good Lord He made you a fool. Only fools are happy in this world."

Uncle Pippin went. And if he did not thank the Lord for being a fool he did at least thank Him devoutly that he still had the use of his legs. He paused when he got to the main road to wipe the perspiration from his brow.

"A reckless woman that—a very reckless woman," said Uncle Pippin sadly.

III

Nan was in the room before Gay had heard any sound. She had never been to Maywood since the night at the Silver Slipper—Gay had never met her alone since then. Occasionally they met at clan affairs, where Nan had always greeted Gay affectionately and mockingly and Gay had been cool and aloof. The clan thought Gay handled the situation very well. They were proud of her.

Gay looked up in amazement and anger from her seat by the window. What was Nan doing here? How dared she walk into one's room like that, unannounced, uninvited? Nan, smiling and insolent, in a yellow frock with a string of amber beads on her neck and long dangling amber earrings, with her blood-red mouth and her perfumed hair and her sly green eyes. What business had Nan here?

"Has she come," thought Gay, "to ask me to be her bridesmaid? She would be quite capable of it."

"You don't look overjoyed to see me, honey," said Nan, coolly depositing herself on Gay's bed and proceeding to light a cigarette. Gay reflected rather absently that Nan was wearing that ring she was so fond of—a ring that Gay always hated—with a pale-pink stone cabachon, looking exactly as if a lump of flesh were sticking through the ring. The next moment Gay felt an odd sensation tingling over her. Where was Noel's diamond? And what was Nan saying?

"And yet I've come to tell you something you'll be glad to hear. I've broken my engagement with Noel. Sent him packing, in short. You can have him after all, Gay."

Long after she had spoken, the words seemed to Gay to be vibrating in the atmosphere. It seemed to Gay a long, long time before she heard herself saying coolly,

"Do you think I want him now?"

"Yes, I think you do," said Nan insolently. She could make any tone—any movement—insolent. "Yes, in spite of

that big diamond of Roger's"—ah, Gay knew very well
Nan had been jealous of that diamond—"and in spite of
the new bungalow going up at Bay Silver, I think you want
Noel as badly as you ever did. Well, you're quite welcome
to him, dear. I just wanted to show you I could get him.
Do you remember telling me I couldn't?"

Yes, Gay remembered. She sat very still because she
was afraid if she moved an eyelash she would cry. Cry,
before Nan! This girl who had flung Noel Gibson aside like
a worn-out toy.

"Of course it will give the clan the tummy-ache," said
Nan. "Their ideas about engagements date back to the
Neolithic. Even Mother! Although in her heart she's glad,
too. She wants me to marry Fred Margoldsby at home,
you know. I daresay I will. The Margoldsby dollars will
last longer than love. I really was a little bit in love with
Noel. But he's getting fat, Gay—he really is. He's got the
beginnings of a corporation. Fancy him at forty. And he
had got into such a habit of telling me his troubles."

Gay suddenly realised that this was true. It struck her
that Noel had always had a good many troubles to tell.
And she remembered as suddenly that he had never
seemed much interested in *her* troubles. But she wished
Nan would stop talking and go away. She wanted to be
alone.

Nan was talking airily on.

"So I'm going to Halifax for a visit. Mother, of course,
won't leave till she knows who is to get that potty old jug.
Do you ever think, Gay, that if Aunt Becky—God rest her
soul—hadn't left that jug as she did, you'd probably have
been married to Noel by now?"

Gay *had* thought of it often—thought of it bitterly,
rebelliously, passionately. She was thinking it again now,
but with a curious feeling of detachment, as if the Gay
who might have been married to Noel were some other
person altogether. If only Nan would go!

Nan was going. She got up and flung another gratuitous
piece of advice insolently to Gay.

"So, Gay dear, just tell your middle-aged beau that you
don't want a consolation prize after all and warm up the
cold soup with Noel."

Really, Nan could be very odious when she liked. Yet somehow she didn't hate her as before. She felt very indifferent to her. She found herself looking at her with cool, appraising eyes, seeing her as she had never seen her before. An empty, selfish little creature, who had always to be amused like a child. A girl who said "hell" because she thought it would shock her poor old decent clan. A girl who thought she was doing something very clever when she publicly powdered her nose with the unconcern of a cat washing its face in the gaze of thousands. A girl who passed as a sophisticate before her country cousins but who was really more provincial than they were, knowing nothing of real life or real love or real emotion of any kind. Gay wondered, as she looked, how she could ever have hated this girl—ever been jealous of her. She was not worth hating. Gay spoke at last. She stood up and looked levelly at Nan. There was contempt in her quiet voice.

"I suppose you came here to hurt me, Nan. You haven't— you can never hurt me again. You've lost the power. I think I even feel a little sorry for you. You've always been a taker, Nan. All through your life you've taken whatever you wanted. But you've never been a giver—you couldn't be because you've nothing to give. Neither love nor truth nor understanding nor kindness nor loyalty. Just taking all the time and giving nothing—oh, it has made you very poor. So poor that nobody need envy you."

Nan shrugged her shoulders.

"Please omit flowers," she said. But her subtle air of triumph had left her. She went out with an uneasy feeling that Gay had had the best of it.

Left alone, Gay sat down by her window again. Everything seemed different—changed. She wished this hadn't happened. It had unsettled her. She had been so contented before Nan came—even happy. Thinking of the new bungalow Roger was building for their home.

"I want to build a house for *you*," he had said, his eyes looking deep into hers with a look that was like a kiss. "A house that will be a home to come to when I'm tired—on a little hill so that we'll have a view, but not a hill like

Treewoofe—too high above all the rest of the world. A house with *you* in it, Gay, to welcome me."

They had planned it together. The clan overwhelmed them with floods of advice but they took none of it. It was to have one window that faced the sea and another that looked on the dreamy, over-harbour hills. And a quaint little eyebrow window in the roof.

They would be able to look through their open dining-room door into the heart of a blooming apple tree in its season—a hill of white blossom against the blue sky—to eat supper there and see the moonrise behind it. There was a clump of cool, white birches at one corner. A spruce bush behind it where dear little brown owls lived. Gay had been so interested in everything. Her bathroom was to be mauve and pale yellow. She would have window-boxes of nasturtiums and petunias and Kenilworth ivy. She was thinking about nice linen—nice little teacups. The wedding was to be in late October. The clan had really behaved beautifully—although Gay knew what they were saying behind her back.

And now everything was tangled up again. Gay walked late that night, in the old Maywood garden that lay fragrant and velvety under the enchantment of a waning moon. The ghost of a lost happiness came and mocked her. Noel was free again. And Gay knew that what Nan had said was true. She *did* want him—with all her heart she wanted him still—and she had to marry Roger in October.

IV

Peter Penhallow was finding out the fun of really trying to get something. After a year in Amazonian jungles, where, when his temper had cooled, he spent most of his time longing to hear Donna's exquisite laugh again, he had come home to make it up with her. Never doubting that he would find her as ready and eager to "make up" as he was. Peter knew very little about women and still less about a woman who was the daughter of Drowned John. He arrived Saturday night, much to the surprise of his family, who had supposed him still in South America, and had promptly telephoned Donna—or tried to. Old Jonas answered the phone and said all the folks were away—he didn't know where.

Peter chewed his nails in frenzy until next morning, when he saw Donna across the church. His darling—unchanged—with the mournful shadows under her eyes and her dark, cloud-like hair. What a pair of fools they had been to quarrel over nothing! How they would be laughing over it presently!

Donna got the shock of her life when she saw Peter looking at her across the church. Outwardly she took it so coolly that Virginia, who was watching her anxiously, threw her eyes up at the ceiling in relief.

Donna had hated Peter furiously for over a year and it seemed now that she hated him more than ever. After the first startled glance she would not look at him again. When church came out he strode across the green to meet her—exultantly, triumphantly, masterfully. That was where he made a fatal mistake! If he had been a little timid—a little less cocksure—if he had shown himself a repentant, ashamed Peter, creeping back humbly for pardon, Donna, in spite of her hate, might have flung herself on his neck before everybody. But to come like this—as if they had parted yesterday—as if he had not behaved outrageously to her when they *had* parted—as if he had not ignored her existence for a year, sending never a word or message—expressing no contrition—coming smiling towards her as if he expected her to be grateful to him for forgiving *her*—which was exactly what Peter *did* expect—no, it was really too much. Donna, after one level, contemptuous glance, turned her back on Peter and walked away.

Peter looked rather foolish. Some boys standing near giggled. Virginia swept after Donna to help her through this ordeal. And, "Don't be so—emotional," was all the thanks she got.

Drowned John wanted to swear but couldn't, realising thankfully that in little over a month more the affair of the jug would be settled and free speech once more be possible. Finally Peter turned away and went home, lost in wonder at himself for putting up with all this just to get a woman.

Peter's next attempt was to stalk down to Drowned

John's, walk into the house without knocking, and demand Donna. Drowned John raved, stamped and played the heavy parent to perfection—yet still—will it be believed? —did not swear. Peter would have cared little for Drowned John if he could have seen Donna but not a glimpse could he get of her. He went home, defeated, asking himself for the hundreth time why he endured this sort of thing. It was really an obsession. Donna wasn't worth it—no feminine creature in the world was worth it. But he meant to have her for all that. He was not going to endure another such year as he had endured among the upper reaches of the Amazon. Sooner would he knock Donna over the head and carry her off bodily. It never occurred to Peter that all he had to do was to ask forgiveness for that night at the west gate. Nor, had it occurred to him, would he have done it. It had been all Donna's fault. *He* was forgiving *her*—most magnanimously, without a word of reproach. And yet she seemed to expect him to crawl on all fours for her.

Eventually, finding it impossible to obtain speech with Donna, Peter wrote her a letter—probably the worst letter that was ever written in the world for such a purpose. Donna got it herself at the post-office and, although she had never seen Peter's large, black, untidy handwriting before, knew at once that it had come from him. She carried it home and sat down before it in her room. She thought she ought to return it to him unopened. Virginia would advise that, she was sure. But if she did, she knew she would spend the rest of her life wondering what had been in it.

Eventually she opened it. It was a blunt epistle. There was no word of repentance—or even of love in it. Peter told her he was leaving in a week's time for South Africa, where he meant to spend four years photographing lions in their native haunts. Would she come with him or would she not?

This take-or-leave-it epistle infuriated Donna, when one "darling" or even an X for a kiss might have melted her into a forgiveness that hadn't been asked for. Before her rage could cool she had torn the letter four times across, put it in an envelope and directed it to Peter.

"I'll *never* forgive him," she said through set teeth. It
was a comfort to articulate the words. It made her feel
more sure of herself. In her heart she was afraid she *might*
forgive him. She dared not leave the letter lying on her
table all night, lest her resolution fail her, so she went
down and gave it to old Jonas to mail on his way to town.
Then, the thing being irrevocable she went to her father
and told him she was going away to train as a nurse,
whether he was willing or not. Drowned John, who was
thoroughly fed up with having a sulky thunderstorm at
table and hearth for a year, told her she could go and be
dinged to her. Whatever theological difference there may
be between "damn" and "ding," there was none whatever
in Drowned John's meaning or intonation.

As for Peter, when he got back his torn letter, he gave
himself up to hate for a time and hated everything and
everybody, living or dead. So matters stood until the night
Dandy Dark's house burned down.

V

The old Moon Man went singing softly through the
quiet September night, under a silvery harvest moon. He
went along by the dim ghostly shore of the Indian Spring
river, past friendly old fields where the wind purred like a
big cat, through woods where the trees were talking about
him, along lanes where there was a stippling of moonlight
on the narrow grassy path and over hills where he paused
to listen to eternity. He was very happy and he pitied the
poor folks asleep in the houses as he went by. They did not
know what they were missing.

It was he who first saw that Dandy Dark's house,
perched on the shoulder of a small wooded hill where the
road turned down to Bay Silver, was on fire. The flames
were already bursting out of the roof of the ell when the
Moon Man thundered on the door and a drowsy hired boy
shuffled down from the kitchen chamber to demand what
was up. The Moon Man told him and then strode calmly
off. Their life was no longer any concern of his. He was not
going to lose another minute of this beautiful night for it.
Behind him he left alarm and confusion. Dandy Dark was

away—nobody knew where. Dandy had taken to staying out late at nights, though as yet nobody knew of it except his wife. But the clan at large knew that something had come over Dandy in the past few weeks. He was changed. Unsociable, uneasy, irritable, absent-minded. Some put it down to the fact that the date for the jug decision was drawing near and argued that the decision must be in Dandy's hands, since he was so manifestly uncomfortable about it. Either that, or something had happened to the jug. Nobody dared ask Dandy about it; he positively snapped now if any one referred to the jug. But everybody more or less was beginning to feel uneasy, too. And now Dandy's house was burning. The hired boy had yelled down the hall for Mrs. Dandy, had roused a neighbour on the phone and had dashed to the barn for ladders. In an incredibly short time a crowd had gathered, but from the first it was manifest that the house was doomed. They had got out most of the furniture and were grimly watching the spectacle when Dandy arrived home.

"Good Gosh," cried Dandy, "where is the jug?"

Incredible as it may seen, nobody had thought about the jug. Everybody stared at each other. There was no one to ask. Mrs. Dandy, when the hired boy roused her, had promptly run out of the front door in her night-dress and fainted in a corner of the garden. Foolish Mrs. Dandy was noted for doing things like that. She had been carried over to Penny Dark's house on the next farm and was being attended to there.

"Doesn't *anyone* know anything about the jug?" howled Dandy, losing his head completely and running wildly about, clawing over the stuff that had been saved from his blazing roof-tree.

"Where was it kept?" shouted somebody.

"In the spare-room closet," moaned Dandy.

Nothing had been saved from the spare room. It was far down the upstairs hall in the ell and the hall had been too full of smoke to reach it.

Peter was standing among the crowd. He had been among the first to arrive and had worked heroically. And now they had not saved the jug. The jug Donna wanted so much—the old jug Aunt Becky had told him tales of in his childhood—the jug that had ruined his elopement and wrecked his hopes. Peter snatched a reeking coat that was hanging on the fence, flung it over his head and dashed into the house. He must save that jug for Donna.

Everyone yelled after him and then went made. The yard was filled with dancing, shouting frantic figures, among which suddenly appeared a raving maniac of a boy from Penny Dark's who gasped out a horrifying question. Where was Donna Dark? She had been staying all night with Mrs. Dandy—she had been sleeping in the spare room—was she safe?

Some women fainted with a better excuse than Mrs. Dandy. Some went shrieking about for Donna. The men gazed at each other and then at the burning house. They shook their heads. It was a madman's attempt to enter that house now. Peter would be burned to death, trying to save Donna—for nobody now doubted it was Donna he had gone to save. He must have heard what the boy was saying before any one else did,

Peter had gone up the blazing staircase three steps at a time, ready to plunge into the inferno of smoke and flame that had been the hall, when he stumbled and almost fell over the unconscious form of a woman lying on the floor at the head of the stairs.

Good God, who was it? She must be rescued, jug or no jug. He picked her up and turned back with a feeling of regret. No hope of the jug now. Poor Donna would be bitterly disappointed. He stumbled down the stairs and out of the door into the seething crowd. The yells and shouts changed suddenly to hurrahs. Peter was a hero. Eager hands took his slim white burden from him. Drowned John, who had just driven in, having heard of the fire but not of Donna's danger until he arrived there—was shaking his hand and sobbing, with tears running down his face.

"God bless you, Peter—you saved her—God bless you for saving Donna—my poor little motherless girl—" Drowned John was almost maudlin—people had to lead him away and calm him down, while Peter stood very still and tried to realise that it was Donna whom he had carried out of Dandy Dark's burning house. Donna!

"She kem up today to help me make the baked damson

preserve," sobbed Mrs. Dandy on the kitchen lounge at
Penny Dark's. "I never did or could seem able to bake
damsons so as to please Dandy. Donna knew how—Dandy's
mother taught her 'fore she died—so I asked her if she'd
come up and do 'em for me. They're all burned up now. It
looked like rain at supper-time and Dandy was away—he's
always away now, it seems to me—so I told Donna she
might as well stay all night. Oh, dearie me, to think wha'
might have happened!"

"The jug's gone, though," said William Y. gloomily.

"The jug? *It* ain't broken?" cried Mrs. Dandy shrilly.

"It's burned up with all the rest of the spare-room
things."

"Oh, no, it ain't." Mrs. Dandy looked very sly and
cunning. "When I put Donna to sleep in the spare room I
took the jug in its box outen the closet and took it down to
my own room. I didn't know what Dandy might of said to
me if I'd left that jug in the same room with *anybody*.
Folks say I'm silly but I'm not so silly as that. And when I
heard Tyler yelling fire I grabbed holt of that box first
thing along with the old teapot with the broken spout I
keep my bit of money in, and run out with them and
dropped them over the fence into the burdocks in the
back yard. I reckon you'll find them there."

Find them there they did, much to everybody's relief.
Donna had come to her senses and had been taken to the
hospital, and everybody went home through the pale-
yellow, windy dawn, telling tales about the fire. One of the
funniest was that of Penny Dark, who, summoned to the
telephone from his bed, had lost his head and torn over to
Dandy's place in his pajamas. Worse still, in trying to
climb over the picket fence back of Dandy's barn, he
slipped and the waist cord of his pajamas had caught on a
picket. There poor Penny had hung, yelping piteously,
until some one had heard him above all the din and
rescued him. Most people thought it served him right for
wearing pajamas. It had been suspected for several years
that he did but nobody ever was really sure, for old Aunt
Ruth had kept his secret well.

"And Happy Dark is home," said Sim Dark. "Walked in
last night after his mother had gone to bed, ate the supper

she'd left, and the went to sleep in his own room. *She* didn't know it till he come down to breakfast this morning. Said he'd met an old crony in Singapore who gave him an old Charlottetown paper to read. It was the one where that fool reporter had writ up the story of the jug. Happy said he thought he might as well come home and see what his chances were for it. His mother's so uplifted she can hardly talk. Just sits and looks at him."

But among all the events of that night, the really tragic one was not talked over at the clan breakfast-tables because it was not known until several days later. Christopher Dark, drunk as usual, had run in at the kitchen door of the burning building unseen of anybody, and had been killed by a falling beam. People supposed he must have been making a crazy effort to save the jug. The clan was properly stirred up over the dreadful end of poor Chris, but under all their horror was a calm conviction that everything was for the best. One disgrace to the clan was ended.

Murray Dark looked at his house proudly when he came home from the funeral.

"We'll soon have a mistress for you now," he said.

Donna sent for Peter as soon as she was allowed to see anybody, and begged him to forgive her. She knew now that he really did love her, in spite of everything, or he would never have dashed into that blazing house to save her. Peter did not undeceive her. He remembered that he had once heard Stanton Grundy say that life would be unbearable if we didn't believe a few lies. The deception sat lightly on Peter's conscience, for he knew that if he had dreamed for a moment that Donna was, or even might be, in that doomed house he would have gone through it from cellar to attic for her.

"But no more eloping," said Donna. "I'll marry you in the open, in spite of Father's teeth."

Drowned John, however, showed no teeth. He told Donna that since Peter had saved her life he deserved to get her and she could go and photograph lions in Africa with his blessing. The first time Peter went to Drowned John's after Donna came home, Drowned John shook hands genially with him and took him out to see his favourite pig. Peter concluded that, after all, Drowned John was a great old boy..

"Well, here's congratulations," said Roger, meeting Peter coming beamingly out of the west gate.

"Thanks. And I hear you're to be congratulated, too."

Roger's face hardened.

"I don't know. Are congratulations in order if you are going to marry a girl who is in love with another man?"

"So? It's that way still?"

"Still."

"And you *are* going to marry her?"

"I am. Congratulate me now if you dare."

VI

Joscelyn Dark wakened one September morning, knowing that something was going to happen that day. She had received some sign in her sleep. She sat up and looked out of her window. The sunlight of dawn was striking on Treewoofe, although the lower slopes were still in shadow. Around it golden grain fields lay in the beauty of harvesting. The air was rose and silver and crystal. The house seemed to beckon to her. All at once she knew what was to happen that day. She would go to Hugh and ask him if he could forgive her.

She had wanted to go ever since the night she had met Mrs. Conrad, but she had not been able to summon up enough courage. And now, in some mysterious way, the courage had come. She would learn the truth. Whatever it might be, sweet or bitter, it would be more bearable than this intolerable suspense.

She could not go before evening. The day seemed long; it hated to go out; it lingered on the red roads, on the tops of the silver dunes, on the red ploughed summer fallow on the shoulder of Treewoofe. Not until it had really gone and the full moon was shining over the Treewoofe birches did Joscelyn dare to set out. Her mother and Aunt Rachel had gone to prayer-meeting, so that there was no one to question her. Old Miller Dark shortly overtook her in his buggy and offered her a "lift," which Joscelyn accepted because she knew it would offend poor old Miller if she refused. In her high rapt mood she did not want to see or ride with anyone. Old Miller was in a great good humour; he had just about finished his history of the clan. Meant to have it published in book form, and would she subscribe for a copy? Joscelyn said she would take two; she wondered if old Miller had put anything about her and Hugh in. He was quite capable of it.

Joscelyn got out at William Y.'s gate. Old Miller supposed she was going to see the William Y.'s and she let him think so. But as soon as he had disappeared around the wooded curve she walked up the Three Hills road to Treewoofe. The air was keen and frosty; the waves far down on the bay quivered as if they were tipsy with moonlight: it was just such another night as her wedding-night had been, eleven years ago. What a fool she had been? Hugh could never forgive her. She was seized with a spasm of panic and was on the point of turning and running madly down the hill.

But Treewoofe was close to her—dear frustrated Treewoofe. She trembled with longing as she looked at it. She pulled herself together and walked across the yard. There was a light in the kitchen but no answer came to her repeated knocks. She felt heartsick. She could not go back without *knowing*. With a shaking hand she lifted the latch and went in. She crossed the kitchen and opened the door into the hall. Hugh was sitting there, alone, by the ashes of his desolate fireplace. In the light that fell over his face from the kitchen she saw the stark amazement on it as he stood up.

"Hugh," cried Joscelyn desperately—she must speak first, for who knew what he might say?—"I've come back. I was a fool—a fool. Can you forgive me? Do you still want me?"

There was a silence that seemed endless to Joscelyn. She shivered. The hall was very cold. It had been so long since there had been a fire in it. The whole house was cold. There was no welcome in it for her. She had alienated it.

After what seemed an eternity Hugh came towards her. His hungry eyes burned into hers.

"Why do you want to come back? Don't you still—love *him*?"

Joscelyn shuddered.

"No—no." She could say nothing more.

Again Hugh was silent. His heart was pounding with a wild exultation in his breast. She had come back to him—his again—not Frank Dark's—his, his only. She was standing there in the moonlight where she had mocked him so long ago. Asking his forgiveness and his love. he had only to put out his hand—draw her to his breast.

Hugh Dark was his mother's son. He crushed back the mad words of passion that rushed to his lips. He spoke coldly—sternly.

"Go back to Bay Silver—and put on your wedding-dress and veil. Come back to me in it as you went away—come as a bride to her bridegroom. Then—I may listen to you."

Proud Joscelyn went humbly. She would have done anything—anything that Hugh commanded. Never had she loved him as she loved him standing there, tall and dark and stern in the moonlit hall of Treewoofe. She would have crawled to him on all fours and kissed his feet had he so commanded. She went back to Bay Silver—she went to the garret and got the box that contained her wedding-dress and veil. She put them on, like a woman in a trance obeying the compulsion of some stronger will than her own.

"Thank God, I'm still beautiful," she whispered.

Then she walked back to Treewoofe, glimmering by in the silver of moonlight and the shimmer of satin.

Uncle Pippin, who was always where nobody expected him to be, thought she was a ghost when he saw her. The excited yelp he emitted might have been heard for a mile. Uncle Pippin didn't approve of it. Well-behaved young women didn't go strolling about on moonlit nights, wearing wedding-clothes. It couldn't be the jug that made Joscelyn do this. So Uncle Pippin fell back on the Spanish blood. A bad business that. Really, nothing but queer things had happened since Aunt Becky died. He sat in his buggy and stared after her until she disappeared. Then he drove home with badly shaken nerves.

Joscelyn had not even noticed Uncle Pippin. She went

on, past the graveyard where her father lay, up the Three
Hills road. For a wonder, no one else saw her. Nobody
ever believed Uncle Pippin had seen her. The poor old
man was getting doty. Imagining things to make himself
important.

The lights of beautiful Treewoofe were twinkling through
the tall slender birches when she came back. Every room
was lighted up to flash a welcome to her—its mistress for
whom it had waited so long. She and Treewoofe were good
friends again. The front door was open—and goblins of
firelight were dancing in the hall beyond it. The mirror
over the mantel was turned face outward, and Hugh was
waiting for her by the fire he had kindled. As she paused
entreatingly in the doorway, he came forward and led her
over the threshold by one of her cold hands. A wedding-
ring was lying on the dusty mantel, where it had lain for
many years. Hugh took it up and put it on her finger.

"Joscelyn," he cried suddenly. "Oh, Joscelyn—*my* Joscelyn!"

VII

Margaret had made many wedding-dresses for other
people with vicarious thrills and dreams but she made her
own very prosaically. Her wedding-day was finally fixed for
the first of October. That would give them time for a bridal
trip to points on the mainland before the date appointed
for the final disposal of Aunt Becky's jug. Neither she nor
Penny felt any elation over the affair. In truth, as the fatal
time drew near, Penny grew absolutely desperate. At first
he thought he would ask Margaret to postpone the wedding again—until after the puzzle of the jug was solved.
That would not affect his chances materially. Then Penny
threw up his head. That would be dishonourable. He
would break the engagement before, if break it he must.
Ay, that would be nobler. Penny felt a fine glow of victorious satisfaction with himself.

He went up to Denzil's, one evening, firmly resolved.
No more shilly-shallying. Jug or no jug, he would be a
free man. He had known yesterday that he could not go
through with it. Margaret had told him that his watch was
wrong. It always infuriated Penny to be told his watch was

wrong. It was not the first time Margaret had offended in a similar fashion. And he was in for marrying a woman like that. What a devilish predicament!

Margaret had evidently been crying. And Margaret was not one of those fortunate women who can cry without their noses turning red. Penny wondered testily why a woman who was engaged to *him* should be crying. Then he thought she might suspect his real feelings on the matter and be weeping over them. Penny felt his heart softening—after all—no, this would never do. He must not be hen-hearted now. This was his last chance. He mopped his brow.

"Mar'gret," he said pleadingly, "do you think we'd better go through with it after all?"

"Go through—with what?" asked Margaret.

"With—with getting married."

"Don't you want to marry me?" said Margaret, a sudden gleam coming into her eyes. It terrified Penny.

"No," he said bluntly.

Margaret stood up and drew a long breath.

"Oh, I'm so thankful—so thankful," she said softly.

Penny stared at her with a dawning sense of outrage. This was the last thing he had expected.

"Thankful—thankful? What the hell are you thankful for?"

Margaret was too uplifted to mind his profanity.

"Oh, Penny, I didn't want to marry you either. I was only going through with it because I didn't want to disappoint you. You don't know how happy it makes me to find out that you don't care."

Penny looked rather dour. It was one thing to explain to a woman that you didn't see your way clear to marrying her after all. It was quite another to find her so elated about it.

"I only asked you out of pity, anyhow, Mar'gret," he said.

Margaret smiled. The Griscom showed there. Penny's great-grandmother had been a Griscom.

"That isn't a sporting thing to say," she murmured gently. "And would you mind—very much—remembering that my name is Margaret—*not* Mar'gret. Here is your ring—and I've something rather important to attend to this evening."

Thus coolly dismissed, Penny went—stiffly, rigidly, with neither handshake, bow, nor backward glance.

Penny was huffed.

The important thing which Margaret had to do was to write a letter. She had not been crying because she was going to marry Penny exactly—she had been crying because suddenly, unbelievably, magically, a darling dream could have come true if she did not have to get married. And now that the marriage was off, the dream *could* come true. The letter was to Nigel Penhallow.

When it was written Margaret felt curiously young again, as if life had suddenly folded back for thirty years. She slipped away in the September moonlight to visit Whispering Winds. It would be hers—dear friendly Whispering Winds. All the lovesome things in its garden would be tended and loved. The little house should be whitewashed twice every year so that it would always be white as a pearl. She would be there in cool, exquisite mornings—in grey, sweet evenings—there to hear little winds crying to her in the night. It would be so deliciously quiet; nobody could ever open her door without knocking. She would be alone with her dreams. She could cry and laugh and—and—*swear* when she wanted to. And she would adopt a baby. A baby with dimples and sweet, perfumed creases and blue eyes and golden curls. There must be such a baby somewhere, just waiting to be cuddled.

She looked lovingly at the trees that were to be hers. Whispering Winds belonged to its trees and its trees to it. One little birch grew close to it in one of its angles. A willow hovered over it protectingly. A maple peeped around a corner. Little bushy spruces crouched under its windows. Dear Whispering Winds. And dear Aunt Becky who had made it all possible. Margaret prayed that night to be forgiven for the sin of ingratitude.

No one in the clan could find out just why the engagement had been broken off. It was inconceivable that Margaret could have done it, although for some reason best known to himself Penny had taken up and was nursing an aggrieved attitude.

"These mysteries will drive me distracted," groaned Uncle Pippin, "but I'll bet that fiendish jug was at the bottom of it somehow."

The clan were astounded when they heard Margaret had bought Aunt Louisa's cottage from Richard Dark, still more astounded when they found she had sold the *Pilgrim's Progress* Aunt Becky had given her to a New York collector for a fabulous sum. Actually ten thousand dollars. It was a first edition and would have been worth thirty thousand if it had been in first class condition. It was plain to be seen now why she had thrown Penny over so heartlessly. Penny himself chewed some bitter cuds of reflection. Who would ever have dreamed that any one would be crazy enough to pay ten thousand dollars for an old book like that? Ten thousand dollars! Ten thousand dollars! But it was too late. Neither he nor the clan ever really forgave Margaret—not for selling the book but for getting it from Aunt Becky in the first place. What right had she to it more than anybody else? Denzil was especially grouchy. He thought Margaret should have gone on living with him and used her money to help educate his family.

"Throwing it away on a house you don't need," he said bitterly. "You'd show more sense if you put what it cost you away for a rainy day."

"Umbrellas have been invented since that proverb," said Margaret blithely.

VIII

Gay was lingering by the gate, watching a big red moon rising behind a fringe of little dark elfin spruces over Drowned John's hill pasture to the east of her. Behind her, through the trees around Maywood, was visible a great, fresh, soft, empty, windy yellow sky of sunset. A little ghost of laughter drifted to her from the hill road. There was, it seemed, still laughter in the world. She was alone and she was glad of it. Just now life was bearable only when she was alone.

For weeks Gay had been dully unhappy—restless—indifferent. The new house no longer thrilled her; everything was tarnished. She wished drearily that she could go away—or die—or at least cease to exist. Life was too perplexing. She could not help thinking of Noel all the time. What was he doing—thinking—feeling? Was he very unhappy? Or was he—wiser? If she only knew the answers to those questions! She would never know them. And in little over a month she had to marry Roger.

She was still there when Noel came. Now that she was not waiting for him—now that she was going to marry Roger—he came. When she lifted her head he was standing before her. Looking like a movie star—handsome and—and—*dapper!* Yes, dapper, just like little Penny Dark. In twenty years' time he would be just like Penny Dark. Gay's head spun around and she wondered if she were going crazy.

"Noel!" she gasped.

"Yes—it's Noel." He came close and took her hand. She looked at him. Had he grown shorter? No, it was only that she had grown used to looking up at Roger. Noel's hair *was* too curly—what had Nan said once about the tongs? Oh, what had got into her? Why was she thinking such absurd things—now at this wonderful moment when Noel had come back to her?

Noel was leaning over the gate, talking rapidly—telling her he had never really cared for Nan. Nan had chased him—hunted him down—he had been bewitched temporarily—he had never really loved anyone but her, Gay. Would she forgive him! And take him back?

Noel had evidently very little doubt that he would be forgiven. He had, Gay found herself thinking, quite a bit of confidence in his own powers of attraction. He put his arms about her shoulders and drew her close to him. For long months she had longed to feel his arms about her so—his lips on hers—his face pressed to her cheek. And now that it had come about, Gay found herself laughing—shaking with laughter. A bit hysterical perhaps—but Noel did not know that. He released her abruptly and stepped back a pace in amazement and chagrin.

"You're—so—so—funny!" gasped poor Gay.

"I'm sorry," said Noel stiffly. This was not at all what he had looked for.

Gay forced herself to stop laughing and looked at Noel. The old enchantment had gone. She saw him as she had never seen him before—as her clan had always seen him. A handsome fellow, who thought every girl who looked at him fell in love with him; shallow, selfish. Was this what she had supposed she loved? Love! She had known nothing about it till this very moment, when she realised that it was Roger she loved. Roger who was a *man!* This Noel was only a boy. And he would never be anything but a boy, if he lived to a hundred—with a boy's fickle heart, a boy's vanity, a boy's emptiness. She had fancied herself in love with him once—fancied herself heartbroken when he jilted her—and now—

"Why, it's all ancient history," she thought in amazement.

As soon as she could speak she told Noel to run away. Her voice still shook and Noel thought she was still laughing at him. He went off in high dudgeon. It was a new and very wholesome experience for Noel Gibson to be laughed at. It did him no end of good. He was never quite so self-assured again.

Gay stood by the gate for a long while, trying to adjust herself. The sky faded out into darkness and the moonshine bathed her. Passing breaths of autumn wind sent showers of silvery golden leaves all over her. She loved the night—she loved everything. She felt as if she had been born again. How lucky Noel had come back. If he hadn't come back she might always have fancied she cared—might never have seen the fathomless difference between him and Roger. To come back so soon—so shamelessly. Hadn't he *any* depth? Couldn't he care really for anybody? But he had come—and his coming had set her free from phantom fetters.

"I suppose if it were not for the jug I'd still be engaged to him—perhaps married to him."

She shuddered. How dreadful that would be—how dreadful it would be to be married to anyone but Roger! It was simply impossible even to *imagine* being married to any one but Roger. God bless Aunt Becky!

Still she had an odd but fleeting sense of loss and

futility. All that passion and pain for nothing. It hurt her that it should seem so foolish now. It hurt her to realise that she had only been in love with love. The clan had been right—so right. That stung a little. It isn't really nice to be forced to agree with your family that you have been a little fool.

But she knew she did not care how right they had been. She was *glad* they had been right. Oh, it was good to feel vivid and interested and alive again—as she hadn't felt for so long. All the lost colour and laughter of life seemed to have returned. The time of apple-blossom love was over. Nothing could bring it back. It was the time of roses now—the deep, rich roses of the love of womanhood. Those months of suffering had made a woman of Gay. She lifted up her arms in rapture as if to caress the night—the beautiful silvery September night.

"Let me brush the moonlight off you," somebody said—a dear somebody with a dear, dear voice.

"Oh, Roger!" Gay turned and threw herself into his arms. Her face was lifted to his—her arms went about his neck of their own accord—for the first time Roger felt his kiss returned.

He held her off and looked at her—as if he could never have enough of looking at her. She was an exquisite thing in the moonlight, with her brilliant eyes and her wind-ruffled hair.

"Gay! You love me!" he said incredulously.

"It will take me a whole lifetime to tell you how much—and I never knew it till an hour ago," whispered Gay. "You won't mind how silly I've been, will you, Roger? You'll find out—in time—how wise I am at last."

Roger met the Moon Man on the way home.

"One *does* get the moon sometimes," Roger told him.

IX

Little Brian Dark was prowling about the roads, looking for some of his Uncle Duncan's young cattle which had broken out of their pasture. His uncle had told him not to come home until he found them, and he could get no trace of them. Rain was brewing and it was a very dark and cold and melancholy October night. A fog had blotted out the end of the harbour road; a ghostly sail or two drifted down the darkening bay. Brian felt horribly alone in the world. His heart swelled as he passed happy homes and saw more fortunate children through lighted, cheery kitchen windows. Once he saw a boy about his own age standing by his mother's side. The mother put her arm about him and kissed him fondly. Brian choked back a sob.

"I wonder," he thought wistfully, "what it would be like to be loved."

Now and then through an open door he caught delicious smells of suppers cooking. He was very hungry, for he had not had his supper. And very tired, for he had been picking potatoes all day. But he dared not go home without the young cattle.

Sim Dark, of whom he inquired timidly, told him he had seen some young beasts down on the shore road leading to Little Friday Cove. Sim felt an impulse of pity for young Brian as he drove away. The child looked as if he didn't get half enough to eat. And that thin sweater was not enough for a cold fall night. The Duncan Darks ought to be ashamed of themselves. After which, Sim went home to his excellent supper and well-dressed family and forgot all about Brian.

Brian trudged down the long grassy road to Little Friday Cove. It was getting very dark, and he was frightened. Little Sam's light gleamed cheerily through the blur of rain that was beginning to fall. Brian went to the house and asked him if he had seen the calves. Little Sam had not, but he made Brian go in and have supper with him. Brian knew he ought not to go in, with the calves yet unfound, but the smell of Little Sam's chowder was too tempting. And it was so warm and cosy in Little Sam's living-room. Besides, he liked Little Sam. Little Sam had once taken him out for a row one evening when the gulf had been like rippled satin and there was a little new moon in the west. It was one of the few beautiful memories in Brian's life.

"We're in for a rain," said Little Sam, ladling out the chowder generously. "My shin's been aching scandalously

for two days." Little Sam sighed. "I'm beginning to feel
my years," he said.

By the time supper was over, the rain was pouring
down. Little Sam insisted that Brian stay all night with
him.

"It ain't fit for you to go out a night like this. Listen to
that wind getting up. Stay here where you're comfortable
and have a look round in the morning for your calves.
Likely you'll find 'em over in Jake Harmer's wood-lot. His
fences are disgraceful."

Brian yielded. He was afraid to go home in the dark.
And it was so warm and pleasant here. To be sure, he
thought uneasily of Cricket. But if Cricket came he would
likely just curl up on Brian's bed and be quite comfortable.
No harm would come to him.

Brian spent the pleasantest evening he had known for a
long time, sitting by Little Sam's blazing fire, petting
Mustard—who was a very nice old cat, though not to be
compared to Cricket—and listening to Little Sam's hair-
raising ghost stories. It did not occur to Little Sam that he
should not tell ghost stories to Brian. It was a long time
since he had had anybody to listen to his tales. Little Sam
had already spent many lonely evenings this fall. He
dreaded another winter like the last. But he did not
mention Big Sam. The Sams had at last given up talking
about one another. Little Sam only pointed Aurora proudly out to Brian and asked him if he didn't think her pretty.
Brian did think so. There was something in the white,
poised figure that made him think of music in moonlight
and coral clouds in a morning sky and all the bits of
remembered beauty that sometimes—when he wasn't too
tired and hungry—made a harmony in his soul.

It was a long time before Brian could sleep, curled up in
the bunk that had once been Big Sam's. The wind roared
at the window and the rain streamed down on the rocks
outside. The wind was offshore and the waves were not
high, but they made a strange, sobbing, lonely sound.
Brian wondered if his aunt and uncle would be very cross
with him for staying away and if Cricket would miss him.

When he finally fell asleep he had a dreadful dream. He
was standing alone on a great, far-reaching plain of moon-

lit snow. Right before him was a huge creature—a creature like the wolf in the pictures of Red Riding Hood, but ten times bigger than any wolf could be, with snarling, slavering jaws and malignant, flaming eyes. Such hate—such hellish hate—looked out of those eyes that Brian screamed with terror and wakened.

The room was filled with a dim greyness of dawn. Little Sam was still snoring peacefully, with Mustard curled up on his stomach. The wind and rain had ceased and a peep from the window showed Brian a world wrapped in grey fog. But the horror of his dream was still on him. Somehow— he could not have told how or why—he felt sure it had something to do with Cricket. Softly he slipped out of bed and into his ragged clothes—softly slipped out of the house and latched the door behind him. An hour later he reached home. Nobody was up. There was a strange car in the garage. Brian tiptoed across the kitchen and climbed the ladder to the loft. His heart was beating painfully. He prayed desperately that he might find Cricket there, warm and furry and purring.

What Brian saw was his Uncle Duncan asleep on his bed. There was no sign of Cricket anywhere. Brian sat down on the floor, with a sick feeling coming over him. He knew what must have happened—what had happened once before. Visitors had come—more visitors than there were beds for. His uncle had given up his own bed and come to the loft.

Had Cricket come? And if so, had he gone away safely? Brian was asking these questions of himself over and over when his uncle woke, stretched, sat up, and looked at him.

"Find the cattle?" he said.

"No-o-o, but Little Sam says he thinks they're in Jake Harmer's wood-lot. I'll go right away and get them."

Brian voice shook beyond control but it was not with fear about the cattle. What—oh, what was the truth about Cricket?

Duncan Dark yawned.

"You'd better. And where'd that cat come from that woke me up pawing at my face? You bin having cats here, youngster?"

"No-o-o, only one—it came sometimes at nights," gasped Brian. It seemed that his very soul grew cold within him.

"Well, it won't come again. I wrung its neck. Now, you hustle off after them cows. You've plenty of time before breakfast."

Later on, Brian found the poor dead body of his little pet among the burdocks under the window. Brian felt that his heart was breaking as he gathered Cricket up in his arms and tried to close the glazed eyes. He felt so helpless—so alone. The only thing that loved him in the world was dead—murdered. Never again would he hear the pad-pad of little feet on the porch roof—never again would a soft paw touch his face in the darkness—never again would a purring thing snuggle against him lovingly. There was no God. Not even a young careless God could have let a thing like this happen.

When night came Brian felt that he could not—*could not*—go to his bed in the loft. He could not lie there alone, waiting for Cricket, who could never come again—Cricket lying cold and stiff in the little grave Brian had dug for him under the wild cherry tree. In his despair the child rushed away from the house and along the twilit road. He hardly knew where he was going. By some blind instinct rather than design, his feet bore him to the Rose River graveyard and his mother's neglected grave. He cast himself down upon it, sobbing terribly.

"Oh, Mother—Mother. I wish I was dead—with you. Mother—Mother—take me—I can't live any longer—I can't—I can't. *Please*, Mother."

Margaret Penhallow stood looking down at him. She had been down to Artemas Dark's with a dress for May Dark and had taken a short cut through the graveyard on her way back, walking slowly because she rather enjoyed being in this dreamy spot where so many of her kindred slept and where the crisp, frosty west wind was blowing over old graves. Was this poor Laura Dark's boy? And what was his trouble?

She bent down and touched him gently.

"Brian—what is the matter, dear?"

Brian started convulsively and got up, shrinking into himself. His painful little sobs ceased.

"Brian—tell me, dear."

Brian had thought he could never tell anybody. But Margaret's soft grey-blue eyes were so tender and pitiful. He found himself telling her. He sobbed out the story of poor Cricket.

"It was all I had to love—and nobody but Cricket ever loved me."

Margaret stood very still for a few moments, patting Brian's head. In those few moments the dream of the golden-haired baby vanished forever from her heart. She knew what she must do—what she *wanted* to do.

"Brian, would you like to come and live with me—down at Whispering Winds? I'm moving there next week. You will be *my* little boy—and I will love you—I loved your mother, dear, when we were girls together."

Brian stopped sobbing and looked at her incredulously.

"Oh, Miss Penhallow—do you mean it? Can I really live with you? And will—will Uncle Duncan let me?"

"Yes, I do mean it. And I don't think there's much doubt that your uncle will be glad to get—to let you come to me. Don't cry any more, dear. Run right home—it's too cold for you to be here like this. Next week we'll arrange it all. And will you call me Aunt Margaret?"

"Oh, Aunt Margaret,"—Brian caught her hand—her pretty slender hand that had so kindly touched his hair— "I—I—oh, I'm afraid you won't love me when you know all about me. I'm—I'm not good, Aunt Margaret. Aunt Alethea says so. And she's—she's right. I didn't want to go to church, Aunt Margaret, because my clothes were so shabby. I know that was wicked. And I—I had such dreadful thoughts when Uncle Duncan told me he'd killed Cricket. Oh, Aunt Margaret, I wouldn't want you to be disappointed in me when you found out I wasn't a good boy."

Margaret smiled and put her arm around him. How thin his poor little body was.

"We'll both be bad and wicked together then, Brian. Come, dear, I'll walk part of the way home with you. You're cold—you're shivering. You shouldn't be out without a jacket on a night like this."

They went over the graveyard past Aunt Becky's grave

and gleaming monument and down the road, hand in hand. They were both suddenly very happy. They knew they belonged to each other. Brian fell asleep that night with tears on his lashes for poor Cricket but with a warm feeling of being lapped round with love—such as he had never known before. Margaret lay blissfully awake. Whispering Winds was hers and a little lonely creature to love and cherish. She asked for nothing more—not even for Aunt Becky's jug.

6
FINALLY, BRETHREN

▼

I

The clan had hardly got its second wind after the reconciliation of Hugh and Joscelyn when the last day of October loomed near—the day when it should be known who was to get Aunt Becky's jug. The earlier excitement, which had waned a little, especially in view of all the approaching weddings—"a lot of marrying this year," as Uncle Pippin said—blazed up again fiercely, coupled with anxious speculations as to what had caused the change in Dandy.

For Dandy was changed. Nobody could deny that. He had become furtive, morose, unfriendly, absentminded. He snapped at people. He went to church regularly but he never lingered to talk with folks after the service. Assemblies at the blacksmith's forge knew him not. Town on Saturday night knew him not. Some thought it was because of the fire but the majority refused that opinion. Dandy had lost practically nothing by the fire, except his spare-room furniture. He was well insured and had an old house on his lower farm to move into temporarily. It must be something connected with the jug. Did Dandy really have to decide who was to get it and was afraid of the consequences?

"Looks like a man with something on his conscience," said Stanton Grundy.

"Can't be that," said Uncle Pippin. "Dandy never had any conscience to speak of."

"Then he must have nervous prostration," said Grundy.

"I shouldn't wonder," agreed Uncle Pippin. "Having that jug for a whole year and mebbe having to settle who's to get it'd be hard on anybody's nerves."

"Do you suppose," suggested Sim Dark horribly, "that Mrs. Dandy has smashed the jug?"

The tension grew as the last of October approached. Drowned John and Titus Dark both reflected that, jug or no jug, they could let themselves go in another week. William Y. had bought a new mahogany table in Charlottetown, and gossip said he meant it as a stand for the jug. Old Miller Dark was holding the final chapter of his history open until he could include the lucky name. Chris Penhallow was looking lovingly at his dear neglected fiddle. Mrs. Allan Dark, whose spirit and determination had so far kept her alive, reflected with a tired sigh that she could die in peace after the thirty-first of October.

"And here's Edith going to have a baby that very week," wailed Mrs. Sim Dark.

It was just like Edith to have a baby at such an inconvenient time. Really, her mother thought vexedly, she might have planned things better than that.

The day came at last. A grey day with a grey wind. Autumn groves that had been an enchantment of gold and spruce-green were leaflessly grey now. Red-ribbed fields on the Treewoofe hill testified to many a glad day's work on Hugh's part. A great pyramid of pumpkins shone goldenly in Homer Penhallow's yard. The gulf was dark blue and the pasture fields adream.

Everybody was at Dandy's, except poor Mrs. Sim— Edith had run true to form—and the Jim Trents, who were quarantined for measles and were at home bitterly wondering if they had served God for naught. Dandy's bulldog, Alphonso, sat on his haunches at the front door as if he never expected to do anything but sit.

"On the whole you are the ugliest brute I ever saw," Peter told him—which didn't hurt the dog's feelings any.

He simply made a blood-curdling sound that gave Mrs. Toynbee a spasm.

"Going to give us anything to eat, Dandy?" whispered Uncle Pippin.

"The wife has prepared refreshments, I believe," said Dandy nervously. He didn't think anybody would have much appetite after they heard what he had to say.

Murray Dark sat and watched Thora as usual—with this difference: that he was wondering how soon it would be decent to begin courting her. If Chris had died a natural death Murray would have waited only three months. But as things were, he thought he'd better make it six. Margaret wore an exceedingly pretty grey silk dress—it had been intended for her wedding one—and looked so young and dainty and happy that Penny felt another dreadful qualm and Stanton Grundy wondered if it mightn't be wise to marry again after all. There must be a good bit of that ten thousand left, in spite of her foolish purchase of that tumbledown little place and all the new furniture they said she had put in it. Stanton determined to think it over. Eventually he decided not to. Which was just as well because Margaret had no longer any hankerings for marriage. She had Whispering Winds and Brian and she was perfectly happy. She no longer even cared about the jug.

Donna still cared a little, but not so greatly. After all, you could not take a jug like that to Africa. She was thinking more of the wedding-breakfast and the decorations of the church. For Peter, who was one of the born wanderers of the earth, found himself roped in for a conventional wedding with all the fuss and frills possible. Drowned John was determined on it. He loved a big colourful wedding, in keeping with the traditions of the clan. He had been cheated out of it on Donna's hurried war bridal with Barry but by—goodness, he wasn't going to be cheated out of it the second time. And thank heaven decent dresses were in again! Donna's wedding-dress, Drowned John decided, should sweep the floor. Donna didn't care. Where she was going with Peter she would wear nothing but knickerbockers. Luckily Drowned John knew nothing of this. It would have seemed more outrageous to him than the lions.

Roger sat and worshipped Gay openly and shamelessly—
her shining hair, her marigold eyes, the charming gestures
of her wonderful hands. He looked so happy that he made
some of them feel a bit uneasy, as if it were flying in the
face of Providence.

Nan was there, darting the mockery of her green eyes
over everything, although she rather avoided looking at
Gay. Thomas Ashley and his wife, of Halifax, were there,
though the clan thought they hadn't any business to be.
They were no relations, although they were visiting the
William Y.'s. Nobody, looking at Thomas's moon face, pursy
old mouth and tortoise-shell glasses, would have dreamed
that he came there fired by a romantic memory. He
wanted to see Mrs. Clifford Penhallow again. He had been
wildly in love with her when he was young and, as his wife
knew bitterly, had never wholly got over it. Thomas was
looking furtively at all the women in the room. Mrs.
Clifford had not come yet. He wondered who the grim,
homely woman under the mantelpiece was.

Hugh and Joscelyn were there, although Joscelyn would
rather have been home, painting the woodwork in the
spare room at Treewoofe. Rachel Penhallow was there, as
happy as it was possible for her to be. Penny Dark had
heard that her bottle of Jordan water had been spilled and
he promptly sent her his, glad to get the absurd thing out
of the house. Rachel had gone off her milk diet at once.
Kate and Frank and their baby were there. The baby cried
a great deal and Stanton Grundy glared at it. Tempest
Dark was there. Lawson and Naomi Dark were there.
Naomi looked a little older and tireder and more hopeless.
David Dark was there, comfortably sure that Dandy at any
rate, would not ask him to open with prayer. Uncle Pippin
was there, wondering why, in spite of all the repressed
excitement, everything seemed a little flat. Not much like
Aunt Becky's levees. Uncle Pippin decided it was because
everyone was too polite. Things weren't interesting when
people were too polite. Aunt Becky had never been too
polite. That was why her levees had been so interesting.

II

The crucial moment had arrived. Dandy had come in and stood before the stove, his back to the mantelpiece. He was deathly pale and it was observed that his hands were trembling. The strain suddenly became almost unbearable. Artemas Dark tried to steady his nerves by counting the roses on the wallpaper. Rachel Penhallow immediately had a feeling that something was going to happen. Mrs. Howard reflected with a gasp that the windows in that house couldn't have been opened for a hundred years. Why had Mrs. Dandy put such a roaring fire in the stove, even on a chilly October day? But she was always a little mad, anyway.

Dandy had once looked forward to this moment, when, clothed with authority, he should stand up before them all and announce Aunt Becky's decision. And now he wished himself dead. He turned suddenly on Percy Dark.

"Would you mind stopping that everlasting drumming on the table?" he asked irritably.

Percy jumped and stopped. He started to say something but Drowned John nudged him fiercely.

"Dry up," said Drowned John.

Percy dried up.

"Come, come, Dandy," said William Y. impatiently. "Step on the juice. We've had enough of suspense. Tell us who's to get it and have it over."

"I—I can't," said Dandy, moistening his lips.

"Can't *what*?"

"Can't tell you who's to get the jug. I—I—don't know. Nobody ever will know—now."

"Look here, Dandy—" William Y. rose threateningly. "What does this mean?"

"It means"—the worst was out and Dandy had a little more courage—"I've lost the letter Aunt Becky gave me—the letter with the name in it. There *was* a name in it—she told me so much."

"Lost it! Where did you lose it?"

"I'm—not sure," hesitated the wretched Dandy. "That is—I'm almost sure it fell into the pig-pen. I always carried it round in a folder in my breast pocket. I never let it out of my possession. One day, some two months ago, I was up in the barn loft forking down straw. You know the flooring is just poles—there was gaps between them. I took off my coat when I got warm working and put it on again when I finished. When I went back to the house I—I missed the folder. I hunted everywhere—*everywhere*. It must have fallen into the pig-pen—the pig-pen is right under the loft, and the pigs must have et it altogether, letter and folder and all."

For a few minutes everybody said nothing very rapidly. Then—

"Damn it!" exploded Drowned John. All the repression of months was in his ejaculation. Everybody forgave him. Titus Dark looked envious. He had got so out of the habit of swearing he was afraid he could never get into it again. Even his horses had learned to understand a milder vocabulary. And a fat lot of good it had done!

Tom Dark remembered he had seen a black cat run across the road on his way to Dandy's. William Y. looked around on the circle of outraged faces. This was what you might call a hellish discovery. The situation demanded careful handling and he felt that he, William Y., was the man to handle it.

"Are you sure you had it in your pocket when you went up into the loft—sure it hadn't dropped out before?"

"Almost sure," stammered the miserable Dandy, who couldn't feel sure even of his own name just then. "I searched everywhere. It's been wearing me to a shadow. The wife said to pray about it. Dang it, I've prayed till I was black in the face."

"And you've no idea what name was in the envelope?"

It seemed incredible that Dandy didn't know *that*.

"I ain't got the least idea," said Dandy. "It was sealed—I never saw so much sealing-wax on the back of any letter. And Aunt Becky made me swear I wouldn't tamper with it."

Drowned John determined to take a hand. William Y. wasn't going to be let run things.

"We'll have to draw lots for it," he said.

"That isn't a Christian way to decide it," said William Y. "Anybody got any other suggestion?"

"Let's vote who's to have it—secret ballot," said Junius Penhallow.

"With everybody putting his own name in the ballot," remarked William Y., with a smile of icy contempt for such a suggestion. "No; I'll tell you what should be done—"

"Here's the Moon Man running across the yard," interrupted Uncle Pippin. "He seems in a mighty hurry."

Those who could look out of the window did so. They saw the Moon Man with his long black coat streaming out behind him in the wind like the mantle of a prophet of old. In a few seconds he had reached the house, crossed the hall and was standing breathlessly in the doorway of the room. The whole clan realised that the Moon Man had one of his really crazy fits on.

"I heard the devil cackling as I came down by the barn," said the Moon Man. "He was in glee over this unholy gathering where envy and all uncharitableness prevail."

His look scorched everybody and left them feeling like cinders.

"It has been revealed to me what I should do."

The Moon Man strode to the table between the two windows—he snatched up Aunt Becky's jug—he hurled it furiously at the mantelpiece. Roger, realising before anyone else, but just too late, what the Moon Man meant to do, sprang up and caught at his arm. He could not save the jug but he deflected slightly the Moon Man's aim. The jug hurtled through the air at Lawson Dark. And Lawson Dark, who had not stood or walked for eleven years, saw it coming and sprang to his feet to avoid it. The jug struck him squarely on the head, crashed like an egg-shell, slid off against the stove and fell on the floor in hundreds of tiny fragments. Harriet Dark perhaps turned over in her grave. Possibly Aunt Becky did, too. But Lawson Dark, with blood trickling from a cut on his forehead, had turned dazedly to his wife.

"Naomi!" he cried, holding out his hands to her. "Oh, Naomi."

III

"Don't it beat hell?" said Sim Dark.

"And we won't ever know who should have had the

pieces," said William Y. disconsolately, as they lingered in the yard, after Roger had taken charge of Lawson and carried him and Naomi off home.

The clan were not inclined to discuss what had happened to Lawson. It savored too strongly of something miraculous and unclan-like. The jug was a safer topic—now.

"That doesn't matter much," said David Dark. "There's thousands of 'em—they could never be stuck together."

"Anyhow, if anybody had got it I reckon he'd never have got home alive," said Stanton Grundy. Tom Dark, who had never cried in his life, was crying because he hadn't got the jug. His wife dragged him hastily off to his car to hide his shame. Joscelyn and Hugh went away together very silently, thinking only of the look on Naomi Dark's face when Lawson had turned to her with his glad cry of recognition. Mrs. Alpheus was furious with both the Moon Man and Dandy. Something—she wasn't quite clear what—ought to be done to both of them. Homer Penhallow and Palmer Dark passed each other without recognition. It was very satisfying to be enemies again. Life had been so darned dull when they had to be friendly. David and Percy Dark nodded shamefacedly to each other and mentioned the weather. The graveyard fracas was forgotten.

"It's a funny world," sighed Uncle Pippin.

"Let's laugh at it then," said Stanton Grundy.

Old Thomas Ashley was not happy. Somebody had come up to him on the verandah and said archly, "Don't *dare* to say you don't know *me*." He stared at her in silence. It was the grim lady who had sat under the mantelpiece. No, he didn't know her—and yet—

"I'm Mavis Dark," she said more archly still.

"Mavis Dark! Impossible!" exclaimed Thomas Ashley.

"Oh, *have* I changed so much?" said Mrs. Clifford poutingly. "Don't you remember that summer you were here?"

Thomas Ashley looked at her. The skin which had been creamy in youth was yellow now—the smooth cheeks were wrinkled—the smooth neck wattled. The sleek, black hair had turned grey—the gracious curves had vanished.

"But—but—you were beautiful then," stammered poor old Thomas.

"You've changed a little yourself," Mrs. Clifford reminded him acidly.

Thomas Ashley went away, lamenting a lost dream. He wished he had never heard of the old Dark jug. But his plump, pretty little wife was not ill-pleased. The ghostly rival of thirty years was laid at last. God bless Aunt Becky's jug!

Tempest Dark, his eyes alight with good-humoured mockery, had decided that he would keep on living. He had found a job that would give him bread and discovered that existence was possible even without Winnifred.

"After all, life's worth living when a comedy like this is played out," he reflected.

"Dang it, I believe there *is* something in prayer after all," said Dandy, when the last car had driven away.

IV

Winter was coming on apace; November wore away. At Treewoofe Hugh and Joscelyn kept glowing fires in every room and laughed at the winds that swirled up from the gulf. Peter and Donna were on their way to Africa. Roger and Gay were not yet home from their honeymoon. Margaret and Brian were nested in Whispering Winds. And one cold evening poor, lonely, hungry Big Sam set out for a walk around the shore to the lighthouse on Bay Silver Point. It was a long walk and he had various rheumatic spots about his anatomy, but there would be some cronies at the lighthouse and Big Sam thought an evening of social intercourse would be better for his nerves than playing tit-tat-to, right hand against left, at home. These short days and long, early-falling evenings were depressing, he admitted. And the Wilkins's shanty was draughty. Perhaps Happy Dark would be at the lighthouse, with his ringing tales of life in the tropic seas. And maybe the lighthouse-keeper's wife might even give them a bite of lunch. But he would not let his thoughts dwell on Little Sam's suet puddings and chowders and hot biscuits. That way madness lay.

There had been a skim of snow that morning, melting into dampness as the sun rose for an hour or two of watery brightness before shrouding himself in clouds. The brief day had grown cold and raw as it wore on and now land and sea lay wrapped in a grey, brooding stillness. Far away Big Sam heard a train-whistle blow distinctly. The Old Lady of the Gulf moaned now and then. A storm was coming up but Big Sam was not afraid of storms. He would come home by the river road; the tide would be too high on his return to come by the Hole-in-the-Wall.

As a matter of fact when he reached the long red headland known as the Hole-in-the-Wall, he blankly realised that the tide was already ahead of him. There was no getting around it. He could not climb its steep rugged sides; and to go back to where a road led down to the shore meant a lot of extra walking.

A daring inspiration came to Big Sam. Since he could not get around the Hole-in-the-Wall, could he go through it? Nobody ever had gone through it. But there had to be a first time for anything. It was certainly bigger than last year. Nothing venture, nothing win.

The Hole-in-the-Wall had begun with a tiny opening through the relatively thin side of the headland. Every year it grew a little larger as the yielding sandstone crumbled under wave and frost. It was a fair size now. Big Sam was small and thin. He reckoned if he could get his head through, the rest of him could follow.

He lay down and cautiously began squirming through. It was tighter than he had thought. The sides seemed suddenly very thick. All at once Big Sam decided that he was not cut out for a pioneer. He would go back out to the road. He tried to. He could not move. Somehow his coat had got ruckled up around his shoulders and jammed him tight. Vainly he twisted and writhed and tugged. The big rock seemed to hold him as in a grip of iron. The more he struggled the tighter he seemed to got wedged in. Finally he lay still with a cold sweat of horror breaking over him. His head was through the Hole-in-the-Wall. His shoulders were tight in it. His legs—where *were* his legs? There was no sensation in them, but they were probably hanging down the rock wall on the hinder side.

What a position to be in! On a lonely shore on a fast-darkening November night with a storm coming up.

He would never live through it. He would die of heart-
failure before morning, like old Captain Jobby who tried
to climb through a gate when he was drunk, and stuck
there.

Nobody could see him and it was no use to yell.
Before him, as behind him, was nothing but a curving,
shadowy cove bounded by another headland. No house,
no human being in sight. Nevertheless, Big Sam yelled
with what little breath he had left.

"Wouldn't you just as soon sing as make that noise?"
queried Little Sam, sticking his head around the huge
boulder that screened him.

Big Sam stared at the familiar spidery nose and huge
moustache. Of all the men in River and Cove to catch him
in this predicament, that it would be Little Sam! What the
devil was he doing, squatted here a mile away from home
on such a night?

"I wasn't aimin' to sing, not being afflicted as some folks
are," said Big Sam sarcastically. "I was just trying to fill my
lungs with air."

"Why don't you come all the way through?" jeered
Little Sam, coming around the boulder.

"'Cause I can't, and you know it," said Big Sam savage-
ly. "Look here, Samuel Dark, you and I ain't friends but
I'm a human being, ain't I?"

"There are times when I can see a distant resemblance
to one in you," acknowledged Little Sam, sitting calmly
down on a jut of the boulder.

"Well, then in the name of humanity help me out of
this."

"I dunno's I can," said Little Sam dubiously. "Seems to
me the only way'd be to yank you back by the legs and I
can't git round the cape to do that."

"If you can get a good grip on my shoulders or my coat
you can yank me out this way. It only wants a good pull. I
can't get my arms free to help myself."

"And I dunno's I will," went on Little Sam as if he had
not been interrupted.

"You—dunno's—you—*will!* D'ye mean to say you'll leave
me here to die on a night like this? Well, Sam Dark—"

"No; I ain't aiming to do that. It'll be your own fault if

you're left here. But you've got to show some signs of sense if I'm going to pull you out. Will you come home and behave yourself if I do?"

"If you want me to come home you know all you've got to do," snapped Big Sam. "Shoot out your Roarer."

"Aurorer stays," said Little Sam briefly.

"Then I stay, too." Big Sam imitated Little Sam's brevity—partly because he had very little breath to use for talking at all.

Little Sam took out his pipe and proceeded to light it.

"I'll give you a few minutes to reflect 'fore I go. I don't aim to stay long here in the damp. I dunno how a little wizened critter like you'll stand it all night. Anyway, you'll have some feeling after this for the poor camel trying to get through the needle's eye."

"Call yourself a Christian?" sneered Big Sam.

"Don't be peevish now. This ain't a question of religion—this is a question of common sense," retorted Little Sam.

Big Sam made a terrific effort to free himself but not even a tremor of the grim red headland was produced thereby.

"You'll bust a blood-vessel in one of them spasms," warned Little Sam. "You'd orter see yourself with your red whiskers sticking out of that hole. And I s'pose the rest of you's sticking out of the other side. Beautiful rear view if anyone comes along. Not that anyone likely will, this time o' night. But if you're still alive in the morning I'm going to get Prince Dark to take a snap of your hind legs. Be sensible, Sammy. I've got pea soup for supper—hot pea soup."

"Take your pea soup to hell," said Big Sam.

Followed a lot of silence. Big Sam was thinking. He knew where his extremities were now, for the cold was nipping them like a weasel. The rock around him was hard as iron. It was beginning to rain and the wind was rising. Already the showers of spray were spuming up from the beach. By morning he would be dead or gibbering.

But it was bitter to knuckle under to Little Sam and that white-limbed hussy on the clock shelf. Big Sam tried to pluck a little honour from the jaws of defeat.

"If I come back, will you promise not to marry that fat widow?"

Little Sam concealed all evidence of triumph.

"I ain't promising nothing—but I ain't marrying *any* widow, fat *or* lean."

"I s'pose that means she wouldn't have you."

"She didn't get the chance to have me or not have me. I ain't contracting any alliance with the House of Terlizzick, maid *or* widow. Well, I'm for home and pea soup. Coming, Sammy?"

Big Sam emitted a sigh, partly of exhaustion, partly of surrender. Life was too complicated. He was beaten.

"Pull me out of this damn' hole," he said sourly, "and I don't care how many naked weemen you have round."

"One's enough," said Little Sam.

He got a grip somehow of Big Sam's coat over his shoulders and tugged manfully. Big Sam howled. He was sure his legs were being torn off at the hips. Then he found that they were still attached to his body, standing on the rock beside Little Sam.

"Wring your whiskers out and hurry," said Little Sam. "I'm afraid that pea soup'll be scorched. It's sitting on the back of the stove."

V

This was comfort now—with the cold rain beating down outside and the gulf beginning to bellow. The stove was purring a lyric of beech and maple, and Mustard was licking her beautiful family under it.

Big Sam drew a long breath of satisfaction. There were many things to be talked over with Little Sam—incidents they could discuss with the calm detachment of those who lived on the fringe of the clan only. What name had really been in the envelope Dandy's pig had eaten. The uncanny miracle of Lawson Dark's restoration. The fact that Joscelyn Dark had got over her long fit of the sulks. The wedding of Peter and Donna and all the expense Drowned John must have gone to. All the things that had or had not happened in the clan because of Aunt Becky's jug. And some amazing yarn of Walter Dark's black cat that had fallen into a gallon of gasoline and come out white.

Really the pea soup was sublime.

After all, them earrings rather became Little Sam. Balanced the moustache, so to speak. And Aurorer—but what was the matter with Aurorer?

"What you bin doing with that old heathen graven immidge of yours?" demanded Big Sam, setting down half drunk his cup of militant tea with a thud.

"Give her a coat of bronze paint," said Little Sam proudly. "Looks real tasty, don't it? Knew you'd be sneaking home some of these long-come-shorts and thought I'd show you I could be consid'rate of your principles."

"Then you can scrape it off again," said Big Sam firmly. "Think I'm going to have an unclothed nigger sitting up there? If I've gotter be looking at a naked woman day in and day out, I want a white one for decency's sake."

Lucy Maud Montgomery

was born on November 30, 1874, in Clifton, Prince Edward Island, Canada. Although few women of that time received a higher education, Lucy attended Prince of Wales College in Charlottetown, P.E.I., and then Dalhousie University in Halifax. At seventeen she went to Nova Scotia to work for a newspaper, the Halifax *Chronicle*, and wrote for its evening edition, the *Echo*. But Lucy came back to rural Prince Edward Island to teach, and lived with her grandmother at Cavendish. It is this experience, along with the lives of her farmer and fisherfolk neighbors, that came alive when she wrote her "Anne" books, beginning with *Anne of Green Gables* in 1908. First published as a serial for a Sunday school paper, *Anne of Green Gables* quickly became a favorite of readers throughout the world, so much so that L.M. Montgomery published eight novels in all featuring Anne Shirley and her family. Lucy Montgomery also wrote the popular *Emily of New Moon* in 1923 followed by two sequels, and *Pat of Silver Bush* in 1933 with its sequel. She and her husband, the Rev. Ewen Macdonald, eventually moved to Ontario. L. M. Montgomery died in Toronto in 1942, but it is her early years of lush green Prince Edward Island that live on in the delightful adventures of the impetuous redhead, the stories Mark Twain called "the sweetest creation of child life yet written."

Anne of Green Gables has been translated into seventeen languages, made into a number of movies, and has had continuing success as a stage play.

The success of these productions inspired *The Road to Avonlea*—enchanting new tales based on characters created by L. M. Montgomery for a television series as well as the new paperback editions.